ST THOMAS'S EVE

Due to illness, Jean Plaidy was unable to go to school regularly and so taught herself to read. Very early on she developed a passion for the 'past'. After taking a shorthand and typing course, she spent a couple of years doing various jobs, including sorting gems in Hatton Garden and translating for foreigners in a City café. She began writing in earnest following marriage and now has a large number of historical novels to her name. Inspiration for her books is drawn from odd sources – a picture gallery, a line from a book, Shakespeare's inconsistencies. She lives in London and loves music, second-hand book shops and ancient buildings. Jean Plaidy also writes under the pseudonym of Victoria Holt.

D1005563

Also by Jean Plaidy
in Pan Books

The Tudor Series

ST THOMAS'S EVE
Jean Plaidy

Pan Books London, Sydney and Auckland

First published 1954 by Robert Hale and Company
This edition published 1966 by Pan Books Ltd,
Cavaye Place, London sw10 9pg
19 18 17 16 15 14 13
ISBN 0 330 10539 6
Printed in Great Britain by
Richard Clay Ltd, Bungay, Suffolk

This book is sold subject to the condition that it
shall not, by way of trade or otherwise, be lent, re-sold,
hired out or otherwise circulated without the publisher's prior
consent in any form of binding or cover other than that in which
it is published and without a similar condition including this
condition being imposed on the subsequent purchaser

With love to
Enid and John Leigh-Hunt

ACKNOWLEDGEMENTS

I WISH gratefully to acknowledge the guidance I have received from the undermentioned books:

History of England, William Hickman Smith Aubrey.

Life of Sir Thomas More, William Roper.

Thomas More, R. W. Chambers.

Life of Wolsey, Cavendish.

Utopia, Sir Thomas More.

A Dialogue of Comfort, Sir Thomas More.

The Latin Epigrams of Thomas More, edited with Translations and Notes by Leicester Bradner and Charles Arthur Lynch.

England in Tudor Times, L. F. Salzman, M.A., F.S.A.

British History, John Wade.

Lives of the Queens of England, Agnes Strickland.

Old and New London, Walter Thornbury.

The Divorce of Catherine of Aragon, James Anthony Froude.

Wolsey (Great Lives), Ashley Sampson.

Early Tudor Drama, A. W. Reed, M.A., D.Lit.

J.P.

ONE

'AND WHO is this man who dares oppose us?' demanded the King. 'Who is this Thomas More? Eh? Answer me that.'

The King was angry. He sat very straight in the royal chair, one slender hand lying on the purple velvet which covered the table, the other stroking the ermine which covered his mantle. He was battling to subdue his rage, to preserve his habitual calm; for he was a shrewd man and his life had taught him that unheated words were more effective than the sword.

He looked from one to the other of the two men who sat with him at the velvet-covered table where lay the documents which had absorbed their attention until the entrance of the man Tyler.

'You, Empson! You, Dudley! Tell me this: Who is this man More?'

'Methinks I have heard his name, Your Grace,' said Sir Edmund Dudley. 'But I know him not.'

'We should be more careful whom we allow to be elected as our London burgesses.'

'Indeed yes, Your Grace,' agreed Sir Richard Empson.

The King's fury was getting the better of him. He was glaring distastefully at Master Tyler, that gentleman of the Privy Chamber who had brought the news; and it was not this king's habit to blame men for the news they brought. Tyler trembled; he was fervently wishing that he had allowed someone else to acquaint the King with the news that his Parliament – owing to the pithily-worded arguments of one of the youngest burgesses – had refused to grant him the sum of money for which he had asked.

There was one other in the room of the palace of Richmond, and he – a boy of thirteen – was staring idly out of the window watching a barge on the river, wishing he were the gallant who accompanied the fair young lady as they went gaily on to

Hampton; he could see them well, for his eyesight was keen. The sun was shining on the water which was almost the same colour as the dress of the young lady. This Prince was already fond of ladies, and they were fond of him. Although young as yet, he was already as tall as many men and showed promise of shooting up to great stature. His skin was fair and his hair had a tinge of red in it so that it shone like the gold ornaments on his clothes.

Now he had forgotten the young lady; he wished to be playing tennis, beating any who challenged him, listening to the compliments they paid, pretending not to hear, while they pretended not to know he listened. For two years he had been aware of such adulation; and how could he, who so loved adulation, feel really sorry that his brother had died? He had loved Arthur; he had admired him as his elder brother; but it was as though he had lost a coarse frieze garment and, because of his loss, found himself the possessor of a doublet of velvet and cloth of gold.

He was conscious that he was a prince who would one day be a king.

And when I am, he told himself, I shall not sit in council with such mumping oafs as Master Dudley and Master Empson. I shall not worry my head with the hoarding of money, but the spending of it. I shall have merry men about me—fat spenders, not lean misers.

'And you, my son,' he heard his father say, 'what of you? Have you heard aught of this fellow More?'

The boy rose and came to the table to stand in homage before the King.

My son! pondered the King. What a king he will make! What resemblance he bears to the hated House of York! I see his grandfather, Edward of York, in that proud carriage.

And the boy's father was faintly worried, for he remembered Edward the Fourth in his latter years when the tertian fever had laid hold of him and, like a mischievous scribe, had added a smudge here, a line there, until an ugly mask had made a palimpsest of his once beautiful face. But not only the fever had done this; it had been aided by the life he led: too much good food, too much good wine; too many women – anyhow, anywhere, from serving-wenches to duchesses. Such debauchery took toll of a man.

I must speak with this son of mine, thought the King. I must set his feet on the rightful path. I must teach him how to save money and keep it. Money is Power, and Power is a King's heritage; and if that king be a Tudor king – a young tree, the prey of sly and subtle pests, in danger of being overcome by older shrubs who claimed that young tree's territory – then that Tudor king must have wealth, for wealth buys soldiers and arms to support him; wealth buys security.

He was not displeased with his own acquisitions; but when he had filled one coffer, he was eager to fill another. Everything he touched did not turn to gold as easily as he would wish. The touch of Midas was in his shrewd brain, not in his fingers. Ah well, he would then thank God for that shrewd brain. War drained the coffers of other kings; it filled those of Henry Tudor. He used war; he did not allow war to use him. He could draw money from the people by telling them that they must do battle with their enemies the French and the Scots; and the people were ready to pay, for they believed that the bread of righteous anger thrown upon the waters of conquest would yield rich booty. But Henry the Seventh knew that war took all the treasure that was offered, demanded more, and in exchange for so much riches gave pestilence, hunger and poverty. So the King, having collected his money, would make a speedy peace; and that which was intended to bring war to the enemies of England, brought wealth to England's king.

He was a king who had suffered from many insurrections; insecure, since he was a bastard branch of the royal tree, grafted on by an indiscreet widowed queen, there had been many to oppose him. Yet each year saw him more firmly seated on the throne. He did not demand the blood of those who planned to destroy him: he only asked for their lands and goods. Thus he grew richer every year.

He now looked at the boy who stood before him, not as a

father might look at his son, but as a king regarding his successor.

Last year, the Queen had died in childbed, and the King was eager to get himself a new wife. This was the only son left to him; and the death of Arthur, so recently a bridegroom, had been a bitter blow. The loss of the Queen was not so important; there were many women in the world – royal women – who would not hesitate to become the wife of the King of England; and it was pleasurable to contemplate that wives brought dowries.

Secretly he was not sorry to see the end of Queen Elizabeth. She had been a good, meek wife; she had given him several children; but she was of the House of York, and reasonable as he was, he had found that hard to forget.

'Well, my son?'

'I have met the man More, Your Grace.'

'Then tell me what you know of him.'

'He is a lawyer, Sire, and it was when I was at Eltham with my sisters that I saw him. He came with Mountjoy and the scholar, Erasmus; for Erasmus was visiting Mountjoy whom he had once tutored.'

'Yes,' said the King; 'and what manner of man was this More?'

'Of medium height, I should say, Sire. Of bright complexion. And he had merry eyes and a way of speech that provoked much laughter.'

'Methinks his way of speech provoked much parsimony in our Parliament. And that we will not have. Is that all you can tell us?'

'That is all, Sire.'

The King waved his hand and the Prince, bowing, went back to his stool.

'He should be heavily fined,' declared the King.

'He is not a rich man, Your Grace,' murmured Empson. 'A scholar, a writer, a lawyer . . . little could be extorted from him.'

The King could trust his henchmen, Empson and Dudley.

They were of his own kind. They had their private greed; they enriched themselves while they enriched the King.

'He has a father, Sire,' said Dudley.

'Who,' added Empson, 'might be good for a hundred pounds.'

'Put him in the Tower.'

'On the charge of possessing a disloyal son, Your Grace?'

'Nay. Nay. You know better than that. Look into his affairs, then bring some charge against him. See what goods he hath; then we will decide on the fine. And do so with all speed.'

The King wished to be alone with his son.

The boy, when he had stood before him, had aroused anxieties within him and temporarily they had swamped his anger at the failure to obtain as much money as he wished. This was because of the boy's appearance; the proud set of the head on the shoulders, the dazzlingly fair skin, the vital hair that was almost the colour of gold, the small sensual mouth, the bright blue eyes had reminded the King so vividly of the boy's maternal grandfather; and he remembered the profligacy of that man.

He felt the need, therefore, to talk with his son immediately.

When they were alone he addressed him: 'Henry.'

The boy rose at once, but his father went on: 'Nay; stay where you are. No ceremony whilst we are alone. Now I would speak to you as father to son.'

'Yes, Father.'

'One day, my boy, you will be king of this realm.'

'Yes, Father.'

'Three years ago, we did not know that you were destined for such greatness. Then you were merely the King's second son, who, your father had decided, should become Archbishop of Canterbury. Now your steps are turned from Church to Throne. My son, do you know that the cares of kingship outweigh the glory and the honour?'

The boy answered: 'Yes, Father.'

But he did not believe this. So it might be with lean, pale men such as his father, whose thoughts were all of filling their coffers; but if a king were young and handsome and the eyes of ladies lightened as they rested upon him, and those of the young men

13

were warm with envy and admiration, that was a different matter. The glory and the honour could outweigh the care; and if they did not do so in the case of Henry the Seventh, Henry the Eighth would see to it that they did so for him.

'Many temptations come to kings, my son. You would do well to study the history of those who have gone before.'

'That I do, Father. My Lord Mountjoy insisted that I did so when he tutored me.'

'There are times when a king is beset on all sides, when traitors rise and threaten him. Then he must act with speed and wisdom.'

'I know it, Sire.'

'You know then why I wish you to be present at our councils. I hope you do not spend your time staring idly through the windows, dreaming of sport and pleasure. I would have you learn from what you hear at these our meetings.'

'I do, Father.'

'There are some who would have sent that fellow More to the Tower and would have had his head on London Bridge for what he has done. But such acts are folly. Remember his: Let the people think that the Parliament guides the King; but let the members of the Parliament know that the King has a hundred ways of striking at them if they obey him not.'

'The people are not pleased,' said the boy boldly. 'They like not taxes, and they say that there have been too many taxes. They murmur against Dudley and Empson.' He dared not say they murmured against the King, but he knew the people would never love his father as he believed they would love his father's son. When he went into the streets they called his name. 'God bless the Prince! God bless Prince Hal!' The sound of their cheers was sweeter than the music of his lute, and he loved his lute dearly. His father could not tell *him* how a king should behave.

'There must be those to do a king's work,' said King Henry, 'and if it be ugly work, then it is the duty of those to bear the reproaches of the people. My son, you will one day be not only a king, but a rich king. When I slew the traitor Crookback at

Bosworth Field and took the crown, I found I had inherited a bankrupt kingdom.'

'A right noble act it was to slay the traitor!' said the boy.

'Yet coming to the throne as we have done is a dangerous way. Never forget it. Be watchful. Above all, learn from those who have gone before. Use the lessons of the past to overcome the dangers of the future. You remind me of your grandfather, great King Edward, for you have something of his lineaments and his stature. Ah, there was a man!'

Father and son smiled as they thought of the boy's grandfather.

With his beauty and charm, thought the King, he lured taxes from his people's pockets and he called them 'Benevolences'. Oh, for such power!

He roamed the countryside as an ordinary gentleman, thought the Prince; and such was his charm and beauty that no woman could resist him. Oh, for such power!

The sun's rays slanted through the windows of Richmond Palace and as the father began to talk to the son of the delights and dangers of kingship, they ceased to think of Thomas More.

*   *   *

Meanwhile in the grounds of a pleasant old mansion in the little village of Stepney, the object of the King's wrath was walking arm-in-arm with one of his greatest friends, his confessor, Dr John Colet, a man whose wit and learning delighted him almost as much as the affection they bore each other.

Colet, some ten years older than Thomas More, was listening gravely to his friend's account of what had happened in the Parliament.

He shook his head. ' 'Twas a brave act, I'll grant you; but there is a point in human nature where bravery may be called folly, and folly, bravery.'

'Is it better to be a brave fool or a wise coward? Tell me that, John. I love the wise; I love the brave; and I love not cowards nor fools. What a perverse thing is life when the wrong partners walk together!'

John Colet was in no mood for laughter. He was alarmed.

'Had it been anything but money, the King would have been the more ready to forgive you.'

'Had it been anything but money, would the King have been begging it from his Parliament? Nay, the King loves money. He loves the colour of gold. He loves the sight of gold in his coffers . . . gold plate . . . gold coins. He rejoices in the knowledge that he is not only a king, but a rich king.'

'Friend Thomas, there is one thing you should take to heart. Now, I am an older man than you are . . .'

'I know it, thou greybeard.'

'Then know this also: If you wish to make an enemy of the King, get between him and the money he hopes to win. Thus – and more quickly than in any other way – can you rouse his wrath. And, Thomas, remember this now and for ever: it is a perilous thing to set yourself against a king.'

'It is an even more perilous thing to set oneself against one's conscience, John. Tell me this: Should the King be allowed to impose such taxes on his people? You yourself have often said it should not be so. Come, admit it.'

'What we have said, we have said in the circle of our friends. It is another matter to say such things in Parliament.'

'I call to mind that there are those of my friends who have lectured in such manner as to attract multitudes. And this they have done in public places.' Thomas put his head on one side and lifted his shoulder in a manner which was characteristic of him. 'I think of one friend, not so far from me at this moment, who has placed himself in high danger by too boldly expressing what are called "dangerous thoughts".'

Colet said impatiently: 'I talked of theology. You have talked of money. There was never a more avaricious king than ours. There was never one more vindictive when his darling money is kept from him. However, there is one thing that pleases me. You are a poor man, my friend. To rob you of your wordly goods would hardly be worth the time of the King's henchmen.'

'Now there we see one of the great compensations in life. Poverty is my shield; it protects me from the onslaughts of mine enemies. But have done with this matter. It was of others that I came hither to talk to you.'

They walked through the orchards, where the fruit was beginning to ripen. 'Ah, John,' said Thomas, 'there'll be a good harvest this year if the wasps and the birds allow it. Hast heard aught of our friend Erasmus of late? Now, John, do not scowl. I know it was a grave blow to you when he would not stay in Oxford and lecture there with you. But it was compulsion that moved him to return to Rotterdam and poverty.'

'He disappoints me,' said Colet. 'He could have stayed in this country. There was work for him to do. Could he not have studied here as much as he wished?'

'Remember what he said to you, John. He said it was you who disappointed yourself. You made a picture of him – far too learned, he says, far too saintly. *He* has not disappointed you, for he has always been himself; it is you who have disappointed yourself by making a false image of him. He is right, John. And I too have disappointed him. I rejoice that he does not love gold as the King does. For you know I told him it was safe for him to bring his money into England, and that he could safely take it out when he wished. My knowledge of the law was at fault – and I call myself a lawyer! Because of it my friend was deceived, and so . . . he was not allowed to take his money home. If he loved his few pieces of gold as the King loves his full coffers, Erasmus would hate me even as does the King. Hath it occurred to you that money bringeth much trouble to me? Now, that is an odd thing, for it is the love of money that is the root of evil; yet I pay so little court to it that I win the King's anger and, I fear, the scorn of my learned friend Erasmus, through my contempt of it.'

'It would seem,' said John Colet, 'that my wise friends are fools. There is Erasmus who must return to poverty in order to perfect his Greek. There is you who must take great pains to provoke the King . . like a boy with a stick bent on teasing a bull.'

'But such an insignificant boy . . . a boy who is not worth the tossing.'

'Believe it or not, even those whose passion is the accumulation of money can have other passions. Revenge, for one.'

'Enough, John. Let us speak of my affairs. I have made a decision which will alter the course of my life.'

John Colet turned to look at his friend. The blue eyes were twinkling, the usually pink cheeks were flushed a rosy red. May God preserve him, thought Dr Colet, for his nature is the sweetest I ever knew, and there are times when I fear it will lead him to trouble.

'Come, let us sit on the seat here and watch the barges sail up the river to London. Then tell me of this decision.' They sat down and John went on: 'You have decided to take your vows?'

Thomas was silent; he laid his hands on his knees and looked across the river to where the willows hung low in the water and the rose-tinted umbels of the flowering rush bloomed among the purple stars of loosestrife, the figwort, with its brown helmets standing guard over them.

Thomas was twenty-six years of age – an age, he had decided, when a man must make decisions. He was fair-haired, blue-eyed, of fresh complexion; and it was the sweetness of expression which people remembered.

Looking at him now, John Colet thought of the friends he loved; there was the great and learned Erasmus, the intellectual Grocyn, the reliable William Lily, and the keen-witted, kindly Linacre; all these men were the great scholars of the day; yet none of them could charm and attract as did Thomas More. Thomas was younger than either Colet or Erasmus, yet both these men counted him as their intellectual equal. He had a first-class brain; he could assimilate knowledge with astonishing speed; he could converse learnedly with humour and a sense of fun, and in the sharpness of his wit he never stooped to wound. Yet it was not only for these qualities that he was loved; it was the sweet kindliness of the man, his courteous manner even towards the humblest; it was the frankness mingling with the courtesy; it was the never-absent sympathy, the understanding of the problems of others and the ever-present desire to help any in distress.

'Nay,' said Thomas. ''Tis not to take the vows.'

John turned to him and grasped his hands. 'Then I am glad that you have at last come to this decision.'

'I am a greedy man,' said Thomas. 'Ah yes, I am, John. I have discovered that one life is not enough for me. I want to live two lives . . . side by side. I would take my vows and be with my dear brothers of the Charterhouse. How that beckons me! The solitude of the cloisters, the sweetness of bells at vespers, the sonorous Latin chants . . . the gradual defeat of all fleshly desires. What victory, eh, John? When the hair-shirt ceases to torment; when a wooden pillow has more comfort to offer than a downy feather bed. I can see great joy in such a life. . . . But, then, I would be a family man. To tell the truth, John, I find that beside this monk within me, there is another – a man who looks longingly at the fair faces of young maidens, who thinks of kissing and caressing them; this is a man who yearns for the married state, for the love of a woman and the laughter of children. I have had to make a choice.'

'I'm glad you have chosen, Thomas; and I am sure that you have chosen well.'

'Then I have not disappointed your hopes of me? I see you did not set me such a high standard as you did our friend from Rotterdam.'

'Nay; I think not of standards. I think how pleasant it will be when you are a family man and I visit you, and your good wife will greet me at your table. . . .'

'And you will listen to my children, repeating their lessons, and you will tell them that you have never known children so skilled in the arts of learning. Ah, John, would it not be an excellent thing if we could live two lives and, when we have reached an age of wisdom, lightly step out of that which pleases us no longer into that one that gives us great pleasure.'

'You are a dreamer, my friend. Indeed, it would bring no satisfaction, for you would be as undecided at fifty as you are at thirty. Each road would have joy and sorrow to offer a man; of that I am sure.'

'There you are right, John.'

'But I'll swear the life you have chosen will be a good one.'

'But is it the right one, John? Is it the right one for me, do you think?'

'It is only at the completion of a man's life that such can be decided.'

'Then tomorrow I ride into Essex,' said Thomas, 'to the house of Master Colt at New Hall. And I shall ask Master Colt for the hand of his eldest daughter in marriage.'

'The eldest! But methought it was one of the younger ones who had taken your fancy.'

Thomas frowned a little; then he smiled, and his smile was one of infinite charm.

'I changed my mind.'

'Oh . . . so you liked the looks of one of the younger girls first, and then . . . you fell in love with her sister. Methinks you are a fickle man.'

'It seems so, John, for first I fell in love with the Charterhouse and a life of retirement; and you see I could not be faithful to that love for long.'

'Ah, but that was not a true love. For all those years you lived with the monks; you fasted and did your penances; but did you take your vows? No. Always you postponed that ceremony. And in the meantime, to please your father, you continued with your law studies. The Charterhouse was never your true love. Then you saw young Mistress Colt, and you thought how fair she was; but you did not ask her father for her. It was only when you saw the eldest girl that you were successfully weaned from your desire to retire from the world. A long and fruitful married life to you, Thomas! May you have many sons and a few daughters . . . for daughters are useful in the house.'

'My daughters will be as important in my eyes as my sons. They shall be educated exactly as my sons will be.'

'Women educated as men! Nonsense!'

'John, what is the greatest gift the world has to offer? You will answer that as I would: Learning. Is it not what you plan to give to the world? How many times have you talked of what you will do with your fortune when it is yours? You worship in the temple of Learning with me. Now would you deny it to one child because its sex is not the same as another?'

'I can see that you wax argumentative. Well, that is what I expect of you. It grows a little chilly here by the river. Let us walk back to the house whilst we talk of this thing. There is not much time, since you say you must ride on towards Essex tomorrow.'

'Yes, I must set out at sunrise.'

'On a mission of love! I will pray for you this night. I will remember the younger daughter on whom your fancy dwelt, and I shall pray that the husband will be less fickle than the lover.'

They walked slowly towards the house, and by the time they reached it they were deep in further discussion.

* * *

John Colt welcomed his guest. He considered the lawyer of London a worthy suitor for his eldest girl. As he said to his wife, to tell the truth he had almost despaired of the girl's getting a husband.

Jane lacked something which her sisters possessed. It was not only that she was a little plain; she lacked also their vitality. She seemed to want nothing but to stay in the country, tending the gardens or working in the house; and she seemed to find the company of the servants preferable to that of her own family or their neighbours. It would be good to see her a wife before her sisters married.

'Welcome to New Hall, friend Thomas!' cried Master Colt, embracing the man he hoped would soon be his son-in-law. 'There, groom! Take his honour's horse. Now, come you into the house. You'll be tired after your journey. We've put supper forward an hour, for we thought you'd be hungry. 'Twill be five of the clock this day. And Jane's in the kitchen. Ah! Knowing you were coming, she must be there to see that the meat is done to a turn, and the pastry of such lightness as was never known. You know what girls are!'

He nudged Thomas and broke into hearty laughter. Thomas laughed with him.

'But,' said Thomas, 'it was to do homage neither to the beef nor to the pastry that I came, Master Colt.'

Master Colt broke into more laughter. He was a man of bucolic manners. He could never look at Thomas More without a chuckle. All this learning! It amused him. What was it for? 'God's Body,' he often said to his wife, 'I'd rather one of our boys was hanged than become a bookworm. Books! Learning! What does it do for a man? Ah, if our Jane were like her sisters, I'd not have her throw herself away on a lawyer from London, whose nose, I'll swear, likes better the smell of parchment than good roast beef.'

Now he said: 'Come, Master More, we'll put some flesh on those bones before you leave us. We'll show you that a veal pie has more nourishment to offer you than Latin verse. Don't you agree? Don't you agree?'

'Take the roast beef of old England to nourish the muscles of the body,' said Thomas. 'And then digest the wisdom of Plato to develop the mind.'

'Your mind won't build you a fine house to live in, Master More; it won't raise a fine family. A man must live by the strength of his body.'

'Or by the agility of his wits as do the King's ministers.'

'Bah! Who'd be one of them? Here today and gone tomorrow. My Lord this and that today, and tomorrow it's "Off with his head!" Nay, fight your own battles, not the King's.'

'I see that you have gleaned much wisdom from your red roast beef.'

Master Colt slipped his arm through that of his visitor. Queer, he thought, he might be a bookworm, but he was a merry man, and in spite of his oddity, Master Colt could not help being fond of him.

He felt proud of his possessions as he took Thomas through the forecourt and into the house. In the hall which occupied the ground floor of the central block, the great table was already set for the meal. Master Colt had little time for new-fangled town manners, and all his household ate at the same table – those servants who were not waiting, below the salt. Thomas looked at the sunlight slanting through the horn windows, at the vaulted roof, at the two staircases and the gallery from which the doors led to the other wings; but he was not thinking of the house. He was wondering what he would say to Jane.

'Come to my winter parlour and drink a mug of wine with me. Can you smell the juniper and rosemary? That's our Jane. She knows much of the herbs that grow in the fields, and she is for ever burning them in pomanders to make the air sweet.'

Master Colt still thought he had to impress on Jane's suitor the wifely qualities of the girl, as though Thomas needed to be impressed, as though he had not already made up his mind.

His host led the way to the winter parlour and called for wine to be brought.

The winter parlour was a cosy place; it contained hangings embroidered in rich colours by the girls, and there was a table about which were placed several stools; Master Colt was very proud of the polished metal mirror and the new clock.

They sat at the table and wine was brought, but Master Colt noticed that his guest merely touched his with his lips for the sake of politeness.

He sighed. Here was a man he did not understand, who did not care what he ate, and loved books better than wine. Yet any husband for Jane was better than no husband at all.

Then through the window he caught sight of Jane with her flower-basket.

'Why,' said Jane's father, 'there is Jane. You have seen her. You're thinking you'd rather have a word with her than drink wine with her father. Well then, slip out into the garden now. You can speak with her before supper is served.'

So Thomas went out of the house to Jane.

* * *

Jane knew he was coming. She was afraid. Her sisters laughed at her for her timidity. She should be grateful, they told her. At last she had a suitor. At last a man was thinking of marrying her. She had better be careful how she acted, for he was not caught yet.

I wish, thought Jane, that I could stay at home with my heartsease and snapdragons, my sweet williams and gilly-flowers. I want to stay and help salt the meat after the killing, and make the butter and cheese, and to see that the servants watch well the roasting meat, to make the bread and pies. I could stay at home and do these things.

But Jane knew that was not what was expected of a girl. She must marry. If she did not, she was scorned; her sisters would marry and shut her out of their confidences; they would laugh at her; they would pity her; even now they called her Poor Jane.

She was Poor Jane because, while she was afraid of marriage, she was even more afraid of not being married at all.

He was very old, this man who had selected her; he was twenty-six, and she was just turned sixteen. Still, it was better to have an old husband than no husband at all. He was very clever, so they said; and he knew much of what had been written in books. But her father did not think very highly of that sort of cleverness. As for June, it alarmed her greatly, for she could not understand half of what Thomas More said to her; and when he began to speak she would think, since he was fond of jesting, that she must surely smile; but she was never certain when the smile should come. Perhaps she would learn. She was sure there were many things which she would have to learn, and that was doubtless one of them.

Still, she continually repeated to herself, and she was sure of the wisdom of this: it was better to marry any man than not to marry at all.

When, in the kitchen, she had heard his horse, she had taken her flower-basket and run into the gardens to hide herself. Today he had come to ask her to marry him. Her father had told her this would happen and that she must accept him and tell him that she would be very happy to become his wife.

Happy to become his wife. . . .

Would her young sister have been happy to be his wife, and would he have been happy to wed her?

She wondered why he had suddenly turned from her sister to

herself; her father had sent her sister away at that time, and again she wondered why.

Life was difficult to understand. If it were only as simple as tending the garden, how contented she would be!

Now she started, and her heart began to beat in real fear, for Thomas was coming towards her.

*   *   *

He saw her bending over the flowers, rosy colour flooding her neck, for her head was bent so that he could not see her face.

I will make her happy, he swore. Poor, fragile little Jane.

'Why, Mistress Colt,' he said. 'Why, Jane, I trust I find you well.'

She curtsied awkwardly, and the flowers fell from her basket.

'You tremble,' he said. 'Jane, you must not be afraid of me.'

'I . . . I am not afraid.' She lifted her eyes to his face. They reminded him of her sister's and he felt a pang of regret. His feelings for the two girls were so different. The younger girl, whom her father had sent away, was a creature of charm and beauty; he had been fascinated by the smooth, clear skin, the childish line of the cheeks, a certain boldness in her eyes that proclaimed her aware of the fact that she was admired. There had been, in her face and form, a certain promise of carnal delight. It was she who had decided him, who had shown him clearly that he must not take his vows, that he must leave the Charterhouse and make a home with a wife.

Was that love? He thought of others who had attracted him. He was no monk; he was no priest. He was a sensual man, it seemed. God had made him thus; and he believed he would have to control such feelings during the course of his life. All his friends had taken orders: Colet, Linacre, Lily. And what were women to Erasmus? He could see that he himself was fashioned of different clay. He wanted to be a saint; but since women moved him, charmed him, he was right not to turn from them; for it was better to be a layman who knew his weakness and tried to make an ideal family life, than a priest who took his vows and afterwards broke them.

25

He had loved young Mistress Colt until he had caught a look in Jane's eyes which had moved him – in another manner, it was true – as deeply as his desire for her sister.

He remembered the day well. They had been at dinner; and dinner was a merry meal at New Hall. Master Colt paid the deepest respect to his food. Why, he had his servants doff their hats with respect when the meat was brought in; his table was covered with so many dishes that it was almost impossible to make room for the wooden platters the family used. They had been at dinner, and Thomas had looked at his loved one, merrily chatting, delighting him with the quickness of her retorts. She had not been an educated girl. What girls were? Ah, that was a great mistake, as he had argued many times both with Colet and Erasmus. If women had souls, they also had brains, and it was as wrong to neglect the latter as the former. No, she was not educated, but he had appreciated her quick mind, that little display of wit. He had pictured his married life. They would sit after supper and he would teach her Latin; he would read her some of his epigrams and later perhaps those he was translating with Lily from the Greek anthology into Latin – but that was looking ahead. Then, when he had educated her, he would astonish his friends; and she would talk with them and be one of them. Yes, she should not only make a home for him, and give him children, she should join him and his friends in discussing theology, the need for reforming some of the old tenets of the Church; they would analyse the works of Plato, Socrates and Euripides; they themselves would write verses and essays which they would read to one another. He had looked forward to those days. He saw himself not only caressing her beautiful body, but feeding her mind. It had been an enchanting picture.

And then, as his glance strayed from her, he had been aware of Jane. Jane, the quiet one whom they all twitted because she was not so ready with her tongue, because she was the eldest and because no man had sought her in marriage.

Jane had been looking at her sister with admiration and envy. Not malicious envy. Jane was of too gentle a nature to experience unadulterated envy. It was merely that she became more insignificant than usual when her sister chattered; and as he watched her, Thomas More found his love for the younger girl infringed by his pity for the elder one.

He had tried to draw her into conversation, but she would keep aloof like a frightened doe. He found her alone in the gardens and he said to her: 'You must not be afraid to speak, little Jane. Tell me, why are you afraid to speak?'

She had said: 'I have nothing to say.'

'But,' he had protested, 'there must be something behind those eyes . . . some thought. Tell me what it is.'

'It would sound silly if I said it. Everyone would laugh.'

'*I* should not laugh.'

Then she told him how she thought the scent of gilly-flowers was the best in the world, and when she smelt it, she would always – no matter where she was – imagine that she was in the walled garden at New Hall. And she told him she feared she was a coward, for when they killed the animals in November, she shut herself in her room, stopped up her ears and wept. And sometimes she wept during the salting.

'Those are kindly thoughts, Jane,' he had said. 'And thoughts that should be told.'

'But they would laugh if I told them. They would say that I am even sillier than they believed me to be.'

'I should not laugh, Jane,' he had told her. 'I should never laugh.'

Then she had answered: 'But you would laugh more than anyone because you are cleverer than any.'

'Nay. Because I know more of what is in books than do your brothers and sisters, the more I understand. For is not understanding knowledge? When people laugh at others it is often because those others differ from themselves. Therefore the ignorant think them strange. But if you study the ways of men, you learn much; and as your knowledge grows there is little to surprise you. The man who travels the world, in time becomes no longer astonished by the looks and customs of men of other lands. Yet the man who lives in his village all his life, is amazed by the habits of the man dwelling but ten miles away.'

'I do not entirely understand your words,' Jane had told him. 'But I understand your kindness.'

'Then, Jane, you are clever, for if more understood the inten-tions behind men's words, the world would be a happier place, and it is those who achieve happiness and lead others to it who are the clever ones of this world.'

Then she had told him how astonished she was that he, who was so much cleverer than others, should not frighten her so much; and that he, who had friends among the most learned of men, should know more than others how to be kind to a simple maid.

After that she would give him her quiet smile, and he would see the pleasure in her face when he spoke to her.

Others had noticed his friendship with Jane; and one day, when he had arrived at New Hall, it was to find that young Mistress Colt had gone away, and, with a sudden shock, he realized that he was expected to marry Jane.

To marry Jane! But it was merely a tender pity that he felt for her. It was her gay, tantalizing sister who had shown him that a monk's life was not for him.

His first impulse had been to ride away or explain his feelings to Master Colt.

Her father might have guessed his reluctance. He said: 'Jane is a good girl. The best in the world. The man who married her would get a good wife.'

Master Colt was not a subtle man; but if Thomas More was not moved by the desire of a country gentleman to get his daughter off his hands, he was deeply touched by the mute appeal of Jane.

He saw at once what he had done. With his kindness he had sown seeds of hope. Jane had a new gown; Jane had won the respect of her family, for which she had always longed, because they believed that a man wished to make Jane his wife.

What could he do? Could he ride away and never return to New Hall? Could he still ask for the hand of the girl with whom he had fallen in love?

And what of Jane? Meek and mild she was; but it was those

of her temperament who suffered most cruelly. And her sister
– what of her? But she was a gay spirit and there would be so
many to admire her. She was very young, and he doubted
whether she had ever thought very seriously about one who
would seem elderly to her.

If he hurt Jane, if he wounded her pride, if he was responsible
for bringing upon her her family's scorn, how could he forgive
himself? He had meant to make her life easier. Could it be
that in his blind folly, he had made it harder for her to bear?

Being the man he was, he saw only one course open to him.
He must turn tenderness into love; he must marry Jane. He
must turn her into a woman such as he wished to have for his
wife. Why should it not be so? She had been a docile daughter;
she would be a docile wife. So he removed the girl he loved from
the picture of domestic bliss and set Jane there in her place. He
saw pleasant evenings when they would sit over their books
while he talked to her in the Latin tongue. And after Latin . . .
Greek.

And so, as Thomas More came into the garden to speak to
Jane, he was picturing the future . . . their happy home, their
children and his learned friends . . . all merry together.

'Why, Jane,' he said, 'we saw you through the window and
your father bade me join you.'

'You are welcome,' she answered with her quiet smile.

And in the garden, with the hot sun upon him and the girl
beside him, her eyes downcast, there came to him a reminder
that he had not yet spoken those words which would make it
impossible for him to turn back. Suddenly he thought of the
quiet of the Charterhouse, of those years when he had lived with
the Carthusian monks, and he longed to be back with them. He
wanted another chance to think, to brood on this matter, to talk
it over with his friends.

But because he was silent so long, she had lifted her eyes to his
face; she had been looking at him for some seconds in anxious
bewilderment before he realized this.

How young she was! How pathetic! How could he leave her
to the mercy of her family? Dear Jane! He guessed what her

life would be if he rode away now. Her sisters would taunt her; the whole family would let her see that she had failed; she would become Jane-of-no-account, in very truth.

Life was unfair to such women.

Pity coloured all his thoughts. It was ever so. When he saw the poor in the streets he could never resist giving alms. His friends said: 'The word goes round among the beggars: "Thomas More comes this way!" And they uncover their sores, and some feign blindness. Make sure that in enriching the beggars you do not beggar yourself.' And he had answered: 'There may be some who are not so poor as they would seem to be; there may be some who feign distress to win my pity and with it money from my pocket. But, my friends, I would rather be the victim of a rogue than that any man should be the victim of my indifference to his suffering.'

Pity. Sweet Pity. A nobler emotion than passion or desire. Here then, he thought, is what I most desire: A happy home. And cannot Jane give me that?

'Jane,' he said, 'I want you to be my wife.'

She stared down at the flowers in her basket.

'What say you, Jane?' he asked tenderly.

'My father wishes it.'

'He does. And you?'

She smiled slowly. 'I shall try to be a good wife to you.'

He kissed her tenderly; and she thought: There will be less to fear with him than with anyone else, for he is the kindest man in the world.

'Then come. Let us go into the house and tell your father that you have consented to become my wife.'

They went into the hall, where the servants were now carrying in the dishes. Thomas was amused by the ceremony which was paid to the food.

'I was about to ask you to salute a new son,' he said to his host, 'but I see that he must keep his place until His Majesty the Ox hath been received.'

And only when the great side of beef was set on the table was Master Colt ready to embrace Thomas. Then, taking him to the head of the table, he proclaimed to those assembled there that his daughter Jane was betrothed to Thomas More.

* * *

Jane was sitting at the window of her new home, which was called The Barge, looking out along Bucklersbury, thinking that she must be the most unhappy woman in the world. But then, Jane's knowledge of the world was slight.

The Barge! She hated it. It was a foolish name to give a gloomy old house. 'The Barge,' Thomas had explained, 'will be our home. Why "The Barge"? you may ask. It is because in the days before the Walbrook was covered, the barges came right to this spot. Oh, Jane, we will wander through the City and we will picture it as it was in days gone by. Then you will see what a wonderful old City it is, and you will love it as I do – more than any other place in the world.'

But Jane could not love it. She could love no place but New Hall. She longed for her garden, for the quiet fields of buttercups and marguerites; she hated this great City with its shops and crowds of noisy people. All through the day she could hear the shouts of traders in the Poultry and the Chepe; she could smell the meats being roasted in the cook shops, and the scents from the apothecaries' of which there were so many in Bucklersbury; the scent of musk mingled with that of spices from the pepperers' and grocers' shops; and she was homesick . . . homesick for New Hall and the single life.

She wept a good deal. Often Thomas would look in dismay at her reddened eyelids; but when he asked what ailed her, she would shrink from him. She had not imagined that married life was like this, and she could not understand why so many people longed for it. Why did they think a girl had failed if she did not achieve it?

She had married a man whose heart was in books. In London he seemed older than he had in the country. Men came to the house; they were older even than her husband; and she would sit listening to their talk without understanding anything they said.

She was foolish, she knew. Her family had always said so. How tragic it was that she, the simplest of them all, should be married to one of the most learned men in England!

There was so much to learn. She had always believed that a wife had but to watch the servants and see that there was no waste in the kitchen. That had been her stepmother's duty. But here at The Barge, much was expected of her.

'Jane,' he had said, 'I will lay the whole world at your feet.' She had thought that was one of the most beautiful things a husband could say to his wife; but she had discovered that his way of laying the whole world at her feet was to attempt to teach her Latin and to make her repeat, by way of recreation, the sermons they heard in St Stephen's Church in Walbrook.

'Poor little Jane,' he said, 'they have neglected your education, but we will remedy that, my love. I said I would lay the whole world at your feet, did I not? Yes, Jane, I will give you the key to all the treasures in the world. Great literature – that is the world's greatest treasure; and the key is understanding the languages in which it is written.'

She was a most unhappy bride. She felt bewildered and lost and wished she were dead.

Surely everything a normal woman needed was denied her. In a book he had written, entitled *The Life of John Picus*, there was a dedication to a woman. She had felt a faint stirring of jealousy, but she had discovered that the woman to whom the book was dedicated was a nun – a sister who lived with the Order of the Poor Clares just beyond the Minories. How could she be jealous of a nun? Even that was denied her. She knew that she had married no ordinary man, and she fervently wished that she had a husband whom she could understand – someone like her father or her brothers, even if there were occasions when he was angry with her and beat her. This harping on the value of learning, in spite of his kindness and gentleness, was sometimes more than she could bear.

He was trying to mould her, to make her into a companion as well as a wife. It was like asking an infant to converse with sages.

Dr Lily came to the house, as did Dr Linacre and Dr Colet; they conversed with her husband, and they laughed frequently, for Thomas laughed a good deal; but a woman could not continue to smile when she had no idea of the cause of laughter.

Sometimes her husband took her walking through the City, pointed out with pride what he considered places of interest.

They would walk through Walbrook and Candlewick Street, through Tower Street to the Great Tower. Then Thomas would tell her stories of what had happened within those gloomy walls, but she found she could not remember which of the kings and queens had taken part in them; and she would be worried because she knew she could not remember. Then he would take her to Goodman's Fields and pick daisies with her; they would make a chain together to hang about her neck; he would laugh and tease her because she was a country girl; but even then she would be afraid that he was making jokes which she did not recognize as such.

Sometimes they would walk along by the river or row over to Southwark, where the people were so poor. Then he would talk of the sufferings of the poor and how he visualised an ideal state where there was no such suffering. He loved to talk of this state which he built up in his imagination. She was rather glad when he did so, for he would not seem to notice that she was not listening, and she could let her mind enjoy memories of New Hall.

At other times they would walk through the Poultry to the Chepe and to Paul's Cross to listen to the preachers. He would glance at her anxiously, hoping that her delight in the sermons equalled his own. He would often talk of Oxford and Cambridge, where so many of his friends had studied. 'One day, Jane, I shall take you there,' he promised her. She dreaded that; she felt that such places would be even more oppressive than this City with its noisy crowds.

Once she watched a royal procession in the streets. She saw the King himself – a disappointing figure, unkingly, she thought, solemn and austere, looking as though he considered such displays a waste of money and time. But with him had been the young Prince of Wales, who must surely be the most handsome Prince in the world. She had cheered with the crowd when he had ridden by on his grey horse, so noble, so beautiful in his purple velvet cloak, his hair gleaming like gold, his sweet face, as someone in the crowd said, as lovely as a girl's, yet masculine withal. It seemed to Jane that the Prince, who was smiling and bowing to all, let his eyes linger for a moment on her. She felt herself blushing; and surely all the homage and admiration she wished to convey must have been there for him to see. Then it had seemed that the Prince had a special smile for Jane; and as she stood there, she was happy – happy to have left New Hall, because there she could never have had a smile from the boy who would one day be the King.

The Prince passed on, but something had happened to Jane; she no longer felt quite so stupid; and when Thomas told her of the coming of King Henry to the throne, she listened eagerly and she found that what he had to tell was of interest to her. Thomas was delighted with that interest, and when they reached The Barge he read her some notes which he had compiled when, as a boy, he had been sent to the household of Cardinal Morton, there to learn what he could. The notes were written in Latin, but he translated them into English for her, and she enjoyed the story of the coming of the Tudor King; she wept over the two little Princes who, Thomas told her, had been murdered in the Tower by the order of their wicked, crookbacked uncle, Richard. She could not weep for the death of Arthur, for, had Arthur lived, that beautiful Prince who had smiled at her would never be a King. So the death of Arthur, she was sure, could not be a tragedy but a blessing in disguise.

Thomas, delighted with her interest, gave her a lesson in Latin; and although she was slow to understand, she began to feel that she might learn a little.

She thought a good deal about the handsome Prince, but a conversation she overheard one day sent her thoughts fearfully to the Prince's father, the flinty-faced King.

John More came to see his son and daughter-in-law. Like Thomas, he was a lawyer, a kindly-faced man with shrewd eyes.

He patted Jane's head, wished her happiness and asked her if she were with child. She blushed and said she was not.

Marriage, she heard him tell Thomas, was like putting the hand into a blind bag which was full of eels and snakes. There were seven snakes to every eel.

She did not understand whether that meant he was pleased with his son's marriage or not; and what eels and snakes had to do with her and Thomas she could not imagine.

But there was something which she did understand.

John More said to his son: 'So, your piece of folly in the Parliament has cost me a hundred pounds.'

'My piece of folly?'

'Now listen, son Thomas. I have been wrongfully imprisoned on a false charge, and my release was only won in payment of a hundred pounds. All London knows that I paid the fine for you. You were the culprit. You spoke with such fire against the grant the King was asking that it was all but halved by the Parliament. The King wishes his subjects to know that he'll not brook such conduct. You have done a foolish thing. A pair of greedy royal eyes are turned upon us, and methinks they will never lose sight of us.'

'Father, as a burgess of London, I deemed it meet to oppose the King's spending of his subjects' money.'

'As a subject of the King, you have acted like a fool, even though as a burgess you may have acted like an honest man. You are a meddler, my son. You will never rise to the top of our profession unless you give your mind to the study of law, and to nothing else. I kept you short of money at Oxford. . . .'

'Aye, that you did – so that I often went hungry and was unable to pay for the repair of my boots. I had to sing at the doors of rich men for alms, and to run up and down the quadrangles for half an hour before bedtime, or the coldness of my body would have kept me from sleep altogether.'

'And you bear me a grudge for that, eh, my son?'

'Nay, Father. For, having no money to spend on folly, I must give all my energies to learning; and knowledge is a greater prize than meat for supper – even if it is not always of the law!'

'Thomas, I understand you not. You are a good son, and yet you are a fool. Instead of giving yourself entirely to the study of the law, what do you do? When that fellow Erasmus came to England you spent much time . . . discoursing, I hear, prattling the hours away, studying Greek and Latin together . . . when I wished you to work at the law. And now that you are accounted a worthy and utter barrister, and you are made a burgess, what do you do? You . . . a humble subject of the King, must arouse the King's wrath.'

'Father, one day, if I am a rich man, I will repay the hundred pounds.'

'Pah!' said John More. 'If you are a rich man you will hear from the King, and I doubt you would remain a rich man long enough to pay your father that hundred pounds. For, my son . . . and let us speak low, for I would not have this go beyond us . . . the King will not forget you. You have escaped, you think. You have done your noble act and your father has paid his fine. Do not think that is an end of this matter.' He lowered his voice still more. 'This King of ours is a cold-hearted man. Money is the love of his life; but one of his light o' loves is Revenge. You have thwarted his Love; you have wounded her deeply. You . . . a young man, who have, with your writings, already attracted attention to yourself so that your name is known in Europe, and when scholars visit this country you are one of those with whom they seek to converse. You have set yourself up to enlighten the people, and you have done this in Parliament. What you have said is this: "The King's coffers are full to bursting, good people, and you are poor. Therefore, as a burgess of your Parliament, I will work to remedy these matters." The King will not forget that. Depend upon it, he will seek an opportunity of letting you know that no subject of his – be he ever so learned, and whatever admiration scholars lay at his feet – shall insult the King and his beloved spouse, Riches.'

'Then, Father, I am fortunate to be a poor man; and how many men can truly rejoice in their poverty?'

'You take these matters lightly, my son. But have a care. The King watches you. If you prosper he will have your treasure.'

'Then I pray, Father, that my treasures will be those which the King does not envy – my friends, my writing, my honour.'

'Tut!' said the shrewd lawyer. 'This is fools' talk. Learn wisdom with your Greek and Latin. It'll stand you in better stead than either.'

Jane was frightened. That man with the cruel face hated her husband. *She* took her father-in-law's warning to heart if Thomas did not.

Often she dreamed of the hard-faced King, and in her dreams his great coffers burst open while Thomas took out the gold and gave it to the beggars in Candlewick Street.

She knew she had a very strange and alarming husband; and often, when she wept a little during the silence of the night, she wondered whether it would have been much worse to have remained unmarried all her life than to have become the wife of Thomas More.

*   *   *

Her position was not relieved by the coming of the man from Rotterdam.

Jane had heard much of him; and of all the learned friends who struck terror into her heart, this man frightened her more than any.

He settled in at The Barge and changed the way of life there.

Sometimes he looked at Jane with a mildly sarcastic smile, and there would be a faint twinkle in his half-closed blue eyes as though he were wondering how such a man as his friend Thomas More could have married the insignificant little wench.

She learned a good deal about him, but the things which interested her were, Thomas said, unimportant. He was the illegitimate son of a priest, and this seemed to Jane a shameful thing; nor could she understand why he was not ashamed of it. He had become an orphan when he was very young, and when those about him had realized his unusual powers he had been sent into a convent of canons regular, but, like Thomas, he could not bring himself to take the vows. He had studied in Paris, where he had given his life to literature; and although he had suffered greatly from abject poverty and had been forced to earn his bread by becoming tutor to gentlemen, so dazzling was his scholarship that he had drawn the attention of other scholars to himself and was recognized as the greatest of them all.

Jane, in her kitchen, giving orders to her maids, could hardly believe that she had this great man in her house and that it was her husband with whom he went walking through the streets of London.

To some extent she was glad of this man's visit; it turned Thomas's attention from herself. They were translating something – to which they referred as *Lucian* – from Latin into Greek, she believed; they would spend hours together doing this work, disagreeing on many points. It seemed to Jane that learned conversation involved a good deal of disagreement. And so it happened that as Thomas must engage himself in continual conversation with Erasmus, with his work as a lawyer and with his attendances at the Parliament, he had less time to give to the tutoring of his wife.

But she, since the smile she was sure she had received from the Prince of Wales, began to feel that perhaps she was not so foolish as she had believed herself to be. On looking back, it seemed that that smile of the Prince's had held a certain appreciation. She was not so foolish that she did not realize that the Prince would look for other qualities in a woman than did Thomas; yet the approbation of such a Prince gave her new courage and confidence in herself.

She listened more carefully to the discourses that went on about her; and when they were in English she found that they were not so dreary as she had believed they must be.

Erasmus disliked the monks: Thomas defended them.

Erasmus declared his intention of one day laying bare to the world the iniquitous happenings which occurred in some of the monasteries of Europe.

He had stories to tell of the evil practices which went on in monasteries. Listening, Jane realized that there was much sin in the world.

In some religious houses, declared Erasmus, lewdness rather

than religion was the order of the day. Abortion and child-murder prevailed; for how, demanded Erasmus, can these holy nuns account for the children they bring into the world? They cannot. So they strangle them as soon as they are born and bury them in the grounds of the nunneries. There are lusts of an unnatural nature between the sexes. . . .

Here the men became aware of Jane's attention, and they lapsed into Latin.

Jane thought: The Prince thought me worth a glance. Perhaps I could learn a little Latin. Though I should never be a scholar I might learn a little, for if I can understand English, why not Latin?

Erasmus spoke in English of one monastery in which there was a statue of a boy-saint, hollow and so light that it could be lifted by a child of five. Yet it was said that only those without sin could lift it. Many came to see the holy statue, and rich men found that they could only lift it when they had paid heavily for the monk's intercession with the saints on their behalf. Only when they had given to the monastery as much money as they could be induced to part with were they able to lift the statue. A miracle? In a way. Worked by one of the monks who, remaining out of sight, removed at the right moment that peg which held the statue on the floor. Then there was the case of the phial of blood, reputed to be that of Christ. Only those who were holy enough could see the blood; and it was deemed a sign from Heaven that a man would only be received there if the blood appeared to him. And the blood? The blood of a duck, renewed at regular intervals. And the phial? It was opaque one side. It cost much money to have the phial turned so that the blood was visible to the devout dupe.

'These practices are wicked,' said Erasmus. 'They bring much gain to the monasteries now, but they will eventually bring much loss. I am sure of it.'

'Is it fair,' asked Thomas, 'to condemn all monasteries because of the evil-doing of some?'

'It is well,' said Erasmus, 'to put all under suspicion and let them clear themselves.'

'But should one be assumed guilty until he fails to prove his innocence?'

'You are too lenient, friend More. The greed of these monks will prove their undoing. One day I shall show their criminal follies to the world; I shall set it out that all may read. Then, my friend, they will wish that they had led the lives of holy men, which are more comfortable than the lives of the wandering beggars they will become. What say you, Mistress More? What say you?'

The mildly mocking eyes were turned upon her. Thomas came to her rescue. 'Jane will doubtless agree with you.'

'Then I am glad of that,' said Erasmus. 'And I hope one day to convince you also. For it is the duty of us men of letters to show the world's wrongs to the world.'

'But we must be sure we have something good to offer in its place, before we destroy that which mayhap could be set to rights.'

'Ah, you and your ideal state! That is still on your mind, is it? You set too high a standard. You think the world is made up of potential saints and martyrs. Does your husband talk to you, Mistress More, day in, day out, of this wonder-world of his?'

'He talks . . . a little,' stammered Jane. 'But I am not clever. I am far from learned and there is much I do not know.'

Thomas smiled at her, his eyes telling her not to be nervous. He rose and put an arm about her shoulders.

'Jane is learning,' he said. 'One day she will understand Latin even as you or I.'

'I fear not,' said Jane. 'I am far too foolish.'

'Why,' said Erasmus, 'so he would bother you with lessons, would he? You see, it is what I expect of him. The world is not to his liking, so he would build an ideal world. A woman is . . . a woman, and he would make a scholar of her!'

'There is no reason, my dear Erasmus, why women, if taught, should not became every bit as learned as men.'

'There is every reason.'

'And what are these?'

'Women are the weaker sex. Do you not know that? They are not meant to cudgel their brains. They are meant to look to the comfort of men.'

'Nay. I do not agree. I believe that we are mistaken in not giving our girls an education equal to that which we give our boys. If we did, we should find our women able to converse with us in Latin while they cooked the dinner.'

'And Mistress More . . . she is proving as apt a pupil as you once were . . . as I was?'

Thomas answered in Latin, because he was aware of Jane's embarrassment. He was always acutely aware of the feelings of others, and suffered their hurt more deeply than he would his own.

And the two men, having found a subject for discussion, would go on happily until the one led to another.

It will not always be thus, thought Jane. One day Erasmus will go away; one day we shall visit New Hall; and one day, who knows, I may learn to converse in Latin!

But that day must be a long way ahead, and meanwhile she must go on trying not to hate her life at The Barge.

*　　*　　*

Had he been wrong to marry?

Thomas was unsure. Sometimes he walked alone through the streets of London and his steps invariably took him northwards across the City; he would find himself walking up Charter Lane until he came to the great buildings in which he had spent those four years of indecision.

He would enter the quadrangle, then go to the chapel or the chapter house; and he would think, not without longing, of the life of solitude and meditation, life that was given up to study and contemplation, life that was unharassed by bodily needs, by the great events which were going on in the outside world.

He thought of the rigorous way of life of the Carthusians, each with his separate house of two rooms, closet, refectory and garden, living his solitary life, speaking to his fellow monks only on feast days, fasting at least once a week, never eating flesh of any sort and thus subduing the appetites of the body; he thought of wearing the hair-shirt by night so that sleep did not come easily, until eventually it was possible to indulge in sleep for only an hour each night; using the wooden pillow, dressing in the coarsest clothes to detract from any good looks a man might possess and so subdue his vanity; he thought of shutting himself away from the world, and perhaps by his example helping to lead others to a holier way of life.

The life of retirement seemed very dear to him when he thought of his home in The Barge of Bucklersbury.

Was Erasmus right? Was it as difficult to create an ideal woman as an ideal world? Was he a fool to try to educate Jane to his intellectual standard? Was he making an unhappy woman of her as well as a fool of himself?

This was the state of the marriage of Jane and Thomas More when Jane found that she was going to have a child.

*　　　*　　　*

A child! thought Jane. This would be wonderful. A boy whom his father would make a scholar? That would delight him; that would turn his attention from his poor, simple wife. If he had a boy to whom he could teach the Latin tongue, why should he bother to teach it to Jane? And must he not be grateful to the simple woman who could give him such a blessing in life?

But, thought Jane, if it is a girl, how happy I shall be, for then he will see that girls should not be made learned. She will teach him what I could not; and she and I will be together; she will love flowers and we will grow them together, and I shall take her to New Hall; and when I show my child to my family, then I shall know that the world was right when it said that the married state is the best state of all.

So the child could make Jane happy as Thomas never could.

*　　　*　　　*

Thomas was gay.

A child! That was the meaning of married life. That was what he wanted. What was the life to be lived in Carthusian solitude when compared with the bringing up of a child? The

42

best tutors in England should be procured for young Master More. They would be glad to come. Dr Lily perhaps? There was the greatest teacher in England. Then there would be Thomas More himself to guide his son.

Those were happy days – awaiting the birth of the child. A son, of course. The first-born should be a son. And after that, more sons and some daughters. And the daughters should be treated in the same way as the sons; no matter what Erasmus, Colet, Lily and the rest said, Thomas was convinced that women should not be denied education. His daughters should prove him to have been right.

But for the present he could dream of his son.

There was laughter in The Barge; and if Jane did not understand all the jokes, she laughed as though she did. She was happy and Thomas was happy to see her happy.

Married life was the best state of all.

*   *   *

His friends were often at the house. Jane did not care. She sat, her needle busy, making clothes for the child. Her body widened and her prestige grew. Who were these scholars? Who was Dr Colet, with his talk of founding schools for children? It was true that he was no longer a mere vicar of Stepney but had been appointed Dean of St Paul's itself. But what did she care for him. Who was Dr William Lily, who had learned Latin in Italy, had travelled widely, had opened a school in London and had, like Thomas, almost become a monk? Who was this Dr Linacre who had taught Thomas Greek? Who was the great Erasmus himself? Clever they might be, but none of them could bear a child!

New dignity and confidence had come to Jane. She sang snatches of songs as she went about the house.

Married life was indeed good and Jane was very happy.

*   *   *

And one summer's day in the year 1505 Margaret came into the world.

43

TWO

MARGARET WAS four years old when she first knew the meaning of fear. Until then her world had been a merry place, ruled by the person she loved best: her father.

The only times when she was unhappy were when he was not at home. Then the old house with its dark staircases, its odd nooks and alcoves, seemed a different place. Margaret would sit in the window seat watching for his return, looking out on the shops of the apothecaries and grocers, thinking that they were not quite the same shops which she had passed, her hand in her father's, while he explained to her the uses of spices and drugs, the scent of which filled the air. Nothing could be quite right in Margaret's eyes unless her father was with her.

When she heard his laughter – and she almost always heard his laughter before she heard him speak – she would feel as though she had found the right answer to a problem which had bothered her in her lessons. She would run to him and stand before him, waiting for him to lift her up.

He would say: 'And what has my Meg learned today?'

Eagerly she would tell him, and draw back to see the effect of her answer. Pleasing him was the most important thing in the world to her. She longed to be able to speak to him in Latin; that, she believed, would please him more than anything she could do.

'Meg,' he once said to her when an answer she had given him had especially pleased him, 'to think that when you were born we hoped for a boy!'

'And you would rather have me than any boy, would you not, Father?'

'Rather my girls than any boys in the world.'

She believed that he meant: rather his Meg than any boys; but he would think of the others – Elizabeth who was three and Cecily who was two – and he would tell himself that it was not right for a father to love one child more than the others. And he was a man who must always do right; she knew that. She was a child and not good like he was; and she could love one member of her family so much that if all the affection she had for the others were rolled into one heap it would be as the moon to the great sun of her affection for him. But she would not ask him if he loved her best; she knew he did; and he knew of her love for him. That was their secret.

Sometimes she would go into that room in which he sat with his friends, and he would take her on his knee or sit her on the table. Then the old, solemn-faced men would look at her, and her father would say: 'Margaret will prove to you that I am right. She is young yet, but you will see . . . you will see.'

Then he would ask her questions and she would answer him. They would say: 'Can this be a maid so young?'

'A maid who will show you, my friend, that a woman's brain is equal to a man's.' Then he would bring his smiling face close to hers. 'Meg, they do not believe that you can learn your lessons. They say that because you are a girl this headpiece of yours will not be equal to the task. Meg, you must prove them wrong. If you do not, they will say that I am right named. For *Moros* . . . that is Greek for fool, Meg; and it will seem that I shall be worthy of the name if I am wrong. Meg, thou wilt not let them laugh at thy father?'

'Nay, Father,' she said scowling at the men. 'They shall not laugh at thee. We will show them who are the fools.'

They laughed and talked to her, and she answered as best she could, with her heart beating fast for fear she should behave like a very little girl instead of a learned young woman of nearly five years old. She was determined to save her father from the mockery of his friends.

So her lessons were more than a task to her; they were a dedication. She *must* master them.

'It is not natural to sit so long with your books,' said her mother. 'Come . . . play with Bessy.'

But if she played with Bessy it was but to teach her; for, she thought, Father will like all his daughters to be clever. It will

45

not do for one of us to be wise and the rest ignorant.

Yet she hoped that Elizabeth and Cecily would not be able to learn as easily as she could, for she wished to remain the cleverest of her father's daughters.

Thus Margaret, even at the age of four, had become an unusually learned little girl.

One day her father brought home a girl of her own age – a shy sad little girl.

Margaret heard his voice and rushed down to meet him; she flung her arms about his knees; then she stood solemnly regarding the little girl who stood beside him, her hand in his.

Her father crouched down so that the three of them were all of a size. He put an arm about each of them.

'Margaret,' he said, 'I have brought a playmate for you.'

Margaret wanted to say that she had no wish for a playmate. Her lessons absorbed her; and she had two sisters with whom she could play. If she wanted a new addition to their household it would have been a boy, so that she could have proved to those friends of her father's how right he was when he said girls could learn as much as boys.

But she knew that she must not make the little girl feel unwanted, for that would surely displease her father.

'This,' he went on, 'is another Margaret. Margaret is my favourite name.'

That made Margaret smile and look with new interest at the little girl who had the same name as herself.

'This Margaret is coming to live with us, Meg.'

'We cannot have two Margarets in one house,' Margaret pointed out. 'If you called me she would think you called her.'

'My wise little daughter!' His laughter was merry but she knew that he had sensed her resentment, and she blushed because she knew it must displease him.

'One of us would have to be given a new name,' she said quickly.

'What other names are there for Margaret?' he asked. 'There is Peg. There is Daisy. There is Meg and Marget. Ah, but we already have a Meg and Marget in our own Margaret. There is

Mercy. One of you will have to change her name, will she not?'

'Yes,' said Margaret, her lips trembling slightly. She knew what he expected of her, and she knew that she could not bear to hear him call another Margaret. He knew it too; that was why he expected her to give her name to this girl.

'It is more blessed to give than to receive.' Often he had told them that. He often said: 'Ah, my Meg, if only men and women would realize that it is the unselfish acts that bring most pleasure, then the world would become full of unselfish people; and perhaps the very act of unselfishness would become a selfish one.'

She knew, with his eyes upon her, that she must make the sacrifice now.

'I . . . I will be Daisy or Mercy,' she said.

He kissed her then. 'My Meg . . . my dearest Meg,' he said; and she thought that if that was the last time he called her by her name she would always remember his voice at that moment.

'Mercy is a beautiful name,' he said, 'for mercy is one of the most beautiful of all qualities.'

'Do you like Mercy?' asked Margaret of the newcomer.

'Yes,' she answered. 'I will be Mercy, because this is your house first, and you were the first Margaret in it.'

Then her father kissed them both and said: 'So my Meg stays with me; and in addition I have brought Mercy into the house.'

Her name was Mercy Gigs and she had been left an orphan. She had no fortune, he explained to Margaret, but her own sweet nature. 'So, Meg, we must take her into our house. I will be Father to her; your mother will be Mother; and you will be Sister to her as you are to Elizabeth and Cecily.'

And so it was that she acquired a new sister, to learn with her and talk with her. She had the advantage of having started her lessons earlier, but she soon realized that Mercy Gigs was a rival, for she had given her devotion to the man who had taken her into his house and become her foster-father, and, like Margaret, her one thought was to win his respect and approval.

She too worked hard at her lessons and tried to startle him with her ability to learn. Now when the friends came and asked how Margaret was progressing with her lessons, there would be two little girls to confront them; and Mercy Gigs, the orphan, could confound them even more than Margaret who was, after all, the daughter of a learned man.

'So Mercy will prove my point completely,' Thomas would say with glee. 'Mercy is going to be as clever as my own children. Mercy shall be given the best tuition with my own children, and she will show you that most feminine minds are as capable of absorbing knowledge as a sponge absorbs water.'

Then Mercy would blush and smile and be very happy.

Later there came a period of anxiety. It began when, one day, her father took Margaret on his knee and told her that he was going away for a little while.

She put her arms about him and bit her lips to hold back her tears.

'But it will not be for long, Meg,' he said. 'I am going into foreign lands. I am going to the universities of Paris and Louvain to see my friends who come to see me when they are here; and perhaps one day, Meg, I shall take you and your mother and your sisters there. How will you like that?'

'I would rather stay here and that you should stay too.'

'Well, Meg, that which we would rather have does not always come about. You will have to look after everybody in the house, will you not? And you will work hard at your lessons whilst I am gone?'

She nodded. 'But why must you go? Why must you go?'

'I am going because quite soon I may want to take my family to France. But first I wish to go there alone, to make sure that it is the place my family would like to live in.'

'Of course we should like to live there if you were there. There is no need for you to go first without us.'

He kissed her and put her down.

Her fears had started then. Not only was this due to the fact that he left for France shortly afterwards, but she knew from the looks of the servants, from the voices of the people who spoke with her mother, and from her mother's worried looks, that something frightening had happened.

He had not told her what it was; and she knew that could only be because she was too young to understand.

She talked of this matter with Mercy. Mercy was wise and quiet; she too had noticed that something was wrong; she too was afraid.

Once when her mother was baking bread in the kitchen, Margaret said: 'Mother, when will my father come back?'

'Soon, my child. Soon.'

'Soon,' said Margaret, 'can be a long time for something you greatly wish for. It can be quick for something you hate.'

Jane touched the small head and marvelled at this daughter of hers. Margaret was far more like Thomas than like herself; she was more like Thomas than any of the others. Whenever she looked at the child she remembered those days soon after Margaret's birth, when Thomas had walked up and down the room with her to soothe her cries; she remembered that Thomas could soothe her as no one else could. She remembered also how Thomas had talked of what he would do for this child, how she was to be a great and noble woman, how delighted he was with his daughter, how she had charmed him as no son ever could have done.

And it seemed that Thomas must have had pre-knowledge for Margaret was all that he had wished. Her cleverness astonished her mother; she had already, though not yet five, started on Latin and Greek, and seemed to find the same pleasure in it that most children would in a game of shuttlecock. Jane could feel satisfied when she surveyed her eldest daughter. Surely she had made his marriage a success when she had given him this quaint and solemn daughter.

'Well, my dearest,' said Jane, 'your father will be away for a few weeks, and I'll swear that that will seem long to all of us. But when he returns you will be all the more pleased to see him because you have missed him so much.'

'Nothing could please me more,' said Margaret, 'than to see him every day.'

Then she went away and gravely did her lessons. Her one aspiration now was to astonish him when he came back.

And eventually he did come back. Margaret must be the first to greet him; and when she heard his voice calling to his family, she sped into the great hall; but Mercy was there beside her.

They stood side by side looking up at him.

He smiled at their grave little faces and lifted them in his arms. He kissed Mercy first; but Margaret knew, and Mercy knew, that that was because he was longing to kiss Margaret more than anyone, for Margaret was his own child and he could never love any as he loved her.

They sat at the big table – the whole household – and everyone was happy because he was home. All the servants, who sat at the table with the family, were happy; and so were those poor travellers who had called in, weary and footsore, because they knew that they could always be sure of a meal in the house of Thomas More.

After the meal, Thomas went first to the schoolroom, and there he marvelled and delighted in the progress his daughters had made. Even two-year-old Cecily had started to learn; and he was, he said, mightily pleased. 'Why,' he declared, ''twas worth being away, for the pleasure it gives me to come back to you.'

But a few days later he took Margaret walking in Goodman's Fields, and made her sit beside him on the grass there; and as they sat, he told her that he had made plans to leave The Barge in Bucklersbury, to leave this City, and to take his family away with him to France.

Margaret cried: 'But . . . Father, you say you love London, and that no other city could ever be home to you.'

'I know, my child. And you?'

'Yes, Father. I love it too.'

'And which would you have – a strange land with your father, or England . . . London . . . and no father?'

'I would rather be anywhere with you, Father, than anywhere without you.'

'Then, Margaret, it will be no hardship for you. "Better is a dinner of herbs where love is . . ." eh? And it will be a dinner of herbs, my dearest, for we shall not be rich.'

'We shall be happy,' said Margaret. 'But why must we go?'

'Sometimes I wonder, my Margaret, whether I have made you grow up too quickly. I so long to see you bloom. I want you to be my little companion. I want to discuss all things with you. And I forget what a child you are. Well, I shall tell you this; but it is our secret. You will remember that?'

'Yes, Father.'

'Then listen. A long time ago, before you were born, before I married your mother, our King asked his Parliament for a sum of money. I was a Member – a very junior Member – of that Parliament, and I argued against the King's wishes. Partly because of the words I spoke, Margaret, the King did not get all the money for which he was asking.'

Margaret nodded.

'When the King is given money by the Parliament, it is the people's money raised by taxes. You do not know what these are, and one day I will explain. But, you see, money has to be taken from the people to give to the King ... a little here ... a little there ... to make a large sum. The cost of food is increased so that some of the money which is paid for it may go to the King. The people had already paid too many of these taxes and the King wanted them to pay more and more. I thought it wrong that he should have the money for which he asked. I thought it wrong that the people should be made even poorer. And I said so.'

'It *was* wrong, Father.'

'Ah, little Meg, do you say that because you see why it was wrong, or because I say so?'

'Because you say so, Father.'

He kissed her. 'Do not trust me too blindly, Meg. I am a mortal man you know. I will say this: I thought what I did was right. The King thought I was wrong. And kings, like little girls ... little boys ... and even babies, do not like people who prevent their doing those things which they wish to do. So ... the King does not like me.'

'Everybody likes you, Father,' she said in disbelief.

'*You* do,' he said with a laugh. 'But everyone, alas! has not your kind discernment. No, the King does not like me, Meg, and when a king does not like a man, he seeks to harm him in some way.'

She stood up in alarm. She took his hand and tugged at it.

'Whither would you take me, Meg?'

'Let us run away now.'

'Whither shall we run?

'To some foreign land where we can have a new king.'

'That is just what I propose to do, Meg. But there is no need for you to be frightened, and there is no need for such haste. We have to take the others wth us. That is why I went abroad . . . to spy out the land. Very soon you, I, your mother, the girls and some of our servants are going away. I have many kind friends, as you know. One of these is a gentleman you have seen because he has visited us. He is a very important gentleman— Bishop Foxe of Winchester. He has warned me of the King's feelings against me, and he has told me that he can make the King my friend if I will admit my fault to the Parliament.'

'Then he will make the King your friend, Father?'

'Nay, Meg, for how can I say that I was wrong when I believe myself to have been right, when, should I be confronted with the same problem, I should do the same again?'

'If Bishop Foxe made the King your friend, you could stay at home.'

'That is true, Meg. I love this City. Look at it now. Let me lift you. There is no city in the world which would seem so beautiful to me as this one. When I am far from it, I shall think of it often. I shall mourn it as I should mourn the best loved of my friends. Look, Meg. Look at the great bastions of our Tower. What a mighty fortress! What miseries . . . what joys . . . have been experienced within those walls? You can see our river. How quietly, how peacefully it flows! But what did Satan say to Jesus when he showed Him the beauties of the world, Meg? That is what a small voice within me says, "All this can be yours," it says. "Just for a few little words." All I need say is that I was wrong and the King was right. All I need say is that it is right for the King to take his subjects' money, to make them poor that he may be rich. Nay, Meg, it would be wrong to say those words. And

52

there would be no peace in saying them. This City of mine would scorn me if I said them; so I cannot, Meg; I cannot.' Then he kissed her and went on : 'I burden this little head with so much talk. Come, Meg, smile for me. You and I know how to be happy wherever we are. We know the secret, do we not? What is it?'

'Being together,' said Margaret.

He smiled and nodded, and hand-in-hand they walked home by the long route. Through Milk Street they went, that he might show her the house in which he was born, for he knew she never tired of looking at it and picturing him as a child no bigger than herself; they went past the poulterers' shops in the Poultry, through Scalding Alley where the poulterers' boys were running with the birds sold by their masters, that there in the Alley they might be plucked and scorched; the air was filled with the smell of burning feathers. And they went on into the Stocks Market with its shops filled with fish and flesh and its stalls of fruit and flowers, herbs and roots; and so home to Bucklersbury with its pleasant aromas of spices and unguents which seemed to Margaret to have as inevitable a place in her life as the house itself.

It was as though he looked at all these places with loving concentration, so that he might remember every detail and be able to recall them when he became an exile from the City which he loved.

As they approached the house he said : 'Meg, not a word to anyone. It would frighten the children. It would frighten your mother.'

She pressed his hand, proud to share their secret.

But she greatly feared that the mighty King would hurt her father before they could escape him.

*   *   *

There was great excitement in the streets; and there was relief mingling with that excitement which was felt in the house in Bucklersbury.

The King was dead. And fear had died with him.

A new King had come to the throne—a boy not yet eighteen.

He was quite different from his father; there was nothing parsimonious about him, and the people looked forward to a great and glorious reign. The household of Thomas More need not now consider uprooting itself.

All over the City the church bells were ringing. In the streets the people were dancing and singing. How could they regret the passing of a mean old King, when a young and handsome one was waiting to take the crown?

Men talked of the terrible taxation demanded by the late King through his agents, Empson and Dudley. Rumours ran through the town. The new King loved his people; he loved to jest and be merry. He was not like his father, who rode in a closed carriage whenever he could, because he did not wish the people to see his ugly face. No, this King loved to ride abroad, clad in cloth of gold and velvet, sparking with jewels; he liked to show his handsome face to his subjects and receive their homage.

'Father,' said Margaret, 'what will happen now that we have a new King?'

'We shall pass into a new age,' he said. 'The old King's meanness curbed everything but the amassing of money by a few people. England will now be thrown open to scholars. Our friend Erasmus will be given a place here, and enough to keep him in comfort while he continues his studies. Avarice will be stamped out. The new King begins a new and glorious reign.'

'Will he give back the money his father took from the people?' asked Margaret.

Her father laid a hand on her head. 'Ah, that I cannot tell you.'

'But how can he begin to please the people unless he begins by doing that?'

'Margaret, there are times when the working of your mind seems almost too great a strain for your years.'

But he kissed her to show that he was pleased with her; and she said: 'Even if he does not, there is nothing to fear, is there, Father. Satan does not whisper to you any more: "The cities of the world are yours. . . ."'

'You are right, Meg,' he told her joyfully.

Dr Colet came to the house, and even he, for a time, ceased to talk of literature and theology while he discussed the new King.

'There will be a marriage of the King and the Spanish Infanta, his brother's widow,' he said. 'I like that not. Nor, I gather, does my lord of Canterbury.'

Margaret listened to them; she was eager to learn everything, that she might afford her father great pleasure by her understanding when these matters were referred to.

'There will have to be dispensation from the Pope,' said Thomas. 'But I doubt not that will be an easy matter.'

'Should it be granted?' asked Colet. 'His brother's widow! Moreover, did he not some years ago make a solemn protest against the betrothal?'

'He did – under duress. He protested on the grounds that she was five years his senior, and he quoted the Bible, I believe. No good could come of such a marriage, he said. But it was his father who forced the protest from him. Young Henry, it seems, always had a mild fancy for the Spanish lady; and his father was pleased that this should be so, for you'll remember, only half of her magnificent dowry had fallen into his hands and he greatly longed to possess himself of the other half.'

'I know. I know. And when the old King decided he would marry Katharine's sister Juana, he felt that, if father and son married sisters, the relationship would be a complicated and unpleasant one. I doubt not that he thought it better to secure Juana's great riches than the remaining half of Katharine's dowry.'

'That was so. Therefore young Henry, whatever his private desires, must protest against his betrothal to his brother's widow.'

'Still, he made the protest,' said Colet.

'A boy of fifteen!'

'It was after the protest, so I hear, that he began to fall in love in earnest with his brother's widow. The toy had been offered him; he thought little of it; it was only when there was an attempt to snatch it from him that he determined to hold it. And now he declares nothing will turn him from the match, for she is the woman of his fancy.'

'Well, she is a good Princess,' said Thomas, 'and a comely one. She will provide England with a good Queen. That will suffice.'

'It will, my friend. It must. Do not forget it is the King's wish. There is no law in this land but the King's pleasure. And it will be well for us to remember that this King – be he ever so young and handsome – like his father, is a Tudor King.'

And Margaret, listening, wondered whether fear had entirely left her. This King – young and handsome though he was – might not give back to the people the money his father had taken from them; he wished to marry his brother's widow mainly because his father had said he should not. Would he prove to be such a good King after all? Could she be happy? Could she be reassured that her father was safe?

*   *   *

One event took place which seemed to the family as important as the accession of the new King to the throne.

Little Jack was born.

Jane was happy. A boy at last! She had always wanted a boy; and right from the first she saw that the boy was going to resemble the Colts.

He had her father's nose already; he had Jane's eyes; and she loved him dearly. But his birth had taken its toll of her health. She was ill for many weeks after Jack was born; and when she got up from her bed she felt far weaker than she had been after her previous confinements.

Still, she was happy. She would not have believed five years ago that she could have been so happy in this old City. London now meant home to her; she even enjoyed walking through the crowds to the Chepe, her maid following her, ordering from the tradespeople. She was not afraid of crowds now; nor was she afraid of Thomas. She had even learned a little Latin, and she could join in the children's conversations with their father.

Sometimes she regretted the fact that not one of her children was a simple little soul such as she herself had been; for even baby Cecily was showing that she would be a little scholar. Yet, thought Jane, I am glad that they are clever. They will not suffer as I suffered; and how sad it would be for one of them to be a dullard in the midst of so many that are brilliant – like a sad piglet in a litter. I should not like that at all. No, let them all be clever; even though they do surpass their mother, even though they must, as they grow up, look upon her as a simpleton.

There was great excitement because the King and the Queen, whom he had married a few days before, were going to be crowned; and London was in Coronation mood. There was no talk but of the accession, the royal marriage, and the Coronation, and all the streets were now being decorated for the last cere-mony. Cornhill, the richest street in London, was hung with cloth of gold, and was a sight to gladden any eye, so Jane was told; she had felt too weak to go and see it for herself, but she had promised the children that she would take them to watch the progress of the King and Queen, and nothing would induce her to disappoint them.

Thomas could not accompany them; he had his duties allotted to him as a burgess of the Parliament; and so, on that sunny June day, leaving the newly-born baby in the care of a nurse, with Cecily clinging to one hand, Elizabeth to the other, and Margaret and Mercy hand-in-hand, the little party set out to watch the King with the Queen ride through the streets from the Tower to Westminster for the crowning.

Jane had decided that Cornhill would be the best place in which to see the procession, for accounts of the beauties of Corn-hill had been spread through the City. Moreover, they had but to go through Walbrook, cross the Stocks Market to the corner where Lombard Street and Cornhill met.

But Jane had reckoned without the crowds. Everyone, it seemed, had decided that this would be the best place from which to see the procession.

Jane felt weak and tired and the heat was making her dizzy. There was nothing she would have liked better than to take her party home; but when she looked at the excited faces of the children, she found it impossible to disappoint them.

'Keep close to me,' she warned. 'Margaret, you keep your eyes on Cecily. And Mercy . . . take Bess's hand. Now . . . keep very close. How hot it is! And so many people!'

'Mother,' cried Elizabeth, 'look at the beautiful cloth. Is it real gold? They *are* goldsmiths' shops, are they not? So perhaps it *is* real gold.'

'Yes, yes; they are beautiful,' said Jane.

Cecily wanted one of the hot pies which were being sold nearby. Elizabeth said she would prefer gingerbread.

'Now, now,' said Jane. 'You will miss the King if you do not watch.'

That made the children forget their hunger.

But there was a long time to wait for the procession. The sun seemed to grow hotter; Jane felt faint as the crowds pressed about her. She became very frightened, asking herself what would happen to the children in this press of people if she were to faint. Her very panic seemed to revive her.

She lost her purse before they had stood there for ten minutes. The thief must have been the young boy who had pressed against her and given her such an angelic smile of apology that she had thought how charming he was.

She should not have come. She should have told Thomas of her intention. Why had she not? Because, she supposed, there were times when she wished to assert her authority over her little family, to say to them: 'I know I am not wise, but I am the mother, and there are times when I wish to make my own decisions. I wish to say that something shall be done and to see that you do it.'

How glad she was when the sound of trumpets and the tramp of horses' hoofs heralded the approach of the procession. The people shouted; the children stood spellbound. And as the excitement grew Jane felt a little better. There had not been much in her purse, and this would be a lesson to her. She would quote Thomas and say: 'Experience is generally worth the price, however dearly bought.'

Now came the knights and squires and the lords of the land – so handsome, some magnificent in their velvet and cloth of gold. But more handsome than any was the King himself. There he rode, so young, so eager for the approbation of his subjects, smiling, inclining his head, a-glitter with jewels. It was worth a little discomfort, even the loss of her purse, to witness such glory.

And there was the Queen – a bride of a few days although she was a widow of some years' standing. She was in her twenties – too old, some said, for such a hearty youth; but she was beautiful – there was no denying that. Her dark hair, which it was said, hung to her feet when she stood, now hung about her shoulders, a black, gleaming cloak; she was dressed in white satin, beautifully embroidered, and her headdress was glittering with multi-coloured jewels. Two white horses bore her litter which was decorated; and cries of 'God Save Queen Katharine' mingled with those of 'God Bless the King.'

Now came the rest of the procession, and so close did the prancing horses come that the mass of people surged back to avoid being trodden on. Jane grasped her children and pulled them towards her, but the pressure increased. The faces of the people seemed to merge into the blue sky and the fanfares and the trumpeting seemed to come from a long way off. Jane fainted.

'Mother . . . Mother!' cried Margaret in alarm.

But Jane was slipping down and was in danger of being trampled underfoot.

'Stop . . . Stop. . . . I beg of you stop!' cried Margaret.

Cecily began to scream, Elizabeth to cry forlornly, while Mercy tried in vain to hold back the people with her little hands.

Then suddenly a strong voice cried: 'Stand back! Stand back! Can you not see! A woman has fainted.'

It was a loud, authoritative feminine voice; and Margaret lifted fearful eyes to a plump woman who was holding a little girl by the hand. Her fat cheeks quivered, her mouth was tight with indignation, and her eyes snapped contempt at the crowd.

Miraculously she had cleared a space about Jane. She put an arm about the fainting woman and forced her head downwards. After a few seconds, to Margaret's delight, the colour began to return to her mother's face.

'The heat, that's what it is,' said the woman. 'I could have fainted myself. And would have done . . . if I had not had the will to stop myself.'

Margaret, grateful as she was, could not help sensing the reproof to her mother in those words. She said: 'My mother is not strong yet. We have just had a baby brother.'

'Then more fool she to come out on such a day!' was the answer to that. 'Where do you live?'

'At The Barge in Bucklersbury.'

'That's not more than a stone's throw from here. I'll take you back. The crowds will be rougher ere long.'

'You are very good,' said Margaret.

'Tilly valley! What could I do? Leave a baby like you to look after a fainting woman in a crowd like this? Ah, mistress, I see you are looking about you. You fainted and I am looking after your children here. Can you stand? Here, lean on me. You two big girls take the little ones and keep a firm hold of their hands. Now, Ailie, you cling to my gown. I am going to force my way through the crowd. Come, mistress. Take my arm. Your children are here, and we'll push them ahead so that they cannot stray from our sight. We'll be in Bucklersbury in next to no time, and that's where you should be before the mob starts roystering."

'You are very good,' said Jane. 'I . . .'

'Now keep your breath for walking. Come along now. Come along.'

Forcefully she pushed a way for them, calling sharply to any that stood in their path. 'Can you not see? I have a sick woman here. Stand aside, you oafs. Make way there.'

And the odd thing was that none cared to disobey her, and under such strong guidance the family soon reached Bucklersbury.

The woman sniffed and looked with scorn about her. 'What odours! What odours!' she declared. 'I'm glad my late husband was not one of these apothecaries with their smells. There are no smells in a mercer's shop but goodly smells. But this . . . poof! I like it not!'

'My husband,' said Jane, 'is a lawyer.'

'A lawyer, eh! What the good year! Well, here you are, and if you will take my advice you'll not go into crowds again in a hurry.'

'You will come in and take a little refreshment?'

The widow said she would, and followed them into the big hall, where she sat down.

Margaret saw that the little girl named Ailie was very pretty and more or less of an age with herself and Mercy. Her golden hair escaped from her cap, and her gown was of richer material than that worn by the little More girls.

'Tell me the names of your girls,' said the widow. 'Nay . . . let them speak for themselves. I'll warrant they have tongues in their heads.'

'We have,' said Margaret with dignity, for although she was grateful for the widow's help in bringing them home, she did not like her overbearing manner. 'I am Margaret. This is my foster-sister called Mercy because her name is also Margaret, and . . . my sisters Elizabeth and Cecily.'

'And I am Mistress Alice Middleton, widow of Master John Middleton, mercer of the City and merchant of the Staple of Calais. Here is my daughter. Alice like myself, so like Mercy there, she is called by a name other than her own. Why, you and she are of an age. That should make you friends.'

The children continued to study each other, and Mistress Middleton turned to her hostess, complimented her on the mead she was offered and told her how she could improve it by using more honey in its making. Still, it was a goodly brew.

She went on: 'Now rest yourself. Keep to the house, for there'll be roystering this night . . . and so there should be, for it is a good day for the land, I'll swear, with such a bonny King come to the throne.'

When she had drunk her mead and had a look at the house, commenting – not always favourably – on its furnishings, she left with her daughter.

'A talkative woman,' said Jane, 'but capable, I'll swear . . . and very kind.'

*   *   *

This was a happy day for Thomas More. The tyrant was dead and in his place was a monarch who promised great things for England.

When Thomas was happy, he liked to take up his pen, and it was natural that his writings should now be concerned with the new reign.

'If ever there was a day, England,' he wrote, 'if ever there was a time for you to give thanks to Those above, this is that happy day, one to be marked with a pure white stone and put in your calendar. This day is the limit of our slavery, the beginning of freedom, the end of sadness, the source of joy. . . .'

He went on to enumerate the virtues of the young King: 'Among a thousand noble companions, does he not stand out taller than any? If only Nature could permit that, like his body, the outstanding excellence of his mind could be visible! This Prince has inherited his father's wisdom, his mother's kindly strength, the scrupulous intelligence of his father's mother, the noble heart of his mother's father. What wonder if England rejoices in such a King as she has never had before!'

Thomas went on to sing the praises of the Queen; he wrote of her dignity and her devotion to religion, of her beauty and her loyalty. There was surely no woman more worthy to be the wife of such a King, and none but the King was worthy to be the husband of such a Queen. Heaven bless such a union; and surely when the crowns had long been worn by Katharine and Henry, their grandson and great-grandson would wear the crown of England in the years to come.

When Thomas recited this composition to John Colet, the Dean of St Paul's remarked in his dry way that the qualities of Henry's ancestors might have been construed differently. For instance, the wisdom of Henry the Seventh might have been called avarice; the kindly strength of Elizabeth of York, meekness dictated by expediency; the scrupulous intelligence of Margaret of Richmond, ambition; the noble heart of Edward the Fourth as lechery and determination to rule at all cost.

'Still,' said the Dean, 'this should be shown to the King. It will surely please His Grace. Much flattery has been poured into the royal ears, but I doubt that any has ever been so elegantly phrased.'

'Flattery?' said Thomas. 'That may be. But, John, it sometimes happens that if a man is shown a flattering picture of himself, he will try to be worthy of that picture. For such reasons it is expedient to flatter kings.'

'Yet when men offer flattery with one hand, they are apt to hold out the other to receive the rewards such flattery may earn. What rewards seek you, friend Thomas?'

Thomas considered this. 'Might it not be,' he said at length, 'that this writing of mine is in payment for his coming to the throne at an opportune time for me? I could sing paeans, my friend, if I had the voice for them, because this King now reigns and there is no need for me to leave the country. Rewards? Perhaps I wish for them. It may be that I long to go on as I have . . . here in London . . . with my family about me. Oh, and perhaps if the King is pleased with my offering, I might ask concessions for Erasmus. It would be good to have him with us again, would it not?'

'It would. Take the verses. Crave audience. I doubt not you will obtain it.'

And so Thomas took his writing to the King.

*　　*　　*

The happiest person in the palace of Westminster should have been its King. None knew this more than the King himself, and he was sullen on finding that it was not so.

It was a glorious thing to be a King. Wherever he went the people hailed him, for he was not only a King; he was a beloved King. Were he not taller than all those about him, he would have been distinguished as their King by the glittering jewels he wore. He was the richest King in Europe; he was only now realizing how rich, for he had only guessed at the amount of wealth and treasure his father had amassed.

The reason for his discontent was his Queen. He liked his Queen. She was older than he was by five years – but as he did not care to be considered a mere boy, he liked this, for it seemed that she helped to add years to his age.

But they were rich; they were young; and they should be gay. There must be lavish entertainment; masques, jousts and pageants could go on for as long as he wished; and at all these ceremonies he should be the very centre of attention as was meet, considering who he was. All festivities should have one purpose: to honour the King, to display the King in all his glory, to show that the King was more skilled, more daring, than any King who had ever lived before him or would come after him.

But his Queen had disappointed him. Alas! she had not his love of gaiety, his passion for enjoyment; they had made her too solemn in that Spanish court of her childhood. She was comely enough to please him: and he was glad to reflect that she was the daughter of two of the greatest monarchs in the world; it pleased him too that he had married her, for marrying her was like snapping his fingers at his father's ghost. He did not care to disparage the dead, but it had rankled to be *forced* to relinquish his betrothed. It was only at that time that he had discovered how fair she was and how much he desired her – her above all women. It hurt his pride to be forced into that protest. And now, every time he looked at her, he could say: 'There is none now to force me to that which I desire not; nor shall there ever be again.' Such thought stimulated his desire, made him more ardent that he would otherwise have been; which, he reminded himself, not without a touch of primness, was all for the good of England, since an ardent man will get himself children more speedily than a cold one.

Yet she disappointed him.

It had happened on the day after the Coronation, when the ceremonies were at their height. He and Katharine had sat on a platform covered with velvet and cloth of gold set up within the grounds of Westminster Palace. What a wonderful sight had met their gaze, with the fountains emitting the best of wine, and more wine flowing from the mouths of stone animals! Many pageants had been prepared for the enjoyment of the royal couple. A fair young lady dressed as Minerva had presented six champions to the Queen, and that was a tribute to her solemnity, for these champions, dressed in cloth of gold and green velvet, were meant to represent scholars. That should have pleased her; and it did. Then drums and pipes heralded more knights who bowed before the Queen and asked leave to joust with the champions of Minerva.

Oh, what a spectacle! And the jousting lasted all day and night!

Then the King disappeared from the Queen's side, and shortly afterwards there came to her a lowly knight who craved leave to joust with the champion. The Queen gave that permission while everyone laughed the lowly knight to scorn until he threw off his shabby cloak and there, in glittering armour, towering above them all, was Henry himself. And Henry must be the victor.

That was all well and good.

But Henry had planned more joys for his Queen. An artificial park had been set up in the grounds of the Palace, with imitation trees and ferns shut in by pales; this contained several fallow deer and was designed to make a seemly setting for the servants of Diana. Suddenly the gates of this park were thrown open and greyhounds were sent therein. Through the imitation foliage they ran, leaping and barking; and out came the frightened deer, to the amusement of all except the Queen – rushing over the grounds and entering the Palace itself. And when all the deer were caught, they were laid, stained with blood, some still palpitating, at the feet of the Queen.

And how did she receive such homage? Shuddering, she turned her eyes away: 'Such beautiful creatures,' she said, 'to suffer so!'

He remonstrated: 'It was a goodly chase. Mercy on us, it was fine, good sport!'

Before the courtiers he had laughed at her squeamish ways. But his voice had been a little threatening when he said: 'You must learn to love our English ways, sweetheart.'

Now, alone with her, as he recalled this incident, his sullen eyes rested upon her. She had not been taught to ride in the chase; she liked better to spend her time with the priests; and it spoiled his pleasure that she should not appreciate the amusements which, he told himself, he had prepared for her. If he did not love her, he might have been very angry with her.

Well, it was a small matter and he would teach her. But perhaps he was not so displeased after all, for it must be admitted that she was a most virtuous woman; her virtue was a light that shone on him; and in the midst of pleasure he liked to be sensible of his own virtue.

Every moment he was feeling less displeased with her; and to soothe himself he planned more revels.

He said to her: 'I shall ride into the tiltyard. I'll tilt against Brandon. He'll be a match for me.' He laughed. 'There are few skilled enough for the task. And after that, we'll have a ball . . . a masque . . . such as was never seen.'

'You are spending much of your father's treasure on these ceremonies,' said the Queen. 'They are costly, and even great wealth will not last for ever.'

'Is it not better to delight the people with pageants and joyful feasts than to store up treasure in great coffers? I would rather be the best-loved King than the richest King.'

'The people murmured against your father's taxes. Would it not be well to alleviate them in some way? Could we not devise some means of letting the people know that you will make amends for your father's extortions? I am sure that my Lord Norfolk and that very clever Master Wolsey would know what should be done.'

The King narrowed his eyes. 'Mayhap. Mayhap,' he said testily. 'But know this: I too know . . . even more than such as Norfolk and Wolsey, what my people want – and that is to see their King, to know that he will make this land a merry one for the people of England.'

Katharine lowered her eyes. This boy whom she had married was a headstrong boy; he must, she was beginning to understand, be continually humoured. She had been wrong to show her disgust when the warm bodies of the deer were laid before her; she must appear to enjoy the extravagant pageants which so delighted him; she must always feign astonishment when he presented himself before her faintly disguised as Robin Hood or some lowly knight. She must remember that he was young; he would grow up quickly, she was sure; as yet he was but a boy who loved a boy's games. And she must never forget that, although he was a boy, he was the most powerful person in the kingdom. There were times when she thought that to put the sceptre in the youthful hands was like giving a wilful, hot-tempered child a sword to play with.

He was smiling now, and his smile could startle her, for there was a malignant cruelty in it which sat oddly on his fair young face. Although she was growing accustomed to it, it made her uneasy.

'I have prepared a treat for the people which will repay them for all they have suffered,' he said.

'Yes, Henry?'

'You remember when I gave orders that those agents of Empson and Dudley should be placed in the pillory?'

'I do.'

'And what happened to them?'

'The mob set upon them, I believe, and stoned them to death.'

The King's smile deepened. 'Now I shall give them a bigger treat. Oh yes. I will repay the people for their sufferings, never fear.'

'Then will you give back what your father took from them?'

'Better than that!' he said. 'Far better. I will give them Empson and Dudley. *They* were the extortioners. They shall be executed on Tower Hill, and I'll warrant you, Kate, the people will come from far and wide to see their blood flow . . . and they will thank their King for avenging their wrongs.'

Words were on her lips, but each day she learned wisdom. So, she thought, you will offer them the blood of your father's unpopular servants, but their money – the money which was wrung from them in cruel taxes so that they were left with little to show for their labour – you will spend on your jewels, your fine clothes and your rejoicing.

'You do not speak,' he said, frowning. 'Like you not my plan?'

There is nothing I can do, she decided.

Ah yes, she was beginning to understand the man whom she had married.

She said quietly: 'The people will rejoice, I doubt not.'

Now he was laughing, embracing her warmly. He loved and needed approval as much as he loved and needed feasting and revelry.

* * *

My Lord Mountjoy was one of those who were with the King when Thomas brought the verses he had written on vellum decorated with the white and red roses of York and Lancaster.

Mountjoy was hopeful; the King had confided to him that he looked to the scholars to make his court bright with learning. Mountjoy was considering writing to Erasmus.

There were also present the King and his chaplain, a man for whom Henry had a deep liking and respect. It was true that he was not a handsome man; his face was slightly marked with the pox, and the lid dragged a little over the left eye, which was not becoming; being in his mid-thirties, he seemed elderly to the King; but although he was, as yet, merely the King's chaplain, Henry was so struck with his discourse that he determined to keep Thomas Wolsey at his side and to heap preferment on him at an early date.

And now came Thomas More, scholar and writer, to offer verses of laudation.

The King held out his hand for the man to kiss. He liked that face; and the royal smile was benign as Henry bade Thomas More rise.

'I remember you,' he said, 'in company with the scholar Erasmus. Was it not at Eltham that we met?'

'It was, Your Grace, and Your Grace's memory of that fact covers me with honour.'

'We like our poets. There is too little learning at our court. We feel ourselves but ignorant when compared with such learned men.'

'Your Grace astonishes the world with his learning.'

The King smiled, meaning to charm; and instinct told him that modesty would appeal to this man with the kind mouth and

68

the shrewd eyes. 'If not with my own,' said Henry, 'with that of my subjects. This is a pretty thing you bring me. Read the verses . . . that all may hear what you have to say to your King.'

Thomas read them, and as he listened the King's heart warmed towards this man. Such elegance of phrase, such finely worded sentiments. He liked what this man had to say of him and his Queen.

'We thank you, Thomas More,' he said when the reading was over. 'We shall treasure the verses. And Mountjoy here has been telling us of that friend of yours . . . Erasmus. We must have him here. I want all to know that I wish to see this court adorned by learned men. I would that I had paid more attention to my tutors. I fear the chase and all manner of sports have pleased me overmuch.'

'Your Grace,' said Thomas, 'your humble subjects ask not that you should become a scholar, for you have a realm to govern. We would beg that you extend your gracious encouragement to scholars in this land of ours.'

'We give our word to do it. We need these scholars. They are the brightest jewels in our crown.'

And he kept Thomas More beside him, conversing lightly of theology and the science of astronomy. The Queen joined in and the King was pleased that this should be so.

There were some men whom he liked, whether they were old or young, gay or serious. He had two of those men close to him now . . . his two Thomases, he called them. One was Thomas Wolsey and the other was Thomas More.

*　　*　　*

Two days after the Coronation Alice Middleton called at The Barge with a posset for Jane.

As soon as she entered the house it seemed to Margaret that she dominated it; but both Margaret and Mercy were pleased that she had brought her daughter with her.

The three children went to one of the window-seats and talked together. Little Alice Middleton, to the astonishment of Margaret and Mercy, had learned no Latin.

'But what will you do when you grow up?' asked Margaret in a shocked voice. 'Do you not wish to please. . . .'

Margaret was stopped by a look from Mercy, which reminded her that as this little girl had no father they must not talk of fathers.

Margaret blushed, and her eyes filled with compassion. Both she and Mercy wished to be very kind to the little girl who had no father. But young Alice was not disturbed.

'When I grow up I shall take a husband,' she said. 'A rich husband.' And she twirled a golden curl which had escaped from her cap, and, fatherless as she was, she seemed very pleased with herself.

Meanwhile her mother was talking in a loud voice:

'This place is not healthful. I'll swear it's damp. No wonder you are not feeling well, Mistress More. But you take a little of this posset, and you'll feel the better for it.'

Jane said it was good of her to call; she repeated her thanks, for, as she said again and again, she did not know how she would have reached home without the help of Mistress Middleton.

'You would have reached home, I doubt not. That which we must do, we find means of doing. . . . So I always say.' And Mistress Middleton smiled as though to imply: And what I say – by the very fact that I say it – it is bound to be right.

Jane was glad that Thomas should come in so that he could thank the widow personally for her kindness.

'Thomas,' she said, 'this is Mistress Middleton, the kind lady who brought me home.'

'Right glad I am to meet you, Mistress Middleton. My wife has told me many good things of you.'

Mistress Middleton eyed him shrewdly. A lawyer! A scholar! she believed. She had not much respect for scholars; she doubted they did as well as mercers of London and merchants of the Staple of Calais.

'A pity, sir, that you had not the time to take your wife and children into the streets to see the sights.'

'A great pity, madam.'

'Thomas,' cried Jane. 'The King . . . he received you?'

Thomas nodded.

'My husband,' Jane explained, 'is a writer.'

A smile curved Alice Middleton's lips. A writer? A writer of words? What was the use of words? Give her good bales of cloth. That was what people wanted to buy. Who wanted to buy words?

Thomas, grateful to the widow, could not help but be amused by her obvious contempt and her refusal to pretend anything else.

'I perceive,' he said, 'that you do not worship at the shrine of Literature.'

'I worship in church like all good people, and in no other place. And Literature? Tilly valley! What is that? Will it build a house? Will it weave a cloth? Will it look after your wife when she falls fainting in the streets?'

'It might inspire a man or a woman to build a house, madam. And before a man builds a house he must have the will to do so. So might it make a man – or should I say a woman? – so long to possess a new gown that she will weave the cloth. As for its looking after a fainting wife: Well, suppose a lady could read of a great pageant, her imagination, enhanced by literature, might be such that she would feel it unnecessary to stand in a press of people in order to see with her eyes that which she could conjure up by a mental effort.'

'Here's clever talk!' said Alice. 'And my eyes are good enough for me. I can weave with the best, and I don't need words to help me. If I can't build a house I can keep one clean. And as for this Latin the scholars talk one with another, I manage quite well, sir, with my native tongue.'

'May I say, madam, that I am convinced you manage . . . you manage admirably.'

'But my husband is a poet,' said Jane in mild reproof.

'Poetry won't bake bread. Nor make a man wealthy, so I've heard.'

'Who speaks of wealth, madam?'

'I do, sir. For in this world it is a useful thing to have. And no

71

matter what you tell me, riches come through work and thrifty living . . . not through writing poetry.'

'True riches belong to the spirit, madam, which uses its own resources to improve itself. We can only call a man rich if he understands the uses of wealth. Any man who piles up endless wealth, merely to count it, is like the bee who labours in the hive. He toils; others eat up the honey.'

'I speak of money not of honey, Master More. It seems you are a man who cannot keep to the point. You may smile. Methinks I should be the one to smile.'

A faint colour showed in the cheeks of Alice Middleton. She liked the man; that was why she was giving him what she would call the edge of her tongue; she would not bother to waste that on those she considered unworthy of it.

His face was pleasant and kindly, she concluded. A clever man, this; yet in some ways, helpless. She would like to feed him some of her possets, put a layer of fat on his bones with her butter. She'd warrant he gave too much thought to what went into his head and not enough to what went into his stomach.

'His verses were dedicated to the King,' said Jane. 'And did the King accept them, Thomas?'

'He did. He took them in his own hands and complimented me upon them.'

His lips were smiling. Margaret left the little girls to come and stand close to him. She was so happy because this King loved him. They had nothing to fear from this King. She took his hand and pressed it.

'So the King likes verses!' said Mistress Middleton, her voice softening a little.

'Ah, madam,' said Thomas. 'What the King likes today, may we hope Mistress Middleton will like tomorrow?'

'And he accepted them . . . from your hands?' demanded Mistress Middleton.

'He did indeed.' Thomas was remembering it all. It was only about his writing that he was a little vain; he made excuses for his vanity. Artistic talent, he was wont to say, is a gift from God. But he was conscious of his vanity, and he mocked himself while he treasured words of praise. And now at this moment he could not help recalling with pleasure the King's delight in his verses.

As for Alice Middleton, she was looking at him with new respect.

For a lawyer and a scholar she had little to spare; for a man who had spoken with the King she had much.

*　　*　　*

The next two years were eventful ones for Margaret. For one thing, two people became very important to her. Both of these were visitors to the house; although one of these was a neighbour and a constant caller, the other lived with them as one of the family.

The first was Alice Middleton who made regular calls. Margaret did not love Mistress Middleton, although she recognized that lady's wish to be kind. Mistress Middleton believed that everyone who did not do as she did must surely be wrong. If any household task was not done according to Mistress Middleton's rule, it was not done in the right way. She would teach them how to bake bread in the only way to bake the best bread, and that was the way she always did it; she would show them how to salt meat in order to make the best of it. She would show how children should be brought up. They should be obedient to their elders; they should be whipped when stubborn; they should be seen and not heard, and not talk in heathen tongues which their elders could not understand.

What disturbed Margaret more than anything was the fact that her father did not feel as she did towards Mistress Middleton. She had watched his face as he listened to her tirades, and had seen the amused twitch of his lips; sometimes he would talk with her, as though he were luring her on to taunt him. She was a rude and stupid woman; yet he seemed to like her rudeness and her stupidity. And Margaret, who followed her father in most things, could not do so in this.

The other person was the exalted Erasmus.

Him, Margaret regarded with awe. He was now more famous

than he had been in the days when he had first come to England. He was known all over the world as the greatest Greek scholar, and he was preparing to write a critical edition of the Greek text of the New Testament.

Margaret *could* understand her father's affection for this great man, for Erasmus was worthy of his regard and friendship as Madam Alice could never be.

This Erasmus was a sick man. There were days when he could do nothing but lie abed. On such days Margaret would wait upon him, bringing to him the books he asked for. He had a great affection for Margaret and she was pleased that this should be so, largely because of the delight it gave her father. Thomas would openly sue for praise for his daughter as he never would for himself, and Margaret felt very tender towards him as she watched his delight in the compliments Erasmus paid her.

Once Erasmus said: 'I do not believe there is another girl – or boy – of this child's age who can write and speak the Latin tongue as she does.' And afterwards her father said to her: 'Meg, this is one of the happiest days of my life. It is a day I shall remember on the day I die. I shall say to myself when I find death near me: "The great Erasmus said that of my daughter, my Meg." '

She thought a good deal about Erasmus. He might be a greater scholar than her father – though she doubted this – but she did not believe he was such a brave man. There was a certain timidity in his manner; this had been apparent once when Alice Middleton was present and had spoken quite sharply to him – for Alice was no respecter of scholars, and the fame of Erasmus had not reached her ears. She obviously did not believe that a poor wisp of a man who, as she said, looked as though a puff from the west wind could blow him flat, was as important as they seemed to think. 'Scholar! Foreigner!' she snorted. The sort of men she respected were those like the King: more than six feet tall and broad with it; a man who would know what to do with a baron of beef and a fat roast peacock . . . aye, and anything a good cook could put before him. She liked not this sly-looking man with his aches and pains. Greatest scholar in the world! That might be. But the world could keep its scholars, declared Mistress Alice.

Margaret said to Mercy: 'No; he has not Father's bravery. *He* would not have stood before Parliament and spoken against the King.'

'He has not Father's kindness,' answered Mercy. 'He would mock where Father pitied.'

'But how could we expect him to be like Father!' cried Meg; and they laughed.

Erasmus spent his days writing what he called an airy trifle, a joke to please his host who loved a joke, he knew, better than anything. He was too tired, he told Margaret, to work on his Testament. He must perfect his Greek before he attempted such a great task. He must feel sure of his strength. In the meantime he would write *In Praise of Folly*.

He read aloud to Thomas when he came home; and sometimes Thomas would sit by his friend's bed with Margaret on one side of him, Mercy on the other; he would put an arm about them both, and when he laughed and complimented Erasmus so that Erasmus's pale face was flushed with pleasure, then Margaret believed that there was all the happiness in the world in that room.

Erasmus poked fun at everybody . . . even at the scholar with his sickly face and lantern jaws; he laughed at the sportsman for his love of slaughter, and the pilgrims for going on pilgrimages when they ought to have been at home; he laughed at the superstitious who paid large sums for the sweat of saints; he laughed at schoolmasters who, he said, were kings in the little kingdoms of the young. No one was spared – not even lawyers and writers, although he was, Margaret noted, less severe with the latter than with the rest of the world.

And this was written with the utmost lightness, so that it delighted not only Thomas, but others of their friends, to picture Folly, in cap and bells, on a rostrum addressing mankind.

He stayed over a year in the house, and while he was there Thomas was made Under-Sheriff of the City of London, which was an honour he greatly appreciated. Alice Middleton, still a constant visitor, was delighted with this elevation.

'Ah,' Margaret heard Thomas say to her, 'how pleasant it is to enjoy the reflected honours! We have neither to deserve them nor to uphold them. We bask in the soft light, whilst the other toils in the heat. The temperate rather than the torrid zone. So much more comfortable, eh, Mistress Middleton?'

'Tilly valley! I know not what you mean,' she told him sharply. 'So you but waste your breath to say it.'

He explained to Margaret as he always explained everything: 'The Mayor of London and the Sheriffs are not lawyers; therefore they need a barrister to advise them on various matters of law. That my Margaret, is the task of the Under-Sheriff who is now your father.'

And when he dealt with these cases he refrained, if the litigants were unable to pay them, from accepting the fees which had always previously been paid. This became known throughout the City. It was about this time that the people of London began to love him.

Margaret was very happy during those two years; she had learned the meaning of fear, and that lesson had made her happier, for with it had come the joy of being without fear. But there was another lesson to learn: It was that nothing in life was static.

First, Erasmus left for Paris, where he hoped to publish *In Praise of Folly*; and that was the end of the pleasant reading and discourse. Then Margaret's mother took to her bed with a return of that weakness which had rarely left her since the birth of little Jack.

What they would have done during this time but for Alice Middleton, no one could say. Alice swept through the house like a fresh east wind, admonishing lazy servants, administering possets and clysters to Jane, boxing the ears of maids and menservants and the children when it seemed to her that they needed such treatment.

Gone was their gentle mother, and in her place was bustling and efficient, though sharp-tongued and heavy-handed, Dame Alice.

The children looked at each other with solemn eyes.

'Will our Mother get well?' asked four-year-old Cecily.

Jack cried at night: 'Where is our Mother? I want our Mother.'

'Hush,' said Margaret, trying to comfort him. 'Mistress Middleton will hear your crying, and box your ears.'

When he fell and cut his knees, or whenever any of the children hurt themselves, it was Mercy who could bind up the wound or stop the bleeding. Mercy had the gentlest of hands, and the very caress of them could soothe a throbbing head.

'I should like to study medicine,' she confided to Margaret. 'I believe it is the one thing I could learn more easily than you could. In everything else I believe you would do better than I. But not in that, Margaret.'

And Mercy began growing herbs at the back of the house; and she became very skilful in these matters. Thomas called her: 'Our young doctor'!

But nothing Mercy grew in her border, and nothing she could do, made Jane well.

*   *   *

One day Jane called her eldest daughter to her.

Jane seemed to have grown smaller during the last few days; she looked tiny in the four-poster bed; and her skin was the same colour as the yellow thread in the tapestry of the tester.

Margaret suddenly knew that her mother would not live long to occupy that bed.

'Margaret,' said Jane, 'come close to me.'

Margaret came to the bed.

'Sit near me,' said Jane, 'where I can see you.'

Margaret climbed on to the bed and sat looking at her mother.

'Margaret, you are only six years old, but you are a wise little girl. You seem all of eleven. I feel I can talk to you.'

'Yes, Mother.'

'I am going to die.'

'No . . . you must not. What can we do without you?'

Jane smiled. 'Dear little Meg, those are sweet words. It is of when I am gone that I wish to speak to you. How I wish I could have waited a while! Another seven years and I could have safely left my household in your hands.'

'Mother . . Mother . do not say these things. They make me so sad.'

'You do not wish for change. None of us does. You will take care of your father, Margaret. Oh, he is a man and you are but a child . . . but you will know what I mean. Margaret, I can die happy because I have left you to your father.'

The tears began to fall down Margaret's cheeks. She wished that she had given her mother more affection. She had loved her father so much that she had thought little of the quiet woman who, she now saw, had taken such an important place in their happy household.

'Mother . . . please . . .' she began.

Jane seemed to understand.

'Why, bless you, Meg, it has been my greatest delight to see that love between you and your father. When we married I was afraid I was quite unworthy of him. I was so . . . unlearned; and at first I was unhappy. I would sit at the table trying so hard to study the Latin he had set me . . . yet knowing I would never learn it to his satisfaction. And then when you were born all my unhappiness vanished, because I knew that, although I could not make him an ideal wife, I had given him someone whom he could love better than anyone in the world. That was worth while, Margaret. I was happy then. And when I saw you grow up and become everything that he had desired, I was even happier. Then there was Elizabeth . . . then Cecily . . . and now Jack. You see, he has, as he would say, his quiver full. And but for me he could not have had you all. That is what I have told myself, and because of it I can die in peace. So do not reproach yourself, my little one, that you love him more than you do me. Love is not weighed. It flows. And how can we stem the flow or increase it? Margaret, always remember, my child, that if you have given him great happiness, you have given me the same. Come, kiss me.'

Margaret kissed her mother's cheeks, and the clammy touch of her skin frightened her.

'Mother,' she said, 'I will call Mercy. Mayhap she will know what would ease you.'

'One moment, dearest Meg. Meg . . . look after them all. My little Jackie . . . he is such a baby. And he is like me. I am afraid he will not be as good with his lessons as you girls are. Take care of him . . . and of little Bess and Cecily. And, Meg, I need not tell you to comfort your father, for I know that your very presence will do that. Oh, how I wish that this could have been delayed . . . a year or two . . . so that my Margaret was not such a child. You are a dear child, a clever child – never was one so clever – but . . . if only you had been a few years older I could be content.'

'Mother . . . please do not fret. I will be as though I have lived twelve years. I will. I swear it. But you will get well. You must. For what shall we do without you?'

Jane smiled and closed her eyes; and, watching, Margaret was filled with terror.

She ran from the room, calling Mercy; but it was Alice Middleton who came into the chamber of death.

*   *   *

A week later Jane was dead; and only a month or so after she was buried, Thomas called his children to him and told them that they should not be long motherless.

He was going to marry a lady capable of looking after them, a lady of great virtue. She was without much education and several years older than himself, but he was convinced that she would be the best possible stepmother for them.

Her name was Alice Middleton.

THREE

WHEN MARGARET was twelve years old fear again appeared
in her life. It seemed like a great cloud which came nearer and
nearer to the house until that day when it enveloped it. The
cloud formed itself into the shape of a man, of great height, of
great girth, on whose head there was a crown. At the age of four,
Margaret had learned to fear kings. And now would the cloud
pass over the house? Would it pass on as, once before, had a
similar cloud?

Much had happened since the death of her mother. The family
still lived in Bucklersbury, but it had become a different household under the domination of Mistress Alice.

It must have been the cleanest house in London; the rushes
were changed once a week, and very little odour came from them.
When they were removed from the house it was only necessary
to go upstairs, not to leave the house for a day until the servants
had cleared it of its filth. Alice was the most practical of women.
She knew exactly how many pieces could be cut from a side of
beef, and she saw that they were so cut; her servants must
account for every portion of fish, every loaf of bread. She kept
strict count of the visitors who called for a meal. She reckoned –
and this matter she took up fiercely with her husband – that
visitors were costing the household purse the whole of twopence
a day, what with food, beds and firing. The family was allowed
only sixty candles a year, and if any burnt out his share before
the year was over, then, said Alice grimly, must that one sit in
the dark. She herself kept the keys of the buttery; she saw that
none had more than his portion of ale or mead. She was the
martinet of the household.

All Thomas's attempts to teach her Latin failed.

'What the good year!' she cried in scorn. 'Would you have me
one of these pale-faced, lantern-jawed scholars? I'll warrant you,
Master More, that I do you more good watching the affairs of

your household than I ever should tampering with foreign speech. The English tongue, sir, is good enough for me.'

But nevertheless she kept a strict eye on the children.

Thomas had instituted what he called his 'School' in the house, and here all the children spent many hours at their lessons. Alice had a habit of peeping at them at odd moments, and if she found them not at their desks she would take them, throw them across a chair and administer a good beating with her slipper.

'Your father has set you these tasks,' she would say, 'and your father is head of this house.' (Not that she would admit such a fact to his face.) 'He'd not whip you himself, being too soft a man, so there's some that has to do his duty for him. Now . . . get to that Latin . . . or Greek . . . or that mathematics . . . or whatever nonsense it is, and if you have not learned it by sundown you'll feel more of my slipper where you won't like it.'

Jack was the chief offender, because he could not love learning as his sisters did. Jack would look longingly out of the window, particularly when horsemen rode by. He would like to be out of London, in the green country, climbing trees and riding horses. Jack sometimes felt it was a sad thing to be a boy possessed of such clever sisters.

Ailie was not overfond of lessons, but she did not care to be too far outstripped by her stepsisters. She applied herself and as she had a cleverness of her own, a natural wit, she could usually appear to know more than she actually did. Her mother had a habit of looking the other way when Ailie misbehaved, so, although she might have been in trouble as much as Jack was, somehow she managed to escape it. She was very pretty, and Alice believed that one day she would make a very good match.

Alice insisted that each of the girls should study housekeeping under her guidance; for what, she had demanded, would be the use of all that learning if when they married – and if only Master More would make the most of his chances they might marry very well – they had no knowledge of how to run a house and keep the servants in order? So each of the girls must, in addition to her lessons, give orders to the servants, decide on the composition of meals and superintend the cooking for a whole week before the task fell to her sister or stepsister. And if anything went wrong, if the bread was burnt or the meat had been subjected to too many turns of the spit, or not enough, then it was not only the servant who felt the mistress's slipper.

Alice was not above giving any member of this large household the measure of her tongue. Even the tutors came in for their share, learned men though they might be. Master Nicholas Kratzer, fellow of Corpus Oxford, who had come to live in the house to teach the children astronomy, particularly irritated Alice.

She laughed him to scorn. 'You, a scholar . . . and cannot speak the King's English! Here's a pretty state of affairs. And supposed to be a learned man!'

'Madam,' he told her with the humility all these great men seemed to display before Alice, for it was a fact that every one of them wilted under her scornful gaze, 'I was born in Munich; and although I cannot speak your tongue well, I doubt you can speak mine at all.'

'Tilly valley!' said Alice. 'And who would want to when they could make themselves understood in good plain English?'

The poor scholar, to the amusement of Margaret and Mercy, was quite at a loss to answer Alice; for, somehow, her method of delivering what she thought to be wise was so authoritative that temporarily it seemed to be so. Therefore, Master Kratzer returned to his study of the stars feeling a little cowed, and as for Margaret and Mercy, they had their ears boxed for laughing – as Alice said, when Kratzer had left them – at a great and learned man.

Richard Hyrde, the great Greek scholar, also lived in the house. Mercy was his favourite pupil, for he was also a student of medicine, and this science appealed to Mercy more than any other. Master Drew and Master Gunnel, considerable scholars, also lived in the growing household in order that they might tutor the children.

Dr Colet and Dr Lily came to the house now and then, but not so frequently as they had at one time, for all Dr Colet's thoughts and energies were now concentrated on the school he had built in St Paul's Churchyard, at which he planned to educate children of all ages, of all classes and all races. This school was his delight; it was a dream become a reality. He had always said that when he was a rich man – and he knew he would be on the death of his father – he would build such a school. Now he watched over it as a mother watches over her child, brooding over it, worrying over it, talking of it continually. Dr Lily shared all his enthusiasm and fears for Dr Lily had consented to become Headmaster of the school.

Thomas had said: 'There is no man in England who could carry out this task with greater skill. But I wanted Lily for my children.'

Colet laughed gleefully. 'I got there first, Thomas,' he cried. 'I have secured him for my children.'

Now that Margaret was aware of the cloud's coming nearer to her home she thought often of Dr Colet's escape from the King's wrath. This had happened a few years before, and they had trembled for the fate which might overtake this beloved friend. The same cloud must have darkened Colet's house then as it now did that of the Mores.

Why must these great men always express their views with such careless unconcern for the consequences? Why could they not be content to talk in private with their friends, and enjoy the happy lives which they had built up for themselves out of their goodness? Dr Colet had his school – the great wish of a lifetime fulfilled – yet when the King planned war with France, he must get into his pulpit and preach a sermon on the folly and wickedness of war.

It was inevitable that he should be called before an angry King; it was by a miracle that he had escaped with his life. But was it a miracle? What a plausible tongue had this great man, what a way with words!

He came to the house afterwards to tell them about it; and he and her father had laughed together until Margaret had feared they would make themselves ill with such immoderate laughter which in her wisdom, she understood was partly the laughter of relief.

83

'But, Your Grace,' Colet had said to the King, 'it is true that I preached against war. Aye, and would do so again. I said: "Few die well who die in battle, for how can they charitably dispose of anything when blood is the argument? Men must follow Christ, the King of Peace . . . not the kings of war." Those were my words, Sire.'

'I know your words, sirrah!' the King cried angrily. 'And I like them not.'

'But, Your Grace,' was the reply, 'I but preached against dishonourable war . . . unjust war . . . and Your Grace must agree with me that there can be no good in unjust war.'

It was at this point, when telling the story, that Colet was overcome with helpless mirth. 'And Thomas, the King looked at me, his little eyes suspicious. Then, suddenly, that tight mouth slackened. He laughed; he slapped my shoulder. "I see, friend Colet," he said. "You spoke not of this just war I would wage against the enemies of England. You spoke of the unjust wars that my enemies would wage on me!" I bowed my head. I feared he might see the laughter in my eyes. For, this King of ours, Thomas, is a King who believes he is God Himself. He believes in all simplicity, in all sincerity, that he himself could not be unjust, could not be dishonourable. The very fact that he acts in a certain way makes that action honourable. What a man! What a King!'

'How easy life must be for him!' mused Thomas. 'He has but to adjust his conscience to his desires.'

'Exactly. And this is what he did. He told himself that his Dr Colet had not spoken against *his* war; he had spoken against unjust war, as he himself would speak, for is he not a just King? He led me out of his privy chamber, his arm about me. You would have been amused to see the faces of his courtiers. They had expected me to appear between two halberdiers, and here I was – His Grace's arm through mine. He embraced me before them all, and he cried: "Let every man favour his own doctor. This Dr Colet is the doctor for me. . . ."'

They might laugh; but such encounters terrified Margaret.

But for a turn of phrase John Colet might not be with them at this time.

Erasmus had stayed in the house during those years, and of all the scholars who came to the house, Alice liked him least.

A 'finicky' man, she declared he was – picking at his food, talking Latin to her husband, laughing with him. Alice was not at all sure that they were not laughing at her. 'And here's a pretty state of affairs when a woman does not know what is being said before her face.'

The climax came when he dropped a ring in the rushes and on recovering it looked at it with such distaste, and wiped it so carefully on a kerchief before restoring it to his finger, that Alice's indignation could not be suppressed.

'So, Master Desiderius Erasmus, you find my house not clean enough for you? You sniff at my rushes, do you, sir? There is one answer to that, and I will give it. If you like not my house, why stay in it? Why not go back to your hovel . . . your native country where houses are so clean that they make you turn up your foreign nose at ours!'

He had tried to placate her, as all tried to placate Alice; but his arguments did not move her. She disliked him, and that was the blunt fact. All the learned tutors – the absent-minded Master Gunnel and the guttural-voiced Master Kratzer, she would endure; but not the sickly, watery-eyed, sarcastically smiling Erasmus. And indeed Erasmus had left England soon after that. He had told Margaret, of whom he was very fond: 'I am a little tired of England, my child; and your stepmother is very tired of me.'

Soon after the great scholar had left them there had occurred the terrible rising of apprentices in the City, and, as Under-Sheriff, her father had played a great part in quelling the rebellion. The rising had come about on account of the citizens' dissatisfaction with the foreigners who lived therein and who, said the citizens, took their livings from Englishmen in their native land. These foreigners brought silks, cloth of gold and merchandise into London and sold them cheaply. Dutchmen brought over timber and leather, baskets and stools, tables and saddles, already wrought; and these they sold in such numbers that there was little work for those who had previously made such goods for their own countrymen.

So it was that during the month of April people gathered in the streets to discuss this matter, and they asked themselves how they could best rid themselves of the foreigners. Thomas Wolsey, now Cardinal, Pope's Legate, Archbishop of York, Chancellor of England and Prime Minister of State, sent for the chief aldermen of the City and told them that it was the King's wish that the foreigners should not be molested, as they brought much trade to the country; but the aldermen, after listening respectfully to Thomas Wolsey, went away and assured each other that their first allegiance was to the City of London, and if the citizens had decided to rid themselves of the foreigners there was nothing they could do about it.

Then came that 'Evil May Day' when the apprentices, with the people behind them, rose and rioted through the streets, sacking and burning the houses of foreigners.

Thomas, as Under-Sheriff, had been able to restore order to some parts of the City. The Cardinal, foreseeing how matters would go, ordered troops to close in on London, and several of the rioters were taken prisoner.

These men and boys were condemned as traitors, but only one of them was executed in the terrible manner – hanging, drawing and quartering – which was the lot of traitors. This one was to prove an example to the people; as for the rest, they provided the King with an opportunity to stage one of those little plays which he so loved, the ending of which was supposed to be a surprise, but which all except the most simple of men knew to be inevitable.

Henry, gloriously clad, a mighty man in sparkling jewels, sat on a lofty dais in Westminster Hall, while before him were brought the condemned men, with ropes about their necks. The Queen must kneel before him · a foreigner herself – and beg the King for leniency since some of the offenders were so young; she asked this as a favour to herself.

The sullen little mouth became less sullen. The King raised

the Queen and said that for her sake he would consider pardoning these wretches.

Then it was the turn of the great Cardinal – magnificent in his scarlet robes – to kneel and crave the King's clemency.

All must watch this spectacle, all must know that a beloved Queen, the mother of the King's own daughter, the Princess Mary, must humble herself before the all-powerful monarch, as must the mighty Cardinal who went about the City in such state that men gathered to see him pass as though he were a King himself; this mighty Chancellor, this great Prime Minister of the realm, also must bow the knee to beg a favour from the King.

And eventually the King allowed himself to smile, to temper justice with mercy, to receive the humble thanks of those miserable men and the gratitude of their wives and mothers who called blessings on him – their most clement King, their most handsome King, who in anger was terrible, but who knew how to relent.

It was a touching scene, begun so solemnly, ending so joyously. The memory of it would put the King in a good humour for days.

And it was not forgotten what an excellent part in quelling the rebellion had been played by Thomas More. The King noted it and discussed it with his right-hand man. They would keep their eyes on Master More. They liked the fellow, both of them.

But life was made up of success and failure, of joy and fear; it was like a game of see-saw.

Just as the King's benevolence was shining upon Thomas More during that month of May, something happened to turn the King's smiles to frowns.

One of the Pope's ships had been forced to call at the port of Southampton, and the King had ordered it to be seized.

A week ago a man had called at the house in Bucklersbury to see Thomas and, when he had gone, Thomas told his family that he had agreed to act as interpreter and counsel in a case which the Pope was bringing against the authorities in England.

Alice said: 'This is a good thing. You will win the case for the King, and the King's favour never hurt anyone.'

'Nay,' Thomas answered her. 'You mistake me. It is not for the King I am briefed, but for the Pope.'

Margaret said nothing; she could only look mutely at her father. He saw the way in which she looked at him, and his eyes conveyed reassurance to her.

But Alice cried: ''Tis a marvel to me, Master More, that some men deem you wise. A bigger fool it has not been my misfortune to meet. Here is a lawyer who advises those who would go to law not to waste their money! Here is a lawyer who spends much of his time saving his clients' money that he may keep himself poor. He has won the King's favour, this Master More, on Evil May Day. That will not do. Therefore he must throw away his advantages by working against the King and serving the Pope.'

'I seek no favours of the King,' said Thomas. 'I seek to defend what is right. The ship does not become the property of the King because it calls at an English port.'

'Anything in this land belongs to the King.'

'Madam, you should enter the law. The King would doubtless favour your advancement. I doubt not that you would reap great honours.'

'I beg of you not to mock me, sir,' said Alice. 'And I beg of you not to be such a fool as to take this case.'

'My folly has already run ahead of your wisdom, madam. I have accepted the brief.'

'More fool you!' cried Alice. But she, like Margaret, was afraid. Like the rest of the family, she did not want change to overtake them. If her tongue was sharp, if she must be subject to fools, in her private opinion they were beloved fools.

The weeks seemed like a year; and the cloud about the house grew darker.

Margaret said to her father: 'I remember, a long time ago when I was a little girl, you told me that the King was angry with you. That was another King, but it seems to me that this King can be as angry – perhaps more angry – than his father'

'That may be so, Meg.'

'Must you do this thing?'

'How could I refuse? The case was brought to me. I know the Pope's cause to be the right one. Would you have me refuse it because I know that, in defending the right, I might offend the King?'

'Let some other do it.'

'Turn away from danger that some other might face it! Or leave it to those who would defy justice for the sake of the King's favour! Nay, Meg! That is not the way to live. You . . . you of all people to ask it!'

'But, Father, I . . .'

'I know, Meg. You love me. But should I be worthy of your love if I turned away from danger? Remember this, Meg. When good fortune is greatest, then is trouble close at hand. For Fortune delights to strike down those who are too high and to raise those who are low; and if we do not anticipate trouble, should it come, we shall face it with greater fortitude.'

So she trembled, and during that day when he went into the courts she found that she could not keep her mind on her lessons. Nor could Elizabeth and Cecily; and when Alice looked in and found Jack astride a stool, dreaming that he was on horseback, and Ailie pulling at the curls which escaped from her cap, and Cecily and Elizabeth whispering together, and neither Mercy nor Margaret attending to their lessons, she merely shook her head at them and said nothing, which was strange for her. There was about her an alertness, as though she were listening for the sound of horses' hoofs which would herald the return of Thomas.

And at length he came home.

'Wife!' he cried. 'Children! Where are you?'

They rushed to greet him, to look into his face; and there they saw a shining triumph.

'Well, Master More?' demanded Alice.

'The case is won.'

'Won?' cried Margaret.

'There could only be one verdict, and I got it.'

He had won the case, even though it had been tried before the great Wolsey himself. He had won the Pope's case, and in doing so he had defeated the King!

Margaret had felt then that that other occasion had been but a rehearsal for this. Henry the Seventh had gone timely to his grave; but the new King was young and healthy.

What will become of us? wondered Margaret.

Mercy was beside her. 'Come, Margaret. Sit down here.'

Mercy forced her on to a stool and placed a cool hand on her forehead.

'Thank you, Mercy.'

'Do not frighten the little ones,' whispered Mercy.

'You are right,' said Margaret. 'We must not frighten the little ones. But Mercy . . . Mercy . . .'

Mercy pressed her hands. Mercy, even though she loved him as Margaret did, even though she saw his danger, could remain serene.

They were at supper when the messenger came. He was the King's messenger; they knew that by his livery.

The King, declared the messenger, desired the presence of Thomas More at his Palace of Westminster. It would be well for Thomas More to take barge at once.

Margaret felt the piece of cob bread sticking in her throat. Her eyes met those of Mercy. Mercy's eyes, beneath her level brows, were full of fear.

*　　*　　*

When Thomas was shown into the royal apartments of the Palace of Westminster, the King was alone with his Chancellor.

Thomas went forward, knelt, and a large hand, a-glitter with emeralds, diamonds and sapphires, was extended to him.

Almost immediately it was snatched away and waved impatiently.

'Rise . . . rise . . .' said the King.

Thomas did so and stood before the royal chair. The sparkling hands were laid on the velvet-covered chair-arms; the big face was flushed, the eyes narrowed.

'We have had news, Master More,' said the King, 'of your conduct in this affair of the Pope's ship.' He glared at Thomas.

'That is why we have sent for you.'

Thomas's eyes strayed for a second to those of the Chancellor, who stood by the King's chair. It was impossible to read the thoughts behind those eyes, but Thomas sensed a certain sympathy, a certain encouragement. During this day in the court he had been aware of Wolsey's approval of his conduct of the case. But what the Chancellor would feel in the absence of the King might be something different from that which he might show in his presence.

'Master More,' went on the King slowly and deliberately, 'you have a fine conceit of yourself.'

Thomas was silent.

'Have you not?' roared the King. 'We hear that this day, when you defended the Pope, you were full of fine phrases. Now, when you should defend yourself, you appear to have lost your voice. What is the meaning of this? What is the meaning of it, eh?'

'Before I begin the case for my defence, Sire, I must know what is the accusation.'

'You dare to stand before us . . . your *King* . . and to ask what is the accusation! Master More, did you, or did you not, deliberately act against your King this day?'

'Nay, Sire. I acted against injustice.'

The King's hands on the arms of his chair were clenched suddenly; they appeared to tremble.

'Did you hear that, Wolsey, did you hear that?'

'I did, Your Grace.'

'He acted against *me* . . . and he calls that acting against injustice! By God's body, what should I do with such a man, eh? Tell me that. You are the Chancellor of this realm. What should I do with him? Clap him into the Tower? Know this, my friend . . . know this: Those who act against the King are traitors. Master More, do you know the death that awaits a traitor?'

'I do, Your Grace.'

'You should . . . as a lawyer. Well . . . well . . . what have you to say? You stand there. . . . Come, come, repeat to me what you said in the courts this day. You . . . you traitor . . . you . . .

you who would work for a foreign power against your own country . . .'

'Your Grace, I was asked by the representative of His Holiness the Pope to argue his case for him. The Chancellor here will tell you that I only did what any lawyer would do.'

'And are you in the habit, Master More, of employing your talents to uphold injustice?'

'Nay, Sire.'

'And if you did not think a case was a just one, you would refuse it. I dare swear?'

'I should, Your Grace.'

The King rose. He put his hands on his hips and rocked on his heels. The little eyes opened very wide and he began to laugh.

'Here, Wolsey!' he cried. 'Here is our man!'

Thomas looked in astonishment from King to Chancellor. Henry walked towards Thomas and laid a hand on his shoulder.

'It grieves us,' he said, 'it grieves us mightily that when we find honest men in our kingdom . . . honest men and brave . . . they are not with us, but against us.' He lifted his hand suddenly and brought it down in an affectionate pat on Thomas's shoulder. 'And when we grieve, Master More, we seek to right the grievance. That is so, is it not, Master Wolsey?'

The Chancellor came forward. ''Tis even so, my gracious lord.'

'Speak to him then, Wolsey. Tell this fellow what I have said of him.'

Then Wolsey spoke: 'Our most gracious King, in his clemency, in his great love of truth and justice, is not displeased, as you might well believe, at the way in which the case went this afternoon. When I told His Grace what had happened, how you, with your learned discourse, with your determination to uphold what you believed right in this matter, had so swayed the court that the verdict went against the holding of the Pope's ship, his most gracious Majesty was thoughtful.'

''Tis so!' interrupted the King. ''Tis so. And I said to Wolsey: "Thomas Wolsey," I said. "Thomas, I like it not when the best men in my kingdom . . . out of their honesty and bravery . . . are not with me, but against me." That is what I said to him. "By God," I said, "we should send for this fellow. He shall work for me in future, for he is a man that I like . . . and he is a man I will have beside me. . . ." '

'I understand not, Your Grace,' said Thomas.

'He understands not my grace!' said the King with a laugh. His eyes were sparkling with benevolence; the little mouth was slack with sentiment. 'Aye, but you shall. You shall see, Thomas More, that I am a King who would surround himself with the best in the kingdom. I like you, Master More. You were against me . . . but I like you. That's the man I am. You dared to speak against your King, but such is your King that he likes you for it.'

Now he stood back like a boy who has all the toys that others envy; and who, because he is wise and kindly, will share those toys with the less fortunate.

'Come here, my friend.' He took Thomas's arm in a gesture of such friendliness that it startled Thomas. 'Don't be afraid of us, Master More. Don't be overcome, my dear fellow. Yesterday you were a poor lawyer. Today the King is your friend. And you, my dear Wolsey, my other Thomas. . . .' He put his arm through that of the Chancellor, and with them walked the length of the apartment 'We have work for a man like you here at court, Master More. We can lift you up. We can honour you with favours . . . and we will. You shall work with our Chancellor here, for he has taken a fancy to you. He likes you. Do you not, eh, Wolsey?'

'I do, my gracious master.'

'Indeed, you do.' The King stopped and looked with the utmost affection at the Cardinal. 'There's not much missed by those shrewd eyes. Now there shall be two Thomases to serve their master . . . two good and honest men. What have you to say, Master More?'

'Your Grace overwhelms me. I know not what to say'

The King began to laugh. ''Twas as good as a play, eh, Wolsey? As good as a masque! Master More, present yourself to the King! By God, Master More, when you entered this room you thought you'd march out of it to a dungeon, I doubt not. You did not know that you would find in it the King's warm regard . . . the King's favour.'

'Your Grace,' said Thomas, 'I know you to be a just King. I did not believe that you would condemn a subject because that subject acted in accordance with what he believed to be right.'

'Well spoken,' said the King soberly. 'Your advancement is certain. You will do well in the service of the Chancellor.'

'Your Grace, I . . . I have my duties as a lawyer. . . '

Both the King and Wolsey had raised their eyebrows, but Thomas went on boldly: 'I have also my duties as Under-Sheriff of the City of London. . . .'

'Enough! Enough!' said the King. 'We shall take care of that. Man, I offer you great rewards. Look at this man here. He was but my chaplain, and I have made him the greatest man in this land . . . under myself. My father raised him up . . . and what was he before that? I'll tell you. . . . No, no. I will not tell you! Suffice it that it was humble . . . *most* humble, eh, Master Wolsey? But I like this man. I like this Wolsey. He is my counsellor and my friend. And so . . . from little I lifted him to greatness. So will I do for you. Now . . . you are overwhelmed. It was a little joke of mine to tease you first, to fill you with fear, then to fill you with joy. You shall be a rich man, Master More. Fortune is favouring you, for the King is giving you his hand in friendship. Go away now . . . and think of the greatness which lies before you. I will let all men see this day how I honour those who are brave and honest men . . . even though they do not always share my views.'

'Your Grace . . .'

'You are dismissed, Master More,' said the King with a smile. 'You shall speak of your gratitude some other time. You need now to be alone . . . to think of this sudden change in your fortunes.'

The King had turned away, calling for a page; and Thomas found himself walking backwards out of the apartment.

* * *

Slowly he made his way down to the river, where his barge was waiting for him.

Never had he been at such a loss for words; never in the whole of his life had he received such a surprise. He had gone to the Palace prepared to defend himself and, instead of having to justify his action in the court of law, had found a more difficult task presented to him. He had tried to refuse an appointment at Court which the King himself had offered, when to refuse it would certainly be looked upon as an affront to His Grace.

Yet refuse it he must. He did not want to go to Court. He was no courtier. He did not want his quiet life to be disturbed. He had his work, his writing, his study, his family. They were enough for him; they gave him all that he desired in life. It was ironical; so many yearned for a place at Court; so many were ambitious; and he who did not seek it, who must refuse it, was having it thrust upon him.

As he was about to step into his barge, one of the Cardinal's servants came running to the river's edge.

Wolsey's retinue were as magnificently attired as though they served the King; they wore a livery of crimson velvet trimmed with gold chains; and even his menials wore scarlet trimmed with black velvet.

'His Excellency the Cardinal begs you to wait awhile,' said the man. 'He would have speech with you. He says the matter is of importance. Will you wait for him in his apartments, sir?'

'Assuredly I will,' said Thomas; and he was conducted back to the Palace.

There he was shown into the apartments of the Cardinal, the furnishings of which were as rich as those of the King. Thomas was taken through many rooms to a small chamber, and when he had waited in this chamber for five minutes, the Cardinal came in.

In his scarlet satin dress and tippet of sable, he dominated the room; and he wore his garments as though they delighted him. There were many stories current regarding the magnificence of the Cardinal. He kept several princely households, in which he stored many treasures. York House and Hampton Court were

95

said to vie with the King s own palaces. He lived in great pomp, surrounded by a large retinue of servants; he had his cofferer, three marshals, an almoner, two yeomen ushers and two grooms; he had clerks of the kitchens, a clerk controller, even a clerk of the spicery; his pages, grooms of the scullery and scalding-houses, grooms of the pantry, porters and yeomen were so numerous that even he did not know their number; and his cook was seen to strut in the grounds of his houses like a minor potentate in damask and with a chain of gold about his neck, carrying a nose-gay or a pomander in imitation of his master, his own servants of the kitchen about him.

The grandeur of Wolsey exceeded, some said, that of the King himself; and because the Cardinal had risen to great heights from a lowly beginning, he was resented by those of high birth, who felt he should not be among them, and envied by those of low birth who felt he should be on their level. Yet he cared not for these criticisms. He cared not that the mischievous Skelton had written verses concerning the state he kept, and that the people were singing them in the streets, asking each other:

> *'Why come ye not to Court?*
> *To which Court?*
> *To the King's Court*
> *Or to Hampton Court?*

> *'The King's Court*
> *Should have the excellence.*
> *But Hampton Court*
> *Hath the pre-eminence.'*

Perhaps those who sung the verses believed they might rouse the King's resentment; but the King was not resentful towards his favourite, for Henry believed that all the magnificence with which the Cardinal surrounded himself came from his own kingly munificence. Henry had set the fountains playing; if he wished, he had but to give the order and their flow would cease. Hampton Court was in reality the King's Court, and the King's Court was Hampton Court. The Cardinal regarded the

King as his puppet; but that was exactly how the King saw the Cardinal; each was unaware of the other's myopia, and while this was so they could feel safe and contented.

The Cardinal, though essentially ambitious, was not an unkindly man. There was no room in his life for malice for its own sake. There was one ruling passion in the Cardinal's life, and that was ambition. To the humble, he was generous; and his servants were fond of him. He had used religion as a ladder to fame and fortune; he used people, and if he found it necessary to destroy them, it was not out of malice or sudden anger; it was merely because they impeded his ambition.

He, like the King, had taken a fancy to Thomas More; he had seen that this man could be useful.

He had also seen what the King had not seen: that Thomas More was not overcome with joy at the prospect of the King's favour. It was not that Thomas More had been at a loss for words to express his gratitude; he had hesitated because he was wondering how to refuse the honours the King was ready to bestow. It was concerning this matter that the Cardinal wished to see Thomas More.

'I am glad that you returned to the Palace,' said the Cardinal. 'I would converse with you. You may speak frankly with me, as I will with you. And you need have no fear that what you say will go beyond these four walls, for my servant, Cavendish, whom I would trust with my life, will see that none overhears us. So . . . speak your mind freely to me, Master More, as I will speak mine to you.'

'What is it that Your Excellency has to say to me?'

'Merely this: You are considering how to refuse the King's offer, I believe?'

'You are right. I shall refuse it.'

'Such procedure would be misguided.'

'I will try to explain to you.'

The Cardinal lifted his well-cared-for hand. 'Save your breath. I understand. You are not an ambitious man. You are a scholar who wishes to be left alone with the work he has chosen. I understand that point of view, although it is a most unusual one. I have read your literary works – and may I compliment you on their excellence? You prefer the secluded life. But if you rebuff the King's friendly gesture, you will be a foolish man. Nay . . . nay . . . mistake me not. I know that if a man does not seek fame, then he sets no store by it. But I do not talk of fame . . . of the advancement which I know could come to a man of your talents. I speak, Master More, of your life.'

'My life?'

'It could easily be at stake.'

'I do not understand you.'

'That is because you do not understand the man whom we have just left. You see him as a mighty King. Pray do not be alarmed. As I said, I shall speak frankly to you, even of the King. You may think I am incautious. But, my friend, if you carried tales of what I say to you now, I should deny them. Moreover, I should find some means of silencing you. But I speak to you thus because I know you are a man who would respect a confidence. I trust you as you trust me. You have just witnessed a little play-acting in the royal apartments. Was it not charming? A humble official believes he has displeased the King; and then he finds that he has pleased him. The King is a boy at heart, Master More. He loves to play, and you have helped him to play a very pretty scene. Now, the King is not always a merry-tempered boy. Sometimes the young cub roars and sometimes he springs; and although I am his very watchful keeper, I cannot always save his victims from those mighty claws; even if I have a will to do so. You marvel? But, listen. I have a fancy for you . . . just as the King has. There are few men in this kingdom with brains and honesty . . . oh, very few. Having found one, I do not intend to let him slip through my fingers. I want you, Master More, to work with me. I can offer you a great career . . . fame . . . advancement . . .'

'Your Excellency . . .'

'You do not want them, I know. But you want to live. You want to go home to your clever children and your wife, do you not? You want to go on conversing with your learned friends. Oh, life is sweet, Master More, when it brings as much to a man as it has brought to you. But think of this: A child plays his games and he loves his toys; but if a toy displeases him, what does he do? He smashes it. Master More, when you played the honourable lawyer this day, you took a great risk. But the boy liked his playlet; he liked his new role. Perhaps he has heard his praises sung too consistently of late. Who shall say? But you pleased him. You played your part so well that the principal actor was able to outshine us all. Now, the King will not be pleased if you do not continue to make him feel pleased with *himself*, if you do not allow him to show the world what a beneficent monarch he is.'

'You are very bold, Cardinal.'

'You were bold this afternoon, Master More. But you cannot afford to risk offending the King twice in one day. Great good luck has attended you; you could not expect that to be repeated. This King of ours is a mighty lion who does not yet know his strength. He is caged . . . but he does not see the bars. I am his keeper. If he felt his strength, if he knew his power, then we might begin to tremble. I believe he would risk his kingdom to satisfy his appetites. That is why he must be fed carefully. It is the duty of men like yourself . . . like myself . . . who wish to serve our country – some because of honour, some because of ambition; what matters it if we serve our country well? – it is the duty of such men to suppress their personal desires. And if we do not, we may find that the King's frown, instead of his smile, is turned upon us.'

'Are you sure that if I refused to come to Court I should find myself persecuted?'

'I believe this would certainly come to pass. Remember, my friend – and I mean "my friend", for I will be yours if you will be mine – I know him. I served his father as I now serve him; and I have watched him grow up.'

'But I have no wish to come to Court.'

'Master More, you have no choice. I remember, when I served his father, that you were in disfavour. You are a man who cannot fail to attract attention. You would not be here in England at this moment had his father lived, unless you now lay under the earth. The young King is not the old King; but, Master More, he is none the less dangerous for that.'

'I wish to live in peace and quietude with my family.'

'If you wish to live at all, Master More, you will not reject the King's honours.' The Cardinal was smiling quizzically. 'Go now, my friend. There is nothing more to say at this stage. I will tell the King I have talked with you, and that the honour he is about to heap on you has overwhelmed you, robbed you of your native wit. I will tell him that I believe our country is fortunate in the learned honesty of Thomas More . . . and the clemency and astonishing wisdom of its King.'

*　　*　　*

Margaret flung herself into his arms when he came home.

'Father!'

He kissed her warmly.

'Why these sad looks? This is a time for rejoicing. The King honours me. He sent for me to congratulate me . . . to tell me of his regard.'

Margaret, her arms about his neck, leaned backwards to look searchingly into his face.

'But you are disturbed.'

'Disturbed! My dearest, you will see your father a courtier yet. I met the great Cardinal, and he also honours me with his friendship. Meg, I am weighed down with honours.'

But she continued to look at him uneasily. The others were surrounding him now.

'What is this nonsense?' demanded Alice.

'The King sent for me to tell me he is pleased with me.'

'Pleased with you for losing him his ship?'

'The Pope's ship, madam!'

'Pleased with you. Pleased! Is this another of your jokes?'

' 'Tis no joke,' said Thomas slowly. 'The King liked what I did this day, and he honours me. I am to go to Court. I am to work with Cardinal Wolsey. When I left this house, Alice, I was a humble lawyer; now I am . . . I know not what.'

Alice cried: ''Tis a marvellous thing and great good luck,

though you have done little to deserve it. Come to the table. Tell us more of this. A place at Court! Tilly valley! I was never so excited in my life.'

How strange, thought Margaret, that the same piece of news could be so differently received by members of the same family. Here was her stepmother already looking ahead to a rosy future, to rich marriages for the young members of the family; and here was her father looking ahead – smiling for their sakes, trying to be pleased with advancement, yet unable to hide from his beloved daughter the foreboding which showed in his eyes.

* * *

That summer was hot and dry, and the sweating sickness appeared in the City.

Thomas was to begin his service to the King by going on an embassy to Flanders. His life had changed; he must be often at the Palace and he spent much time with the Cardinal. The first trouble which his elevation brought were his absences from home.

'I wish we were a humble family,' said Margaret passionately to Mercy. 'Then we might stay together and attract no attention to ourselves.'

'We should have no education,' Mercy reminded her. 'And can you imagine Father as a man of no education? No, as he says, there is good and bad in life; and there is bad in the good and good in the bad; and the only way to live is to accept the one with the other. Enjoy one; endure the other.'

'How wise you are, Mercy!'

'It is borrowed wisdom . . . borrowed from Father.'

Mercy was happy that year in spite of the pending departure of Thomas, and the reason was that there was a new member of this ever-growing household. This was John Clement, a protégé of the Cardinal's, a young man in his late teens who was to accompany Thomas as his secretary and attendant on the mission to Flanders.

John Clement was a serious and very learned person – a young man after Thomas's own heart – and a warm welcome was given him in the house of his new master. Young Clement quickly became a member of that happy family group, but he found that she who interested him most was not one of the Mores, but Mercy Gigs.

He sought every opportunity of talking with her. He was several years older than she was, but it seemed to him that he had never met a girl of her age so solemnly self-contained; and if she was not quite so learned as Margaret, her scholarship lay in that subject which most interested him.

He never forgot the rapt expression in her eyes when he told her that he had studied medicine at Oxford.

'You are interested in medicine, Mistress Mercy?' he asked.

'In nothing so much.'

Now they had a subject which they could discuss together; Thomas watched them with pleasure. My little Mercy is growing up, he thought. They are all growing up. In two or three years it will be necessary to find husbands for Mercy and Margaret – and Ailie too, though she will doubtless find one for herself.

It was a dream materializing, an ideal becoming palpable. When he had decided on giving up the monk's life for that of a family man, he had visualized a household very like the one which was now his. Had he ever imagined such love as he had for Margaret? Nay, the reality was greater than he had foreseen. And when she marries she must never leave me, he thought, for without Margaret I would not wish to live. And Mercy here is as dear to me as are my own children. Did ever a man possess such a learned and affectionate daughter as Margaret, such charming children as those who made up his household? And Alice herself, she was neither a pearl nor a girl, but he was fond of her; and he knew that her sharp words often hid kindly motives. Where could he find a better housekeeper? And surely she was the best of mothers to his children, for it was well to have a touch of spice in the sweetest dish. There might be times when his beloved children were in need of chastisement, and how could *he* administer a whipping? He was a coward where such matters were concerned. What could he whip his children with but a peacock's feather? Yet Mistress Alice shirked not the task.

He was a lucky man. He must not complain that his life away from his family was not all that he could wish. So many men craved the King's favour; so many would have been honoured to call the Cardinal their friend. He wanted too much of life. He must make the best of his new honours; he must steal away from them as often as he could, to be with his books and his family; and he must be grateful to God for the good life which was his.

Was ever man so loved? Very few, he believed. Only yesterday, when the children were talking together of what they wished for most, he had wandered by and heard their talk. Mercy had said: 'If I could wish for something, I would wish I were Father's true daughter.'

And when he had found her alone, he had said to her: 'Mercy, you have no need to wish for what is already yours. To me you are exactly as though you are my true daughter.'

She had blushed and faltered and said: 'Father, I meant that I wished I were your daughter as Margaret, Elizabeth and Cecily are.'

'That matters not at all, Mercy, my child. I see you as my daughter – my true daughter – as much as any of the others. You are as dear to me.'

'I know it, Father,' she said. 'But . . .'

'But, Mercy, if that love which is between us two is as strong as the love which is between me and the daughters of my own body, what difference can there be! You delight me, Mercy. You are all that I could wish for in a daughter. You must not wish for something which is already yours . . . in all that matters. I remember when you were a little girl and I took you to task for some small fault, your distress hurt me as much as the distress of any of the others would have done.'

She caught his hand and kissed it. 'In those days,' she said, 'I sometimes committed those faults that you might talk to me alone . . . even though it was to reprimand me.'

'Poor little Mercy! You felt you were left out then? You were the foster-child? You wished to have attention . . . even if, to gain it, you must seem at fault?'

'It was that,' she answered. 'But it was also that I might have the pleasure of standing before you and that you should be thinking of me . . . me . . . alone. Me . . . by myself, without Margaret.'

'Oh, Mercy . . . Mercy . . . you must not have such a high opinion of me. We must not set up gods on Earth, you know.'

She said: 'I have set up nothing. I have lifted up my eyes and seen.'

He laughed. 'Now to talk sense. Your wish was that you could be my true daughter. Now that you know there was no need for such a wish, what other wish have you, my child? Suppose I were a king with all the wealth in the world at my disposal, and I said I would grant you a favour, what would you say?'

She did not hesitate. 'I would ask for a big house to which I could bring the sick and care for them, and gradually learn more and more, that I should know not only how to cure but prevent disease.'

'That's a noble wish, Mercy. Would I were a king . . . solely that I might grant it.'

So he watched her with John Clement, and his heart warmed towards them both; for he wished his girls to marry and have families. That was the happiest life, he was sure; he had proved it. And while Thomas was preparing to depart on his embassy, Mercy and John Clement were often together, and they talked of the terrible sickness which had taken a hold of the City.

' 'Tis a marvellous thing,' said Mercy, 'that there is not a single case of sickness here in Bucklersbury.'

'I have a theory on that matter,' said John Clement eagerly. 'This street lacks the maleficent odours of other streets. Here we do not smell unpleasantness, but sweetness . . . the smell of musk, the smell of spices and perfumes and unguents.'

'Do you think, then, that the sickness comes from evil smells?'

'I believe this may be so; and if this street, as I believe has been the case in past epidemics, has not a single sufferer of the sweat while scarce a house in the rest of the City escapes, then might there not be something in the theory?'

Mercy was excited.

'Why,' she cried, 'when Erasmus was here he condemned our houses. He did not like them at all. He said the rooms were built in such a way as to allow no ventilation. Our casements let in light, but not air; and the houses are so draughty. He said our custom of covering our floors with clay on which we laid rushes was a harmful one – particularly as in the poor cottages those rushes are not changed for twenty years. I know how angry Mother used to be when he complained about our rushes, although they were changed once a week. He said we should have windows that opened wide. He said that we ate too much – too many salted meats. He said our streets were filthy and a disgrace to a country that called itself civilized.'

'He sounds a very fierce gentleman.'

'He was . . . in some ways. In others he was mild. But I think there may be something in what he said about our houses, do you not, Master Clement?'

'I do indeed.'

'I am terrified that the sickness will come to this house. But I am glad that Father is leaving the country just now. He at least will get away from these pestiferous streets. You also, Master Clement. . . . But . . . it would be terrible if anything happened here . . . while he is gone. What should I do if any take the sickness?'

'You can do nothing about the draughts and the lack of good air in the house, of course. But I believe more frequent sweetening would prevent the disease coming here. Here is a good mixture for any afflicted: marigold, endive, sowthistle and nightshade – three handfuls of all; seethe them in conduit water – a quart of this; strain into a vessel with a little sugar. This will remove the sourness. Let the patient drink it. The patient should keep warm and lie in his bed when first the sweat takes him. If he is dressed, keep him dressed; and if he is undressed let him stay undressed, but cover up the bed . . . cover it well. I have known men and women recover when so treated.'

'Marigold, endive, nightshade and sowthistle. I will remember that.'

'I will tell you how to make the philosopher's egg. Now, that is an excellent remedy for the sweat. It can be prepared in advance and you can keep it for years. In fact, it improves with keeping.'

'That would delight me greatly. Do tell me.'

'You take an egg and break a hole in it and take the yolk from the white as cleanly as you can. Fill the shell with the yolk and some saffron; then close the ends with egg-shell. Put it in the embers and leave it until it be hard and can be made into a fine powder.'

Ailie came over to where they sat; she eyed them mischievously.

'What is it that interests you so much that you forget aught else?' she wanted to know.

'Master Clement is telling me how to make the philosopher's egg.'

'The philosopher's egg! You mean that which changes base metals into gold or silver? Oh, Master Clement, I beg of you to tell *me* your secret.'

'You misunderstand,' said John Clement soberly.

'The philosopher's *egg*,' explained Mercy. 'You think of the philosopher's stone.'

'And what magic powers hath this egg?'

'It cures the sick,' said Mercy.

'I would rather the stone,' said Ailie.

'Heed her not,' said Mercy with some impatience. 'She loves to jest.'

Ailie stood by smiling at them, and John Clement went on: 'You will need white mustard, dittony and termontell with a dram of crownuts; you must also add angelica and pimpernel, four grains of unicorn's horn if you can get it. All these must be mixed with treacle until they hang to the pestle. I will write this out for you to keep. When this substance is made it can be put into glass boxes, and kept for years. Its great virtue is that the longer you keep it the better.'

'Oh thank you. I shall never forget your kindness.'

Ailie went to Cecily and whispered: 'See how friendly they are becoming.'

'What is it he gives her?' asked Cecily.

'It is a love-letter,' said Ailie. 'To think that Mercy should have a lover before me.'

'Love-letter! You are wrong, Ailie. It is a recipe for some medicine, I'll swear.'

'Ah, my dear little Cecily, that may be. But there are many kinds of love-letters.'

And Ailie pouted, for she said she liked it not that any of the girls should have a lover before she did.

Alice laughed at the two young people. 'Master More, what strange daughters you have! They love Latin verse better than fine clothes, and exchange recipes when other youths and maidens exchange love-tokens.'

'That may be,' said Thomas, 'but with my family – and this fits every member of it – with my family, I am well pleased.'

'Tilly valley!' said Alice; but she herself was no less pleased.

*   *   *

Thomas wrote home regularly while he was away from them.

They must write to him for, he said, he missed them sorely, and it was only when he received their letters that he could be happy. He wanted to hear everything, no matter how trivial it seemed to them; if it concerned his home, that was enough to delight him. 'There is no excuse for you girls,' he wrote. 'Cannot girls always find something to chatter about? That is what I want you to do, my darlings. Take up your pens and chatter to your father.'

There was always a special compliment if Jack wrote anything. Poor Jack, now that he was growing up he was beginning to realize how difficult it was for a normal, healthy boy to compete with such brilliant sisters. Alice said it was God's rebuke on his father for having prated so much and so consistently about the equality of men's and women's brains when all the rest of the world opined that men were meant to be the scholars. Here are your brilliant daughters, perhaps God had said. And your son shall be a dullard.

Not that Jack was a dullard by any means; he was merely normal. He could not love lessons as he loved the outdoor life. Therefore his father wrote to his son very tenderly and cherished his efforts with the pen, encouraging him, understanding that all cannot love learning as some do.

He wrote enthusiastically to Margaret. He could not help it if writing to Margaret gave him pleasure which was greater than anything else he could enjoy during his sojourn abroad.

He was writing a book which had long been in his mind, he told her. It consisted of imaginary conversations between himself and a man who had come from a strange land which was called *Utopia*. They discussed the manners and customs of this land. The writing of this book was giving him great pleasure, and when he came home he would enjoy reading it to her.

'I showed one of your Latin essays to a very great man, Margaret. He is a great scholar, and you will be gratified when I tell you who he is. Reginald Pole. My dearest, he was astonished. He said that but for the fact that I assured him this was so, he would not have believed a girl – or anyone your age, boy or girl – could have done such work unaided. My dearest child, how can I explain to you my pride? . . .'

He was a very proud man. He kept his children's writings with him, that he might read them through when he felt dejected and homesick; nor could he refrain from showing them to his friends and boasting a little. His pride and joy in his family was profound.

'My dearest children,' he wrote to them, 'I hope that a letter to you all may find you in good health and that your father's good wishes may keep you so. In the meantime, while I make a long journey, drenched by soaking rain, and while my mount too frequently is bogged down in the mud, I compose this for you to give you pleasure. You will then gather an indication of your father's feelings for you – how much more than his own eyes he loves you; for the mud, the miserable weather and the necessity for driving a small horse through deep waters have not been able to distract my thoughts from you. . . .'

Then he went on to tell them how he had always loved them and how he longed to be with them:

'At the moment my love has increased so much that it seems to me that I used not to love you at all. Your characteristics tug at my heart, so bind me to you, that my being your father (the only reason for many a father's love) is hardly a reason at all for my love for you. Therefore, most dearly beloved children, continue to endear yourselves to your father, and by those same accomplishments, which make me think that I had not loved you before, make me think hereafter (for you can do it) that I do not love you now. . . .'

And so they waited, while the sweating sickness passed over Bucklersbury, for the return of the father whom they loved.

* * *

One day after his return when the family were gathered at the table, Thomas said to them: 'I have a surprise for you all. There is to be a new addition to our family. I hope you will all make him welcome. I find him an interesting and charming person. I am sure you will too.'

'Is it a man?' asked Ailie, her eyes sparkling.

'It is, daughter.'

'Not a grey-bearded scholar this time, Father!'

'Half right and half wrong. A scholar but not a grey-bearded one. He is, I gather, some twenty years of age.'

'It is to be hoped he has not the finical manners of that Erasmus,' said Alice. 'I want no more such foreigners in the house.'

'Nay, Alice, he is not a foreigner. He is an Englishman; and I doubt you will find him over-finical. He is of a very good family, I must tell you, and he comes to study the law with me.'

'Father,' cried Margaret, 'how will you have time to help a

young man with his studies, do your law work and serve the King and the Cardinal? You do too much. We shall never have you with us.'

'Do not scold me, Meg. I'll warrant you'll like Friend Roper. He is a serious young man, a little quiet, so he'll not disturb you overmuch. I think he will be ready to join our family circle.'

So William Roper came to the house – a young man of quiet manners and seeming meekness, but, Margaret noticed, with an obstinate line to his mouth. There was one thing about him that Margaret liked, and that was his devotion to her father. It was quite clear that the young man had decided to follow in Thomas's footsteps whenever possible.

John Clement, who had returned to the household of the Cardinal, came to the house whenever he could; and in a few months it became clear that Will Roper and John Clement looked upon The Barge in Bucklersbury as their home.

Margaret was thirteen when Will Roper came; he was twenty; yet in spite of the difference in their ages, Margaret felt as old as he was. As John Clement sought Mercy's company, Will Roper sought Margaret's; and this fact made Ailie pout a little. There was she, by far the prettiest of the three of them, and yet the two eligible young men at the house seemed to seek the friendship of Margaret and Mercy.

'Not,' she said to Cecily who was herself a little frivolous, 'that we could call such as John Clement and Will Roper *men*; one is always sniffing herbs and cures, and the other always has his nose in his law books. Now that Father is at Court, perhaps he will bring home some real men . . . for you, Cecily, and for me. I doubt whether Margaret or Mercy would be interested.'

Alice worried Thomas when they were alone: 'Now that you have such opportunities, you must see to husbands for the girls.'

'Why, Alice, there are some years to go yet.'

'Not so many. Mercy, Margaret and my girl are thirteen. In a year or two it will be time to settle them.'

'Then we may wait a year or two yet.'

'I know. I know. And by that time who knows what honours will be heaped upon you! It is all very well to be wise and noble and to prattle in Greek, but it seems to me you would be wiser and more noble if you thought a little about your children's future.'

He was thoughtful, and suddenly he laid his hand on her shoulder.

'In good time,' he said, 'I promise you I will do all that a father should.'

Those were the happy days, with few cares to disturb the household. They had grown accustomed to Thomas's working with Wolsey now. He came home at every opportunity, and they would laugh at his tales of how he had managed to slip away from the Court unseen.

At that time the only troubles were petty annoyances. There was an occasion when Thomas went to Exeter to see Vesey, the Bishop, and he came home quite put out; and while they sat at the table he told them why this was so.

'I had some of your work in my pocket . . . a little piece from each of you . . . and the best you have ever done. Well, I could not resist the chance of showing them to the Bishop, and, to tell the truth, it was that which I was longing to do all the time I was with him. So, at the first opportunity I brought out this piece of Margaret's. He read it, and he stared at me. "A girl wrote this!" he said with astonishment. "My daughter Margaret," I answered lightly. "And her age?" "She is just thirteen." And, my dear one, like Reginald Pole, he would not have believed me had I not given him my word. He would not hand the piece back to me. He read it through and through again. He walked about his room in some excitement and then unlocked a box and produced this.'

They crowded round to see what he held up.

'What is it, Father?' asked Jack.

'A gold coin, my son, from Portugal'

'Is it valuable?'

'It is indeed. The Bishop said: "Give this to your daughter Margaret with my compliments and good wishes, for I never saw such work from one so young. Let her keep it and look at it now and then and be encouraged to grow into that great scholar which I know she will become." I begged him to take back the coin. I refused to accept the coin. But the more I refused, the more earnest he became that I should accept it.'

Ailie said: 'But why, Father, did you not wish to take it?'

'Because, my daughter, I wished to show him the work of the others which I had in my pocket. But how could I show it? He would think I was asking for more gold coins. I have rarely been so disappointed. I felt cheated. I wanted to say: "But I have five clever daughters and one clever son, and I wish you to know how clever they all are." But how could I?'

They all laughed, for now he looked like a child – a little boy who has been denied a treat, Margaret told him.

'Well, here is your coin. Meg, do you not like it?'

'No, Father. Every time I look at it I shall remember it brought disappointment to you.' Then she put her arms about his neck and kissed him. 'Father, you must not be so proud of your children. Pride is a sin, you know – one of the deadly sins. I am going to write some verses for you . . . about a father who fell into the sin of pride.'

'Ah, Meg, I shall look forward to hearing them. They will make up for the disappointment the Bishop gave me.'

In the evenings they would gather together and talk and read; sometimes they would sing. Thomas had taught Alice to sing a little. She had begun under protest. She was too old, she declared, to join his school. And did the man never think of anything but learning and teaching? Latin she would not touch. As for Greek, that was more heathen than anything.

He would put his arms about her and wheedle her gently: 'Come, Alice, try these notes. You've a wonderful voice. You'll be our singing bird yet.'

'I never heard such nonsense!' she declared. But they heard her singing to herself when she sat stitching, trying out her voice; and they knew that one day she would join in; and she did.

Margaret felt that with the passing of that year she had grown to love her father even more – so much more, as he had said, that it seemed that previously she could hardly have loved him at all.

His book *Utopia* taught her more about him. She understood from it his longing for perfection. She enjoyed discussing it with him. 'My pride in you, Father, is as great as yours in your children. Methinks we are a very proud pair. And, Father, there is one thing that pleases me more than any other: That is your tolerance in this matter of religion.' She quoted: ' "King Utopus made a decree that it should be lawful for every man to favour and follow what religion he would, and that he might do the best he could to bring others to his opinion, if he did it peaceably, gently, quietly and soberly, without hasty and contentious rebuking and inveighing against others. . . ." I like the views of King Utopus on religion. I feel them to be right.'

'Ah, Meg, what a wonderful world we could have if men could be induced to make it so.'

On one occason he said to her: 'My dearest daughter, there is one matter which I wish to discuss with you. It is something between us two, and I want no other to know of it.'

'Yes, Father?'

'You know that at one time I considered taking my vows. Meg, it is a strange thing but the monastic life still calls to me.'

'What! You would leave us and go into solitude?'

'Nay, never! For you are dearer to me than all the world . . . you . . . you alone – and that is not counting the rest of the family. I once said to Colet, when he was my confessor, that I was a greedy man. I wanted two lives; and it seems I am a determined man, for I want to live those two lives side by side, Meg. While I live here in the midst of you all, while I am happy among you, still I crave to be a monk. While I live with you, I am happy with you, and I believe we are meant to be happy for a saintly life need not be a gloomy one, I still continue those practices which I followed when I was in the Charterhouse.' He undid the ruff about his neck and opened his doublet.

'Father!' she whispered. 'A hair-shirt!'

'Yes, Meg. A hair-shirt. It subdues the flesh. It teaches a man to suffer and endure. Meg, it is our secret.'

'I will keep it, Father.'

He laughed suddenly. 'Will you do more than that? Will you

wash it for me . . . and in secret?'

'Assuredly I will.'

'Bless you, Meg. There is none other to whom I could confide this thing and be certain of understanding.'

'There is nothing you could not confide in me . . . nor I in you.'

'Your mother, God bless her, would not understand. She would ridicule the practice. So . . . I thank you, daughter.'

When she took the shirt and washed it in secret, she wept over it, seeing his blood upon it. Sometimes she marvelled to see him so merry and to know he was wearing that painful thing. But he never gave a sign to the others of the pain he was inflicting on himself. If he was a monk at heart, he was a very merry monk.

There was great excitement when the Greek Testament, which Erasmus had edited and reconstructed, was received into the Mores' home. Thomas read it aloud to the family. Alice sat listening, although she could not understand it, her fingers busy with her needle.

Those were happy days. Looking back, a long time afterwards, Margaret realized that the change came from an unexpected quarter, as such changes usually do. A German monk named Martin Luther had during that eventful year denounced the practices of the monks and the Catholic Church, as Erasmus had denounced them before him; but whereas Erasmus mildly disapproved, this man was bold and passionate in his denunciation; and whereas Erasmus had taken refuge behind his scholarship and attacked with an almost light-hearted cynicism, the German monk did so with passionate indignation; whereas Erasmus had written for the initiated, Luther was fulminating for the multitude.

The climax came when this man Luther nailed to the door of a Wittenberg church his ninety-five theses against Indulgences. And when he did this he had fired the first shot in the battle of the Reformation which was to shake Europe, divide the Church and plunge the world which called itself Christian into bloodshed and terror.

Men and women began to take sides; they were for the Pope or for Martin Luther. Erasmus crept back to his desk; he was no fighter. It was said that he had laid the egg which Martin Luther hatched; but he wished to be remote from conflict; he wished to live peaceably with his books.

But as Margaret saw it, her father was of a different nature; he was a man with firm opinions. He could agree with much that Erasmus had written, but if it was a matter of taking sides he would be on the side of the old religion.

But that had not yet come to pass.

The happy evenings continued, broken only by the shock produced by the death of Dean Colet, who was struck down by the plague. They wept sincerely for the loss of this old friend.

But, as Thomas said, he had had a good life. He had seen his dearest wish realized – and what more could a man ask? His school was flourishing under the headmastership of William Lily; and his life had not been an idle nor a short one.

Margaret marvelled afterwards that she had not paid more heed to the rumblings of that storm which was breaking over Europe. It was due, of course, to Willam Roper, who was now seeking her company on every occasion, asking her to walk with him alone, for, he declared, conversation between two people could be so much more interesting in private than in a crowd.

There was a further excitement. One day a very handsome young man came to the house to see Thomas. He was a rich young courtier named Giles Allington, and Ailie, who had received him with her mother, seemed much amused by him, although she did not allow him to know that.

Ailie, when she wished, could be quite charming. She was the prettiest of all the girls, golden-haired, blue-eyed, tall and graceful. She took great pains to preserve her beauty and was for ever looking into her mirror. In vain had Thomas teased her. Often he repeated to her those epigrams which he had translated with William Lily. The one which concerned Lais, who dedicated her mirror to Venus, was a gentle warning. 'For,' said Lais, 'the woman I am, I do not wish to see; the woman I was, I cannot.'

'And that, my dear daughter, is what happens to women who attach great importance to beauty, for beauty is like an unfaithful lover; once gone, it cannot be recalled.'

But Ailie merely laughed and kissed him in her attractive way. 'Ah, dearest Father, but no woman believes her lover is going to be unfaithful while he is faithful; and as you yourself have said, why should we worry about tomorrow's evils? Does not the Bible say, "Sufficient unto the day is the evil thereof"?'

Thomas could not resist her charms, and for all that she set such store by those pleasures which he deemed to hold no real value, for once he found she could score over him with her feminine logic.

So Ailie continued to make lotions for the freshening of her skin, and kept her hands soft and supple, avoiding any household tasks which made them otherwise. As for Alice, she looked the other way when Ailie refused to do such tasks. If Alice wished to see all the girls married well – which she certainly did – she wished Ailie to make the most brilliant marriage of all.

So came Giles Allington, heir to a rich estate and title, with the manners of the Court, and jewels in his doublet; and for all that he was a court gallant, he could not hide his admiration for Ailie as she concealed her interest in him.

'Where she learned such tricks I do not know,' said Cecily wistfully.

' 'Twas not in this house,' said Elizabeth.

'There are some who are born with such knowledge, I believe,' said Mercy. 'And Ailie is one of them.'

So it seemed, for Ailie grew very gay after the visit of Giles Allington, and although she was interested in Master Allington's lands and titles rather than in himself, she grew prettier every day.

'She blooms,' said Cecily, 'as they say girls bloom when they are in love.'

'She is in love,' said Margaret. 'For a girl can be in love with good fortune as well as with a man.'

Giles Allington came often to the house in Bucklersbury; and Alice and her daughter talked continually of the young man.

Alice declared herself pleased that Thomas had won the King's favour and that he was now a man of no small importance. Will Roper was of good family, and he was as a son of the house; John Clement was slowly rising in the service of the Cardinal, and he looked upon this family as his own; and now the handsome and wealthy Giles Allington came to visit them. They were rising in the world.

Life went on pleasantly in this way for many months.

When the King and his lords went to France to entertain and be entertained by the French and their King with such magnificence and such great cost that this venture was afterwards called 'The Field of the Cloth of Gold,' Thomas went with the party on the business of the King and the Cardinal.

And it was at this time that William Roper declared his feelings for Margaret.

Margaret was now fifteen – small and quiet. She knew that – apart from her father – she was the most learned member of the family; but she had always seen herself as the least attractive, except in the eyes of her father.

Ailie was a beauty; Mercy had a quiet charm which was the essence of her gravity, a gentleness, the soothing quality of a doctor – and that was attractive, Margaret knew; Elizabeth, now that she was growing up, showed herself possessed of a merry, sparkling wit which, like her father's, never wounded; Cecily was pretty and gay; Jack was jolly and full of fun. And I, pondered Margaret, I have none of their charms, for although when I have a pen in my hands, words come quickly, they do not always do so in conversation, except perhaps with Father. I most certainly lack Ailie's beauty; I am solemn rather than gay like Jack, who says things which, by their very simplicity, make us laugh.

It had always seemed to Margaret, on those rare occasions when her thoughts unwittingly strayed to the subject, that she would never marry. This did not perturb her for she had had no wish to do so.

And now . . . William Roper.

He asked her to talk with him, and they went into Goodman's

Fields, where she had so often walked with her father. 'It is not easy,' said Will, as they walked through the grass, 'to talk in the house.'

'We are such a big family.'

'The happiest in London, I trow, Margaret. It was a good day for me when I joined it.'

'Father would be pleased to hear you say that.'

'I should not need to say it. I'll swear he knows it.'

''Tis pleasant for me to hear you say it, Will.'

'Margaret . . . tell me this . . . how do you feel about me?'

'Feel about you? Oh . . . I am glad that you are with us, if that is what you mean.'

'I do, Margaret. Those words make me very happy . . . happier than if anyone else in the world had said them.'

She was astonished, and he went on quickly: 'You are a strange girl, Margaret. I confess you alarm me a little. You know more Greek and Latin than any other girl in England.'

She was silent, thinking of Ailie, in a new blue gown, exclaiming at her as she sat over her books: 'Latin . . . Greek . . . Astronomy . . . Mathematics. . . . There is more to be learned from life, Mistress Margaret, than you can find in those books!'

Ailie was right. Ailie had been born with that special knowledge.

'Margaret,' went on Will, 'I . . . I am not so alarmed by you as I once was, for there are times when you seem to me like a very young girl.' He turned to her smiling. 'You know what my feelings are for you, Margaret?'

'Why yes, Will. You like me . . . you like Father . . . you like us all.'

'But I like you better than any of them.'

'Not better than Father!'

'Oh sweet Meg, one of the things I love so much in you is your love for your father. I admire him more than any man I know; but Margaret – do not be shocked – I admire his daughter more.'

She laughed to hide her embarrassment. 'That sounds like one of Father's puns.'

'I must tell it to him.'

'Nay, if you do . . . he will know . . .'

'Oh Meg, dost think he does not know already?'

'But . . . why should he?'

'I think I must have made my feelings clear to all except you, so it is high time that you began to understand me. Margaret, I want you to marry me.'

'But . . . I am not going to marry.'

'You are young yet. I doubt your father would think it seemly for us to marry for a while. But you are fourteen. . . . Perhaps in a year or so . . .'

'But, Will, I had decided I should never marry. And you have disturbed me. It seems now that I shall not be able to think of you as I do of the others, like John Clement and Giles Allington.'

'But I do not wish you to think of me as you think of them. Oh, Margaret, you have not grown up yet. You have been so busy being a scholar that you have not yet become a woman. You could be both. That is what I wish, Meg: for you to be both. Say no more now. Think of this matter – but not too much so that it oppresses you. Become accustomed to the idea of marriage. Think of it, Meg. It is not that I wish to take you from your father. I do not. I would never take you from him, because I have seen that love which is between you, and it is a rare love. I know that. Nay. I am sure he would wish us to live under this roof . . . here as we do now You would be my wife. That would be the only difference. I beg of you, think of this matter. Promise me you will think of it, Margaret.'

'I . . . I will. . . . But I do not think I shall want to marry.'

They walked back to the house slowly and thoughtfully.

*　　　*　　　*

The year 1521 provided a turning-point in the lives of Margaret and her father.

Thomas was drawn more and more into Court business. To Margaret, from whom he hid nothing, he said: 'I feel like a fly in a web. Mayhap at one time I might have made a mighty effort . . . I might have escaped . . . but now the sticky threads hold me fast.'

'But the King is fond of you. He and the Cardinal find you useful.'

'You are right, Margaret, and I will say to you what I would say to no other : Both the King and the Cardinal are only fond of those who can be useful to them, and only so long as they are useful. A man can grow out of his usefulness.'

There was one matter which shocked Thomas deeply. It concerned both King and Cardinal, and taught him much concerning these men; yet when he looked back he realized that it had taught him little that he had not known before – rather it had confirmed his opinion.

The Cardinal had drawn closer to Thomas in those years during which they worked together. To Thomas he was sometimes frank, and when he was sure they were quite alone he would discuss the King in such a manner that, if it were known, might have cost him his head. Such was the measure of his trust in Thomas.

There was in the Cardinal an overweening pride. He believed himself indispensable to the King; and indeed it seemed that this might be so. The King made few decisions without his chief minister beside him. The King was content to amuse himself, knowing that matters of state rested in the capable hands of Thomas Wolsey.

There was no one – apart from the King and Lady Tailbois – who, in the first place, had been more delighted than the Cardinal when the King's natural son had been born to that lady. This had happened some four years ago, a year after the birth of the Princess Mary.

Now, in the year 1521, when the Queen had failed to give the King a son to follow Mary, the Cardinal was faintly disturbed by the affair and he opened his heart to Thomas.

'Why, Master More, when the boy was born, His Grace was like a child with the finest toy that has ever been given to him. He had a son – and for years he had been longing for a son. The Queen's abortive attempts at child-bearing have worried him considerably, for, as you know, he sets great store upon his man-hood; and although it is His Grace's custom to blame his partner in an adventure if blame should be necessary, there has been in him a slight fear that he may not be able to get him a son. Elizabeth Blount – or Lady Tailbois, if you wish – has proved him capable of getting a son; and little Henry Fitzroy is the apple of his eye. I was delighted in His Grace's delight. But the years have passed and there is still no male heir to the throne – nor even another girl. Master More, the King is restive, and the Queen does not grow younger. If she were not such a great Princess, and if I did not fear to offend the Spaniards I would suggest the marriage should be dissolved and another Princess found for him—one who could give him sons as Elizabeth Blount has shown that she can do.'

'But there could be no honourable reason for dissolving the marriage,' argued Thomas. 'The Queen is the most virtuous of ladies and . . . she is not past bearing children.'

'You have a fondness for Her Grace, I know; and she favours you. I, myself, have the utmost respect for the lady. But a Queen's piety is one thing, her usefulness to her King and country is another. The main object of a royal marriage is to get heirs, and that she has not done with any marked success.'

'These matters are surely in the hands of God.'

The Cardinal smiled his slow, cynical smile. 'My friend, if God is slow to act, then it is sometimes necessary for a King's ministers to act without Him. Ah, would the lady had not such powerful relatives! Imagine . . . a new Queen. A French princess or a protégée of the Emperor Charles of Spain? Think what I could do . . . keeping them in suspense . . . having them both in fear that I should ally England with the other. A French princess, I think, would at this time hold the balance of power to greater advantage.'

'My lord Cardinal,' said Thomas, 'the gown you wear proclaims you to be a man of God, but the words you speak . . .'

But Wolsey interrupted: 'The words I speak betray me as the Lord Chancellor, the Prime Minister of England. I serve England, which I believe it is my duty to do.'

Nay, thought Thomas, you serve neither God nor England; you serve Thomas Wolsey.

Yet Thomas More understood Thomas Wolsey; he understood that the humble scholar, the tradesman's son, finding himself possessed of a quick brain and great wisdom, together with a quality which could charm a King, could not but rejoice in these possessions. Wolsey was not, by nature, a bad man, but a man made bad by an overwhelming ambition; he was a man who enjoyed his wealth and delighted in it more because he had earned it.

It was all very well for such as Norfolk, Suffolk or Buckingham lightly to assume the honours which they had inherited by their birth; but the man who had inherited no such glory, who by his quick and clever cunning had created honours for himself, naturally prized them the more highly. And how great Wolsey's pride must have been when he considered those noblemen, and could reasonably believe that had they been born the sons of Ipswich merchants, they would doubtless have remained Ipswich merchants for the whole of their lives.

Nay, Wolsey was not entirely bad, for he was kind to his servants and they loved him. All he asked of them was that they should pay homage to his greatness; then he would be the benevolent father to them, caring for them, feeding them and, in his way, loving them.

He had illegitimate children. Not that he was a sensual man. His union with the woman of his choice would seem to lack nothing but regularity. He did not consort with women promiscuously; there was only one woman. As he had decided to use the Church as his ladder to fame, he was denied marriage; therefore he dispensed with the marriage ceremony; but, being a normal man, he did not intend to dispense with all that marriage would have brought him. So he had settled into a quiet and steady relationship which, but for the facts that there had been no ceremony and he was a priest, would not have seemed different from the marriage of Thomas More himself.

He loved his children, but his love took a different form from that of Thomas; and yet Thomas saw that in some ways it was similar. Thomas wished to give his children that which he most treasured; Wolsey wished to shower on his children what he most treasured in the world – power and riches. His son, who was still a boy, was already Dean of Wells and Archbishop of York and Richmond, and thus the possessor of much wealth and power in his own right.

Not a bad man, but a man who worshipped, according to Thomas, false gods. But as Thomas told himself this he knew that Wolsey would say of him: A clever fellow, but a fool in some ways, for he seems to have no idea how to advance his fortune.

Now Wolsey talked of state affairs and how it would be a simple matter to get the King's approbation of his plans. The King was immersed in a new love affair – a saucy girl had taken his attention and made big demands upon it.

'The daughter of Thomas Boleyn. Doubtless you know him. Well, Master Boleyn will enjoy some favour, I doubt not, when his pretty daughter Mary whispers her requests into the King's ear. He found the girl when we went to France last year. She has pleased him ever since. We shall see the brother's advancement too. George Boleyn is a bright boy. It must be his Norfolk blood – at least, I doubt not Norfolk would tell us so. I believe there is a younger girl . . . in France just now. We much watch this family, for a man like Thomas Boleyn will give himself airs if favoured too highly. If little Mary becomes too demanding we shall have to find another lady for His Grace. Ah, Master More, you like not this talk. You would have the King's household like your own in Bucklersbury. But there are few families like yours in the kingdom. That is why I must take such pains to enlighten you.'

This sign of the Cardinal's favour would have delighted most men; it made Thomas uneasy; it meant that he was in danger of being more closely entangled in that from which he longed to escape.

He was disappointed in the young King. Henry seemed bent on pleasure, and much of that treasure which had been left by his father had already been squandered – not only on war, but on futile displays like this last one of the Field of the Cloth of Gold.

What useful purpose had been served? It was known now that England could squander wealth to glorify the King and his Court; and that France could do the same for its gay young King. But what of that? Both these monarchs were developing into lechers whose minds could be continuously occupied with devising new sensations in amorous adventurings, rather than in studying a wise state policy.

England had Wolsey; and all Englishmen should be glad of that, because with all his pride, with all his ambition and his love of pomp, Wolsey was a great statesman.

Yet how he was hated by some! It was largely due to Wolsey's carelessly expressed hatred of the Duke of Buckingham that Thomas became aware of new and terrible elements about him.

It was Buckingham's duty at this time to hold the gold bowl in which the King washed his hands; and on one occasion – doubtless to avenge a slight which either Buckingham had given Wolsey, or Wolsey imagined he had, and to show his intimacy with the King – when Henry had washed his hands, Wolsey dipped his own into the bowl and proceeded to wash them.

This was more than the noble Duke could endure, for he could never forget that royal blood ran in his veins and that he was related to Edward the Fourth. That he should be expected to hold the bowl while the son of an Ipswich merchant washed his hands was intolerable. He immediately threw the water over Wolsey's feet.

The King might be amused at this incident and Wolsey might appear to take it lightly, but Buckingham had offended that great pride of the Cardinal's, and no man could do that with impunity.

Now Thomas witnessed the beginning of that terrible feud which could only end in tragedy.

Buckingham had forgotten two things when he made an enemy of the Cardinal. He was in a dangerous position, for his royal blood was something Henry had never liked; he also possessed great wealth, which Henry liked very much. He was one of the richest peers in England.

It was therefore a simple matter for the Cardinal to murmur a few well-chosen words into the royal ear. The King could be reminded that were Buckingham executed on a capital charge, his wealth would become the property of the King; moreover, Buckingham had boasted of his royal blood, and it was not difficult to find someone who had heard the haughty Duke's statement that if the King died without heirs he, Buckingham, would be very near the throne.

The Duke was summoned by the King, and came to Court thinking that he was to be asked to take part in some jousting or jollity. He found himself in the Tower, tried by his peers – none of whom dared find him anything but guilty, since this was the will of the King. Old Norfolk, his friend, must find him guilty, though he shed tears as he did so.

The murder of the Duke shocked England and the Continent as well as Thomas More. It showed what manner of King was this fair-faced boy on whom the marks of lechery and good living had not yet appeared. The handsome boy was exposed as a cruel boy; bluff King Hal had set out on his career of royal murder, to which the deaths of Empson and Dudley were but a prelude.

Thomas now longed more than ever for the solitude of his home, for converse with his friends. Erasmus had written to him: 'So you have deserted the scholars for the sake of the Court. Our learned philosopher has become a courtier.'

'Yes,' muttered Thomas; 'but most reluctantly.'

There had been a time when it had been said among scholars that the three most learned men in the world were Erasmus of the Netherlands, More of England and Budé of France; but now More's name was no longer mentioned in this connection. A young Spaniard, Vives, had taken his place.

Yet those in the King's Court knew nothing of that lost eminence which had meant so much to Thomas. They saw him about the Court, and they knew him as a man destined for greatness.

'Thomas More is rising in the world,' they said.

He could not tell them that he did not wish to rise in the world, but to continue to shine in his own.

Meanwhile Martin Luther had published his book, which he called *Babylonish Captivity of the Church*. The Pope was up in arms and Europe was divided. The Cardinal had another secret conversation with Thomas More.

'His Grace has been expressing much interest in you of late, Master More.'

'Indeed? And for what reason?'

'There are two people in the world whom he hates, fears and envies, while he most jealously observes them. Doubtless you know to whom I refer?'

'The rulers across the water?'

'You are right. The mighty Emperor Charles, who rules other lands besides his native Spain, is one. And perhaps, more than the King hates Charles, he hates the King of France. They know each other well; they are of an age; they are both seekers after pleasure and sensation. Charles and Francis are servants of the Pope. Charles is the Most Catholic King; and Francis is the Most Christian King. Our King has no title to set beside those two, and that grieves him. He feels that this is a matter on which you, more than any other man, can help him.'

'I?'

The Cardinal laid his hand on Thomas's shoulder. 'You under-estimate yourself. Go now to His Grace. He would have speech with you. Be not too modest. Luck favours you. Go in . . . and win your honours.'

It was with disturbed thoughts that Thomas made his way to the royal apartments.

*　　　*　　　*

When Thomas entered the King's audience chamber it was to find him with those three friends and statesmen, the Duke of Norfolk, the Duke's son the Earl of Surrey and Henry's brother-in-law the Duke of Suffolk.

This, Thomas realized, was honour indeed, to be received in

such company. Here was the King, familiarly talking with his friends, and smiling to receive Thomas More among them; but as he knelt before the King, Thomas was aware of the speculating eyes of the three noblemen.

All were well known to him.

Suffolk was not only the King's brother-in-law, but his greatest friend; a dashing handsome fellow, he had accompanied Henry's sister Mary to France when she had married old Louis, and when, after a few months of life with the vital young Mary, the French King had died, Suffolk had, with great daring, married her before their return to England. But Henry had forgiven that rashness long ago.

The old Duke of Norfolk, Lord Treasurer and Knight of the Garter, was a sturdy old warrior, proud head of one of the noblest families in the country, and was still reaping the rewards of his victory at Flodden Field.

His son, Surrey, slightly older than Thomas, was a gallant soldier, shrewd and high in the favour of the King in spite of the fact that his wife was the daughter of the recently murdered Duke of Buckingham. The King was amused by Surrey at this time, and he liked those who amused him. Surrey – the grim, stern soldier – had become enamoured of his wife's laundress, and there was much ribald comment throughout the Court concerning Surrey and Bess Holland.

'Ha,' cried the King. 'Here comes Master More to join us. We were talking of this madman Luther, Master More. You have seen this new outrage of his, I doubt not?'

'I have, Your Grace.'

'By God, I have a mind to answer him with my own pen. Now, you are a master of words, and it is on this matter that I wished to speak to you.'

'Your Grace honours me.'

'We have read some of your writings and found merit in them. We are giving orders that this evil composition of the German monk's shall be publicly burned in St Paul's Churchyard. We are instructing Bishop Fisher to preach a sermon against him. Master More, this man is an agent of the devil. Now . . . my friends, leave us. I would speak alone with our friend here on literary matters.'

The three noblemen retired, and the King smiled at Thomas.

'Now, my friend, we can get down to work. Since I read this . . . this . . . what shall I call it? . . . this evil document . . . I have felt an anger burning within me. I hear the voice of God urging me to act. This cannot go unanswered, Master More; and it needs one to answer it whose writing will astonish the world. Who better than the King of England?'

'Your Grace has written this book?'

'Not yet . . . not yet. I have made my notes . . . notes of what I wish to say. They shall go ringing round Europe. If I had the fellow here in my kingdom he should suffer the traitor's death. But he is not here. I cannot chastise his body, so I will answer him with words. I will show you what I shall call my *Assertion of the Seven Sacraments*, and you will see that what I intend to do is to answer this monstrous piece of writing of this villainous monk. Now, come hither. This is what I have prepared.'

Thomas took the notes which were handed to him. 'And my duty, Your Grace?'

Henry waved a hand 'Well . . . you will arrange them . . . and set them into a form that . . . you know of. You are a man of letters. You will see what has to be done. I am a King. I have my affairs of state to attend to, but I have written the core of the thing. You will . . .' The King waved his hands in an expansive gesture. 'But you know what is your task, Master More. To make this into a book. I have chosen you out of my regard for you.'

'Your Grace is determined to honour me'

'As I am always ready to honour those who please me . . whose learning adds lustre to this realm. Now, Master More, your duties from now on will be undertaken in my small ante-chamber, to which I shall now conduct you. You shall have everything you require, and I should like the task completed with all expediency. Spare not the evil-doer. We will talk to the world . . . even as he has. And we will speak in literary language, Master More; for they tell me you are a master of such language. You are excused all other duties. My friend, do this task well and you will be rewarded. Ah, it pleases you?'

'Your Grace could not have given me a task which delights me so much. To have a pen in my hand once more and on such a composition! It is something which I have wanted for a long time.'

The King's hand came down on his shoulder; it was a heavy blow, but its very heaviness expressed not only approval, but affection. The eyes were shining with pleasure; the cheeks were flushed.

'Come, Master More. This way.'

The King threw open the door of a small room which was richly carpeted and hung with exquisitely-worked tapestry.

When Thomas saw the young woman, she was on the window-seat in an ungainly attitude, her legs tucked under her skirt. Her bodice was low-cut and her dark hair fell about her bare shoulders. What astonished him in that half-second was that she did not rise when the King entered, but threw him a saucy smile.

The King stopped and stared at her. Then she must have become aware of the fact that he was not alone. She jumped to her feet and fell on her knees.

'What do you here, girl?' demanded the King.

'I crave Your Grace's pardon. I . . . but . . . I thought . . . Your Grace desired my presence here.'

'Get up,' said the King.

She rose, and Thomas recognized her as Mary Boleyn, the King's mistress. Her gaze was almost defiant as she looked at Thomas. There was in that look a certainty that the King's displeasure could not last.

'You have our leave to retire,' said the King.

She curtsied and took two or three steps backward to the door. Thomas noticed how the King watched her, his mouth slackening, his eyes a brighter blue.

'Come in, come in, man,' he said almost testily. 'Ah, there is where you may sit. Now, look you, these notes are to be made into a great book. You understand me? A great book! You know how to write books. Well, that is what you must do for me.'

The King's attention was straying, Thomas knew; his thoughts had left the room with that dark-haired girl.

Henry said: 'If there is anything you want, ask for it. Start now. See what you can do with these notes . . . and later . . . when you have something ready, you may bring it to me.'

The King was smiling. His mood had changed; he was already away with the girl who had just left.

'Do your work well, Master More. You will not regret it. I like to reward those who please me. . . .'

The King went out, and Thomas sat down to look at the notes.

He found it difficult to concentrate. He thought of the King and the dark-eyed girl; he thought of Surrey and Bess Holland; he thought of the sharp eyes of Suffolk, the wily ones of old Norfolk, and of Thomas Wolsey, who was cleverer than any of them.

And he longed, as he had never longed before, for the peace of his home.

*   *   *

Adjusting the King's notes was a pleasant task, except that it kept him more than ever away from his family. Many times he had been on the point of slipping home to Bucklersbury when a messenger had come to tell him that the King was asking why he was not in his presence.

Henry liked him. He liked the way in which the work was shaping. He read it and re-read it; and he glowed with pride.

'Ah,' he would cry, 'here's the answer to Master Luther. Read it, Kate.'

The Queen would read, and she also was delighted, for she hated the German monk even more than Henry did.

'Would I had him here . . . that German monk!' the King would cry. 'He should die . . . die for the insults he has heaped upon my mother. For my mother is the Church. Ha, Kate, you will see what we shall do with this trumpeter of prides, calumnies and schisms. He is a member of the Devil. He is a low-liver. Mark my words on that. Only the immoral could lose the faith of their fathers in such a way. We are bound to the See of Rome. We could not honour it too much. Anything we could do would not be too great. I swear it.'

'Your Grace will forgive me,' interjected Thomas, 'but those words you have uttered would, in a court of law, be called maintaining papal jurisdiction in England.'

'What's that? What's that?' cried Henry.

'I was thinking, my lord King, of the Statute of Praemunire.'

'Ha!' laughed the King. 'Here's a lawyer for us, Kate. A writ issued against a King in his own realm, eh? Ha, Thomas More, they are right to call you an honest man. You do well to speak thus before your King. He likes you for it. But I say this: So do I love the Papacy that I would hold nothing back to defend it. Remember, Master More, from that See we receive our Crown Imperial.'

'I must put Your Highness in remembrance of one thing,' said Thomas. 'The Pope, as Your Grace knows, is a Prince, as you are yourself, and is in league with other princes. It could fall out that Your Grace and His Holiness may at some time vary in your opinions. I think therefore that his authority might be more lightly touched upon in the book.'

'But I tell you, Master More, so are we bound to the See of Rome that we could not do too much to honour it.'

'Then it is my bounden duty to remind Your Grace again of the Statute of Praemunire.'

'Have no fear, Master More. Have no fear. We know well how to look to these matters. And continue with us as you always have been. We like your honesty.'

And as the book progressed, so did the friendship between Thomas and the King and Queen. He must sup at the King's table; he must walk with the King on the terraces; and he must linger at the Palace until darkness fell, for the Queen had heard that he knew as much of the spheres that moved in the heavens as any man at Court; and the Queen wished him to instruct her.

'The King himself would like to be there at the instruction,' said Henry. 'For while governing this kingdom here on Earth, he would like to learn something of the kingdom of the skies.'

So in the evenings Thomas would be on the balconies of the Palace, the Queen on his left hand, the King on his right, the courtiers ranged about them while he pointed out the constellations to the watching group.

'How the King favours this man!' said the courtiers. 'He is next to the Cardinal himself in the King's favour.'

They would note the Queen's smile as she pointed out how brilliant Orion was that night, and humbly asked if she was right in assuming that the two brilliant points of light in the western sky were the twins, Castor and Pollux, and was that Procyon down in the west-south-west?

They would hear the loud, booming laughter of the King as he declared that the constellation called Cassiopeia did not to him look in the least like a lady in a chair; they would notice how many times the glittering hand would come down upon the sombrely-clad shoulder of Thomas More.

'The King seems more interested in the Pleiades than in Mary Boleyn!' it was whispered among the ladies who watched such matters, for many of them hoped that one day the royal eyes would be turned from Mary Boleyn towards them.

When the book was finished, and such learned men as Fisher, Stephen Gardiner and Wolsey himself had studied it and declared it to be of sound good sense in perfect literary style, the King was so pleased that he said he would have no more of Master More in attendance; in future it should be *Sir* Thomas More.

* * *

Henry the King was deeply gratified. The book was acclaimed throughout Europe by all those who stood against Martin Luther. It was hailed now as a work of genius. The Pope was delighted with his English champion, but he demurred a little at bestowing the title asked for; he had to consider the wrath and jealousy of Francis and Charles, of whom he lived in perpetual fear. But eventually Henry's bribes and offers of friendship prevailed, and the King of England was known throughout the Catholic world as 'Defender of the Faith.'

But Martin Luther was not the man to ignore the publication

of the book; he poured scorn on it and the King of England at the same time. Henry nominated Sir Thomas More to answer Luther in the name of the King of England.

Thomas had not only his title; he was now made Under-Treasurer of the Exchequer – Norfolk himself was the Treasurer – and so had become an important member of the King's Council. Thus did the man in the hair-shirt become one of those ministers in constant attendance upon the King.

Luther wrote scurrilous attacks on Henry; Thomas replied with equally scurrilous attacks on the German monk. And Margaret, reading those replies which her father was writing in the name of the King, would often feel depressed and uneasy. It seemed to her that she had lost the father she had once known. The gentle, courteous man had become a master of invective. It made Margaret shudder to read: 'Reverend brother, father, tippler, Luther, runagate of the order of St Augustine, misshapen bacchanal of either faculty, unlearned doctor of theology ...' How could her gentle father have written such words? How could he have gone on to say that Luther had called his companions together and desired them to go each his own way and pick up all sorts of abuse and scurrility – one to gambling houses, another to the taverns and barbers' shops, another to the brothels?

What is the Court doing to my father? she asked herself.

When he came home she saw the change in him. There was a fierceness of manner about him. She knew that the hair-shirt, which she still washed for him, was worn more frequently; she knew that he used a piece of wood for his pillow, so that he might not find easy sleep. There was a new emotion in his life which had never been there before; it was hatred for the heretics.

She had to talk to him.

'Father,' she said, 'you have changed.'

'Nay, daughter, I am the same as ever.'

'I do not altogether understand,' she said, 'for you and Erasmus at one time would talk of the wickedness in the monasteries. You planned to set certain matters right in the Church. This Martin Luther ... does he not think as once you and Erasmus did?'

She thought of Erasmus, essentially a scholar. Now that the work he had started had been taken up by another, he wanted none of it; he would retire to his scholar's desk, to the life of reflection, not of action. Margaret felt that that was the life her father should have chosen. But the King had forced him to the forefront of the fight, and it was the King's battle; he was using words which the King would have used. If he had been any other man she would have believed he did so in order to curry favour.

'A change has been wrought in these affairs, Meg,' he said. 'Erasmus and I once sought to set right what was wrong. This monk seeks to destroy the Church and to set up in its place another which is founded on heresy.'

'But those words you have written of him . . . I . . . I could not believe that you had written them.'

'I have written them, Meg. Doubt not that. As I see it, we have to fight a greater evil, in those who would *destroy* the Church, than we had when we fought those who only abused it. Meg, the Church still stands . . . the Holy Catholic Church. To destroy it would bring horror to the world. Evil would break its bounds. At all costs the Church must be upheld. Oh yes, let us have evil driven from the monasteries, let us have a stricter rule for our priests if we must . . . but those who seek to destroy the Church must be themselves destroyed, for if we allow them to destroy the Church, then evil will prevail.'

'But this monk, Father . . . can you really call him a heathen?'

"I can, Meg, and I do.'

'Yet he claims to be a man of God. It is not God whom he reviles; it is the Church of Rome.'

'But the Church of Rome is the Church of our fathers. You know that, Meg.'

She looked at him and thought: For the first time in my life I doubt his wisdom. I have never known this ferocity in him before. I have never before known him show such anger as he does towards these heretics.

'Father,' she said uneasily, 'the King has said that if this heathen – meaning the monk Luther – does not recant, he should be burnt alive. Burnt alive, Father! *You* cannot believe that that should be done! You used to say that we should be kind to others, treat them as we ourselves would be treated.'

'Meg, if your right hand was evil, if it was touched with a poison that would infect the rest of your body, would you not cut it off?'

She was silent, but he insisted on an answer. 'Yes, Father.'

'Well, then. The suffering of the body is as naught to the eternal damnation of the soul. If, by setting the flames at the feet of this monk Luther, we could restore his soul to God, then would it not be well to burn him alive?'

'I do not know.'

'Meg, it is a glorious thing to subdue the flesh, to become indifferent to pain. What happens to these bodies cannot be of importance. And if those who deny God are to suffer eternal damnation, what can a few minutes in the fire mean to them?'

Margaret covered her face with her hands. I have lost a part of him, she thought.

He drew her hands from her face and smiled at her; all the gentleness was back in his eyes.

She saw that he was tired, that he longed to escape from the life at Court, to retire to the quietness and peace of family life.

It was a strange revelation to find that she did not entirely agree with him. Yet how she loved him! Even more, now that she believed she had detected a certain weakness in him, than she had when she had loved him for all his strength.

She almost wished that he had not educated her so thoroughly, that he had not trained her mind to be so logical. She wished that she could have gone on seeing him as perfect.

He was begging her to return to the old relationship. He wanted to laugh and be gay.

'Now you have talked to me, Margaret,' he said. 'You have examined me with many questions, and you look at me quizzically, and you are turning over in your mind what I have said, and you doubt the wisdom of my words. Very well, my Meg. We will talk of this later. Now I have something to say to you. Can you guess what it is?'

'No, Father.'

'Well then, it is about Will.'

'Will Roper?'

'Who else? Do you not like him a little, Meg?'

She blushed, and he smiled to see her blush. 'I like him, Father.'

'He loves you dearly. He has told me so.'

'I would rather he did not burden you with his foolish feelings.'

'Is it foolish to love you? Then, Meg, I must be the most foolish man on Earth.'

''Tis different with us. You are my father, and it is natural that you and I should love.'

''Tis natural that Will should also. He is good. I like him. I like him very much. There is no one I would rather see as your husband, Meg. For although he may not be as rich or handsome as our gay young Allington, although he may not make a lady or a duchess of you one day . . . he is none the worse for that.'

'Do you think I should care to be a lady or a duchess, Father? I am not like your wife, who has been so proud since she has become Lady More.'

He laughed. 'Leave her her pleasures, Meg. They are small ones, and we understand her delight in them, do we not? But to return to Will: you are fond of him, I know.'

'As I am of the others. To me he is no more than . . . any of them.'

'But, Meg, he is personable and clever . . . a pleasant boy. What do you look for in a man?'

'He seems to me to be over-young.'

'He is seven years your senior.'

'Still, he seems young. He lacks seriousness. He is no great scholar. If he had written something like *Utopia* . . . something that showed his ideals and . . . Oh, you have set us a high standard, Father. Your daughter measures all men against *you*, which means that she finds them sadly lacking.'

He laughed those words to scorn, but he could not help showing his pleasure.

Now he was himself again, full of laughter, enjoying every moment. This evening they would be together . . . all of them; they would converse in Latin as they were wont to do; and Alice would chide them, but only mildly. Her title, to her, was a bright bauble. They all smiled to see her face when the servants addressed her as 'My Lady.'

It was good to have him back, to forget his fierceness against heretics, to sing and be gay as in the old days.

* * *

Perhaps there is always something good in what seems to be evil, thought Margaret. She longed for the days when her father had been a humble lawyer and Under-Sheriff of the City; she remembered with a tender pain the walks through the City; but this was not the case with all the members of the family.

Ailie was bright-eyed with happiness as she came into the schoolroom where Margaret sat with her books.

How lovely she is! thought Margaret. And more beautiful now that she is a member of this distinguished family than she was in the days of our humility.

Ailie pulled off the net which held back her golden hair from her face. That beautiful hair now fell about her shoulders and down to her waist.

'Such news, Meg! I am to be married. My Lady Allington! What do you think of that?'

'So Giles is to be your husband?'

'I shall be the first in the family to find one.'

'That does not really surprise us.'

'To tell the truth, Meg, it does not surprise me. Giles says what a good thing it is that Father has written this book with the King and become such an important person at Court. His father could not withhold his consent to a union with the stepdaughter of Sir Thomas More. Oh Meg, is it not a marvellous thing . . . what great happenings are set in motion by such little things? A mere book is written and *I* become Lady Allington!'

Margaret laughed. There was that in Ailie which amused her as it did her father. Perhaps Ailie was selfish because she saw herself as the centre of the world, but it was a charming little world, and Ailie herself was so pretty and pleasant in her ways that it was impossible not to love her.

'Ailie, you will go away from us, for Giles will not live here.'

'He will certainly have his estates to attend to. But, depend upon it, I shall insist on many visits to my darling family.'

'Then I doubt not that there will *be* many visits, for I believe you will have your way as Lady Allington just as you have as Alice Middleton.'

'So do not fret, dearest Meg. We shall be together often. I shall bring you tales of the great world. I shall tell you what the ladies are wearing and what new dances are being danced . . . and all Court matters which Father never notices. Meg, it will be your turn next . . . yours or Mercy's. I wonder who will first find a husband.'

Margaret turned away, but Ailie was looking at her slyly.

'There is Master Clement who comes here so often. Have you noticed how he looks first for Mercy? It would not greatly surprise me if our solemn Mercy told us she was to be Mistress Clement one day.'

'Mercy is too interested in her studies to think of aught else.'

Ailie laughed. 'John Clement *and* her studies both interest Mercy very much. There they sit, heads close together, talking of drugs and disease. Sometimes when I see them I think I shall die of laughter. I do indeed, Meg. I say to Giles: "You talk of my beauty . . . of my charming ways . . . and that is by far the best way of courtship. But there are other ways, I have discovered, for I live in a strange household. Some lovers exchange recipes and talk of the internal organs of the sick instead of the eyelashes of the loved one." '

'Ailie, have done with such frivolous gossip.'

'I will not. For 'tis a strange thing, Meg that, when a girl has found a husband, she is anxious for all her friends to do the same. However solemn, however learned they may be, I want them to be married as I shall be.' Ailie began to dance a stately measure with an imaginary partner, tossing back her hair, smiling coquettishly into the face she saw in her imagination. 'This is the newest Court dance, Meg. Giles taught it to me. Oh, how I long to be at Court, to dance in the great halls while the King's minstrels play in the gallery. I shall have rich gowns, Meg, and jewels. . . . I shall be the happiest girl in the whole world . . . and all because Father has won the King's regard; for Meg, had he not done so, I do not think Giles's father would have readily given his consent to our marriage.'

'You think of nothing but yourself, Ailie. Might not Father rather be at home as he used to be?'

'How could he prefer that! Giles says that the King is as fond of his as he is of Master Wolsey . . . and mayhap more . . . for while the Cardinal makes great efforts to please the King, Father does it without effort; while the Cardinal has to be a worshipper of the King, Father has but to be himself. Nay, we are going up, Meg. Up and up. Father will win more honours yet, and there are many who will be ready – nay, eager – to wed his daughters. But some of these, I vow, look not farther than their own home.'

Ailie was looking at Margaret slyly, and Margaret said: 'Enough of this. Is it not your turn to be housekeeper this week, and have you not your duties to perform?'

'Lady More will not be hard on the future Lady Allington. So rest in peace, dear Meg. I'll swear Will Roper is a pleasant fellow, but now that our fortunes are rising, do not be rash, Meg.'

'I do not understand you.'

'What? Have you then become a fool? You . . . the cleverest of your father's daughters! Listen to me, Margaret: if you do not look to Will Roper, then he looks to you.'

Margaret packed up her books and set them on a shelf; her cheeks were burning.

'You are making a mistake, Ailie,' she said, 'when you think that everyone shares your desires for the married state.'

That made Ailie laugh, and she went on laughing as Margaret, in a most dignified manner, walked out of the room.

* * *

Now she must continually think of Will Roper. When, during mealtimes, she lifted her eyes, she would invariably find Will's upon her. While she studied she would find thoughts of Will coming between her and her work.

It was disturbing.

Then she noticed a change in Will. Often when she looked up she would find him staring into space, and if she caught his eye suddenly, he would start and smile at her; and she would know that his thoughts had been occupied with matters which did not concern her.

He would spend a long time alone and seemed to find great pleasure in his own company.

He has changed his mind, thought Margaret. He does not wish to marry me after all. Can it be that his fancy has turned to someone else?

She was astonished by her feelings. Could it be that, not desiring marriage with Will, she desired him to marry no other? She began to think of what the house would be like if he left it. Her father was away so much; how would it be if Will were not there at all?

Her father . . . and Will! She had come to think of them together. She realized how pleased she had always been when her father spoke well of Will.

One day, when she was alone in the schoolroom, Will came in. He carried a book under his arm. She thought it was a law book until she saw that it was the Greek Testament of Erasmus.

'Oh, Margaret, I am glad to find you alone,' he said. 'I want to talk to you. No, don't be alarmed. . . . It is not about marriage. It is another matter which gives me much concern.'

'Please tell me, if it is on your mind, Will. I have seen that something has bothered you of late.'

'I do not know how you will receive this news, Margaret. I have been reading this Testament, and I have pondered on what I have read. I have also read *Babylonish Captivity of the Church*, and I have come to this conclusion, Meg: there is no truth other than this which comes out of Germany.'

'*Will!*'

'I know. You are alarmed. You will hate me now. Your father has expressed his views strongly . . . and your views, of a surety, are his views on this matter. I had to tell you. I do not believe that Martin Luther is a bad man. I believe he is honest and God-fearing. I believe he seeks a better way of life for the world, and, Margaret, I believe that he, and he alone, has fallen upon the ' truth.'

Margaret stared at him; his eyes were bright and his cheeks flushed; he looked quite unlike the mild law-student whom she had known for the last three years. He looked resolute and noble.

She thought: He knows that this confession of his may mean that he will be banished from the house, and yet he makes it. He knows that it will turn Father from him, and yet he makes it. He knows that Father is one of the brightest stars at the Court, and he knows that heretics are punished in this land. Yet he comes to me and says he will become a Lutheran.

Oh, Will, she thought, you fool . . . you *fool*!

But she was moved by his courage, even though it was inspired by what her loyalty to her father insisted must be his wrong thinking.

She began to repeat her father's arguments, to prevent her thoughts running she knew not whither.

'The man is trying to tear the Church asunder.'

'What of Erasmus? What of your father in the days when they were writing *In Praise of Folly* and *Utopia*?'

She said: 'They exposed certain evils in the Church. They wished these matters to be righted. This man Luther defies the Holy Pope and the whole Church. He would set up a new Church in its place.'

'But, Meg, if that were the true Church . . . is it not a good thing to set it up in place of the false one?'

'You would then deny the faith of your fathers?'

'I want a simpler way of worshipping God. I want to examine the Scriptures more carefully. I do not want to say, "My fathers thought this, therefore must I think it." I have thought much of Martin Luther, Meg. Can *you* deny that he is a great man? Think of him – the son of poor parents, thrown upon the world

at an early age, begging his bread and studying . . . always studying. Meg, he reminds me of your father, for like him he studied
the law, and like him he went into a monastery. And while he
was there, he found much that was evil, and he determined to
fight it with all his might. Margaret, think. These Indulgences
against which he rails – are they good? I ask you: Can people
buy, with money, forgiveness in Heaven? Picture him on that
October day in Wittenberg . . . so boldly marching up to the
church door and there nailing upon it his theses. He knew of
the danger he was in. He knew that the whole Catholic world
was against him. But he cared not, Meg, because he knew that
what he did was right. He is a great man; he is a man of genius;
he is a *good* man whose teaching I would follow.'

Margaret was deeply moved. There was so much truth in what
Will said. She had rarely in her life been so grieved as when
across Europe abuse had been flung by this monk of Germany,
and by her father in the name of the King. What a terrible
thing it was when two good men, because they could not agree
on certain points, must forget courtesy and good manners, and
fling insults at one another!

She said sternly: 'I do not know what Father will do when he
hears of this.'

'Nor I, Meg.'

'He would not wish to harbour a heretic under his roof.'

'That is so. Margaret, I love you. It is for that reason that I
could be silent no longer. I could not continue with you under
false pretences. Nor can I govern my thoughts. I trust you will
understand me. Speak to me, Margaret. Tell me that you will
try to understand how I have fought these thoughts.'

'You . . . you should not fight them. All thoughts should be
examined.'

'Margaret . . . you . . . you will tell your father now, I know.
Then I shall go away from here. That is something I cannot
endure. . . .'

He had turned to her, but she ran from him, out of the
schoolroom.

* * *

How thankful she was that it was daytime and there was no one else in the bedroom. She lay on the bed which she shared with Cecily, and drew the curtains . . . shutting out the house . . . shutting out everything but her thoughts.

Will . . . a heretic! And her father hated heretics! They had inspired him with a fierceness, a hatred of which she had not believed him capable.

This was terrible – nothing more terrible could have happened. Those two were against each other.

She remembered the change in her father, his fierceness against the heretic, his absolute belief in the Church of Rome.

He is wrong to be so certain, she thought. And Will is wrong to be certain that Luther is right. Why must there be this hatred between men? Why cannot they love God simply, without dogmas that must be disputed?

Jesus had told men to love one another. Yet how could they obey that command when they disputed together with such ferocity, and instead of love fostered hatred?

Love must become the ruling passion of the world. If her father was to follow the teaching of Jesus Christ, he must not hate Martin Luther because his views differed from his own; nor must Luther hate her father and the King for similar reasons.

Why could they not say: 'You believe this and I believe that. But let us go our ways in peace. Let us brood on these matters which delight us, and in so doing, if perchance we find the truth, then that is a great and glorious thing which we can show to the world; and let us light it with love, not hatred, so that all may see it.'

She sat up in bed and touched her burning cheeks. She, being Margaret, must see herself as clearly as she saw others. Margaret's brain must examine her heart. She stood between two men – Will Roper and her father – and now she would admit that they were the two whom she loved best in the world. She loved them both so much that she could not bear to be without either of them. A cause for dispute had raised itself between them; it

143

was like an ugly dragon whose nostrils gave out the fire of hatred.

She must turn that hatred into love. She knew suddenly that she was ready to practise deceit if necessary to achieve that end.

Margaret More looked into her mind and discovered that the most important things in the world to her were that her father and Will Roper should continue to be friends, and that she should keep them near her that they might all be happy together. Who was right – the Pope or Martin Luther? She did not know; and she realized with a mighty shock that she believed neither of them was wholly right nor wholly wrong. In any case she wondered whether she would be prepared to take sides if she could believe that one was right and one was wrong.

She wanted to live in harmony with the men she loved.

*　　　*　　　*

Now that she knew herself, she was too honest to feign ignorance.

She rose from the bed and went in search of Will.

He was still in the schoolroom where she had left him. He was standing by the window staring out disconsolately. If he was a man who had found the truth, he looked as if he had lost all else he cared for in doing so.

He turned as she entered. 'Margaret!'

She went to him and smiled up at him. Then he put his arms about her.

'Margaret ... dearest Meg. ... Then you did love me?'

'I know not whether I did or did not,' she said. 'I only know I do.'

'Margaret ... now?'

'Yes, now!' she said emphatically. 'For when our thoughts come, as you say, they must be examined. Will, some time ago you asked me to marry you. I answer you now: I will.'

'But, Margaret ... your father ...?'

'He has said he is pleased.'

He kissed her, and she thought: How strange it is! I am no longer Margaret More, the solemn little scholar. I do not care for the arguments in books. I care nothing but that Will loves me and that I can live the rest of my life with him and with Father.

'You are laughing, Meg. Why, you are different.'

'I am happy,' she said. 'I see that it is because I am in love. Do you not like me thus?' Now she seemed coquettish, even as Ailie.

'Meg, I love you now and for ever. But I feel this cannot really be happening, and that I shall wake up in a moment.'

'It is real . . . real as our life shall be.'

He took her to the window-seat and kept his arm about her.

We shall be here together, she was telling herself. Life is good. It must be so. I will make it so.

'Meg . . . how happy I am! I never thought . . . You seemed remote . . . far too clever for me . . . and now . . . when I had given up hope . . .'

'You should never give up hope, Will. Never . . . never. . . .'

'How you laugh, Meg. I have never heard you laugh like this.'

'It is the laughter of happiness, Will. That is the best sort of laughter. Not to laugh in derision at the misfortunes of others . . . not to laugh with relief because you feel remote from those misfortunes; but to laugh because you are happy . . . happy . . . because you have found that life is good.'

'When did you decide that you would marry me?'

'I think it must have been a long time ago, but I knew it only when you spoke to me just now. I knew then that I loved you.'

'When I told you . . . when I *confessed*?'

'It was seeing you, Will, so sure that you were right. . . .'

'Then you, too, feel as I do.'

'I? I feel nothing but love. Sometimes I think I never have. I loved Father and I wanted to be clever to please him. You see, that was love of Father, not love of learning. Now I know that I love you too. So I have two people to love, and I love you both so much that there seems hardly room for anything else in my life.'

'Margaret! Is this *Margaret*?'

'Yes, it is the same Margaret. She was there all the time, I suppose, but she was hidden by the solemn scholar. She did not know herself. She saw herself as others saw her. Now she has seen herself as she is.'

They talked of marriage and he said: 'What will your father say? Will he consent now?'

She was silent, amazed at herself, amazed that she who had never thought to deceive her father, could think of deceiving him now.

But she had become a woman who thought in terms of love. It only mattered that there should be amity in her house; that she, the woman, should hold her home together; and so make peace and love between those whom she loved more than her own life.

Therefore she was ready to temporize.

She said to herself: There is no need to tell Father. He has much to occupy his mind. He should not be worried with Will's affairs. Moreover, Will may discover that he has not yet found the truth. Who knows, in a short time he may come to the conclusion that there is no truth in the teaching of this man Luther. Then shall we have had our storms for nothing. I can neither lose Will nor Father; therefore the two I love must love each other. Today let us think of love; and let us hope that tomorrow there will be no need to think of anything but love.

So now she said to Will: 'Father is so rarely at home. It is a pity to worry him with your doubts and your leanings. Moreover, men's minds change. Perhaps he will change; or you will change. For the time, let us keep this secret. You and I will discuss these matters when we are alone . . . and only then . . .'

And she smiled at him, wondering whether she would be able to mould his thoughts to her father's way of thinking, or her father's to his.

She thought tenderly: They are obstinate, both of them. They are brave, and they will never accept other than what they believe to be the truth.

But she would wait.

Meanwhile she had discovered love, and for the time being she had determined that nothing should disturb it.

FOUR

Margaret was married in the July of that year. Will continued to live in the house, and none was more happy than Thomas in his daughter's marriage. He saw his new son-in-law as a serious young man – he did not know of his new religious opinions – who would rise in his profession; he would be a devoted husband, an affectionate father; he would not want to go to Court; he would be content to stay in the heart of the family. His beloved daughter was married, but not lost to him.

Ailie too was married, and she left the house to live in state in her husband's country mansions or his London house.

The family star was steadily rising.

Ailie visited the house often. When she was in London she was continually in and out. She had discovered that, much as she wished for gaiety and excitement, the family circle in Bucklersbury meant more to her than she had realized. She confessed to the girls: 'I feel sentimental about home . . . and when I say *home*, I mean this house; for nowhere else can be home to me in quite the same way.'

She was not displeased with marriage. Her Giles adored her; he was ready to satisfy every whim, and there was nothing that pleased Ailie more than having her whims satisfied; nevertheless, sometimes she would talk of the old family gatherings round the fire in winter, and out of doors in summer, of the dreams they discussed, the tales they had invented, the songs they had sung; and there would be a wistfulness in her voice.

She delighted in her fine jewels; she was gratified to display them when she came home, and endeavoured to arouse the envy of the girls; but when she went away it seemed that she was often the one who was a little envious.

She had tales to tell of the grandeur of Giles's father's country estates. She had been to Court and had even spoken to the King.

She would gather the girls about her and talk of the King. 'So gay . . . so eager for the balls and the masques.' And the Queen? Ailie would grimace lightly when she talked of the Queen. 'She is old . . . and so serious. Older than His Grace; and methinks he is considering the fact with some displeasure. Of course, there is his boy, Henry Fitzroy, to prove that he has not been faithful to the Queen, and that he can get himself sons. . . . And now he is deeply enamoured of Mary Boleyn.'

Cecily enjoyed listening to the stories.

She would urge Ailie to continue, while she plied her with eager questions. 'And what is the girl like? Is she very beautiful?'

'I would not say that. But she has something . . . something that men like. She is plump and full of fun and laughter . . . and the King has loved her for a long time . . . a long time, that is, for him.' Then Ailie would stifle her laughter. 'We must not let Margaret hear such talk. Dear Margaret. She likes to think everyone is as pure and noble as she is herself. And the King, my dear, has heaped titles on Mary's father. He is the Steward of Tonbridge, Keeper of the Manor of Penshurst . . . and I don't know what else. And George . . . the brother . . . is not forgotten. George is very attractive. Oh, very handsome! And such poetry he writes! And he has such a way of making the revels successful. The King likes him, as he likes all those who amuse him.'

'As much as he likes Father?' asked Cecily.

'Oh, quite different! With Father he is solemn. Father is a statesman-courtier. George Boleyn is a courtier-statesman.'

'Yet they are both poets.'

'I wish you could see him, Cecily. You would fall in love with him. George, I mean. Oh, assuredly you would.'

And the frivolous creature would go on to describe the balls and banquets, the dresses and jewels, so that it was clear that, although at times she missed her home, Ailie was enjoying life.

And Margaret? She also was happy, but her happiness was tinged with uneasiness. Always she was afraid that discord would flare up between Will and her father. She read with Will; she fortified herself with reasoning which, should the need arise, she could put before her father. She would also be ready with her father's reasoning to set before Will.

And who was right? She, who for Will's and her father's sake had studied both points of view, could not say.

There came a day when Will did not return to the house. She knew that he had set out that afternoon to visit some of his friends. These were mostly merchants in the City, some English, some German traders from the Hanseatic ports. It was Will's custom to visit one of the houses of these merchants where they would agree to congregate, and there to read and discuss the Lutheran doctrines.

Supper was eaten; yet Will had not come home.

To the inquiries of the family, Margaret said: 'He has some business in the City which I knew must keep him.'

But she was frightened; she was always frightened on such occasions, for she knew that since the King had become 'Defender of the Faith', heresy in England was looked upon as a crime.

She went to that bedroom which she now shared with Will, and she sat at the window all through the night. But he did not come home.

* * *

Thomas entered the small private closet that adjoined the splendid Council Chamber of the Cardinal.

Wolsey was looking grave. 'I am concerned about your son-in-law,' he said.

Thomas was astonished. How could the Cardinal be interested in insignificant Will Roper or Giles Allington?

'Your son-in-law Roper,' explained Wolsey. 'He has been caught with some heretics in the house of a London merchant.'

'What! Will Roper . . . with heretics!'

'So it would seem. And bold withal. He declares that he holds the beliefs of these people and that, had he the chance, he would proclaim his beliefs from a pulpit.'

'But . . . I can scarcely believe this. You . . . you are sure?'

Wolsey nodded grimly. 'It is a sad affair. A heretic — the son-in-law of a member of the King's Council! We cannot have that said, Master More.'

'My lord Cardinal, I do not understand. It seems impossible to believe this. Where is he now?'

'Doubtless he will be in your house, whither I sent him. His friends will be punished . . . severely. But as regards your son-in-law . . . .I sent him home and bade him have a care in future.'

'You mean . . . that he is as guilty of heresy as these others?'

Wolsey nodded.

'Then, my lord, should he not be judged with them?'

The Chancellor-Cardinal, that master of nepotism whose illegitimate sons held offices which, at their tender age, they could not possibly administer, smiled tolerantly at his assistant.

'The son-in-law of the Under-Treasurer! Indeed not!'

'So, because he is my son-in-law, he will go unpunished while the others suffer?'

'Oh, come, come, Master More. We will hush up this matter. But, I beg of you, see that nothing of this nature occurs again.'

Thomas was pacing up and down the apartment. Will . . . a heretic! Margaret's husband! And he knew nothing of it. Did Margaret know?

A new emotion had come into his life since his wordy battle with Martin Luther; he had not known that he could feel such fierce hatred as he felt for that monk and the people who followed him. Margaret was as astonished as he was by the depth of his feelings. Why did he feel thus? She was right to remind him that he had said with Erasmus that there were anomalies in the Church which must be stamped out; she had been right to remind him that, in a perfect state, he had visualized freedom of opinion. Why, then, had he changed so suddenly, lost that meekness, that understanding of others who did not share his views? Did he really believe that Martin Luther, the monk who had risked his life, who had given his burning energy to reforming the old religion into a new one, was a rogue?

When he had written *Utopia* he had imagined a state governed by wise men. But when he visualized the future, he was certain that drastic change, such as Luther advocated, could mean nothing but misery and bloodshed, the smashing of an institution which, while it was not ideal, had its roots in righteousness. The man Luther, it seemed, would smash the Catholic Church, and in so doing he would destroy all those who were as equally determined as he was; then would he set in its place another edifice, as yet untried, which would, Thomas did not doubt, grow up with all the frailty which now beset the Catholic Church.

How could such a disaster be prevented? Only by stamping out the heretic, by making sure that the change did not take place. For the sake of the many who would be bound to suffer cruelly in a mighty war of religion, the few upstarts must be made to suffer. They must be punished as a warning to the people. Those who considered following them must be made to fear the consequences.

Death – torture even – of the few, was a small price to pay for the death and torture of many, for the chaos which, as he saw it, must surely come to the world if the movement was tolerated and allowed to grow.

Thomas had believed when he wrote *Utopia* that in an ideal state freedom of religious thought was essential; but before such freedom could be given, there must be the ideal state.

He himself suffered physical torture daily. His body was tormented perpetually by his hair-shirt, and at this time he had taken to whipping it with knotted cords; in the small chamber which he occupied as his sleeping apartment, he lay with a piece of wood for a pillow. The afflictions of the body, he believed, were as nothing to the triumph of the spirit. If he believed that heretics must be punished, he must punish himself. He believed that those who declared they gave their lives to a spiritual cause would care no more than he did for the torments of the body.

These ideas, he felt, came to him as a divine inspiration. He must do all in his power to preserve the Holy Catholic Faith which had its roots in Rome; for this reason he had exercised all his talents in his writing against Luther. He saw himself as one of those who must lead the fight. He was no Erasmus, who, having thrown the stone that shattered the glass of orthodox thought, must run and hide himself lest he should be hurt by the splinters.

And now . . . one of those whom he must fight was his own son-in-law; moreover, he was the husband of her whom he loved more than anyone on Earth.

Wolsey watched the man with some amusement. They were growing farther and farther apart – he and the Under-Treasurer. More disapproved of the Cardinal's policy, and did not hesitate to say so. A brave man, this, thought Wolsey, but a misguided one; he is a man whose talents would take him far, but whose emotions will hold him back and doubtless ruin him, for in the political arena there is no time for a man to serve anything but his ambition. And of Wolsey, Thomas often thought: A clever man, a shrewd and wise and greatly talented man, but a man who puts his own glory before honour, who will serve his ambition rather than his God.

And now, mused the Cardinal, he is turning over in his mind whether or not this man Roper should be spared the consequences of his action merely because he has a father-in-law in a high place. To what depth of folly will this man's idealism carry him?

Wolsey shrugged his shoulders. He had done what he considered his duty towards a friend and fellow councillor by covering up the misdemeanours of a near relative. Now he washed his hands of the matter. His mind was occupied with affairs of greater moment that were pending in Europe. Pope Leo was sick. How long could he last? And when the new Pope was sought among the Cardinals, who would that man be?

What a splendid climb it would be from Ipswich to Rome, from a humble tutor to a mighty Pope. A Pope was a Prince even as was a king, and the Pope stood equal to Charles of Spain, Francis of France and Henry of England.

Why should his new Holiness not be Cardinal Wolsey?

And since his mind was occupied with such great matters, how could he give more than the lightest attention to the consideration of the King's philandering or to this matter of the foolish son-in-law of Sir Thomas More?

*　　*　　*

Thomas shut himself into that small private room in which he tortured his body. He leaned against the locked door.

What could he do? Love and Duty stood before him. Which was he to obey? His duty, he knew, was to refuse the intervention of the Cardinal, to send Roper from his house, to say: 'This man is a heretic. He is one of those who would undermine the Church and bring bloodshed to the land.'

But Love involved his daughter Margaret, and only now did he know fully what she meant to him. She loved Roper, and he could not think of this matter without imagining Margaret tormented and tortured, turning from him to her husband or from her husband to him. But if he were strong enough to torture himself, he could not bear to hurt Margaret.

Yet it was wrong, was it not, that some guilty ones suffered whilst others went free?

But . . . his own son-in-law . . . and Margaret's husband!

He must speak to Margaret first.

He called one of the servants and asked that Margaret should be told that he wished to speak with her. She would know, of course, what was wrong, because Will had been detained for a day and night, and he would have told her why he had been allowed to come home. Therefore she would know that the news of his arrest must have reached Thomas's ears.

Moreover, when Thomas had arrived at the house, Margaret had not been at hand to greet him; doubtless she was in the bedroom which she shared with Will, talking to him. Was she trying to make him accept her father's views? Or was she . . . but this he shuddered to contemplate . . . was she too a heretic?

At length she came and stood before him; her face was pale and there were dark shadows under her eyes; and as she stood there with the marks of anxiety and suffering on her face, he knew that his love for his daughter was so strong that it would turn him from his duty.

'Well, Margaret,' he said, 'so your husband is a heretic.'

'Yes, Father.'

'You knew of this?'

'I did.'

He ought to ask her that further question: And you, Margaret? But he could not ask it; he was afraid of the answer.

'Why did you not tell me? You and I have always shared everything, have we not?' Almost immediately he was contrite. 'But he is your husband. . . . A husband's place is before a father's. . . . You were right in what you did. Of course you were right.'

He saw the tears in her eyes now. She came to him and put her arms about him. He rested his cheek against her hair.

'Oh, Margaret . . . my dearest daughter.'

'Father,' she said, 'how can anyone mean more to me than you do?'

'Hush, my daughter. You must not say that.' All his resolutions were crumbling. He saw himself as weak as other men. He understood the Cardinal's gross action in bestowing favours on his beloved sons. How could he, who so loved his daughter, blame the Cardinal for loving his sons?

'We must be truthful, Father. We always have been. I knew before I married Will that he was leaning towards the new faith. I must tell you everything that is in my mind. I knew your mind and I knew his . . . and, strangely, because they were different and because I feared a quarrel between you, it was then that I knew I loved him even as I love you, and that what I cared for more than anything in the world was to guard the peace between you. So I married Will, and I have known that he was meeting these merchants . . . and I knew what books he has been reading . . . and I know how his thoughts run.'

'He has made his thoughts . . . your thoughts?'

'Father, you have always said that I was your clever daughter. You have said that my mind equals that of any man you know.'

'I believe that to be true, Meg.'

'Yet in this matter my mind is so clouded that I fear you are mistaken in me. When I listen to Will I see there is reason in what he says; and I think that is perhaps because I love him. Then I know *your* mind, and I see reason in your beliefs; perhaps that is because I love you. Father, I do not believe it is important whether men follow Luther or the Pope . . . as long

as they obey Christ's commandments. I have tabled the differences and pondered them. Are they real differences? Neither
creed excludes Love; and Love is surely the whole meaning of
good in life, is it not? Father, I know your thoughts. You think
that these differences of opinion will eventually bring bloodshed,
and you are doubtless right. In fact, is it not already happening
in some degree? It would be a terrible tragedy. So in all you do
and in all you say there is reason, there is love of your fellow
men. Will believes that these questions raised by Martin Luther
must be examined; and if Luther is right, his way must be followed . . . no matter what the cost. In a way *he* is right. You
see, I am swayed . . . this way and that. And I know that the
most important thing in the world is that men should live in
amity together and love, not hate each other. I know that the
two I love best must assuredly do that, and that I will do all in
my power – for this seems the most important thing in the world
to me – to make them.'

'That is women's reasoning, Meg,' he said.

'I know it. You have said that there should be no differences
between the education of men and women. Might it not be that
a woman's reasoning on certain matters could be more clear,
more precise, more true than that of a man?'

'That could be so, Meg.'

'Oh, Father, you must try to understand Will.'

'Margaret, we must try to turn him from his folly. But for the
fact that I have a high place at the Court, he would not be with
us now.'

'I know. He would be in some prison awaiting his sentence.'

'He has broken the laws of the country as well – as I see it –
as the law of God.'

'Will thinks that if he keeps the law of God as he understands
it, it matters not if he breaks the law of the country.'

'We should refuse to accept this concession, Margaret. If he
has stated such views, he should be ready to defend them.'

'He is ready, Father. He is not lacking in courage.'

'That is true. It is I who am the coward.'

'You?'

'Because, Meg, I love you so much that I could not bear to refuse to accept this favour. There are some things I have not learned to bear. Once I wished to be a monk, yet I could not resist my dreams of a family life. Now I wish to be an honest statesman, and I cannot be that if it will bring suffering to my beloved daughter.'

She smiled. 'Oh, Father, do not be a saint. Do not torture your body with whips and this hair-shirt. You are yourself. You are our beloved father. We do not want a saint. And if your love makes you weak . . . then that is yourself . . . far more lovable than any saint. Father, if you could only be less determined to do what you think is right! If only you could be more like other men! You have written your replies to Luther for the King. Any statesman might have done it, were he blessed with your gift for writing. Cannot it be left at that? What have heresies and religious opinions to do with our happy home?'

'They are part of the world about us, Meg. They are here with us, like the sun and the light. You may shut your doors, but the light will find some way of penetrating. Will you help me to recall your husband from his heresy?'

'As to that I cannot say,' she answered. 'There is one thing I wish to do, and that is to foster love between you, to bring you back to that state which you once enjoyed. I cannot help it, Father. Perhaps it is because I am a woman. But I want you and Will to love each other. I want us all to be happy. I know that is right for us.'

He embraced her tenderly. He said: 'I shall talk with your husband, and I shall pray for him. I trust ere long I shall call him home.'

'Father, I too shall pray for him and for you. I shall pray that all may be well between you, and that he who is right shall call the other home, so that you may be together – the two whom I love – in friendship, amity and devotion.'

And when Margaret left him, Thomas fell on his knees and prayed for the soul of William Roper, and that his daughter's wishes should be granted.

*   *   *

Following that, there were disputes and arguments between Thomas and Will. In these Will waxed hot, and Thomas was always calm; which meant that Will must come out the worse from the dispute.

With his wide knowledge of the world and men, with his skill with words, Thomas's arguments must seem the more sound. Thomas was a practised lawyer; Will was a very young and inexperienced one. Will became, quite naturally, a little less sure of his ideas.

Margaret was glad of this, for she saw that the obstinacy of her father was slightly greater than that of her husband; and she continued to wish above all things for peace between these two.

Will no longer consorted with the merchants, no longer attended illegal meetings. He felt he owed it to his father-in-law to abstain; for if Thomas suffered because he had accepted a concession which it was against his conscience to accept, Will suffered equally. He would not put his father-in-law in a false position again. For that reason he would no longer run risks; no longer did he speak openly of his beliefs; he studied in the privacy of his apartment, and he talked no more of his ideas except with Margaret and her father.

Margaret had one great matter with which to occupy her mind during that year. She was to have a child.

Now, more than ever, Thomas regretted that he could not spend much time at home. But events were moving fast. Wolsey had been deeply disappointed when, on the death of Leo, Adrian, Cardinal of Tortosa, became Pope instead of Wolsey, Cardinal of York. But Adrian was a sick man, with little hope of occupying for long the Papal chair, and Wolsey's eyes were still on Rome; his ambition had grown to such an extent that it seemed to blind him to all else.

Margaret's emotions were divided between her joy in the unborn baby and her anxieties for her father who was becoming even more important at the Court. She could never forget that day when she had learned that he had aroused the displeasure of Henry the Seventh; she remembered also the law-suit when there had been a dispute over the possession of the Pope's ship.

That had been the beginning of advancement; but whither did advancement lead? So many men had found the axe waiting for them when they reached the top of the ladder which led to fame.

Now Thomas had been elected Speaker of the Parliament.

England was at war that year with France and Scotland, and Thomas had succeeded in delaying the collection of those taxes which Wolsey had imposed for the purpose of carrying on the war. Thomas was against war; he had always been against it. If he talked continually thus, what would become of him?

The Cardinal was now openly hostile towards Thomas. He was suffering acute disappointment over the election of the Pope. It seemed incredible to him that a man could be as foolish as Thomas More, so blind to his own chances of advancement.

As he left Parliament Wolsey forgot his usual calm so much as to mutter, so that several heard him: 'Would to God, Master More, that you had been in Rome before I made you Speaker of this Parliament.'

Wolsey went straight to the King, and a few days later Thomas was told that he was to be sent on an embassy to Spain.

*　　*　　*

How could he leave London when Margaret was soon to have a child? He was beset by fears. How many women died in childbirth? It was the birth of Jack which had led to Jane's death. He *must* be beside Margaret when her child was born.

She had said: 'Father, I hope you will be near me. Do you remember when I was a very little girl and the pain was better when you sat by my bed, holding my hand?'

He had answered: 'Meg, thus shall it be now. I shall be with you.'

But Spain! The strain of working for the King was beginning to undermine his health; he was often painfully fatigued. He did not believe he could keep in good health if he undertook the long journey in a trying climate. He thought of the many weary months away from his family. Was it too late even now to break away from the life of the Court which he did not want?

Greatly daring, and saying nothing to his family, he craved

audience with the King. It was immediately granted, for Henry liked him for himself, and there were times when he wished to desert his frivolous companions and be with this serious-minded man. It gave him pleasure to see himself as a serious King who, while often gay could also appreciate the company of a scholar.

Thomas had asked for a private interview, so the King sent all his courtiers from him, and when they were alone he turned to his protégé with a pleasant smile.

'Well, Thomas, what is this matter of which you would speak?'

''Tis the embassy to Spain, Your Grace.'

'Ah, yes. You will be leaving us soon. We shall miss you. But Wolsey thinks you are the best man we could send.'

'I fear the Cardinal is mistaken, Your Grace.'

'Wolsey . . . mistaken! Never! Wolsey knows your talents, my friend, as well as I do.'

'Your Highness, I feel myself unfit for the task. The climate does not agree with my health, and if I am ill I cannot do justice to Your Grace's mission. I feel that if you send me thither you may send me to my grave. If Your Grace decides that I must go, then you may rest assured that I shall follow your instructions to the very best of my ability. But I fear the journey, Sire; I greatly fear the journey.'

The King looked gravely at the man before him. He had grown thin, Henry saw. That was too much poring over books. Not enough good food. From what the King had heard, the fellow did not pay enough attention to what he ate; he did not drink wine. Poor Thomas More! He did not know how to live. And he was married to a woman older than himself. The King frowned at the thought, for it reminded him that he was in a similar position; and it was a position which he was beginning to find irksome.

Poor Thomas! thought Henry. He has his misfortunes . . . even as I. And he lacks my good health.

'There is another matter, Sire,' went on Thomas. 'My daughter, recently married, is expecting her first child; and I should die of anxiety if I were not at hand.'

The King slapped his knee. 'Ah, so that's it, eh? That's it, friend Thomas.' Henry's eyes filled with tears. 'I like well such fatherly devotion. So should we feel for our daughter, the Princess Mary, were she in similar plight. But you have a big family in Bucklersbury, eh, Thomas? You have a fine son, I hear.'

'Yes, Your Highness. Three daughters, a son, a foster-daughter and a stepdaughter.'

'I like to hear that, Thomas. Would it surprise you if your King told you that – in some respects – he envies you?'

'Your Highness is gracious indeed. And I know that in some ways I have been a lucky man.'

'Lucky indeed! A fine son, eh? Would to God I could say the same. And this child of yours . . . this daughter . . . Let us hope she will be brought to bed of a fine boy.' The King brought his face closer to that of Thomas. 'And we consider it meet that her father should be in London . . . be here when his grandson comes into the world. Rest happy, my friend. We shall find another to send on that embassy to Spain.'

That was the extent of Thomas's favour with the King.

Yet, delighted as she was to hear the news, Margaret was uneasy.

The King's favour was pleasant while it lasted, but now it seemed to her that her father had won it at the cost of the Cardinal's friendship.

*   *   *

Margaret had quickly recovered from her confinement, and it was a very happy family that lived in Bucklersbury during those months.

Thomas was delighted with his grandson.

'But,' he said, 'now that my secretary, John Harris, is living with us and I have a grandson, this house is not big enough; and in the years to come when I have many grandsons and granddaughters – for the other girls will marry one day and I trust that they, like Margaret, will not leave their father's roof – I must have a bigger house.'

So he bought Crosby Place in the City – a beautiful house, the tallest in London, built of stone and timber and situated close to Bishopsgate.

One day he took Margaret along to see it.

They went through the great rooms of this house which was so much grander than the one they were now occupying. Margaret stood with her father in the great hall, looked up at the vaulted roof and tried to imagine the family in it.

'You like it not?' said Thomas.

'Well, Father, you have bought it, and doubtless we shall make it ours when we settle in, but . . .'

'But?' he insisted.

'I know not. Perhaps I am foolish. But it is not like our house.'

'Propria domus omnium optima!'

'But we should make this our house, Father. Yet . . . I cannot see it as ours. There is an air of gloom about it.'

'You are fanciful, daughter.'

'Indeed I am. Why, when we have the family here and we sit talking and singing together . . . then it will be our home . . . and quite a different place from the one it is now.'

'Richard Crookback lived here for a time,' said Thomas. 'I wonder if that is why you feel this repulsion. I wonder if you think of him and all the miseries that must have been his. Is that it, Meg?'

'It might be.'

She sat on a window-seat and looked thoughtfully at her father.

'Come, Margaret, what is your mind?'

'That we shall make this place our home.'

'Come, be frank with me.'

'It is just a foolish thought of mine. We have often talked of the house we would have . . . when you have not been with us.'

'And it has not been like this?'

'How could you expect it to be? Where should we find all that we have planned? Moreover, if there could be such a house we should have to pull it down once a week and rebuild it, because we have added to it and altered it so persistently that it could not stay the same for more than a week. There is Mercy with her hospital; and there is the library that I have built for you; there is the chapel which Mother thinks should be attached to all great houses. . . . And Jack, of course, has set all this in the midst of green fields.'

He was silent for a few seconds. Then he turned to her. 'Why, Meg,' he said, 'did I not think of this before? We will build our own house. And all of us shall have a hand in it. We shall build what we would have. There *shall* be Mercy's hospital, your mother's chapel, your library for me and Jack's green fields. . . .'

'But, Father, you have bought this place.'

'We can sell the lease.'

'Father, it sounds wonderful, but could it really be done?'

'Why not? I am high in the King's favour, am I not? I have money which I have not spent. That is the answer, Meg. We will not live in this gloomy house which is full of unhappy ghosts. We will seek our own land and we will build our own house . . . our ideal house.'

'As you would build an ideal state,' she reminded him.

'A house is easier to build than a state, Meg, and I doubt not that, with the help of my family, I can do it.' He was as excited as a boy. 'There I shall pass my days with my children and my grandchildren about me. My father will have to be with us soon. He and his wife are getting too old to be alone. Elizabeth, Cecily and Mercy must marry and fill our new house with children. It must be outside the City . . . but not too far out. We shall have to be within reach of London, for I am still bound to the Court. And Meg . . . Meg, whenever I can, I shall slip away. I shall come home. Let us go. Let us decide where we shall live. I can scarcely wait to discuss this with the others. Meg, we will call a conference this night; and the land shall be bought without delay and the ideal house shall be built . . . and we shall live in it happily for many years.'

They walked home, talking of the house.

Thomas was as good as his word. In a short time he had sold

his lease of Crosby Place to a rich Italian merchant friend who was looking for a house in London.

Antonio Bonvisi, the merchant from Lucca, settled in at Crosby Place and Thomas bought land in Chelsea.

* * *

Building their ideal house occupied the minds of the family so much that they gave little thought to what was happening about them.

The Cardinal had again been disappointed of his hopes of the Papacy. On the death of Adrian, Giulio de' Medici, called Clement the Seventh, was elected. The Emperor Charles came to London and was made a Knight of the Garter. This meant that Thomas was taken from his family to be in constant attendance at the Court, but it was regarded as an annoyance rather than a fact of political importance.

It seemed more interesting that that great friend of the family, Dr Linacre, who was now the King's physician, brought the damask rose to England. It should be awarded a special place of honour in the Chelsea gardens. There was again war with France; but that seemed remote, for meanwhile the house at Chelsea was being built.

It stood back from the river, with about a hundred yards of garden between it and the water. There were four bay windows and eight casements, allowing a superb view of the river. The centre block was occupied largely by the great hall, and there were numerous rooms in the east and west wings.

'Mercy,' Thomas had said, 'once you said your dearest wish was to own a hospital of your own in which you could tend the sick. Now that we are building at Chelsea, that hospital shall be yours.'

And so it was built, separated from the house by pales; for Mercy had said: 'What if I should have contagious diseases in my hospital? I could not have my patients passing them on to my family.'

They had never seen Mercy quite so happy as she was when she showed Dr Clement over the hospital. It seemed that when she had the young doctor there, Mercy had all she desired in life – John Clement, her family, and her hospital on the other side of the pales.

There was Thomas's library and the chapel in a separate building – just as they had pictured it.

Elizabeth and Cecily planned the gardens; and Jack decided where they would grow their wheat, keep their cows and have their dairy. Alice designed her buttery and her kitchens; Thomas planned his library, gallery and chapel, with Margaret to help him.

It was to be a house in which one family, who had discovered the means of being happy, would live together, cherishing each other.

Will and his father-in-law were now the best of friends, although Will was not altogether weaned from the new ideas. Thomas prayed for him; Will prayed for Thomas; Will was wavering, for it seemed to him that a man such as his father-in-law, who seemed so right in all other matters, could not be entirely wrong on what seemed to Will the greatest matter of all.

By the end of the year they had moved into the house.

They were a bigger family now, for Thomas's father, the judge, Sir John More, and his wife came to live with them.

In spite of his cynical views on marriage, Sir John had taken a fourth wife and lived amicably with her. He had ceased to fret about his son, and he would often laugh when he remembered how he had worried in the old days because Thomas had paid more attention to Greek and Latin than to law. He admitted that he had been wrong. He had seen Thomas as an ordinary man; and, like the rest of the household, he now knew that to be an error.

He was content in his old age to rest in this great house at Chelsea, to wander in the gardens watching the gardeners at work, now and then discussing a point of law with Thomas, who never failed to give him that deference which he had given him as a young and obscure student. Occasionally he worked in the courts at Westminster; he was treated with greater respect as the father of Sir Thomas More than he was as a judge of these courts.

It was a very happy family that lived in the house at Chelsea.

* * *

Soon after they were established there, Sir John Heron, the Treasurer of the King's Chamber, approached Sir Thomas concerning his son Giles. Sir John admired Sir Thomas More and, having heard of the large house which had been built in the village of Chelsea, he would esteem it a favour if his son might live there with the Mores, after the fashion of the day.

Alice was a-twitter with glee when she heard this.

'The Herons!' she cried. 'Why, they are a most wealthy family. I shall look after that young man as though he were my own son.'

'And doubtless will endeavour to turn him into that,' said Thomas wryly.

'I have told you, Master More, that I shall cherish the young man. . . . He shall be my son in very truth.'

'Nay, by very law, Alice . . . the law of marriage. I'll warrant that before you have seen him you have decided that he will make a suitable husband for one of the girls.'

'They are becoming marriageable. Have you not noticed that?'

'I have indeed.'

'Well, then, it is time we had more such as Master Giles Heron in our household, for one day he will inherit his father's goodly estates.'

'And that is a good thing, for I doubt young Giles will ever win much for himself.'

'Tilly valley! Is it a clever thing, then, to be turned against a young man merely because one day he will inherit his father's fortune?' demanded Alice.

'It is wise, you would no doubt tell me, to be turned towards him because he will inherit one.'

'Now, Master More, will you endeavour to arrange a marriage between this young man and one of your daughters?'

'I would rather let one of my daughters and the young man arrange it themselves.'

Alice clicked her tongue and talked of some people's folly being past all understanding. But she was pleased with life. She enjoyed living in the big house at Chelsea; she had more maids than she had ever had in her life. Her daughter had married well; she would do her duty by her stepdaughters and see that they followed in Ailie's footsteps; and she would never forget for one moment that she was Lady More.

She went down to the kitchen, her marmoset following her. She went everywhere with her. She scolded the little thing, but it was an affectionate scolding, the sort of scolding she was fond of bestowing on her husband.

Good marriages for them all, she reflected. Either Elizabeth or Cecily should have Giles Heron, who ere long would inherit his father's title and lands. Elizabeth it must be; she was more suitable for the position. Cecily was inclined to be slothful, to lie about in the sunshine, under the trees or in the orchard, or wander about gathering wild flowers, spending too much time with her pet animals. Yes, Elizabeth, with her sharp wits, would make the better Lady Heron. Moreover, Elizabeth was the elder and should therefore marry first, for it was a bad thing when a younger sister married before an elder. Not, thought Alice complacently, that there should be any difficulty in finding a good husband for Cecily, a girl whose father was in such high favour at Court.

Fortune had taken a very pleasant turn.

'Lady More!' She whispered that to herself as she went about the house.

*　　　*　　　*

Giles Heron protested when his father told him that he would live for some time in the household of Sir Thomas More.

As Giles took barge for Chelsea, he was thinking of his father's remarks:

'There are two daughters. A match between our house and theirs would bring great benefits, my son. Sir Thomas More is in as high favour at Court as any man – not excluding the

Cardinal himself, some say. You will one day have land and property. I would like to see added to that the favour of the King's favourite minister.'

That was all very well, but Giles was not interested in ambition. This river trip would have been most enjoyable to him if he could have idly drifted downstream, stopping perhaps to lie on the bank, breaking into song, chatting with merry companions; and then, when he was tired, turning the barge homewards. Instead of that, he was on his way to a new home; and he was uneasy.

Who wanted favour at Court? Not he. What did it mean? Constant work, constant fear that you would displease some high official of the Court – mayhap the King himself. Then you began to realize how much happier you had been lying in the sun, idling the hours away.

Then there was this daughter of Sir Thomas More. It was said that his daughters were almost as learned as he was. The girls were prim creatures who spent their days in a schoolroom writing Latin verses. Latin verses! Scholars! Giles wanted to laugh hysterically at the thought. He frantically sought in his mind for one little phrase which his tutors had taught him and which he might manage to quote; but his mind was a blank.

He had seen Alice Allington, a real little beauty, and not seeming very learned except in matters of manners and general fascination. But she was only a stepdaughter – no blood relation to the learned Sir Thomas More. He doubted if he would find another such as Alice Allington in the Chelsea house.

And one of these girls – there was, fortunately, a choice between two – he must try to make his wife. For, his father had said, if you do not, depend upon it others will. These girls have more than fortune. You yourself have wealth, but the More family can give you what you lack: the interest of the King himself. Marry one of these girls and the King, I am sure, could be induced to smile on you. Thomas More is reputed to be an upright man, a man who seeks no gain for himself; but I'll warrant he'll not be averse to taking a little for his daughters, since by all accounts he has a very deep regard for them.

Giles pictured the girls. They would be small, for sitting at a table, poring over books, did not develop the body; they would be pale; they would doubtless stoop; they would be ugly; they would give no attention to personal adornments; they would have Latin instead of good looks; they would have Greek instead of charm.

'O God in Heaven,' prayed Giles Heron, 'save me from a daughter of Sir Thomas More.'

He had reached the privy stairs, and, leaving his servants to tie up the boat and take his baggage into the house, he mounted the stairs and went through the wicket gate.

He stood looking over the pleasantly sloping lawns, at the gardens of flowers, at the young trees and the house itself.

Slowly he made his way towards that great building. Which of the rooms, he wondered, was the schoolroom? He had heard of that schoolroom in which the wisest men in Europe taught the son and daughters of Sir Thomas More. He pictured the grey-bearded, solemn-faced tutors; they would be scornful of him. And the girls? They too. Perhaps they would despise him so much that they would beg their father not to let him marry one of them. Giles was hopeful by nature.

How beautiful it was on that summer's day! He could smell the scent of newly-cut grass; and in the distance he could hear the sound of voices. He heard laughter too; that was the last thing he had expected to hear in this domain, but doubtless it came from someone on land nearby, for voices carried far in the country. Mayhap it was some of the servants. Or were the servants as solemn as the family? Did they have to learn Latin and Greek along with their household tasks?

He stopped as a boy appeared from a clump of trees to the right. This boy's gown was open at the neck; his face was hot for he had been running. He stopped short when he saw the visitor. Giles judged him to be about fifteen years of age.

'Good day to you,' said Giles. 'Am I right in thinking these are the gardens of Sir Thomas More?'

'Good day to you,' said the boy. 'And you are right. You must be Giles Heron.'

'I am. Would you please tell me who you are?'

'John More. Always known as Jack. We are worried about the rabbits. They are behaving in such an odd way. They are huddled together and making the strangest noises. I came to look for Father. He would know what to do. Would you . . . come and look at them?'

He turned without more ceremony and began to run. Giles followed him through the trees to a stone wall, on which sat a peacock displaying his gorgeous tail.

The stone wall enclosed a small garden, and in this a girl was kneeling by several rabbit hutches.

'What ails you, Diogenes?' she was saying. 'Tell me, my little one. And you, Pythagoras, you are frightened. What do you see?'

'Any sign of what troubles them?' asked Jack.

'No.'

'This is Giles Heron. I found him coming up from the river.'

'Good day to you,' said the girl. 'Do you know anything about rabbits? We have not had them long. Only since we have been at Chelsea. Can you imagine what could make them as frightened as that?'

Giles looked at her; her face was flushed; her fair hair was escaping from her cap; and her blue eyes showed her anxiety. It was clear that she was thinking more of the rabbits than of the newcomer. He thought her rather quaint, comparing her with the young ladies whom he met at Court.

'It might be a stoat or a weasel,' said Giles. 'It is terror which makes them behave thus.'

'But where? I can't see anything. . . . Can you?'

'A dog, mayhap?' suggested Giles.

'But Socrates and Plato love the rabbits.'

Diogenes, Pythagoras, Socrates and Plato! thought Giles. Was that not what he would have expected? Even their pets must be named in Greek. Yet both the girl and the boy disarmed him.

The girl went on: 'All the pets love each other. Father says that is because they have been brought up together and know they have nothing to fear from one another. He says that there would be no fear in the world if only everybody understood everybody else. So . . . I don't think they are frightened by the dogs.'

Giles looked about the walled garden, and his quick eyes caught a pair of gleaming ones in the foliage a few yards from the hutch.

'There!' he cried. 'Look.'

They followed his gaze. .

'A weasel,' said Giles. 'That explains much.'

'We must drive it off,' said the girl.

Giles caught her arm. 'Nay. It may be dangerous. You stay here. . . .'

Just at that moment a great dog came bounding into the garden, followed by a monkey. There was an immediate movement in the bushes; the dog paused for half a second; and then he was bounding over to the bushes, barking wildly and leaping with great excitement.

The monkey followed. Giles was still holding the girl's arm. He had forgotten Court manners and all ceremony in the excitement of the moment. They were all tense, waiting to see what the animals would do.

It was the monkey who went into the attack. Suddenly she leaped into the bushes. The girl caught her breath; Giles tightened his grip on her arm. They heard a squeaking and a scuffle in the bushes; and the monkey emerged, her bright eyes gleaming, a chatter of gibberish escaping from her little mouth.

'It's gone!' cried Giles in great excitement. 'The monkey has driven it off.'

'Marmot!' cried the girl. 'You brave creature!'

The monkey ran to her and climbed on to her shoulder. The dog leaped about her, barking wildly.

'All you did, Master Plato, was make a noise. You were the herald; but Marmot was the heroine. She is the victor. Do you like her, Master Heron? She is my mother's, and she was given to her by one of our friends from foreign parts. She is very happy here in the summer, but we have to take great care of her in the winter.'

'She is certainly a brave creature,' said Giles. 'But . . . I have not heard your name yet.'

'Have you not? I'm Cecily More.'

'Oh!' cried Giles with a lifting of his spirits. 'You er . . . you are . . . in actual truth?'

She looked surpised. 'I do not understand.'

He smiled. 'I thought that mayhap you would be very small and pale and humped through bending over your desk.'

Cecily laughed at that.

'And,' went on Giles, laughing himself with the immensity of his relief, 'firing questions at me in Latin.'

'Margaret is the clever one of the family. Mercy, too. You may have heard of them. Margaret is quite a scholar, but she is merry too. She takes much delight in writing in Latin and Greek; and with Mercy it is all mathematics and medicine. Elizabeth, who is my elder sister, is clever too. Poor Jack and I . . . we are not so clever. Are we, Jack?'

'I am the dunce of the family,' said Jack. 'I can just manage to write a little Latin and follow their speech.'

'You will feel yourself to be a learned scholar when you compare yourself with me,' said Giles.

'Then welcome!' cried Jack. 'I shall enjoy appearing to be learned for once.'

Cecily said: 'It is pleasant, is it not, Jack, to welcome someone to this house who does not think that a knowledge of Greek is the most important thing in the world?'

'And what, Mistress Cecily, do you think is the most important thing in the world?'

'At the moment, to make sure that the rabbits are safe and that the weasel cannot come back and frighten them.'

'He will not,' said Giles. 'The monkey gave him a great fright. He will remember. Animals have long memories sometimes.'

'Is that so?' said Cecily. 'I am glad of it.'

'You love animals, do you not?' asked Giles.

'Yes. And you?'

'My dogs and horses.'

'I love dogs and horses and the little helpless ones besides . . .

like rabbits and birds. We have fowls and dear little pigs.'

'You have a farm, then?'

'Well, we have some land and animals. We grow much for ourselves. That is what we always wanted when we lived in Bucklersbury. They are cutting the grass in the home-field now. I should be helping. So should Jack. But I saw what was happening here. . . .'

'I should not have thought you would have had time to keep so many animals.'

'But we are a big family. Each has his own. Father says that we may have what pets we like. The only rule is that we must care for them, see that they are fed and looked after in every way. The peacock there is Elizabeth's. He is beautiful, do you not think so? He is rather haughty too, for he'll not take food from anyone but Bess . . . unless he is very hungry. He is asking for you to admire him.'

'He is as vain as a Court gallant.'

'Are Court gallants as vain as that?' asked Cecily.

'Some are much more vain.'

'*You* are one of them, are you not?'

'Ah, but out of my setting. Here, among the learned, I feel humble. But you should see me at Court. There I display my fine feathers and invite admiration.'

'I should like to see you do that,' said Cecily.

'Who knows, you may one day. Yet if I stay here for a little while, as your father and my father have arranged that I shall, doubtless I shall see myself so clearly that I shall know there is nothing to be vain about.'

'I do not believe you are vain,' said Cecily, 'because the very basis of vanity is that those who possess it are unaware that they do so. They think the puffed-up vision *they* see is the true one.'

'I see you are very wise,' said Giles.

'Nonsense. See how Marmot regards you, Master Heron. She likes you.'

'Does she? Her bright eyes look at me suspiciously, I fancy.'

'She is looking at you with interest. If she did not like you she would be making strange noises of irritation.'

'I am glad one member of the family has taken to me.'

'She is not the only one,' said Cecily with disarming frankness. 'Here is another.'

She made a gay little curtsy – not at all what Giles would have expected from such a learned little scholar.

'And here is another,' said Jack. 'Let us go to the hayfields. We should be helping there.'

It was all very different from what Giles had expected. In the hayfield Sir Thomas More himself was sitting against a hedge, drinking some beverage from a jug, and his daughters were about him.

Was this Sir Thomas More, the Under-Treasurer, the friend of the King and the Cardinal?

'Welcome! Welcome!' he cried. 'I am glad you came when we are all at home. The hay must be cut at the right moment, and right glad I am to be at home at such a time. You are thirsty, doubtless. Come, join us. Have you a tankard for Master Heron, Meg? And give him a piece of that cob loaf.'

Giles was introduced to the family. The Mistress of the house made him very welcome; and even Mistress Roper, the eldest daughter, whose fame as a scholar had reached even him, alarmed him not at all.

Cecily and Jack sat beside him and told how the monkey had driven off the weasel.

It was quite pleasant there, lying in the shade of the hedge and taking refreshment, joining in the conversation and laughter.

Afterwards Jack showed him the grounds and stables, the orchards, barns, outhouses and, finally, the dairy.

Supper proved to be a merry meal taken at the long table on the dais in the great hall. The food was simple; and there was a newcomer, whom no one seemed to know, who had called just as the meal was about to be served and was given a place at the table.

Conversation was perhaps a little clever, and there was Latin – classical allusions, which Giles did not understand, but when this was the case, he found he had no need to join in, and that Lady

More was always ready to poke fun at her scholars, and to smile at him as though to say : 'We are the clever ones.'

When the meal was over they sat on the lawn, for the day was still hot; and some of them brought out their lutes and there was singing.

Giles Heron was very happy that night. He felt that, instead of coming to a strange household and perhaps a hostile one, he had come home.

He sat next to Cecily and listened to her sweet singing voice. He had already decided that by falling in love with and marrying Cecily he might please not only his father, but himself.

*   *   *

When Sir John Heron, Treasurer of the King's Chamber, told his friend Sir John Dauncey, Knight of the Body to the King, that his son Giles was to marry one of the daughters of Sir Thomas More, Sir John Dauncey was reflective.

His thoughts turned to his son William, and he lost no time in seeking him out.

It was possible to talk frankly to William, for William was a most ambitious young man, and would not have to be told twice to seize any advantages which came his way.

'I hear Giles Heron is to marry one of More's daughters,' he said to his son. 'Master Heron has been quick. But there is still one daughter left.'

William nodded. He did not need to have the implication of those words explained. There was no need to point out the advantages of a match between himself and one of the daughters of so favoured a man.

'I must call at the house in Chelsea,' he said.

His father smiled his approval. There was no need to say : 'Do not make the reason for your call too obvious. More is a strange man, and his daughters will doubtless be equally strange. The matter must be tackled with some delicacy.'

William would know. He was ambitious enough to approach every advantageous situation with the utmost tact and delicacy.

*   *

The summer was passing. Among the trees in the orchard, Dorothy Colly, Margaret's maid, was playing with Margaret's young son Will. An apple, part of whch had been destroyed by the wasps, fell suddenly to the grass, and the baby began to crawl towards it.

'Come away, my little man, come away,' said Dorothy. 'Don't touch it, darling. Ugh! . . . Nasty!'

The baby crowed and Dorothy picked him up and cuddled him. He was very like his mother, and Dorothy loved his mother, who had treated her more like a friend than a servant, teaching her to read and write, giving her respect and affection.

'You're a lucky boy,' she said. 'We're all lucky here in Chelsea.'

She thought of coming to the house – her life before, her life after.

As soon as she entered the house or the grounds a feeling of peace would steal over her. She knew this was due to the influence of the master, for to be in his presence was to be filled with a determination to live up to his high standards.

At this moment she could hear Lady More at the virginals, practising in her laboured way. Yet even such sounds were harmonious coming from this house, for to hear them was to remember that her ladyship, who had no great love of music, practised the lute and the virginals so that when her husband came home she might show him what progress she had made. Even Lady More had been mellowed by the sweetness of her husband's nature.

It was true that when she stopped playing she would declare that she had done with wasting time for that day; and to reassure herself she would doubtless scold some defaulter in the kitchens; but the next day she would be practising on the lute or the virginals.

Dorothy's heart began to beat faster, for, coming towards her, was Sir Thomas's secretary, John Harris.

John was an earnest young man, fully aware of the importance of his work. He sought to emulate his master in all ways, even adopting that habit of walking with his gown not properly set on the shoulders, and the left shoulder lifted a little higher than the right. Dorothy noticed this, and it made her smile become a little tender.

He was deep in thought and did not immediately see Dorothy. She spoke first: 'Good day to you, Master Harris.'

He smiled, pleasure transforming his face. 'And a very good day to you,' he said, sitting down beside her and smiling at the baby.

'How big he grows!' said John. ·

'His sister is nearly as big as he is. So you are not at the Court today, Master Harris?'

'No. There is work to do at home.'

'Tell me, do they really think so highly of the master at Court?'

'Very highly indeed.'

Dorothy pulled up a handful of grass and frowned at it.

'You are not pleased that it should be so?' he asked.

'I was thinking that I would like to see all the girls as happily married as is Mistress Roper. She was married before the master became so important. Master Roper was here . . . they grew to know each other . . . and they eventually married. I was thinking that that is the best way in which to make a marriage.'

'You are thinking of William Dauncey?'

She nodded. 'Mistress Elizabeth does not seem to understand. Of course, he is very handsome . . . and very charming to her . . . but there is a light in his eyes which, it would seem to me, is put there by his love of the advancement Sir Thomas More can provide, rather than for Sir Thomas's daughter.'

'Dorothy, you are a discerning woman.'

'I love them so much. I have been with them so long. Mistress Elizabeth is very clever with her lessons, but that is not being clever in the ways of the world. I wish that some quiet young gentleman like Master Roper would come here to study, and Mistress Elizabeth gradually get to know him. And I would like to see her take him instead of Master Dauncey.'

'You have served Mistress Roper for a long time, Dorothy. She has educated you and moulded your thoughts, and you think that everything she does is always right. The baby is the perfect baby.

Master Roper is the perfect husband. There are some who would say that Master William Dauncey is not such a bad match. His father has a high post at Court. What more could you want?'

'Love,' she said. 'Disinterested love. Ah, I have said too much.'

'You need have no fear, Dorothy. But let me say this: When Mistress Roper married, her husband was caught fast in heresy. Heresy, Dorothy! Is that then more desirable than ambition?'

She was thoughtful. 'His heresy,' she said, 'grew out of his searching for the right, his determination to do what he considered best. Ambition - such as Dauncey has - is for self-glorification. There lies the difference.'

'Mistress Dorothy, you are wondrous learned.'

'My mistress has taught me to read; she has given me books. She has taught me to form my own opinions - that is all.'

Dorothy picked up the baby and held him against her. 'Sometimes I wish that the master were not so well received at Court,' she said. 'I would rather see him more often at home . . . with good people about him . . . like you, John Harris . . . than with the most handsome gallants of the Court.'

Then Dorothy left him and walked to the house.

How peaceful was this scene! she thought.

Now came the sound of someone playing the lute. It was too well played to be Lady More. Now she heard Cecily's and Elizabeth's voices, singing a ballad.

'Please God keep them happy,' prayed Dorothy. 'Let us go on just like this . . . for ever and ever . . . until we are called to our rest.'

There came the sound of other voices, singing with the girls - Giles Heron's and William Dauncey's.

Dorothy shivered. The voices of the young men reminded her that life was continually changing.

Too many honours were being thrust upon the master, and honours brought envy; they brought the sycophants, the false friends, who were like wasps that fed on the lovely fruit until it was ruined and dropped from the branches.

*　　*　　*

That year came the winter of the great frost.

There was no keeping the house warm; the bleak winds penetrated into every room, and there was ice on the river. Blizzards swept across the country.

Mercy was hardly ever at home; she had so many sick people in the hospital. Margaret and Elizabeth were often there helping her.

Mercy was very happy. The hospital was her life. Although others might deplore Sir Thomas's rise in the world, Mercy could not. But for his making a fortune in the service of the King, he could not have supplied the money which she needed to keep her hospital in being. But she was careful in the extreme. There was nothing extravagant about Mercy; she worked hard and enjoyed working hard. She remembered Erasmus's criticism of English houses, and she had no rushes in her hospital; there were windows that could be opened wide; and her success with her patients was gratifying.

Mercy enjoyed those days when her foster-father came to inspect her work. He would go among the patients, a joke on his lips. 'Laughter is one of the best medicines,' he told her; and she was contented to have him with her whether he praised or questioned what she did.

She would not admit to herself that she was not completely happy; she, who was so frank on all other matters, knew herself to be evasive in this.

She would not admit to herself that she loved Dr Clement. It is merely, she told herself, that there is so much talk of weddings and that makes me wonder if I shall ever be a bride. Ailie and Margaret are married; and now Cecily will have Giles Heron, and Elizabeth her William Dauncey; and because of all this I too look for love.

Had it not always been so? The little foster-sister had always feared that she was not quite a member of the family, in spite of everyone's attempts to assure her that she was. Now from Court came two gallants eager to wed the daughters of Sir Thomas More; but none came to woo his foster-daughter.

Not that Mercy expected it. She laughed at the idea of plain

Mercy Gigs being wooed by such a dashing gentleman as William Dauncey.

Moreover, Mercy did not want a Court gallant; she wanted Dr Clement.

And he? Why should he think of Mercy Gigs? But he did think of her – oh, as a friend, as a girl who was interested in medicine, as one who spent her time working in her hospital and who liked to ask his advice on certain matters.

She must not be deluded. She was a nobody. She was an orphan on whom the Mores had taken pity; however much they tried to make her forget that, she must not. And John Clement? A young man of good family, high in the service of the great Cardinal, looked on with favour by the King's physician, Dr Linacre. As if he would think of Mercy Gigs as anything but a friend.

Ah yes, she reminded herself, all this talk of marriages makes me want what the others have. I want to be loved by a husband even as, when I was a child, I wished to be loved by their father.

Cecily and Elizabeth had come over to the hospital on this day, although it was as much as they could do to plod through the snow even that far.

They seemed quite pretty – both of them – with a certain glow upon them. That was being in love. Cecily was the happier perhaps; she was more sure of her Giles. But Elizabeth – more reserved than her younger sister – was she a little anxious about William Dauncey? Did she know – as others did – that he was an ambitious young man who believed her father could advance him? Poor Elizabeth! Like Mercy, she wished for marriage. Was she loving the ideal of marriage more than the man who would make it possible? Mercy uttered a silent prayer for Elizabeth. Cecily would be happy with her Giles. He was a lazy boy, good-natured, frank, not hiding the fact that his father had wished him to marry a Mistress More, and that he was delighted to find such a marriage to his liking. He had not William Dauncey's tight-lipped ambition. And was she right, Mercy wondered, when she thought that even Dauncey had changed since he had visited the house? Was his laughter, when he joined their family group and played their games and sang with them, was it a little less forced than it had been?

The two girls laughed as they shook the snow out of their clothes.

'Why, Mercy, what a day! If the blizzard starts again, we shall be snowed up and unable to get out at all . . . and no one will be able to get to us.' That was Elizabeth.

Cecily said: 'And you must come over to dinner today. Someone is coming, and he'll be disappointed if you're not there.'

Mercy flushed; she knew, by Cecily's quick glance at Elizabeth, who was coming.

'If the weather is so bad, your guest may not arrive.'

'I doubt if he'll come by barge. The ice is quite thick on the river. Oh, Mercy, what a lovely fire!' Cecily held out her hands to the blaze.

'I was lucky, I gathered much furze and bracken during the autumn. I had those of my patients who were recovering go out and get it for me. We believe that exercise is good, and so is fresh air.'

'We?' said Cecily almost archly.

'You and Dr Clement, I suppose,' said Elizabeth.

'He is learned in these matters.'

'Father says,' said Cecily, 'that one day the King might take him into his personal service, and Dr Linacre thinks that he is the best young doctor he has known. That will doubtless mean that the King will soon hear of it.'

Oh, yes, thought Mercy, he is all that. He is rising in the world, and when he has gone far enough some nobleman of high rank will decide that he is a good match for his daughter.

And John himself? He was as ambitious in his way as Dauncey was in his. He wished to discover new ways of defeating sickness. The favour of the King might help him to do that.

Cecily and Elizabeth did not know that when they talked of the cleverness of John Clement and his chances at Court, they were showing Mercy, more clearly than she had ever seen before, how foolish she had been to dream.

'So,' insisted Cecily, 'you must come to dinner and be early. You will then be able to talk to him of the latest remedies for the pox. I am sure that will make entertaining dinner talk.'

'We just came to tell you this,' said Elizabeth. 'Mother is in a fine mood this morning. It is Margaret's turn to keep house this week. Poor Margaret! Mother is puffing about the kitchen, warning them all that if the beef is not thoroughly basted, some-one will suffer. There is much running to and fro . . . and all because Dr John Clement has become such an important per-sonage. It is hard to remember that he was scarcely more than a boy when he first came to us to attend Father on his way to Flanders. The humble secretary has become a great doctor.'

Ah, thought Mercy, too great for me.

Just as the girls were about to leave, a young boy arrived. He was white-faced, and the snow nestled in his hair, so that, on account of the gauntness of his features, he looked like a white-headed man.

'What is it, Ned?' asked Mercy, recognizing him as one of the boys from Blandels Bridge.

'It's my father, Mistress Mercy. He's lying on the straw like a dead man. But he's not dead. He just stares with his eyes wide open, and he can say naught. My mother says to come to you and ask you to see him.'

'You cannot go all the way to Blandels Bridge in this weather,' said Cecily.

'He may be very ill. I must go.'

'But the snow is deep. You could never reach there.'

'It is less than half a mile; and Ned came here.' She looked at his feet. He was wearing a pair of shoes which had belonged to Jack, for Margaret's task was to see to the needs of the poor, and this she did with the help of her family's clothes.

'You will not come back with us, then?'

Mercy shook her head. She must stifle weakness. She was a doctor first. This was her hospital; she believed it must be the love of her life, for Dr Clement – her affectionate friend, though he might be – could not marry her.

'Then you will miss dinner.'

'I fear so. I do not know how long I must stay at the cottage.'

'Mercy,' said Cecily, 'come and have dinner and go there afterwards. Perhaps John Clement will escort you.'

There was temptation. She pictured dinner in the beloved home, herself saying grace as she used to in the old days; she imagined the interesting conversation, and then, afterwards, riding pillion with John Clement to the cottage by Blandels Bridge, listening to his diagnosis of the patents's ailment, offering her own.

But sickness did not wait for such pretty, comforting scenes. Speed was everything in fighting sickness. A life could be lost by the delay of five minutes, let alone hours.

'Nay,' she said. 'I must go at once. Ned, wait for me. I must bring a few simples with me.'

So Elizabeth and Cecily went back to the house on the other side of the pales, and Mercy trudged through the snow to Blandels Bridge.

The blizzard beat at her; the familiar landscape had become unfamiliar, a thick white cloth was laid over everything, disguising the shapes of hedges and cottages.

But Ned knew the way. She followed him blindly. Soon her fingers were numb, her feet icily cold. The journey – usually a walk of ten minutes – took the greater part of an hour.

She thought: I shall miss him then. It is so long since I have seen him. He is so busy that he comes to see us but rarely. And when he does . . . I cannot be there!

They had reached the cottage. The rushes stank. There seemed no air in the place, yet it was bitterly cold. The woman who had been sitting on a stool shivering as she watched the man on the floor, brightened when she heard Mercy's voice without.

'God bless you for coming!' she cried as Mercy entered the cottage.

And when Mercy looked into her eyes, she thought: That must be my reward.

She knelt by the man on the dirty straw, and laid a hand on his burning forehead. He began to cough.

'He has been coughing like that for hours,' said the woman. 'It seems as though the cough will choke him.'

Mercy said: 'When the weather improves, I want to take him to my hospital. It is not good for him to be here.'

The man's piteous eyes held Mercy's. He seemed to be begging her to make him well.

She took one of the phials from her bag which she had brought, and gave him its contents. The close, cold atmosphere of the room made her shiver, and the smell from the rushes sickened her.

She thought: If only I could get him away from here . . . into one of my warm rooms, with blankets and a comfortable pallet on which to lie. If I could give him hot soup, fresh air, who knows . . . I might cure him.

'How is he, Mistress Mercy?' asked the woman.

'He is very sick.'

'Is he going to die?'

Mercy looked into the panic-stricken eyes. How could she say: 'I can do nothing for him here'? How could she say: 'Clean out these foul rushes'? Why, to disturb them now would double the danger. He was not so far gone in disease she could not save him. If it were not for the weather, she would go to her foster-father's house; she would get strong men, and boards on which to place this man, and carry him away from this foul-smelling place which was his home. But how could she do this in a snow-storm?

Mercy closed her eyes and prayed for guidance and, as if by some miracle, the door opened and there, seeming strong and all-powerful, was Dr John Clement.

'John!' she cried in delight. 'You . . . here?'

'Indeed yes, Mercy. The girls told me where you were, and I came to see if I could help.'

'Thank God!' she said. 'It is the answer to a prayer.'

'And the patient?'

He knelt in the rushes and looked into the sick man's face.

'This place . . .' said Mercy, and John nodded. 'If I could get him to the hospital,' she went on, 'care for him there . . I

183

believe I could nurse him back to health.'

John was silent for a while. Then he said: 'I rode here. I tied my horse to a stake by the cottage. We could put him on the horse and get him to the hospital.'

'Through the snow?'

John's answer was to look round the room, at the foul rushes and the earthen walls, damp and noisome.

'He cannot live if he stays here.'

'Can he live if he is taken out into the cold?'

'In a case like this, we have to take a chance.'

'You would take this chance, then, John?'

'I would. Would you?'

'Yes,' she said. 'I would do as you would.'

Happiness came in strange places at strange times. The snow was blowing in Mercy's face; she was wet and numb with cold, yet warm with pleasure.

She had rarely been so happy in her life as she was when she was walking through the snow with John Clement, the sick man, whom they held on John's horse, between them, while the pale-faced boy led the horse.

*   *   *

There was a double wedding that summer.

The marriages of Elizabeth with William Dauncey and Cecily with Giles Heron were to be celebrated in the private chapel attached to one of the mansions belonging to the Allington family.

Ailie – now Lady Allington – was delighted to have her family with her for this occasion.

Ailie was a happy person. Her husband adored her; she had a child now, but that fact had changed her little; she was still the gay and fascinating Ailie.

With great pleasure she showed her mother the kitchens of the house. They were older than those of Chelsea and far more grand.

Alice sniffed her disapproval of this and that, trying hard to find fault while she congratulated herself that it was her daughter who had made the best match of all.

'Look, Mother. Have you seen these ceilings? Giles is most proud of them. You see how cleverly they are painted. You'll find nothing like that in modern houses. Look at these painted cloths. They all represent scenes of some battles. Do not ask me which, I beg of you, for I do not know. In the great hall we have Flemish tapestry which is every bit as fine as that which my Lord Cardinal has in Tittenhanger or Hampton Court.'

'Tilly valley!' said Alice. 'What happens in the kitchen is of more importance than painted hangings or Flemish tapestry, I tell you. That has to be tested yet.'

Ailie kissed her mother; she loved to tease . . . to tease them all, her half-sisters, her stepfather, her mother and her husband. And it was very pleasant to have them all with her again.

Margaret spoke to her of William Dauncey. 'Elizabeth loves him, but does he love Elizabeth? Or is he thinking solely of what Father can do for him?'

'Well,' said Ailie, confident in her own charms, 'if he does not love her, then it is for her to make him do so. And if he will not . . .'

Ailie shrugged her shoulders, but, glancing at Margaret, decided not to finish what she had begun to say. Instead, she added: 'Why, they'll be happy enough, I doubt not. Master Dauncey is a young man who will go far and, believe me, my dear Margaret, it is by no means unpleasant to be the wife of a rising star.'

'Is that so, then?' said Margaret. 'I know what it is to be the daughter of one; and I would rather Father were less favourably looked upon at Court, so that his family might look upon him the more often.'

'Father! Oh, Father is no ordinary man. Father is a saint!'

Then Ailie left her sister; she was a busy hostess, and there was much to which she must attend, for her mansion at Willesden was filled with the most distinguished guests.

Her glance had gone to my Lord of Norfolk, recently the Earl of Surrey, who had succeeded to the title on the death of his father a year or so before.

Ailie curtsied before him and told him how honoured she was to see him at her house. Strange man! He was scarcely conscious of Ailie's charm. He looked grim, as though he had never given a thought to anything but matters of state. It was difficult to believe that his wife was giving him a lively time on account of her laundress, Bess Holland, for whom this grim man had a passion which he could not resist.

Norfolk was aloof, believing that he greatly honoured the Allingtons by attending at their house, being conscious that he was a great nobleman, head of one of the highest families in the land, and – although he dared not say this to any – he could not help reminding himself that the Howards of Norfolk were as royal as the Tudors. The recent death of his father-in-law, Buckingham, was a terrible warning to him, a reminder that he must keep such thoughts to himself, but that did not prevent his private enjoyment of them.

No; he would not be here this day but for his friendship with Sir Thomas More. There had occurred in the July of this year an incident which had startled all men who stood near the throne, and had set them pondering.

The King had said to the Cardinal one day when they were in the grounds of that extravagant and most luxurious of country houses, Hampton Court: 'Should a subject be so rich as to possess such a house?' And the Cardinal, that clever, most shrewd of statesmen, whose quick wits had lifted him from obscurity to a place in the sun, had thrown away the riches of Hampton Court in his answer: 'A subject could only be justified in owning such a place, Sire, that he might give it to his King.'

No more could people sing 'Which Court? The King's Court or Hampton Court?' For now Hampton Court was the King's Court in very truth.

Something was happening between the King and the Cardinal; it was something which put a belligerent light in the King's eyes, and a fearful one in those of the Cardinal.

Norfolk, that ambitious man, that cold, hard schemer – soft only to Bessie Holland – believed that the favour so long enjoyed by the Cardinal was less bright than of yore. This delighted Norfolk, for he hated Wolsey. His father had instilled in him that hatred; it was not only brought about by envy of the favour Wolsey enjoyed; it was not only the resentment a nobleman might feel for an upstart from a humble stratum of society; it was because of the part this Duke's father had been forced to play in the trial of his friend, Buckingham. Buckingham, that nobleman and kinsman of the Howards, had been condemned to death because he had not shown enough respect to one whom Norfolk's father had called 'A butcher's cur.' And one of Buckingham's judges had been the old Duke of Norfolk who, with tears in his eyes, had condemned him to death, because he had known that had he done otherwise he would have lost his own head. This would never be forgiven. However long the waiting must be, Wolsey must suffer, not only for the execution of Buckingham, but for the fact that he had forced Norfolk to condemn his friend and kinsman.

But, besides being a vengeful man, the Duke of Norfolk was an ambitious one. He did not lose sight of the fact that when Wolsey fell from grace there would be only one other clever enough to take his place. It would be well to be on terms of friendship with that man. Not that that in itself presented a hardship. If anyone, besides Bess Holland, could soften the heart of this hard man, it was Thomas More. I like him, thought Norfolk, puzzled by his own feelings. I really like him . . . for the man he is, not only for the greatness which may very well be his.

So it was that Norfolk wished to be More's friend. It was a strange matter – as strange as such a proud man's love for a humble laundress.

Thus was the Duke of Norfolk attending the double wedding of the daughters of a mere knight and the sons of two more mere knights.

Thomas was now approaching him. None would think, to look at him, that he was a brilliant scholar of world fame, and on the way to becoming one of the most important statesmen in the kingdom. He was more simply dressed than any man present, and it was clear to see that he thought little about his clothes. He walked with one shoulder higher than the other – an absurd habit, thought Norfolk, for it gave him an appearance of deformity.

But now Thomas stood before him, and Norfolk felt that strange mixture of tenderness and exasperation.

'I have never seen you so gay, Sir Thomas.'

'I am a lucky man, my lord. My two daughters are marrying this day, and instead of losing them I am to gain two sons. They will live with me – these two new sons – when they are not at Court, in my house in Chelsea. All my own daughters are married now, and I have lost not one of them. Do you not think that is a matter for rejoicing, my lord?'

'Much depends on whether you can live in amity with this large family of yours.'

Norfolk's eyes were narrowed; he was remembering his own stormy family life with its recriminations and quarrels.

'We live in amity at Chelsea. You should come to see us one day my lord, when your barge takes you that way.'

'I will. . . . I will. I have heard of your household. It is said: "*Vis nunquam tristis esse? Recte vive!*" Is that how you achieve your happiness, Master More?'

'Perhaps we strive to live rightly in Chelsea. That may be why we are such a happy family.'

Norfolk's eyes were brooding. He changed the subject abruptly. 'There is something brewing at the Court.'

'My lord?'

'The King has created his bastard Fitzroy, Duke of Richmond and Somerset.'

'He loves the boy.'

'But such great titles . . . for a bastard! Might it not be that His Grace feels he may never have a legitimate son?'

'The Queen has been many times disappointed; poor lady, she feels this sorely.'

Norfolk came close and whispered: 'And will feel it more sorely still, I doubt not.'

They went together to the great table on which was laid out

a feast so magnificent that it was said it might have graced the tables of the King or the Cardinal.

There was beef, mutton, pork; there was roasted boar and many kinds of fish, with venison and pies of all sorts. There was even turkey – that newest of delicacies imported into the country for the first time that year.

There was drink of all sorts – wine, red and white; malmsey, muscatel and romney; there was metheglin and mead.

And while the company feasted, minstrels played merry tunes in the gallery.

It was after the banquet and during the ball that followed it, that Mercy, standing aside to watch the dancers, found Dr Clement beside her.

'Well, Mercy,' he said, 'this is a merry day indeed. And right glad you must be that, although your sisters are marrying, like Margaret, they are not leaving the family roof.'

'That is indeed a blessing. I think it would have broken Father's heart if any of them had wanted to leave home. It was bad enough when Ailie went.'

'How would he feel if you went, Mercy?'

'I?' She blushed. 'Oh . . . as he did when Ailie went, I suppose. She is a stepdaughter; I am a foster-daughter. He is so good that he will have us believe that he loves us all as his own.'

'I think he would be unhappy if you left, Mercy. But . . . why should you leave? You could stay there . . . with your hospital, and I should be at Court. . . . Like your father, I should seize every opportunity to be with you.'

She dared not look at him. She did not believe that she had heard him correctly. There could not be all that happiness in the world. Surely she could not have her beloved father, her family, her hospital *and* John Clement!

He was close to her, slipping his arm through hers.

'What say you, Mercy? What say you?'

'John . . .'

'You seem surprised. Did you not then know that I love you? Have I presumed too much in letting myself believe that you love me too?'

'Oh John,' she said, 'do you mean . . . do you really mean . . . that *you* love *me*?'

'When you say *you*, you say it as though I were the King; and when you say *me*, you say it as though you were the humblest serving-girl. Why, Mercy, you are clever; you are good, and I love you. I beg of you, cast aside your humility and tell me you will marry me.'

'I am so happy,' she said, 'that I cannot find the words.'

'Then there must soon be another marriage in this family.'

What a happy day that was! Thomas smiled at each member of his family in turn. Would he rather have had the celebrations in his own home? Not when he looked at the proud smiles of Alice and her daughter. And as for Elizabeth and Cecily, they would have been equally happy wherever the ceremony had taken place.

It was not the banquet with its turkeys, the rich apartments with their painted hangings nor the distinguished guests that were important; it was the blissful happiness of each member of his family. And here was Mercy, as happy as any of them, and John Clement beside her; which could mean only one thing.

The merriment continued. There were morris dancers with bells on their legs; there were riders on hobby horses and there was the more stately dancing of the guests. Ailie was anxious to show that her attendance at Court had not been wasted, and the entertainment she could give her friends – if less luxurious than that given at the King's Court – was such to which the King himself could have come and found pleasure.

And later, Ailie, in her own chamber, surrounded by her sisters, who had gone thither to rest awhile, allowed them to examine her dress, which was of blue velvet and made in the very latest fashion. The velvet overdress was cut away to show a petticoat of pale pink satin; the lacing across the bodice was of gold-coloured ribbons.

Before them all Ailie turned and twisted.

'You like it, then? It is the very latest fashion, I do assure you. It is cut in the French manner. Do you like my shoes?' She extended a dainty foot for them to see. 'Look at the silver star on them. That is most fashionable. And you should all be wearing bands of velvet or gold about your necks. That is the very latest fashion. And see the sleeves! They fall over the hands. They are graceful, are they not?'

'Graceful?' said Elizabeth. 'But are they comfortable? It would seem to me that they might get in the way.'

'Mistress Dauncey,' cried Ailie, looking severely at her half-sister, 'do we wear our clothes to be comfortable? And what matters it if the sleeves, as you say, get in the way? They are graceful, and it is the only way a sleeve should hang.'

'I care not,' said Elizabeth, 'whether it is the latest thing from France or not. I should find it most uncomfortable.'

Ailie was conspiratorial. 'You know who started this fashion, do you not? But of course you do not. How could you? It was one of the maids of honour. It seems that she decides what we shall and what we shall not wear.'

'Then more fool you,' said Cecily, 'to let one woman decide what you should and should not wear.'

'*Let* her decide! We can do no other. She wears this sleeve because of a deformity on one of her fingers. Then it must seem that all other sleeves are ugly. *She* has a wart on her neck . . . a birthmark, some say; so she wears a band about it; and all see that such bands are so becoming that any without are quite unfashionable. She is lately come from France, and she is Anne . . . the daughter of Sir Thomas Boleyn. She is Mary's sister; and all the men admire her, and all the women are envious, for when she is there, though she may have an ugly finger and a wen on her neck, it seems that everyone else appears plain and insignificant.'

Margaret interrupted with a laugh: 'Oh, have done, Ailie! Have done with your frivolous maids of honour. Have done with your Frenchified Anne Boleyn, and let us talk of something that really matters.'

FIVE

THERE WERE several children in the house now. Margaret had a little girl, and Cecily and Elizabeth both had babies. If Elizabeth had not found complete happiness in her marriage, she had great hopes of finding it in her children.

In the streets the people were singing:

> *'Turkeys, carps, hops, pippins and beer*
> *Came into England all in one year.'*

And that year was the one of the great frost and the marriages of Elizabeth and Cecily.

Margaret thought of that year and the year that followed it as the happy years. So much seemed to happen in the family circle that they were all blinded to what was happening outside . . . all except Thomas.

There were times when, with his family about him, Margaret would notice that he stared beyond them with a strangely remote look on his face. It might be that they were in the orchards gathering the fruit, or sitting at table, talking, laughing together.

Once she slipped her arm through his and whispered: 'Father, of what do you think?'

His answer was: 'Of all this, Meg, of this family of mine . . . this perfect contentment. On the day I die – no matter how I die – I shall remember this moment and say that my life brought me much joy.'

Then their eyes had met, and for a moment there was understanding between them as there never was between him and any other.

'Father,' she had cried out in panic, 'I like it not when you talk of death. You frighten me.'

'Fear not, Meg,' he had answered, 'for who knows when death will come? Rejoice, Meg, in that uncertainty. You would be weeping if you knew I had a month to live. You were laughing a moment ago, though I might not have a day.'

'Father, I long for the time when you will leave the Court.'

Then he had smiled his sweet smile and had said: 'Let us be happy in this moment, Meg. Is it not as happy a moment as any could ask?'

There was so much to think about, so much to talk about during those two years. One child was having difficulty with her teeth; another cried too much; another had too many colds. These were such important matters. How could they stop for a moment to consider what was happening in the Courts of Europe? The King of France had been taken prisoner at Pavia and carried to Madrid; Cardinal Wolsey's foreign policy was less successful than it had previously been. There was a certain subject about which there was much whispering in Court circles, and it was known as the King's Secret Matter.

But to the family living in the pleasant house on the bank of the Thames, life was good. The babies were a source of amusement and delight; the Latin verses composed by their mothers provided much entertainment when read aloud. It was enjoyable to stroll in the gardens on a summer's night and watch the stars with Master Kratzer; it was so amusing to try to make Alice take an interest in astronomy and to listen to her scathing comments.

There was the fun of feeding the animals, watching them grow and teaching them tricks; there were the flower gardens to be tended; there was the pleasant rivalry between Elizabeth with her gilly-flowers and Cecily with her daffadowndillies; there was the fun of trying out new dishes. Ailie would come with the very latest recipes and show them how peacocks were served at a Court banquet, and how to make sugarbread and marchpane the royal way. There was the great tapestry to work on in hours of leisure; there were the herbs to be gathered in the surrounding fields, so that Mercy could make them into medicines and Alice use them for flavouring or garnishing a dish.

They were very happy during those two years.

Mercy was married to her Dr Clement, but she lived with them still, dividing her time between the house and the hospital. Thomas had given them the old house in Bucklersbury as a wedding present, and the girls were busy making tapestry to hang in Mercy's new home; but she continued to live at Chelsea during those two happy years. When she went to live in Bucklersbury, Margaret would spend more time at the hospital, but that was not to be yet.

Every evening there were prayers in the private chapel with the family assembled; at meal-times it was always Mercy who read from the Scriptures. They would discuss together what she had read, and there would be interesting argument.

There were three new additions to the family during those years.

One was a poor man, Henry Patenson, who had need of succour. He had a certain sharpness of wit, and since it was not known what task could be given him in the household, he himself suggested that, as all great men whose work led them to the society of the wise needed a fool to amuse them in their leisure hours, Henry Patenson should become the fool of Sir Thomas More.

Thus Henry Patenson joined the household.

Then there was little Anne Cresacre, who came to Chelsea as the betrothed of Jack. Poor little girl, she was very frightened. She knew that she was going to live among the learned, and that terrified her; but she had been so delighted to find that her future husband was the dunce of the family that she saw him as a natural protector. As for Jack, he had himself often felt inadequate among the scholars, and understood her feelings and was able to reassure her. Consequently, Anne Cresacre found that, although her future husband's learned family might terrify her, he did not.

Moreover, Lady More took her to her heart – for she was a very rich little girl – but all the same, riches or no riches, she must learn how to manage a household and take over the arrangement of domestic matters in turn with the other girls.

The third visitor was a painter from Basle – a young man full of enthusiasm and ideals, who had come to England to seek his fortune.

Erasmus – whom Thomas had visited on his trips to Europe and between whom there had been continual correspondence – discovered this man, and he wrote to Thomas asking him to receive him in his house. 'His name,' he wrote, 'is Hans Holbein, and I believe him to be a clever man at his craft. He wishes to come to England in order to earn some money. I beg of you, do all you can to help him.' Such a plea to Thomas could not be made in vain.

He welcomed the young man to his house, and so there was yet another to join the happy family group. He would sit sketching whenever the light allowed, listening to their talk, learning to speak their language, delighted because he could capture their expressions and draw them all with loving care.

'This man hath genius,' said Thomas to Alice.

At which Alice laughed. 'Genius! He was sitting out in the east wind yesterday, sketching away. He'll catch his death, I'll warrant. And *I* shall have to nurse him. *I* shall have to spend my time, which I can ill afford, making hot possets for him. And you call that genius!'

Thus during the happy years life went on.

* * *

Ailie came one day with news hot from Court.

'Such a pother! It is Mistress Anne Boleyn. What do you think? She hath betrothed herself to Henry, Lord Percy. The eldest son of the Earl of Northumberland, if you please! Trust Mistress Anne to pick one of the noblest peers in the land.'

'Then the girl hath good sense,' said Alice. 'For why should she not reach for the best plum on the tree?'

'And he was ready to fall to her touch,' cried Alice, 'like a very ripe plum. Humble Anne Boleyn to mate with a Percy! So to Town comes my Lord of Northumberland, and poor little Percy hath been soundly berated. My lord Cardinal, in whose service he is, himself administered the scolding. And such a scolding! 'Tis said that poor Percy has not stopped weeping yet.

And Mistress Anne? That's a different matter. She has been going about the Court flashing her eyes, swearing she will not be told whom she is or is not to marry. But back she is gone to Hever Castle, and there she will stay for a while, so 'tis said.'

'And what will you do for your fashions now?' asked Margaret wryly.

'She has left us a few. Methinks we must wait until she returns to Court, which, some say, will not be long.'

'Come and help me feed the peacocks,' said Elizabeth. 'I never heard such fuss, and all over one stupid girl!'

*   *   *

Early in the following year, the King sent for Sir Thomas More. He was in his new Palace of Hampton Court, and he suggested that Thomas should take a walk with him, for he had heard that Thomas had made some pretty gardens round his house in Chelsea; he would like to discuss his own plans for altering the gardens at Hampton Court.

So they walked side by side, the man in the sombre garments, his left shoulder a little higher than the right, his gown unadorned by jewels of any sort, and the gigantic, sparkling figure in doublet of purple velvet lined with ermine, his person sparkling with rubies and emeralds worth a fortune.

Now the King talked of the pond garden he would make; he talked of the beds of roses – red and white roses growing together side by side – symbols of the rival houses of Lancaster and York; and these should be enclosed by a wall, the pillars of which were to be made of stone and should be engraved with Tudor roses. All those who looked should see how the roses of York and Lancaster bloomed and faded while the Tudor rose altered not, engraved as it was on pillars of stone. The King enjoyed exploiting his fondness for allegory.

'Now, friend Thomas, what do you think of my pond garden? Have you anything to compare with that at Chelsea?'

'Nay, Sire. Our gardens are simple ones, tended mostly by my family.'

'Ah, that happy family of yours!' The King's heavy hand was

on his shoulder; the King's flushed face was near his own and the little mouth was close to Thomas's ear. 'I'll tell you a secret, Thomas, that I believe I have told you before: I envy you, man. Your King envies you. A happy family! How many grand-children are there now? Six. And grandsons. . . . And your son soon to wed and provide you with more, I doubt not. You are a good man, Thomas More; and God has showered his favours upon you. Yet, Thomas, would you say your King was an evil-doer?'

Into Thomas's mind there flashed a procession of murdered men – Dudley, Empson and Buckingham at the head of them; he thought of Elizabeth Blount, flaunting the King's natural son among her friends; he thought of wanton Mary Boleyn, and the quiet, long-suffering Queen Katharine. Was this King an evil-doer?

What great good fortune that the King did not expect an answer to that which he considered a question so absurd that none could take it seriously!

'Nay, Thomas,' he went on. 'I hear Mass many times a day. I am a devout man. I have dedicated my life to my country. You, my statesman, my Councillor who has lived close to me, know that. Is it not therefore a marvellous thing that God should deny me that which I most crave! Not for myself do I crave it. Nay. It is for this realm. Thomas, I must have a son. I need a son. I need a son for England.'

'Your Grace is young yet.'

'I am young. I am in the full vigour of my youth and man-hood. I could have sons. I have proved . . . I have no doubt of that. And when a man and woman fail to produce an heir, when they wish above all things for a son, there is one explanation only of that Master More. They have displeased Almighty God.'

"Your Grace, have patience for a while. The Queen has given you a healthy daughter.'

'A healthy daughter! Much good is she! I want sons . . . sons. . . . I am King of England, Thomas More; and it is necessary for a King to give his country an heir.'

Thomas was silent and the King frowned as he went on: 'There is a matter which lies heavy on my conscience. The Queen, as you know, was my brother's wife ere she became mine. You are a learned man, Master More, a religious one. You read your Bible. God inflicts a penalty on those who commit the sin of incest. That is what I fear I have done in marrying my brother's wife. Every son has died . . . every son the Queen has borne has died. Is that not significant? Is that not a sign from Heaven that I am a victim of Divine judgement? The more I study this matter, the more certain I become that I have offended God's Holy Laws in my marriage.'

Thomas was deeply shocked. He had heard rumours of the King's Secret Matter, and he had dreaded being asked to give an opinion. He thought of the Queen, that grave and gracious lady, who had offended none but the King; and him she had offended merely because she was growing old and unattractive and had been unable to provide him with a male heir.

The King had stopped in his walk and turned to face Thomas. He rocked on his heels; his face was creased with emotions – sentiment, cruelty, cunning and simplicity, and chiefly with his determination to make Thomas see him as he saw himself.

'I was against this marriage ere I made it. You remember the protest I made?'

Thomas looked in surprise at the King. 'I remember, Sire.'

'There you see, I did not wish to enter into the marriage, then. She was, after all, my brother's widow.'

Thomas dared not say: You protested on your father's orders. It was when you made the protest that you determined to marry Queen Katharine.

Thomas was aware of the selfish cruelty, the predominant desire in the King to see himself as a righteous man. It would not be worth risking his displeasure by making such a remark. It would be folly to anger him at this stage. At this moment Henry was so carefully nursing his conscience that any man who dared suggest that his conscience was really his own desire would surely forfeit his head.

'But . . . I married her,' went on the King. 'I married her, for she was a stranger in a strange land and she had been brought to us for marriage with the heir of England. And, because she was my wife, I cherished her and I loved her, as I still do. To part with her . . . that would be a bitter blow to me. You, who have married two wives and lived with them in amity, know that. It is nearly twenty years since I married the Queen. A man cannot cast off, without a pang, a woman to whom he has been married twenty years. Yet, though I am a man – aye, and a loving husband – I remember first that I am a King. And, Master More, if it were demanded of me to cast off this wife of mine and take another . . . though this matter were hateful to me, I would do it.'

'Your Grace should not sacrifice his happiness so lightly,' said Thomas, seizing the opportunity the King had given. 'If a King has his duty to his country, a husband has his duty to his wife. And if the crowning of a King is a holy sacrament in the eyes of God, so is the ceremony of marriage. You have a daughter, Sire, the Princess Mary. . . .'

The King waved his hand impatiently.

'That gives us much anxious thought. This country has never been happily ruled by a woman. You know that, Master More. And you, who call yourself a religious man, should ponder this: Is an incestuous marriage a holy one? Can it find favour in the sight of God? And what of a man and woman who, disturbed by their conscience, *continue* to live in such a marriage? Nay, this state of affairs cannot go on.' The King smiled slyly. 'Nor will my Ministers allow it. Warham, the Archbishop, and Wolsey, the Papal Legate, are bringing a secret suit against me.'

'A secret suit against Your Grace!'

The King nodded mournfully. 'A pretty pass when a King's subjects act thus against him. Mark you, I have tried to be an honest man over this matter and, much as I deplore the action of Warham and Wolsey, I yet admit they act with reason and within their rights.'

So it has come to this! thought Thomas. The King is indeed determined to cast off his wife since he has made Warham and Wolsey accuse him of incest.

'You see,' said the King, 'I am a King who is beset on all sides – by his love for his wife, by the demands of his ministers, by the reasoning of his own conscience. You are an important member of the Council, and there are many who set store by your opinions. You have many friends – Bishop Fisher among them. When this matter is discussed between you, I would have you obey *your* conscience as I am obeying mine. I would have you cast your vote not for Henry the man and Katharine the woman, but for the good of this land and its future heirs.'

'My Lord King, you honour me too much, I feel myself inadequate to meddle in such matters.'

'Nay, nay,' said the King. 'You underestimate your powers.' His voice was kind still, but his eyes flashed a warning. This matter was very near his heart, and he would brook no interference. This was a matter of conscience – the King's conscience and no one else's, for the King's conscience was such a mighty monster that it would tolerate no interference from the consciences of others. 'Come. You agree with these men who will bring a suit against me, do you not? You know, as they know, that your King and Queen are living together in sinful incest. Come! Come! Be not afraid. We ask for the truth.'

'Since your Grace asks for the truth, may I ask for time – time that I may consider this matter?'

The King's eyes were narrow, his mouth sullen.

'Very well, then. Very well. Take your time.'

He turned away abruptly, and several courtiers, who had been watching from a safe distance, asked themselves what Sir Thomas More had done to offend the King.

* * *

One of the sights to be seen in the City, rivalled only by that of the marching watch on Midsummer's Eve and the Eve of St Peter, was the ceremonious procession which attended the great Cardinal on all his journeyings. Before him, about him and behind him, went his retinue of servants, extravagantly clad in black velvet with golden chains about their necks; the lower servants were conspicuous in their tawny livery. And in the centre of all this pomp, preceded by the bearers of his silver crosses, his two pillars of silver, the Great Seal of England and his Cardinal's hat, rode the Cardinal himself, in his hand an orange, the inside of which had been replaced by pieces of vinegar-soaked sponge and other substances to counteract the pestilential air; the trappings of his mule were crimson velvet and his stirrups of copper and gold.

He went with as much ceremony as if he were the King himself.

He passed over London Bridge, and the people watched him in sullen silence. They blamed Wolsey for all their ills. Who was Wolsey? they asked themslves. A low-born man who, by great good luck, lived in the state of a King. When taxes were too high – and they always were – they blamed Wolsey. And now that the King wanted to replace the Queen, they blamed Wolsey for that. The people wanted an heir to the throne, yes; but the more serious among them remembered that the Queen was the aunt of the Emperor Charles of Spain; they might not be troubled on account of the Emperor's humiliation, which he would undoubtedly feel if his aunt were cast off, but they feared his armies. So . . . they blamed Wolsey.

He was on his way to France now, and in his retinue rode Sir Thomas More.

The great Cardinal was more deeply perturbed at this time than he had ever been before.

Fortune was turning against him. Had he looked too high when he had coveted the Papal Chair? Ah, if only he instead of Clement had been elected Pope, all his anxieties would be at an end. There he would have been content to rest, at the pinnacle of fame. There he would have had no need to fear any man. He had climbed to great heights, and now he was on a narrow ledge, his foothold precarious; he must retain a very careful balance if he were to continue to climb. About him snapped those angry, jealous wolves – Suffolk, Norfolk and their followers. There was only one man who could save him from those ravening beasts, and that was the most dangerous of them all – the King.

The secret court which he and Warham had called, that the King's marriage might be proved incestuous, had failed because of the obstinacy of the Queen, who insisted that her marriage with Arthur had never been consummated; therefore there were no grounds on which legality could be denied. Wolsey's foreign policy had resulted in his winning for England the enmity of both France and Spain; and now the Pope, on whose help he had relied in this matter of the royal divorce, had been captured during the sack of Rome and was a prisoner in the Emperor's hands.

His mission to France was an uneasy one. He must talk with Francis; he must tell him of the King's doubts regarding the legality of his marriage; he must try to arrange a match between the Princess Mary and the son of Francis; he must cautiously hint that he was looking for a future Queen of England in France. Perhaps the Princess Renée, sister of the Queen of France? Perhaps Francis's own sister, the talented Marguerite de Valois?

Everything depended on the successful termination of the King's Secret Matter; and this was a most delicate matter even for a great statesman to handle. To juggle with the politics of Europe was one thing; to secure the gratification of the King's desires another.

Still he who had achieved so much would achieve this also. What perturbed him was the growing truculence of Norfolk, and particularly of Suffolk – for Suffolk, the King's brother-in-law and his greatest friend, had the King's ear; and there were times when Wolsey felt that Suffolk would not have dared to treat him so scurvily, had he not done so with the sanction of the King.

And at the root of this uneasiness was one factor; the King was no longer that careless boy who could be fed with the sugar plums of masques, jousts and fair women while the able hands of his shrewdest statesman steered the ship of state, which was England, along its perilous journey. This King had done with playing the careless boy; he had come to realize that the fascination of power-politics was as great as a new feast or a new woman. He was breaking the bars of his cage; he was testing his strength; he was roaring with pride in his own glory. And he was saying: 'I will have all . . . all . . . I will be King in very truth. I will have my rich entertainments, and I will stand on the bridge of my ship, and if any attempt to come between me and my desires they shall not live long to do so.'

On went the procession – all the pomp and glory – and in the midst of it rode an apprehensive man.

Thomas, riding along unnoticed in the glittering throng, was also pensive. All his sympathy was for the Queen. Poor lady, what had she done to deserve this humiliation? Had she wished for marriage with the King in the first place? He doubted it. He remembered her, serene and dignified, at the Coronation. Yet she had accepted her fate with meekness; she had tried to love the King, and she had been a faithful wife to him; the second was to be expected, for she was a virtuous woman; but her love for the King must have been sorely tried during these last years.

Now was his chance to leave his post, to tell the King the state of his mind, to say boldly: 'Sire, I resign my post, for you will wish to have about Your Highness those ministers who can help you to obtain the divorce.'

It was a relief to rest at Rochester on the journey to France, and there to stay in the company of his old friend, Bishop Fisher.

It was pleasanter still to have a private talk with Fisher after Wolsey had sounded him.

In the small panelled room, the two friends were serious together. They talked solemnly of the terrible calamity which had befallen the Pope; then their talk turned on the King's Secret Matter.

How could the divorce be concluded without the sanction of the Pope? And how could the Pope give his consent to the King's divorce from a lady who was a close relation of the man who held him prisoner, even if he was satisfied that he should grant a divorce?

'These are grave matters, my friend,' said Bishop Fisher.

'Grave indeed,' said Thomas, 'for where they will end I do not know.'

And the next day, the Cardinal, with Sir Thomas More in his entourage, left for Canterbury, and so to France.

*   *   *

The sweating sickness had again come to England; it roamed through the streets of the City like a hungry beast who was nourished on the filth which filled the malodorous gutters and the fetid air inside the houses. Men, women and children took the sweat; they lay down where they were, in a state of exhaustion, and died unless they could be roused from the coma into which they fell. This horrible pestilence was no respecter of persons; it struck at beggars and the highest in the land.

In the streets, the people were muttering together, telling each other that it was clear why God had sent this affliction. He was displeased. And why should He be displeased? The Secret Matter was no longer secret; they knew that the King wished to put the Queen from him; and there was no denying the rumour that the woman he wished to make his Queen was Nan Bullen – his mistress, so it was said. Who was this woman? The daughter of a knight. She was no royal Queen.

All the hatred the people felt for the upstart Wolsey they now allowed him to share with the upstart Anne Boleyn.

God was angry with England, and this was His way of showing it; there was the reason for a further visitation of this terrible pestilence.

The King was also angry. He had been deprived of the presence of his beloved mistress, who he desired to make his wife more than he desired anything on Earth. What had she said to him? 'Your mistress I will not be; your wife I cannot be.' But he must be her lover even if, as she implied, the only way in which he could be was by making her his wife.

And now she had left the Court.

Wolsey had done this. What had happened to Wolsey? He had lost a little of his arrogance. He now knew that the King had not given him his confidence, and that when he, Wolsey, had been trying to negotiate a marriage with one of the princesses of France, the King had already firmly made up his mind that he would have none other than Anne Boleyn. Wolsey now knew that it was mainly Anne Boleyn who had set the King searching his conscience; but he had learned that important factor too late.

Now a sad and anxious Cardinal had advised his royal master that, since the people were angered against the Lady Anne, it would be wise at this stage to send her back to Hever.

So Henry was alone and wretched, longing for her, asking himself why it was that, surrounded as he was by the cleverest men in the world, there was not one of them who could settle this matter to his satisfaction.

There was a message from Hever.

The sweat cared nothing for the wrath and anguish of the King himself. Anne Boleyn – more precious to the King than his kingdom – had become a victim of the sweating sickness.

Now the King was in terror. He wept and stormed and he prayed. How could God put the King's beloved in danger! Had he not been a good King . . . a good man . . . always striving to do God's will! And was it not solely for the good of England that he would take Anne to wife?

He could for his physicians, and the only one who was at Court was his second, Dr Butts. The King threatened this man while he beseeched him to save the Lady Anne, before he dispatched him in all haste to Hever.

Then he sat down and, weeping, wrote to her: 'The most displeasing news that could occur to me came suddenly at night. . . .' He wept as he wrote of his laments, of what it meant to him to hear that his mistress, whom he esteemed more than all the world, and whose health he desired as he did his own, should be ill. He told of how he longed to see her and that the sight of her would give him greater comfort than all the precious jewels in the world.

And when he had written and dispatched this letter, he paced up and down his apartment, weeping and praying; and all the time longing for Anne, cursing the fate which kept them apart, promising himself how he would reward those who helped him to marry Anne, promising revenge on all those who continued to keep them apart.

In the Court the news spread: The Lady hath the sweat. This will doubtless impair her beauty, even though she should recover. Could she do so and be so charming when and if she returned to the Court?

Important events were being decided in a lady's bedchamber at Hever Castle.

* * *

Great sorrow had touched the house in Chelsea.

Margaret had been to the village, taking some garments to one of the families, and she had seemed quite well when she had returned to the house. She had sat with them at the supper table and had joined in the talk. Then, as she had risen, she had tottered suddenly and had been obliged to catch at the table to support herself.

'Margaret!' cried Mercy in terrible alarm.

'What is it?' demanded Alice.

'Let us get Margaret to bed at once,' said Mercy. 'She is sick, I am afraid.'

'Margaret sick!' cried Alice. 'Why, she was eating a hearty meal a moment ago!'

'Yes, Mother, I know. But don't hinder me now. Will! Jack! Father . . . help me.'

It was Will who carried her to her room. Now her eyes were tightly shut and the beads of sweat were beginning to form on her face; she was shivering, yet burning hot.

Thomas followed. He caught his daughter's limp hand.

'O Lord God,' he prayed silently. 'Not Margaret. . . . That I could not endure.'

Will was beside himself with anxiety. 'What shall we do, Mercy? Mercy, in God's name, what *can* we do?'

'Cover her up. Keep her warm. No; don't attempt to undress her. I will try the philosopher's egg. I have it ready, God be thanked.'

She lay on the bed, no longer looking like Margaret; her face was yellow and the sweat ran down her cheeks.

'Please,' begged Mercy, 'everybody go. There is nothing you can do. Leave her with me. No, Will; you can do no good. Make sure that the children do not come into this room. Father . . . please . . . there is nothing . . . nothing you can do.'

Mercy's thoat constricted as she looked into his face.

How will he bear it? she asked herself. He loves her best in the world. She is his darling, as he is hers. How could either endure life without the other?

'Father . . . dearest Father . . . please go away. There is nothing . . . nothing to be done.'

But he stood numbly outside the door as though he had not heard.

Margaret ill of the sweat! Margaret . . . *dying*!

Elizabeth and Cecily had shut themselves in their rooms. There was nothing to be done; that was the pity of it. They said to each other that if only there was something they could have done it would have been easier to bear. But to sit . . . waiting . . . in such maddening inactivity. . . . It was all but unendurable.

Alice took refuge in scolding anyone who came near her. 'The foolish girl . . . to go to the cottages at such a time. She should have known. And they tell us she is so *clever* . . . ! And what is Mercy doing? Is she not supposed to be a doctor? Why does she not cure our Margaret?'

Will paced up and down. He could find no words. Margaret, his beloved wife, so calm, so serene; what would he do if he lost her? What would his life be without Margaret?

Giles Heron was all for riding to the Court; he would bring Dr Linacre himself, he declared. What did it matter if Dr Linacre was the King's first physician? Margaret was a member of that family which was now his, and she was in danger. He must get the best doctors for her. He could bring Dr Butts . . . and Dr Clement. He would bring all the greatest doctors in the country.

Dauncey said: 'You would find yourself in trouble, brother. You . . . from an afflicted house . . . to ride to Court!'

Dauncey was astonished that he could be so affected. What

was Margaret to him? What could Margaret do to advance his fortunes? Nothing. He trembled, it was true, that her father might catch the disease and die, and that Dauncey's biggest hope of achieving favour at Court would be lost. Yet he was moved, and faintly astonished to find himself sharing in the family's anguish. He had grown fond of them; he had enjoyed their merry games; and, strange as it was, he knew that if any calamity came to them it could not fail to touch him. So there was a streak of sentiment in this most ambitious young man after all.

Thomas shut himself up in the private chapel.

What could he do to save Margaret? What could he do but pray? Now he thought of her – Margaret, the baby, the child, the prodigy who had astonished all with her aptitude for learning. He could think of a hundred Margarets whom he loved, but the one who meant most to him was the loving daughter, the Margaret who was his dearest friend and best companion, who was nearer to him than anyone in the world.

'O God,' he prayed, 'do not take my daughter from me. Anything . . . anything but that.'

He did not leave the chapel. He stayed there on his knees. The hair-shirt lacerated his skin, and he wished its pain were doubled.

Will came to him and they prayed together.

'Ah, son Roper,' said Thomas, 'what religious differences are there between us now? We ask one thing, and that we wish for more than anything in the world. She must not die.'

'I cannot contemplate life without her, Father,' said Will.

'Nor I, my son.'

'They say that if she does not recover during the first day there is no hope.'

'The day is not yet over. How was she when you left her?'

'Unconscious. She lies there with her eyes fast shut, oblivious of the world. I spoke her name. "Margaret," I said. "Margaret, come back to me and our children. . . ." '

'Will, I beg of you, say no more. You unnerve me.'

He thought: I have loved her too well; I have loved her more

208

than all the world. When she was born she gave me contentment; she was the meaning of life to me. She *is* the meaning of
life. Have I loved her too well? Oh, how easy it is to torture
the body, to wear the hair-shirt, to flagellate the flesh, to deprive
the body of its cravings. Those pains are easy to suffer; but how
bear the loss of a loved one . . . how endure life when the one
you love more than your own life, more than the whole world is
taken from you?

'If . . . if aught should happen to her . . .' he began.

Now it was Will's turn to implore him not to go on. Will
could only shake his head while the tears ran down his cheeks.

But Thomas continued: 'I would retire from the world.
Nothing could keep me leading this life. Oh, my son, I could
not go on. If Margaret were taken from me, I would never
meddle with wordly affairs hereafter.'

'Father, I implore you . . . I beg of you not to speak of it. Do
not think of it. She will get well. She must get well. Let us pray.
Let us pray together. . . .'

So they knelt and prayed, and if Will saw God as Martin
Luther saw him, and if Thomas saw God as the Pope saw Him,
they each knew that their prayers were being offered to the same
God.

Thomas rose suddenly. His spirits were lifted.

He said: 'Will, when Margaret was a little girl – scarcely two
years old – and we were visiting her mother's old home, New
Hall in Kent, Margaret, playing in a field, was lost and could
not find the gate through which she had come into the field and
which opened on to the path which led to the house. She was
frightened, for dusk was settling on the land. Frantically she ran
about the field, and still she could not find the gate. Then suddenly she remembered that I had told her that when she was in
trouble she must ask the help of her Father upon Earth or her
Father in Heaven. "And, Father," she said when she told me
this some time later, "I had lost you, so I knelt down and asked
God the way home. And when I arose from my knees I was no
longer frightened. I walked calmly round the field until I came
to the gate." I had missed her, as it happened, and had gone to

look for her, and as she came through the gate and ran towards me, she said: "Father, God showed me the way home." What a beautiful thought it is, Will. What a comfort. I have been on my knees now . . . frightened . . . panic-stricken, as Margaret was. I was lost and I could not find the gate which led to the home I knew . . . to the happiness I knew. "God," I have prayed, "show *me* the way." '

'Father, you look changed. You seem . . . serene . . . as though you *know* she will get well.'

'I seem calmer, my son, do I not? I *am* calmer. I feel as she felt when she rose from her knees. My panic has gone. I know this, son Roper, God will show me the way, as he showed Margaret. My mind is calm; thoughts cease to chase themselves in my head. I am going to the house to see how she is. Come with me, Will.'

Mercy met them at the door of the sick-room.

'No change,' she said, 'I have tried to wake her. If we cannot wake her, she will die.'

'Mercy, I want you to give her a clyster.'

'Father, she is too ill.'

'She is so ill, Mercy, that she cannot be much worse . . . short of death. Do this, I beg of you. Administer this clyster. We must wake her, must we not? Then we *will* wake her.'

'Father, I am afraid. It is too violent, and she is very ill indeed.'

'Mercy, you are imprisoned in fear. Yes, my love, you are afraid because you love her even as I do. She is not your patient; she is your sister. You wrap her up; you watch over her; but you will not take a risk because you are frightened. I have prayed. I feel I have been in close communion with God and, Mercy, I am not afraid. I want you to be calm . . . to forget that this is our beloved Margaret. If she does not wake she will die. We must wake her, Mercy. We *must*. You agree that is so. Give her the clyster.'

Mercy said quietly: 'I will do as you wish, Father. Leave me with her.'

Half an hour later Mercy came out of the sick-room.

Her eyes were shining.

'She is roused from her sleep,' she said. 'Father . . . Will . . . she asked for both of you.'

They went to her and one knelt on either side of the bed.

Margaret, weak and only just able to recognize them, let her eyes wander from one to the other.

*   *   *

Three men were very happy after the next few days. Each had feared to lose the one he loved best in the world, and each experienced the great joy of seeing the return of the loved one to health.

These men were Will Roper, Sir Thomas More and the King of England.

*   *   *

Margaret was about the house again, although thin and pale. Her father seemed unable to let her go out of his sight.

They would wander together through the orchards and the flower gardens, and sometimes he would remind her of the pleasures they had shared during her childhood; they would laugh and sometimes weep together, over their memories.

He spoke to her, more frankly than he did to the others, of Court matters; and sometimes they would read together from Erasmus's Testament.

Margaret's convalescence consisted of many happy hours.

He would care for her in a hundred ways; he would get her a shawl from the house, for fear the wind might be too strong; he would not let her walk on the grass after rain lest her feet should be made damp. He rejoiced to see her gradual return to health, and often she would weep, contemplating the sorrow her illness had brought to her family, and in particular she wept for Will and her father.

The bond between Sir Thomas and his daughter was stronger than it had ever been.

One hot day, when they were sitting in the gardens, being overcome by the warmth of the day he opened the neck of his gown, and little Anne Cresacre, who was sitting near him, caught a glimpse of the strange garment he was wearing next to his skin. Anne's big eyes were round with wonder; her lips began to twitch. Could it be a hair-shirt! But only monks wore those . . . monks and hermits. Little Anne, who was often uncertain in this household of clever people, found that when she was at a loss, irrepressible laughter overcame her.

It was Margaret who followed her look and who rose from her seat and said: 'Father, the air grows cold.' She buttoned up his gown and was angry with Anne for her youth and her stupidity, and because she had dared to giggle at a great and saintly man.

He, seeing what had happened and understanding it, smiled at Anne, who, aware of his kindness, was instantly ashamed. She rose and, murmuring that she was wanted in the kitchens, hurried away.

Thomas turned his smile on his daughter, and it grew very tender. He remembered that when Alice wished to know what happened to his shirts and why they were not given in with the ordinary linen to wash, it was Margaret who had answered her, to prevent his telling the truth; for Margaret could not bear to listen to the ridicule which she knew Alice would heap upon him. 'I wash Father's shirts, Mother, with things of my own. I have always done it, and I shall always do it.' 'What nonsense!' Alice had said. 'Why should you do such a thing when there are maids here to do it?' But Margaret had quietly said that it was her affair, and she said it with such determination that even Alice did not pursue the subject.

Thomas now suggested a walk by the river, and as they set forth he said: 'You would protect me then from the scorn of the young and the gay?'

'The stupid child!' said Margaret. 'I wanted to box her ears.'

'You are too hard on her, Meg. She is but a baby. You must not expect all to be as serious as you were at her age. Have patience with little Anne. She is a good child; and I believe she loves our Jack and that he loves her. Let us ask no more of her than that she shall love him and make him happy.'

'Oh, Father, what matters it after all? The important thing is: how go affairs at the Court?'

'Events move fast, Meg.'

'Is the King as determined as ever to cast off the Queen?'

'I fear so.'

'And if he succeeds in arranging the divorce, he will marry Anne Boleyn?'

'I believe that to be his intention. Meg, I think it will not be long before your father loses his honours and becomes a humble man again. You smile, Meg. One would think I had told you that my fortune was made.'

'So it will be if you are home with us all as you once were. If you take up your duties in the City as you once did. . . .'

'I doubt that I could pick up the threads as easily as that, Meg.'

'Never mind. I should be happy to see you leave the Court for ever.'

'We should be very poor.'

'We should be rich in happiness. You would not have to go away from England or be absent at Court. We should have you with us always.'

'What a happy day it will be when I come home and tell you I have given up my honours!'

'The happiest day we have ever known. And will it be soon?'

'As I said, events move fast. The King will let me go. He knows my views. He has not urged me to change them. He hints that he respects them. I think that must mean, Meg, that when I ask leave to retire from Court, he will readily grant it.'

'I long for that day.'

'It is a sad affair, Meg, to watch the rapid descent of those who have climbed to great heights. I think of the Cardinal.'

'How fares it with him, Father?'

'Badly. Meg, it is a sorry sight; it is a sorry thought.'

'The King has no more need of him?'

'The Cardinal has set up false idols, Margaret. He has worshipped pomp instead of honour; he has mistaken riches for the glory which comes with righteous work. Poor Wolsey! He has too many enemies; the King is his only friend . . . a fickle friend.

The Cardinal has offended the Lady Anne. He broke the marriage she desired with Percy; he insulted a relative when he attempted to deprive Eleanor Carey of the post of Abbess of Wilton; but worst of all she knows that he has urged the King to marry one of the French Princesses. They are false steps in his slippery career. He felt so sure of his power. Who is this Anne Boleyn? he asked himself. She is another such as her sister Mary! There he finds his mistake, and the King's mistress is his enemy. He could not have a greater, for she it is who commands the King. Moreover, Norfolk and Suffolk wait for the King to turn his back on the man he once loved; then they will rush in to attack him. He is a sad, sick man, Meg. Poor Wolsey!'

'He has been no real friend to you, Father.'

'He is no true friend to anyone or anything but his own ambition; and now, poor soul, he sees the falseness of *that* friend. Fame! What is fame? Men congratulate themselves if they attain to fame, empty though it is; and because they are light-minded they are lifted to the stars by the fickleness of opinion. What does fame do to a man? Though he be praised by all the world, if he has an aching joint, what does fame do for him? And Wolsey has many an aching joint, Meg . . . and an aching heart. His policy abroad, so successful at one time, has turned sour. He has aroused the hatred of the Emperor without gaining the love of the King of France. Our King cares only for one thing, for he is a single-minded man, and he thinks of little else day and night but ridding himself of Queen Katharine and marrying Anne Boleyn. Wolsey has one hope now – the successful outcome of the case which he and Campeggio are about to try here in London. If Wolsey can arrange the divorce, I doubt not that he will ere long win back the King's favour. If he does not . . . then the King will turn his back on him; and if His Grace continues to look the other way, the wolves will descend on my lord Cardinal, and they will have no mercy, Meg. There are too many slights to be avenged, too many resentments festering.'

'And then, Father?'

'Then, Meg, that will be farewell to his glory, farewell to his pomp and his riches. We shall no longer see our Cardinal ride in state through our streets. Pray God we do not see him riding to the Tower.'

'And you?'

'Here is the way out, Meg. Depend upon it, the King has little use for me. He knows my mind. He will accept my resignation. It will save him the unpleasant task of dismissing me as, Meg, all will be dismissed who do not pander to his wishes.'

'Father, I long for the day of your resignation.'

''Twill not be long now, Meg. I assure you of that.'

*   *   *

The Cardinal's glory was dimmed. None knew it more than he himself. His fate was clear when Campeggio, whom all were expecting to give a verdict in favour of the divorce, with characteristic vacillation rose and adjourned the Court, suggesting that it should be recalled and continued in Rome.

Then the Duke of Suffolk, who, all knew, spoke with the authority of the King, rose in hot anger and, glaring not at Campeggio, but at Wolsey, cried: 'It was never merry in England since we had Cardinals among us.' That was the signal, recognized by all; the King had thrown Wolsey to his enemies.

Events followed rapidly.

The Cardinal returned to his house in Westminster surrounded by his servants, who trembled with him, for he had been a kindly, gracious master. And there they waited for the coming of Norfolk and Suffolk.

They did not have to wait long.

They came in the name of the King and demanded that he deliver the Great Seal of England into their hands.

*   *   *

The King sent for Sir Thomas More.

Margaret went down to the barge with him.

'Depend upon it Meg: this will mean one thing. When your father returns he will be stripped of his honours. I shall receive my marching orders with the stricken Cardinal.'

'And, dearest Father, how different from Wolsey's will be your feelings. You will rejoice. You will come home to your family, a happier man.'

And she stood at the top of the privy stairs, waving to him and smiling.

She had never felt so happy to see him depart.

*　　*　　*

The King received Thomas gravely.

'We have a matter of great importance to discuss with you,' he said. 'You have worked in close company with Thomas Wolsey, have you not?'

'I have, Your Grace.'

The King grunted. He glared at his minister. He could not, even at this moment, resist a little acting. He wished to alarm Thomas More; and then speak what was in his mind.

There was, it seemed, only one man worthy to succeed to the office just vacated by Wolsey. The office of Chancellor was the highest in the land, and could only be given to a man capable of filling it. His Councillors had discussed this with the King. A knowledge of the intricacies of the law was a necessity, Norfolk had said. The new Chancellor must be an honest, upright man to whom the country could look with confidence and trust. The Councillors agreed that there was only one man in the country who could satisfactorily fill the office. This decision of his Councillors had set the King pondering. The Church had been reasonable over this matter of unlawful marriage with Katharine – all except one Bishop, that fool Fisher. He had hummed and ha-ed and maddened the King. But why should a King upset himself over the intransigence of a Bishop? That man should be adequately dealt with when the time came.

Henry did not forget that Sir Thomas More was not in favour of the divorce, that he had supported the Queen; yet he knew, as well as did his Councillors, that Thomas More was the man most fitted to step into Wolsey's shoes. It must be so. Henry was sure of this; so were Norfolk, Suffolk and every member of the Council. Wolsey himself had said, when he knew he was to fall, that there was only one man capable of following him, and that that man was Sir Thomas More.

This man More had a strange effect on all men, it seemed. Even when his opinions differed from theirs, they respected him to such an extent that they must continue to love him.

The King ceased to frown. His smile was turned on Thomas.

'We have good news for you. We have always had a fondness for you. Did we not say so when you first came to us? You remember that affair of the Pope's ship?' The King's smile was now benign. 'Now, we have a task for you. We said we would make your fortune, did we not? It is made, Thomas More. We like your goodness, your honesty, that respect the whole world has for you. We look for one on whom to bestow the Great Seal, and we say to ourselves: "Ah, Thomas More! He is the man for us. He shall be our Lord Chancellor." '

'Lord Chancellor, Your Grace!'

'Now, Thomas, you are overwhelmed. I know. I know. 'Tis a mighty honour. Yet we have given this matter much thought, and we are assured that there is no man in the kingdom who deserves the honour more than you do. Your country needs you, Thomas. Your King commands you to serve your country. Your work with Wolsey, your knowledge of affairs, your love of learning, your erudition, your knowledge of the law . . . You see, do you not? You see that if I did not love you as I do, did I not respect you as a learned and an honourable man, I still must make you my Chancellor.'

Thomas looked with concern at the dazzling figure before him. 'Your Grace,' he said, 'I must speak to you frankly. I am unsuited to the task.'

'Nonsense! There is not a man in this realm whom the task becomes more. We command you to it, Thomas. We will have no other. It is your bounden duty to your King and your country to accept. We will take no refusal.'

'My lord, Your Highness, your most gracious Majesty, I must speak as my conscience commands me. I cannot give my support to the divorce.'

The King's eyes seemed to disappear in his fleshy face. He flushed and drew back. He was silent for a few moments, as though he were considering which of his roles to play. He might roar: 'Send this traitor to the Tower.' On the other hand, he might continue to play the part of benign monarch who respects an honest man.

He needed this man. He was the only man in the realm fitted for the task. All agreed on that. The learning and integrity of Sir Thomas More, the respect he had inspired on the continent of Europe, were necessary to England.

The King decided.

'Thomas,' he said, 'you have your conscience, and I have mine. By God's Body, I have been worried enough in my thoughts by my most sinful and incestuous marriage. I know the pain of a nagging conscience. And on this matter, Thomas More, you and I are not of one mind. I regret it. Thomas, I regret it mightily. But as a man of conscience, I respect a man of conscience . . . mistaken though I know him to be. For, Thomas, you are a learned man. I doubt it not. You are a good man, and we are proud to have you as a subject. You have been favoured by God. I know of that family at Chelsea, and one day, Thomas, I am going to visit Chelsea. I am going to see it for myself. I am going to give the kiss of friendship to those merry daughters of yours, to that jolly wife. Yea, that I will. You have been favoured in your family. . . .' His voice sank almost to a whisper. 'You do not understand how lonely a man can be – even though he be a King – who lacks that which God has given you with lavish hands. Thomas More, there are a few matters which you do not understand as worldly men understand them. And this is one of them. But I am a man of wide views. I understand you . . . even though you understand me not. And, Thomas, I will have you for my Chancellor and no other. And this matter which plagues me day and night shall put no barriers between us two. Dismiss it, Thomas. It is no affair of yours. Come, Chancellor More. Take the Great Seal of England, and your King will put the seal of friendship on your brow.'

Henry leaned forward and kissed Thomas's forehead.

It was not for the Lord Chancellor to meddle in this matter of the divorce, thought the King. That was the task of the clergy. He had two new friends in mind from whom he hoped much: Thomas Cranmer and Thomas Cromwell.

It would seem that I have fancy for these Thomases, thought Henry; and he smiled pleasantly as he looked into the face of his new Lord Chancellor.

SIX

Margaret would never forget rushing to greet him when he returned in his barge. She would never forget the jaunty smile on his face; but while he might deceive others, he could never deceive her.

'Father?'

'Well, Meg, see you not the change? The Under-Treasurer left you earlier this day. The Chancellor is now arrived.'

'Chancellor, Father . . . *you*?'

'A worthy Chancellor, though a humble one, as says my lord of Norfolk.'

'But . . . the King's divorce?'

'I have told him that I can have no hand in it; and it seems he accepts my refusal to do so, as Norfolk accepts my humble birth. And, Meg, with so many ready to accept so much that is unpalatable to them, I was perforce obliged to accept that which I would fain refuse.'

'It is not a good thing, Father. It is not a matter for jokes.'

'It is not good, Meg, and therefore is it meet that we should joke, for by doing so we can make light of what we cannot refuse to undertake.'

'Could you not have refused?'

'I tried, Meg.'

'But . . . surely you have a free choice?'

'I am the King's subject and as such must obey the King's command. Come, let us to the house. I'll warrant you'll smile to see the family's reception of this news.'

Slowly they walked towards the house, and Margaret's heart was full of misgiving.

* * *

Lord Chancellor!

The family received the news with wonder.

Alice was mockingly proud. 'So, Master More, you have made a great man of yourself in spite of all.'

'Rather say, wife, that they have made a great man of me in spite of myself.'

Alice looked at him with beaming pride. 'To think that a husband of mine should be the Lord Chancellor!'

'Why, Alice, you have grown two inches taller, I'll swear.'

Alice was in no mood for raillery. 'This means we shall need more servants. Why, who knows whom we shall have visiting us now. Mayhap the King himself!' Alice grew a shade paler at the thought. 'Now, Thomas, should His Grace honour us, I shall need to know a day or more ahead.'

'Shall my first duties as Chancellor be to warn the King that if he should visit Lady More he must give her good warning?'

'Have done with your nonsense! 'Twould not be unknown, I trow, for the King to visit his Chancellor. Why, he was so much in and out of the houses of the last Chancellor that people did not know whether they were at the King's or the Cardinal's Court.'

'And now the Cardinal's Courts are the King's Courts. Has it occurred to you that all the last Chancellor's possessions are now the property of the King? Do you not tremble for your own, Alice? For remember, they are the property of the new Lord Chancellor, and why should the new one fare better than the old?'

'Have done with such foolish talk.'

'Well, Alice, here is something you will like better. There is to be a visitor this night for supper.'

'A visitor. Who is this?'

'His Grace of Norfolk.'

'Tilly valley! And it already three of the clock! Tilly valley! What shall I do? I should have been given notice.'

'But, Alice, since you need twenty-four hours' warning of a King's visit, is not three hours enough for a Duke? Commoners call five minutes before a meal, and may have a seat at our table.'

'My Lord Norfolk!' cried Alice, growing red and white at the thought.

'His Grace will honour us, Alice. He made a delightful speech when I took the Seal. He stressed my virtues which, he said, were so great that they made him indifferent to my humble birth.'

Alice bristled, but she was still thinking: His Grace of Norfolk! The first nobleman in the land . . . and here to supper. Next it will be His Grace the King. I know it.

'And, Alice, my dear, do not fret,' said Thomas, 'for such a second-rate compliment is only worthy of a second-rate supper. Let us be natural with this noble Duke. Let us treat him as we would a passer-by who looks in to join us at supper. After all, he will expect no more of us – because we are such humble folk.'

But Alice was not listening. She must to the kitchen at once. She must see that the beef received the necessary basting. Had she known they were to be so honoured she would have got one of the new turkeys. She was going to make her new sauce, adding the chopped roots of the wild succory and water arrow-head. She would set her cook making further pies. And her latest pickle should be set upon the table. She would show my lord of Norfolk!

'Now, Master More, do not hinder me. If you *will* ask great noblemen to supper, then you must give me time to attend to them.'

And she was off, bustling down to the kitchens, sniffing the savoury smells; excited and a little fearful.

'Come, come, you wenches. There's work to be done. My Lord Chancellor has a guest for supper tonight. I'll doubt any of you have ever served a noble Duke before, eh, eh?'

'No, my lady.'

'Well, then, now you will learn to do so, for it would not surprise me if we shall one day have at our table a guest who is far greater than His Grace of Norfolk. Do you know whom I mean? Do you, wench?'

Alice gave one of the girls a slap with a wooden ladle. It was more an affectionate pat than a blow.

Alice allowed herself one minute to dream that at her table sat a great, glittering man who shouted to her that he had never tasted a better meal than that eaten at the table of his Lord Chancellor.

'Tilly valley!' she cried. 'This is not the way to prepare supper for His Grace of Norfolk!'

* * *

The old Judge stood before his son; his hands were trembling and there were tears in his eyes.

'Thomas, my son . . . my dearest son. . . . Thomas, Lord Chancellor of England. So you have the Great Seal, my son. *You* . . . my son, Thomas.'

Thomas embraced his father. 'Your son first, Father; Chancellor second.'

'And to think that I scolded you for not working at the law!'

'Ah, Father, there are many routes to fame.'

'And you found a quick one, my son.'

'I took a byway. I confess I am a little startled still to find where it has led me.'

'Oh, Thomas, would that your mother could have lived to see this day. And my father . . . and my grandfather. They would have been proud . . . proud indeed. Why, your grandfather was only a butler of the Inn; he was, it was true, at the head of the servants and kept the accounts. Would that he could have lived to this day to see his grandson Lord Chancellor of England. Oh, Thomas, my son! Oh, proud and happy day!'

Later Thomas said to Margaret: 'You see, daughter, how there is much good in all things. I am glad to have pleased your grandfather, for he is feeble, and I fear he may not be long for this life. I believe his delight in me is almost as great at this moment as mine has always been in you. And, Margaret, it is a happy child who make a fond father a proud one, think you not?'

'If I were less fond,' she said, 'I think I should find greater enjoyment in my pride.'

He kissed her. 'Do not ask too much of life, my wise daughter; ask for little, and then, if it comes, you will be happy.'

*　　　*　　　*

It seemed to Margaret that the one who was least changed by his elevation was her father.

He was delighted with his importance only when he could use it to do good for others. He had shown to the King the drawings Hans Holbein had made of his family, and the King had been impressed with them; so Master Holbein had, regretfully, left the house at Chelsea to take up his quarters at Court as painter to the King at a salary of thirty pounds a year.

'It is a large sum,' said Hans, 'and I am a poor man. I shall mayhap find fame in Hampton Court and Westminster, but will it give me as much joy as the happiness I have enjoyed in Chelsea?'

'With a brush such as yours, my friend,' said Thomas, 'you have no choice. Go. Serve the King, and I doubt not that your future is secure.'

'I would as lief stay. I wish to do more pictures of your family . . . and your servants.'

'Go and make pictures of the King and *his* servants. Go, Hans; make the best of two worlds. Take up your quarters at the Court, and come to Chelsea for a humble meal with us when you feel the need for it.'

Then Hans Holbein embraced his friend and benefactor, and said with tears in his eyes: 'To think that I should wish to refuse an offer such as this. You have put a magic in your house, dear friend; and I am caught in its spell.'

Yes, those were the things which Thomas greatly enjoyed doing. At such times it was worth while holding a great office.

But he was uneasy – far more uneasy than he would have his family realize.

The King was spending more and more time with Cromwell and Cranmer; they were the two to whom he looked for help in this matter of the divorce, and no other matter seemed of any great importance to him. The Cardinal had slipped down to disgrace and death, and the descent had been more rapid than his spectacular climb to grace and favour. He had first been indicted upon the Statute of *Praemunire*; but Thomas Cromwell had cleared him of the charge of high treason, so that Wolsey had been ordered to retire to York; but before he had long rested there he was charged once more with high treason and had died of a broken heart at Leicester on his way to London.

Thomas Wolsey had come to the Chancellorship with everything in his favour; Thomas More had come to it with everything against him. Wolsey had not realized his peril until within a year or so of his decline and death; More was aware of his from the moment he received the Great Seal.

* * *

William Dauncey came to his father-in-law on one of those rare occasions when Thomas found time to be with his family.

There was a determined light in Dauncey's eyes.

'Well, son Dauncey, you would have speech with me?'

'I have thought much of late, Father,' said Dauncey, 'that things have changed since you became the Chancellor of this realm in place of the Cardinal.'

'In what way?'

'When my lord Cardinal was Chancellor, those about him grew rich, for he shut himself away and it was a matter of some cost for any to put their desires before him. Yet, since you have become Chancellor, any man may come to you. He may state his case and receive judgement.'

'Well, my son, is that not a good thing? Why, when my lord Cardinal held the Great Seal there were many cases which must go unheard because there was no time to put them before him. 'Tis easier for me. My interests are not so many, and I am a lawyer to boot. Do you know that when I took office there were cases which men were waiting to present for ten or twelve years! And now, my son – I grow boastful, but this matter gives me great pleasure, so forgive my pride – I called yesternoon for the next case, and I was told that there were no more cases to be heard. So proud was I that I invented a little rhyme as I sat there. This is it:

> *'When More some time had Chancellor been,*
> *No more suits did remain.*
> *The like will never more be seen*
> *Till More be there again.'*

'Yes, Father,' said Dauncey impatiently, after he had given his polite laugh. 'That is good for those who would wish their cases to be heard; but it is not so good for the friends of the Chancellor.'

'How so, my son?'

'When Thomas Wolsey was Chancellor, not only the members of his privy chamber but even the keepers of his doors took great gain to themselves.'

'Ah,' said Thomas. 'Now I understand. You feel that a daughter of this Chancellor should be at least as profitable as a door in the house of the last.'

'Profit?' said Dauncey. 'But there is no profit. How could I take gifts from those whom I brought to your presence when in bringing them to you I could do no more for them than they could do for themselves?'

'You think I am at fault in making myself accessible to all who desire to see me?'

'It may be a commendable thing,' said Dauncey stubbornly, 'but it is not a profitable thing for a son-in-law. How could I take reward from a man for something which he could get without my help?'

'I admire your scrupulous conscience, my son.' He smiled at Dauncey. Dauncey yearned for advancement. He was not a bad boy; he but obeyed his father, Sir John Dauncey, in his determination to rise. Now Dauncey looked downcast; he did not always understand his father-in-law. Thomas laid a hand on his shoulder. 'If, my son, you have some matter which you wish to place before me, if you have a friend whom you wish to help, well then, you could always put this matter before me. I might hear the cause of a friend of yours before that of another if it could be done. But remember this, son Dauncey – and I assure you this on my faith – that if my father himself stood on one side of me and the Devil on the other, and in this instance the Devil's case was the right one, then must I decide in favour of the Devil. Come, walk with me in the gardens. You too, son Roper. I like to have you with me.'

And he put his arm through Dauncey's, for Dauncey was looking ashamed; and he spoke to him with the utmost kindliness.

It was not Dauncey's fault that he had been brought up on ambition. Moreover, he had softened somewhat since he had come to Chelsea.

*   *   *

Alice was in a flurry of excitement, making preparations for the wedding of Jack to Anne Cresacre. This was to be the peak of her achievements so far; there had been other marriages in the family; ah, yes, but those had been the marriages of Thomas More, later *Sir* Thomas; now the son of the Lord Chancellor was to be married.

Alice was a little disappointed that the King would not be among the guests. She listened to the talk when they did not always think she listened; she heard some of the remarks which had passed between Margaret and her father, and also some of the hints which the Duke of Norfolk – who called at the house quite frequently, to Alice's delight – and she gathered that Thomas, as was to be expected, was not making the most of his opportunities. He was deliberately opposing the King, and all because the King wanted a divorce and Thomas did not think he should have it.

'What the good year!' said Alice to herself. 'This man of mine is a most foolhardy person. He is so careless of his position that he treats it with indifference; and yet, as regards this matter of the King's he is most firm and resolute. 'Tis nothing but stubborn folly, and I am glad that my lord of Norfolk agrees with me.'

Well, the King would not be at the wedding; nevertheless, it was to be a grand affair. She had bought the young couple one of the new portable clocks which were such a novelty, as they were unknown in England this time last year. It was pleasant to be in a position to buy such things.

Such a feast she would prepare! All should marvel at the good table she kept in Chelsea. She had planned this feast again and again, altering an item here and there, until Margaret cried out in dismay that if she were not careful she would find her feast falling short of perfection because she would forget what she had decided for and what against.

She puffed about the kitchen, taking a look at the boar which was being soaked in vinegar and juniper; she went out to the sties to study the fatness of the pigs which would be killed; she went to the cellars to see how the mead and metheglin were maturing. She inspected her pickles, which must be the best she had ever produced.

Hourly she admonished her servants. 'Do not forget. This is no marriage of a mean person. This is the marriage of the son of the Lord Chancellor of England.'

'Yes, my lady. Yes, my lady.'

My lady! she thought blissfully. My *lady*!

Ah, this was the good and pleasant life. Her only fear was that Thomas would do something to spoil it, for indeed Thomas seemed to have no understanding of the great dignity which should be his. It was all very well for him to poke fun at her, to laugh at *her* dignity. She must have her dignity. She did not forget she was the wife of the Lord Chancellor, if he was so foolish as to forget the dignity he owed to his office.

She would have ceremony in her household. He was wrong to welcome into the house every humble traveller who, hearing there was a chance of a good meal at the table of Sir Thomas More, arrived at mealtimes. He was wrong always to wear the same sombre dress. Not a jewel on his person! And when it was remembered how glorious had been the Cardinal, and how the crowds had gathered in the streets of London to see him pass . . . well, puffed Alice, it is enough to make a woman wonder what manner of man she has married. He had no sense of his power, of his dignity.

Recently Giles Heron had occasion to bring a case to the courts against a certain Nicholas Millisante. But would Master More favour his own son-in-law? Indeed, he would not. Master Giles had gone confidently to court. Naturally, the somewhat easy-going Giles had expected his father-in-law to decide in his favour and . . . Thomas had decided against him!

'A fine thing!' Alice had chided. 'So the affairs of your family mean nothing to you? People will say that the Lord Chancellor has no power, since he is afraid to give a verdict in favour of his own son-in-law.'

'What matters that, Alice, if they know that the laws of England are just?'

'Tut, tut,' said Alice to herself. 'Tut, tut' was my lord of Norfolk's favourite expression, and Alice was ready to ape the manners of the great, even if Thomas was not.

Thomas scorned all pomp and show. A week ago, when Norfolk had called unexpectedly on matters of business, Thomas had actually been singing in the choir of Chelsea Church. There he had been, wearing a surplice like an ordinary man; and Alice was not surprised that the sight of him, so undignified, had shocked the Duke.

'God's Body! God's Body!' Norfolk had cried. 'My Lord Chancellor playing parish clerk! Tut-tut, you dishonour the King and his office, Master More.'

Had Thomas been contrite? Not in the least. He had merely smiled that slow maddening smile of his and answered: 'Nay, your Grace, I cannot think that the King would deem the service of God a dishonour to his office.'

And there had been His Grace of Norfolk lost for words, while Thomas smiled and was so sure of himself. Yet the Duke had not been angered by that sharp answer; he had seemed most friendly with Thomas, both during the meal and afterwards in the gardens.

But Alice herself would remember the dignity due to his office, if others did not. And she would have her servants remember also. In Chelsea Church each morning after prayers she had insisted that one of his gentlemen should come to her pew and tell her of the departure of her husband, although she knew the moment when he must leave the church. This gentleman of her husband's must bow before Alice and say: 'Madame, my lord is gone.'

Then she would bow her head and solemnly thank him. It was a ritual which made the others smile. But let them smile, said Alice. Someone must remember the dignity of the house.

Now one of her serving-maids came to her to tell her that there was a poor woman at the door who would have speech with her.

'There are always poor women at the door!' she cried. 'They come here begging from this house, because they know the master's orders that none should be turned away without a hearing. It seems to me that beggars are given more honours here than are noble dukes.'

But this poor woman had not come to beg, she assured Lady More. She had a pretty dog, and as she had heard of Lady More's fondness for these animals she had brought it along in the hope of selling it to her ladyship.

Alice was immediately attracted by the engaging little creature. She gave the woman a coin and welcomed yet another pet into the house.

*   *   *

It was only a week or so after the wedding when the absurd controversy about the dog arose.

Alice was annoyed. A beggar-woman, roaming near the house, saw the dog being carried by one of the servants and immediately declared that it had been stolen from her.

The servant retorted that this was nonsense. My lady had bought the dog. If the old beggar-woman did not go away at once she would be tied to a tree and whipped.

Alice was indignant. To dare to say I stole the dog! I! Does she not know who I am? The wife of none other than the Lord Chancellor!

But the beggar-woman would not go away. She loitered on the river bank, and one day when she saw the Lord Chancellor himself alight from his barge she accosted him.

'My lord! Justice!' she cried. 'Justice for a poor woman who is the victim of a thief.'

Thomas paused.

'Mistress,' he said with that grave courtesy which altered not whether he addressed a duchess or a beggar, 'what theft is this you wish to report?'

'The theft of a little dog, your honour. I wish to regain what I have lost.'

'If you are speaking the truth, and the animal has been stolen from you, then must it be restored to you. Who now has possession of your property?'

'Lady More, your honour.'

'And is that so? Well then, come to my hall tomorrow morning when I try the cases, and we shall hear yours against Lady More.'

He went smiling to the house and there spoke to Alice.

'Alice, you are summoned to the courts tomorrow morning.'

'What foolish joke is this?'

'No joke. 'Tis true. You are accused of theft, wife and must needs come to answer the charge.'

'*I* . . . accused of theft!'

'Of a dog.'

'So it is that beggar!'

'She says you have her dog.'

'And I say I have *my* dog.'

'In a court of law, Alice, it is not enough to say an article is yours if another claims it. It must be proved.'

'You cannot mean that you would ask me to go to the courts on a matter like this!'

'I do, Alice.'

She laughed in his face; but he meant it, she realized to her astonishment. She thought it was a most unseemly thing that the Lord Chancellor should summon his own wife to appear before him, and on the word of a beggar too! They would be the laughing-stock of all, she doubted not.

She dressed herself with great care and set out with the dog as Thomas had bidden her. She would show dignity if he did not. She would show the world that if Thomas was unfit for the office of Chancellor, she was not unfit for the position of Chancellor's wife.

And in the hall, there was my Lord Chancellor with his officers about him.

'The next case which we must try this day,' he said, 'concerns the possession of a small animal. Let us have a fair hearing of this matter. This lady declares the dog was stolen from her and therefore belongs to her; this lady declares she bought him and therefore he belongs to her. Now let us place the little dog on the table here. Lady More, stand you back at that end of the hall; and, mistress, you stand at the other. You will both call the dog, and we will see whom *he* considers to be mistress; for, I verily believe this is a matter which the dog must decide.'

Imperiously Alice called the dog to her, and lovingly the beggar-woman called him; and he, the little rogue, did not hesitate; he did what he had been wanting to do ever since he had seen her; he ran, barking excitedly, to the beggar-woman.

'There can be no doubt,' said Thomas, 'that the dog has once been the property of this lady, and her story that he was stolen from her is doubtless a true one.'

The beggar-woman held the dog tightly against her, and Alice, seeing this, knew herself defeated. She knew too that Thomas had been right in this matter, although she deplored his undignified manners.

The beggar-woman said to her: 'Lady, he has fattened since he was in your care. You can offer him a better home than I can. Take him . . care for him as you have done. I see it would be for the best that he should be yours.'

Alice was touched, as she always was by animals and those who loved them.

She saw that the old woman really loved her dog and that it was no small sacrifice to give him up.

Alice hesitated. She said: 'The judgement of this court went against me. The dog is yours. But if you would like to sell him, I am ready to buy him of you.'

And so the matter was settled amicably and to the satisfaction of all; but Alice could not help pondering on the strange ways of her husband.

* * *

The great day came, as Alice had known it would.

The King was to dine at Chelsea.

All that activity which she had set in train for the entertainment of a noble duke was intensified.

Alice could scarcely sleep at night; and when she did she dreamed of serving at her table beef that was almost burned to a cinder. She dreamed of seeing black piecrust on her table. She called out in the agony of her nightmare.

She could not stop talking of the great event. 'Do you wenches realize that it is tomorrow that the King comes! Hurry, hurry, I say. We shall never be done in time.' Then she would smile and think of His Grace sitting at *her* table, smiling at her. 'His Grace the King, so I have heard, likes to see the blood flow rich and red from his beef. We must make sure that there is not one turn too many of the spit. I hear he has a fancy for his pastry to be well baked . . .'

Never had the servants lived through such days. Preparations were started four days ahead, and Alice could speak of nothing else during that time. All the girls were pressed into service. Ailie must come and stay, and tell all she knew of Court manners and Court etiquette. 'For,' said Alice, 'your father is a dullard in such things. It is beyond my understanding why they have called him a wise man.'

So again and again Ailie told of the King's habits and how food was laid at a Court banquet; and Alice wept because she had not gold platters to set before the King.

And at length the great day came.

She was at her window when the royal barge sailed along the river.

'The King!' she murmured, touching her coif nervously to

make sure that it was exactly as it should be. 'The King is coming to dine at my table!'

She saw him alight. Who could mistake him, surrounded though he was by dazzling courtiers?

The jewels on his clothes caught the rays of the sun. What royalty! What magnificence!

Alice marshalled the family together They stood, as Ailie had said they should, in the hall, waiting to receive him. Thomas watched them all, and he was smiling as though he found this convention somewhat amusing. Amusing! Alice was beside herself with anxiety. Would the beef be done to a turn? How were they faring in the kitchen? She should be there . . . yet she must be here.

And now she heard the great booming voice. 'Why, this is a pleasant place you have here at Chelsea, Master More. We have heard much of it. Norfolk has sung its praises when he has sung yours.'

And now the King was stepping into the hall.

Alice went forward and sank to her knees. All the rich colour had left her face; she was trembling.

'Why, Lady More,' said the King. 'Rise . . . rise . . . good lady. We have heard much of your excellence. We have come to see for ourselves what it is that calls our Chancellor so frequently from our Court.'

Alice had risen uncertainly. 'Your Grace,' she stammered. 'Your . . . most . . . gracious . . . Grace. . . .'

The King laughed; he liked her. He liked reverence. It was good to see how his subjects stood in awe of him. He placed his great hands on her shoulders and kissed her heartily.

'There . . . there . . . We are as glad to come as you are to have us. Now we would see this family of yours.'

One by one they came forward. The King's eyes smouldered as they rested on Jack. A fine healthy boy! He felt angry when he saw the fine healthy boys of other men. Now the girls. He softened. He was fond of young girls. Lady Allington was a fair creature, but all women other than Anne were insignificant to him now; when he compared them with the incomparable they could interest him but little. He gave Lady Allington a kiss for her beauty; and he kissed the others too. Thomas's girls were hardly beauties . . . but pleasant creatures.

Afterwards he sat at the table with the family about him; his courtiers who had accompanied him ranged among the family.

It was an appetizing meal. The food was simple, but well cooked; he complimented the lady of the house and it did him good to see the pleasure he gave her in so doing.

The conversation was interesting – he could rely on More to make it so; and naturally that matter which was becoming more and more a cause of disagreement between them was not mentioned in such company.

More was at his best at his own table – gay and witty, anxious to show the cleverness of his children, particularly the eldest girl. The King liked wit and laughter, and, in spite of the man's folly at times, he liked Thomas More.

It pleased Henry to see himself as the mighty King, accustomed to dining in banqueting halls, the guest of kings and princes, yet not above enjoying a simple meal at the humble table of a good subject.

After the meal he asked Thomas to show him the gardens. Taking it that this meant he wished to talk with his Chancellor alone, the courtiers stayed in the house discoursing with the family.

Alice was beside herself with pride.

This was the happiest day of her life. She would talk of it until the end of her days.

Now she must slip away from the company – she could safely leave the entertaining of her guests to her daughters for a short while – and go to the top of the house, whence she could command a view of the gardens; and there, walking together, were the King and his Chancellor. Alice could have wept for joy. About the Chancellor's neck, in a most affectionate manner, was the arm of the King.

The wonderful visit was nearing its end. With what pride did Alice walk down to the royal barge, receive his words of congratulation and make her deep respectful curtsy!

'I shall remember Your Majesty's commendation of my table to my dying day,' she said.

The King was not to be outdone. 'Ah, Lady More, I shall remember my visit to your house to the end of my life.'

Alice was nearly swooning with delight; and, oddly enough, the others were almost as delighted. They stood in respectful attention while the royal barge slipped along the river.

Alice cried: 'To think I should live to see this day! If I were to die now . . . I should die happy.'

'I rejoice in your contentment, Alice,' Thomas told her.

She turned to her family. 'Did you see them . . . in the gardens together? The King had his arm . . . his *arm* . . . about your father's neck.'

'Then he loves Father well,' said Will. 'For I believe that to be a mark of his highest favour. I have never heard of his doing that with any other than my lord Cardinal.'

Thomas smiled at their excitement; but suddenly his face was grave.

He said slowly: 'I thank our Lord, son Roper, that I find the King my very good lord indeed; and you are right when you say that he favours me as much as any subject in this realm. But I must tell you this: I have little cause to be proud of this, for if my head would bring him a castle in France, it should not fail to go. That, my dear ones, is a sobering thought.'

And the family was immediately sobered – except Alice, who would not allow her happiest day to be spoilt by such foolish talk.

* * *

Death touched the house in Chelsea during the early months of the year 1532.

The winter had been a hard one, and Judge More had suffered through this. He had caught cold, and all Mercy's ministrations could not save him. He grew weaker; and one day he did not know those about his bedside.

He passed peacefully away in the early morning.

There was much sorrow, for it seemed that no one could be spared from this home.

Thomas declared that he was sorry he had given the house in Bucklersbury to his son and daughter Clement, for it meant that he saw much less of them than if they had continued to live in Chelsea. There had been regrets when Hans Holbein had left the house and Mr Gunnel had taken Holy Orders. It was a large household, as Thomas said, but none could be spared from it.

They mourned the old man for many weeks, and one day, in April of that year, when Margaret and her father were walking together in the gardens, he said to her: 'Meg, we should have done with grieving, for I believe that your grandfather was a happy man when he died; yet had he lived a few months longer he might have been less happy.'

'What do you mean, Father?'

'Like Mother, he took great pride in my position; and it is a position which I may not always hold.'

'You mean that you are shortly to be dismissed?'

'No, Meg. I do not think that. But I think that I might resign. Oh, Meg, I am happier about this matter than I have been since that day, nearly three years ago, when I was given the Great Seal. Then I saw no way in which I could refuse; now I believe I can resign.'

'The King would let you go?'

'Events have been moving, Meg, though sluggishly, it may seem, to those outside the Court. It is now four years since the King made his wishes for a divorce known to us, and still there is no divorce. That is a long time for a King to wait for what he wants. He grows impatient, and so does the Lady Anne. When I was given the Great Seal, you will remember, the Cardinal, who had managed the affairs of this country for so long, was falling out of favour and there seemed no one else capable of taking his place. So was I pressed into taking office. But now matters have changed. The King has at his elbow two clever men, from whom he hopes much. He loves them dearly because they work for him . . . solely. They have no mind but the King's mind, no conscience but the King's conscience, no other will than his. They have two brilliant suggestions which they have put before the King, and the King likes those suggestions so much that I believe he will follow both of them. Cromwell suggests that the King should break with Rome and declare himself Supreme Head of the Church of England; in which case he would have no difficulty in gaining the divorce he wants. That is Master Cromwell's suggestion. Cranmer's is equally ingenious. He declares that, since the marriage of the King and Queen was no true marriage, there is no need for divorce. The marriage could be declared null and void by the courts of England. You see, Margaret, these two men have, as the King says, "the right sow by the ear." I, His Grace would tell you, have the wrong sow's ear in my grasp.'

'Father, as Chancellor, you would have to agree with these two men?'

'Yes; that is why I believe nothing will be put in the way of my resigning from the Chancellorship. There is a very able man, a great friend of the King's, and one who he knows would willingly work for him. That is Lord Audley. I doubt not that the King would be willing enough that I should hand the Great Seal over to him.'

'Father, that means that you would be home with us . . . you would go back to the law . . . and we should be as we were in Bucklersbury.'

'Nay, Meg. I should still be a member of the Council, and a lawyer cannot leave his practice for years and take up the thread where he dropped it. Moreover, I am not as young as I was in those days.'

'Father, I know. I have watched you with great anxiety. We will nurse you, Mercy and I. Oh, I beg of you, give up the Great Seal. Come home to us as soon as you can.'

'You must no longer be anxious for me, dearest Meg, for this poor health of mine gives me the reason I shall need, and which the King will like, for giving up the Chancellorship.'

'I long for that day.'

'And poverty, Meg? Do you long for that? We shall be poor, you know.'

'I would welcome it. But it will surely not be our lot. Will is well placed in his profession.'

'This is a big house and we are a large household. Meg, in spite of our big family and the positions they have secured for themselves, we shall be poor.'

'We shall have you home, Father, and out of harm . . . safe. That is all I ask.'

'So, Meg, I will continue my little homily. Do not grieve because my health is not as good as it was, since because of it I shall come home to you. And do not grieve for your grandfather; he died the father of the Lord Chancellor; and had he lived he might have died the father of a much humbler man.'

She took his hand and kissed it.

'I shall remember life's compensations, Father. Never fear. And how deeply shall I rejoice when you leave the Court, for that has been my dearest wish for many a long day.'

'Dear Meg, I may not be blessed with good health and the King's favour – but I'd throw all that away for the blessing of owning the dearest daughter in the world.'

*　　　*　　　*

Margaret was waiting. She knew that it must happen soon. The King had now declared himself to be Supreme Head of the Church. Her father was detained at Court, and she heard that Bishop Fisher had become ill with anxiety.

They were at church one morning – a lovely May morning when the birds sang with excitement and the scent of hawthorn blossom filled the air.

Morning prayers were over, and suddenly Margaret saw her father. He was standing by the door of that pew in which the ladies of the family sat. Margaret took one look at him and knew.

He was smiling at Alice, who had risen to her feet and, in some consternation, was wondering what he was doing there at that hour. He bowed low to her as his gentleman was wont to do, and he said : 'Madam, my lord is gone.'

Alice did not understand.

'What joke is this now?' she demanded.

He did not answer then, and they walked out of the church into the scented air of spring.

Margaret was beside him; she slipped her arm through his.

'What nonsense is this?' demanded Alice as soon as they had stepped out of the porch. 'What do you mean by "My lord is gone"?'

'Just that, Alice. My Lord Chancellor is gone; and all that is left to you is Sir Thomas More.'

'But . . . I do not understand.'

''Tis a simple matter. I have resigned the Great Seal and am no longer Chancellor.'

'You have . . . what?'

'There was naught else I could do. The King needs a Chancellor who will serve him better than I can.'

'You mean that you have resigned? You really mean that you have given up . . . your office?'

Alice could say no more. She could not bear this sunny May morning. All her glory had vanished.

Her lord had gone in very truth.

SEVEN

THEY GATHERED about him that night – all those whom he called his dear children. Mercy and John Clement came from Bucklersbury, for the news had reached them. Ailie had heard, and she also came to the house in Chelsea that she might be with him at the time of his resignation.

'My children,' he said when they were all gathered together, 'there is a matter which I must bring to your notice. We have built for ourselves a fine house here in Chelsea; we have many servants to wait upon us; we have never been rich, as are some noble dukes of our acquaintance. . . .' He smiled at Alice. 'But . . . we have lived comfortably. Now I have lost my office and all that went with it; and you know that, even in office, I was never so rich as my predecessor.'

He smiled now at Dauncey – Dauncey who had hinted that he did not take all the advantages that might have been his. But Dauncey was looking downcast; his father-in-law was no longer Chancellor, and Dauncey's hopes of advancement had not carried him very far. He had a seat in Parliament, representing, with Giles Heron, Thetford in Norfolk; Giles Allington sat for the County of Cambridge, and William Roper for Bramber in Sussex. This they had achieved through their relationship with the Chancellor; but all that seemed very little when compared with the favours which had been showered on Wolsey's relations. Moreover, wondered Dauncey, did these people realize that a man could not merely step from high favour to obscurity, that very likely he would pass from favour into disfavour?

Dauncey and Alice were the most disappointed members of the household; yet, like Alice's, Dauncey's disappointment was over-shadowed by fear.

Thomas went on: 'My dear ones, we are no longer rich. Indeed, we are very poor.'

Margaret said quickly: 'Well, Father, we shall have the comfort of your presence, which will mean more to us than those other comforts to which you refer.'

Ailie said: 'Father, Giles and I will look after you.'

'Bless you, my dear daughter. But could you ask your husband to take my big household under his wing? Nay, there will be change here.'

'We have always heard that you are such a clever man,' Alice pointed out. 'Are you not a lawyer, and have not lawyers that which is called a practice?'

'Yes, Alice, they have. But a lawyer who has abandoned his practice for eleven years cannot take it up where he left it. And if he is eleven years older and no longer a promising young man, but an old one who has found it necessary to resign his office, he is not so liable to find clients.'

'What nonsense!' said Alice. 'You have a great reputation, so I have always heard. You . . . Sir Thomas More . . . but yesterday Lord Chancellor!'

'Have no fear, Alice. I doubt not that we shall come through these troubles. I have been brought up at Oxford, at an Inn of Chancery, at Lincoln's Inn, also in the King's Court; and so from the lowest degree I came to the highest; yet have I in yearly revenues at this present time little above one hundred pounds. So we must hereafter, if we wish to live together, be contented to become contributaries together. But, by my counsel, it shall not be best for us to fall to the lowest fare first. We will not therefore descend to Oxford fare, nor to the fare of New Inn, but we will begin with Lincoln's Inn diet, which we can maintain during the first year. We will the next year go one step down to New Inn fare, wherewith many an honest man is contented. If that exceed our ability too, then we will the next year after descend to Oxford fare; and if we cannot maintain that, we may yet with bags and wallets go a-begging together, hoping that for pity some good folks will give us their charity.'

'Enough of your jokes!' cried Alice. 'You have thrown away your high post, and we are not as rich as we were. That is what you mean, is it not, Master More?'

'Yes, Alice. That is what I mean.'

'Then more's the pity of it. No; don't go making one of your foolish jokes about More's pity ... or such kind. I have no pity for you. You're a fool, Master More, and it was by great good luck, and nothing more than that, that you took the King's fancy.'

'Or great mischance, Alice.'

'Great good luck,' she repeated firmly. 'And His Grace is a kindly man. Did I not see him with mine own eyes? It may be that he will not accept your resignation. I am sure he likes you. Did he not walk in the garden with his arm about your neck? Ah ... he will be here to sup with us again, I doubt not.'

They let her dream. What harm was there in dreaming? But the others knew that the King had no further use for him; and those who knew the King's methods best prayed that the King might feel nothing but indifference towards his ex-minister.

They brought out their lutes, and Cecily played on the virginals. They were the happy family circle. There was not one of them during that evening – not even Alice nor Dauncey – who did not feel that he or she would be content if they could all remain as they were this night until the end of their days.

But they knew that this was not possible.

Even the servants knew it, for the news had reached them.

How could the household go on in the same comfortable way? Some of them would have to go; and although they knew that Sir Thomas More would never turn them away, that he would find new places for them – perhaps in the rich households of those whom he had known in his affluent days – that brought little comfort. There was no one who, having lived in the Chelsea household, would ever be completely happy outside it.

*　　　*　　　*

A year passed.

They were very poor during that year; the house at Chelsea was indeed a large one and there were many living in it to be fed. Yet they were happy. The hospital continued to provide succour for the sick; there was little to spare in the house, but it was always shared with those who were in need. There was always a place at the table for a hungry traveller, and if the fare was simpler than before, it appeased the hunger. Alice took an even greater pride in her cookery; she discovered new ways of using the herbs which grew wild in the fields. They collected fern, bracken, sticks and logs, which they burned in the great fireplaces; and they would gather round one fire to warm themselves before retiring to their cold bedrooms.

Still, it was a happy year. They would not have complained if they could have gone on as they were.

Alice grew angry when the abbots and bishops collected a large sum of money which they wished to present to Thomas. He had written much, they said; the Church was grateful; and they deemed that the best way in which they could show their gratitude was by presenting him with the money. Thomas, however, would not accept it. 'What I have done,' he said, 'was not for gain.'

So Alice scolded him for what she called his misplaced pride, and they continued to live in simplicity.

Patenson the Fool had left them in tears to work with the Lord Mayor of London; and Thomas, knowing that poor Patenson was a very poor Fool indeed, whose idea of wit seemed to be to laugh at the physical appearances of others, arranged that he should be passed from one Lord Mayor to the next Lord Mayor so that he might not suffer through the decline in fortune of one of his masters.

There were some members of the household who were lulled into a feeling of peace, who believed that life would go on humbly and evenly in the years to come. They did not realize that Thomas More had played too big a part in the affairs of the country to be allowed to remain outside them.

So gradually had matters been changing at Court that they were almost unnoticed by those outside it. The King had declared himself to be the Supreme Head of the Church of England. His marriage with Queen Katharine was declared null and void. He had been forced to this procedure by the pregnancy of Anne Boleyn. He was determined that if she gave him a son it should not be born out of wedlock; and he would wait no longer.

Margaret knew that the shadows were moving nearer.

One day a barge pulled up at the stairs, and in it came a messenger.

Margaret saw him as she was playing with her babies, Will and Mary, on the lawns. Her heart leaped, and then she felt the blood thundering in her head. Her children were looking at her wonderingly; she took their hands and forced herself to walk calmly towards the approaching messenger.

To her great relief, she saw that he was not wearing the King's livery.

He bowed low on seeing Margaret.

'Madame, this is the house of Sir Thomas More?'

'It is. What would you of him?'

'I have a letter here. I am instructed to hand it to no other.'

'Whence do you come?'

'From my lords the Bishops of Durham, Bath and Winchester.'

She was relieved.

'Please come this way,' she said, 'and I will take you to Sir Thomas.'

He was in the library, where he now spent the greater part of his time. He could be happy, she thought, then; he could remain in perfect contentment as he is now. Our poverty matters not at all. He can write, pray and laugh with his family. He asks no more than that. 'O God,' she prayed silently, as she led the messenger to her father, 'let him stay as he is. . . . Let him always be as he is now.'

'Meg!' he cried when he saw her.

The little ones ran to him; they loved him; they would sit on his knee and ask him to read to them; he would read them Latin and Greek, and although they could not understand him, they took great pleasure in watching the movement of his lips and listening to the sound of his voice.

Now they caught his skirts and laughed up at him.

'Grandfather . . . here is a man for you.'

'Father,' said Margaret, 'a message from the Bishops.'

'Ah,' said Thomas. 'Welcome, my friend. You have a letter for me. Let little Will take our friend to the kitchens and ask

245

that he may be given something of what they have there, that he may refresh himself. Could you do that, my little man?'

'Yes, Grandfather,' cried Will. 'Indeed I can.'

'Then off with you.'

'Take Mary with you,' said Margaret.

The two children went off with the messenger, and as soon as they were alone Margaret turned to her father. 'Father, what is it?'

'Meg, you tremble.'

'Tell me, Father. Open your letter. Let us know the worst.'

'Or the best. Meg, you are nervous nowadays. What is it, daughter? What should you have to fear?'

'Father, I am not as the others to be lightly teased out of my anxieties. I know . . . as you know . . .'

He put his arm about her. 'We know, Meg, do we not? And because we know, we do not grieve. We are all death's creatures. I . . . you . . . even little Will and Mary. Only this uncertain air, with a bit of breath, keeps us alive. Meg, be not afraid.'

'Father, I beg of you, open the letter.'

He opened it and read it. 'It is a letter from the Bishops, Margaret; they wish me to keep them company from the Tower to the Coronation. They send me twenty pounds with which to buy myself a gown.'

'Father, this is the beginning.'

He sought to comfort her. 'Who knows, Meg? How can any of us know? At this magnificent Coronation, who will notice the absence of one poor and humble man?'

Then she knew that he would refuse to go to the Coronation; and while she longed that he should accept the invitation of the Bishops and bow to the will of the King, she knew that he would never falter in his way along the path which he had chosen.

*　　*　　*

There had never been such pageantry as that which was to celebrate the crowning of Queen Anne Boleyn.

In the gardens at Chelsea could be heard the sounds of distant triumphant music, for the river had been chosen as the setting for the great ceremony in which the King would honour the woman for whom he had so patiently waited, and for whose sake he had severed his Church from that of his father.

Many of the servants from Chelsea had gone forth to mingle with the crowds and enjoy the festivities of that day, to drink the wine that flowed from the conduits, to see the new Queen in all her beauty and magnificence.

Margaret had not wished to mingle with those crowds.

On that lovely May day she sat in the gardens at home. Her father, she knew, was in his private chapel, praying, she guessed, that when his testing time came he would have the strength to meet it nobly.

May was such a beautiful time of the year; and it seemed to Margaret that never had the gardens at Chelsea seemed to offer such peaceful charm. Those gardens were beginning to mature; the flower borders were full of colour; there was blossom on the trees, and the river sparkled in the sunshine. From far away came the sounds of revelry. She would not listen to them. They were distant; she must not think of them as the rumbling of the coming storm. The buzzing of bees in the garden was near; the scent of the flowers, the smell of fresh earth – they were the home smells. Sitting there in the heat of the sun, she reminded herself that she was in her home, far from the tumult, at peace in her backwater.

Why should the King care what her father did? she soothed herself. He was of no importance now. Who would notice that Sir Thomas More was not present at the Coronation?

She recalled that meeting of his with the Bishops, whom he had seen after he had received their letter.

'My lords,' he had said in his merry way, 'in the letters which you lately sent me you required two things of me.' He was referring to the money they had asked him to accept and the invitation which they had asked him to accept also. 'The one,' he went on, 'since I was so well content to grant you, the other therefore I might be the bolder to deny you.'

They had protested that he was unwise to absent himself from the Coronation. What was done, was done, they pointed out. By staying away from the ceremony, they could not undo the marriage of the King with Anne Boleyn and set Queen Katharine on the throne.

Then he had spoken in a parable. He had told them the story of an Emperor who had ordained that death should be the punishment for a certain offence except in the case of virgins, for greatly did this Emperor reverence virginity. Now, it happened that the first to commit this offence was a virgin; and the Emperor was therefore perplexed as to how he could inflict this punishment, since he had sworn never to put a virgin to death. One of his counsellors rose and said: 'Why make such an ado about such a small matter? Let the girl first be deflowered, and then she may be devoured.'

'And so,' added Thomas, 'though your lordships have in the matter of the matrimony hitherto kept yourselves pure virgins, take good heed that you keep your virginity still. For some there may be that by procuring your lordships first at the Coronation to be present, and next to preach for the setting forth of it and finally to write books to all the world in its defence, therefore are desirous to deflower you; and when they have deflowered you they will not fail soon after to devour you. Now, my lords, it lieth not in my power that they may devour me, but God being my good Lord, I will so provide that they shall never deflower me.'

These words would be noted by many who had heard them. And what would the King say to their utterance? And what would he do?

These were the questions Margaret asked herself as she sat in the sunshine.

We can be so happy here, she thought. And he is no longer Lord Chancellor. He is of no great importance now.

But, of course, he would always be of importance while men listened to his words and he had the power to turn their opinions.

From the river came the sounds of rejoicing. In vain did Margaret try to shut out these sounds.

*   *   *

Was she really surprised when the persecutions began?

The first came at the end of the year after the King's Council had published the nine articles which justified all he had done in ridding himself of one Queen and providing himself with another.

Thomas was accused of having written an answer to the nine articles and sent it abroad to be published. Thomas had written no such answer. He was still a member of the King's Council, and as such would consider that his membership debarred him from discussing the King's affairs except in Council.

Nothing could be proved against him and the matter was dropped; but to his family it was an indication of how the winds were beginning to blow.

The King was angry with Thomas, as he was with all those who did not agree with him or who made him question the rightness of his actions.

A few peaceful months passed, but every time Margaret heard strange voices near the house she would feel beads of sweat on her brow, and she would place her hand over her heart in a vain attempt to quell its wild leaping.

Another charge was brought against him. This time he was accused of accepting bribes.

Here, thought those who had been set to bring about his downfall, was a safe charge to bring against him, for surely any man in his position must at some time have accepted a gift which could be called a bribe. It was possible to produce people who had presented him with gifts during his term of office, but it could not be proved that any of these had been bribes, or that the donors had gained aught from such gifts. Instead, it was shown how his son-in-law Heron had lost a case which he had brought, and that even the rather comic case, in which his wife had been involved, had gone against her. No, there was no way of convicting him on the score of bribery.

The King was irritated beyond measure by the folly of the man. He knew well that there were many in his kingdom who thought highly of Sir Thomas More and who might change their opinions regarding the King's recent actions if only such a highly respected man as Sir Thomas More could be made to come to heel.

Friar Peto, of the Observants of Greenwich, had actually dared preach a sermon against the King, declaring from the pulpit that if he behaved as Ahab, the same fate would overtake him. This was prophecy, and Henry was afraid of prophets unless he could prove them false – and only the King's death could prove Peto false.

The Carthusians, with whom More had a special connexion, were preaching against the marriage.

Fisher, Bishop of Rochester, was another who dared to take his stand against the King.

'By God's Body,' said Henry, 'I do verily believe that if this man More would state in his clever way that he is with me in all I do, he could have these others following him.'

But More would do no such thing; he was an obstinate fool.

If he could be proved false . . . ah, if only he could be proved false!

The King himself wanted to have nothing to do with More's downfall. He wished to turn his back, as he had in the case of Wolsey; he wished to leave More to his enemies. This was not so easy as it had been in the case of Wolsey, for More had few enemies. He was no Cardinal Wolsey. Men loved More; they did not wish him harm. Audley, Cranmer – even Cromwell – became uneasy over the matter of More's downfall.

That was why, when More was accused of taking bribes, with his clever lawyer's words and his proof of this and that, with his knowledge of the law, he was able to rebut the charges.

It was even so with regard to the matter of the lewd nun of Canterbury.

Elizabeth Barton, a mere serving-girl, who had been cured of a terrible sickness by, some said, a miracle, became a nun in the town of Canterbury. She had made certain prophecies during trances, and when Thomas was Chancellor, the King had sent him to examine the woman. Thomas had been impressed by her holiness and, with Fisher, inclined to believe that she was not without the gift of prophecy. Elizabeth Barton had declared that if the King married Anne Boleyn he would, within six months, cease to be King of England. Six months had passed since the marriage, and here was Henry still in firm possession of the throne.

Elizabeth Barton was a fraud; she was a traitor and she should suffer the death penalty.

The King was pleased, for those who had believed the nun's evil utterances were guilty of misprision of treason.

What of my lord Bishop of Rochester? the King asked the devoted Cromwell. What of our clever Sir Thomas More?

Here again he was defeated, for Thomas the lawyer was not easily trapped. He could prove that, as a member of the King's Council, he had always refused to listen to any prophecy concerning the King's affairs.

That was an anxious time for Thomas's family. Now they felt fresh relief. Nothing could be proved against him in this affair of the nun of Canterbury and once more, after an examination, Thomas returned to his family.

It was small wonder that they would sometimes catch a look of alarm in one another's eyes, that sometimes one of them would appear to be alert, listening, then that fearful disquiet would settle on the house again.

* * *

The King was fretful.

His marriage was not all that he had believed it would be. He had a child – but a daughter. He was fond of young Elizabeth, but she was not a son; and it was sons he wished his Anne to give to him.

Moreover, Anne the wife was less attractive than Anne the mistress had been.

The King was beginning to feel great need to justify his behaviour. He wanted all the world – and certainly all his own countrymen – to see him as the righteous man who had rid himself of an ageing wife and married an attractive one, not for his own carnal desires, but for the good of the country.

He was very angry with Thomas More, who, while he had

done nothing against the King which the law could condemn, yet refused to express his approval of the King's actions. When the list of those who had been guiltily involved in the case of the nun of Canterbury was brought before Henry, he refused to allow Thomas's name to be removed.

But he could do no more about that matter at the moment.

He would pace up and down his apartments with some of his intimates about him.

'It grieves me,' he cried. 'It grieves me mightily. I have honoured that man. What was he before I took him up? A miserable lawyer. I made him great. And what is his answer? What does he offer me? Base ingratitude! A word from him, and there could be peace among these monks. Even Fisher himself could doubtless be persuaded by his old friend. Yet . . . Thomas More will not accept me as Head of the Church! By God's Body, this is treason! He holds that the Pope is still Head of the Church! That's treason, is it not? Was there ever a servant to his sovereign more treacherous, more villainous, or subject to his prince so traitorous as he? What have I given him? Riches. Power. Favour. And what does he give me? Disobedience! I ask nothing but that he does what others of my servants have done. He has but to acknowledge my supremacy in the Church. Audley . . . Cromwell . . . Norfolk, my friends . . . was ever King so plagued?'

He was asking them to rid him of this man.

The little eyes were hot and angry, but the mouth was prim. All over the continent of Europe, Sir Thomas More was respected. The King's conscience must not be offended.

'Bring this man to obedience.' That was what the little eyes pleaded with those about him. 'No matter how . . . no matter how you do it.'

*   *   *

Norfolk took barge to Chelsea.

Margaret, on the alert as she ever was, saw the Duke coming, and ran down to meet him.

'My lord . . fresh news?'

'Nay, nay. 'Tis naught. Where is your father? I would speak with him at once.'

'I'll take you to him.'

Thomas had seen the Duke's arrival and had come down to greet him.

'It is rarely that we have had this honour of late,' he said.

'I would speak with you alone,' said the Duke; and Margaret left them together.

'Well, my lord?' asked Thomas.

'Master More, you are a foolish man.'

'Have you come from the Court to tell me that?'

'I have. I have come straight from the King.'

'And how did you leave him?'

'Angry against you.'

'I regret that. I regret it deeply.'

'Tut, tut, what is the use of such words? You could turn his anger into friendship if you wished it.'

'How so?'

'Tut, I say again; and tut, tut, tut. You know full well. You have but to agree to the succession of the heirs of Anne Boleyn and the Act of Supremacy. And, Master More, when you should be called upon to sign these Acts, you must cast aside your folly and do so.'

'I would accept the former, because it is the law of this land that the King and the Council may fix the succession. Even though that would mean setting aside a lawful heir for the sake of a bastard, the King and Council can, in law, do it. But I would never take the Oath of Supremacy.'

Norfolk tut-tutted impatiently. 'I come as a friend, Master More. I come from the Court to warn you. The King will not brook your disobedience. He seeks to entrap you.'

'Several charges have been brought against me, but I have answered them all.'

'By the Mass, Master More, it is perilous striving with princes. Therefore I would wish you somewhat to incline to the King's pleasure, for, by God's Body, Master More, *Indignatio principis mors est.*'

'Indeed, indeed,' said Thomas with a smile. 'The indignation of this Prince is turned against Thomas More.'

'I intend no pun,' said Norfolk impatiently. 'I ask you to remember it, that is all.'

'Is that all, my lord?' said Thomas. 'Then I thank you for coming here this day, and I must say this: In good faith, the difference between your Grace and me is but this: that I shall die today and you tomorrow.'

The Duke was so exasperated that he took his leave at once and strode angrily down to the barge without coming into the house.

This annoyed Alice, for she had seen his arrival and hastened to change her dress and put on her most becoming coif; and lo and behold, when she went down to receive her noble guest, it was but to see his abrupt departure.

*   *   *

Gloom hung over the house.

Mercy had called, anxious and pale.

'How go matters, Meg?' she asked.

'Mercy, come out to the gardens where we can be alone. I cannot talk to you here, lest Mother overhears.'

In the quiet of the gardens, Margaret said: 'He has gone before another committee.'

'Oh, God in Heaven, what is it this time?'

'I know not.'

'His name is still on the Parliament's list of those guilty with Elizabeth Barton.'

'Oh, Mercy, that's the pity of it. He has confuted them with his arguments, but it matters not. They still accuse him. Why do they do this, Mercy? I know . . . and so do you. They are *determined* to accuse him. He is innocent . . . innocent . . . but they will not have it so.'

'They cannot prove him guilty, Margaret. He will always triumph.'

'You seek to comfort us, Mercy. Often I think of the happy times . . . when we were cutting the hay, or walking in the gardens, sitting together . . . singing, sewing . . . reading what we had written. Oh, Mercy, how far away those days seem now, for we can never sit in ease or comfort. Always we must listen . . . always be on the alert. A barge comes. Will it stop at our stairs? we ask ourselves. There is a sound of a horse on the road. Is it a messenger from the King . . . from the new Councillor, Cromwell?'

'Meg, you distress yourself.'

But Margaret went on: 'He used to say when he was particularly happy: "I shall remember this moment when I die. I shall remember it and say that my life was worth while . . ."' Margaret broke down and covered her face with her hands.

Mercy said nothing; she clasped her hands together and felt she would die of the deep distress within her.

She thought: We are realists, I and Margaret. We cannot shut our eyes to the facts as the others can. Bess, Cecily, Jack, they love him . . . but differently. They love him as a father, and I believe that to Meg and me he is a saint as well as a beloved father.

'I remember,' said Margaret suddenly, 'how Ailie came to us and showed us the fashions. Do you remember? The long sleeves? It was that woman . . . the Queen. That woman . . . ! And but for her, Mercy, he would be with us now . . . perhaps he would be reading to us . . . perhaps he would be laughing . . . chiding us for some folly in his merry way. And now, Mercy, he is standing before a Commission, and we do not know of what he is accused; and we do not know when he will come home . . . *if* he will come home.'

'Margaret, this is not like you. You . . . so reasonable, so rational. Margaret, you the cleverest of us all . . . to give way to grief, to mourn for what has not yet come to pass!'

'Oh, Mercy, do not stand there and pretend to be so calm! There are tears in your eyes. You have the same fears. Your heart is breaking too.'

Mercy looked at her, and the tears began to flow silently down her cheeks.

'And all for a woman,' cried Margaret in sudden anger, 'a

woman with a deformed hand and a mole on her throat that must be covered with a jewel. . . . For beautiful sleeves . . . for Frenchified manners . . . our father must . . .'

'Don't say it, Meg. It has not happened yet.'

They looked at each other and then began to walk silently back to the house.

*　　　*　　　*

He did come home from the Commissioners; he came merrily. Will was with him in the barge when Mercy and Margaret ran down to meet him.

He embraced the girls warmly. He saw the tears on their cheeks, but he did not comment on them.

'Father . . . so you have come back !' said Margaret.

'Yes, daughter, your husband and I came back together.'

'And, Father, all is well?'

'All is well, my daughter.'

'You are no longer on the Parliament's list? You are no longer accused with the nun of Canterbury?'

'It was not of that that they wished to talk.'

'Then what?'

'I was accused of urging the King to write his *Assertion of the Seven Sacraments.*'

'But, Father, he had started to write that when he called you in.'

'Ah, my dear daughter, it was as good a charge as the others, so, I beg of you, do not complain of it.'

'Father, they are seeking to entrap you.'

'They cannot trap an innocent man.'

'How could they have accused you of this matter?'

'His Majesty was determined to honour the Pope in his book, and he did so. And now it appears he would like to accuse me of writing this book, but for the fact that it is so well done, and he likes better the praise he has received for writing it. But it is said that I have caused him, to his dishonour, to put a sword in the Pope's hand to fight the King.'

'Oh, Father !'

'Have no fear, Meg. I have confounded them. For did I not warn the King of the risk of incurring the penalties of *prae-munire*? I reminded them of this, and that the book was the King's book; that he himself had said I had but arranged it to his wishes. They could scarcely bring such a matter against me when the King has so clearly said that the book was his own – aye, and has received the title of Defender of the Faith for having written it.'

'If he is repudiating authorship of the book, then he should abandon the title it brought him,' said Mercy.

'You are right, daughter. I said: "My lords, these terrors be arguments for children and not for me." '

Will's brow was furrowed. He said: 'But, Father, what of the Parliament's list? Have they struck your name from it?'

'By my troth, son Roper, I forgot that matter in this new one.'

Will spoke tartly in his anxiety. 'You did not remember it? A case that touches you so near, and us all for your sake!'

Margaret looked anxiously from her husband to her father. Thomas was smiling; Will was angry.

'I understand not, sir,' said Will, 'why you should be so merry.'

'Then, Will, let me tell you. And I will tell my dear daughters also. This day I have gone so far, I have spoken my mind so clearly to these lords who cross-examined me, that, without great shame, I could not now turn back.'

He lifted his eyes and looked beyond them. He was smiling, but those about him were conscious of a deepening of their fear.

*　　*　　*

It seemed wrong that the weather should be so beautiful. Surely there had never been a more lovely April. Margaret could not bear the brightness of the spring sunshine. They went about their work silently, forcing their smiles. Everyone in the household knew that it could not be long before he was called before the Commissioners to sign the newly-coined Oath of Supremacy. How would he be able to extricate himself from this trouble? Now he would be presented with the necessity to sign or not to sign. The first would mean a return to the King's pleasure; the other . . . ? They did not know; they dared not think.

Easter Day came, and he, determined not to brood as they did, trying to laugh at their fears, being more gay than even was his wont, had arranged to go with Will to St Paul's to hear the sermon.

On that lovely spring day they set out by barge.

He would not be back until late in the day.

'I shall be within a few minutes of Bucklersbury,' he said, 'and I cannot pass so close without calling on my son and daughter Clement.'

Mercy was waiting for him with a heavy heart. Each time she saw him she wondered whether it would be the last.

'John,' she cried to her husband, 'how *can* I greet him merrily? How can I?'

'You must,' John answered. 'Who knows, this storm may pass.'

Dinner was on the table waiting for him, and she went out along the Poultry to meet him.

She saw him coming, his arm through that of Will Roper; they were deep in discussion, doubtless talking of the sermon they had just heard.

He embraced her warmly when they met; but his searching eyes saw what she could not hide, and that which he must be seeing in the faces of every member of his family now.

'Why, daughter, it is good indeed to see you. And how do I find you? Merry and well?'

'Merry and well,' she repeated. 'Merry and well, Father.'

He put his arm through hers and they walked thus to Bucklersbury; he smiling, a son and daughter on either side of him, happy to be with them, for although they had neither of them been born son and daughter of his, he would have them know that he considered them as such.

Friends and acquaintances greeted him as they passed along. There was warmth in the smiles of these people. They remembered him when he had been Under-Sheriff of the City; they remembered him as the incorruptible Lord Chancellor. But Mercy interpreted the looks in their eyes – fear, pity, warning.

The blow could not be far off.

Margaret, who loved him perhaps more poignantly than any of them, would have him sign the Oath; Margaret would have him do anything so that she might keep him with her. Mercy knew that. And if she, Mercy, could have pleaded with him, would she have urged him to sign the Oath?

She differed from Margaret. Margaret's love was all-important to her. He was, after all, Margaret's father, and if Margaret could keep him with her she would not care what it cost. But Mercy would never ask him to do what was against his conscience. Mercy would have him do what was right . . . whatever the consequences to himself and his family.

But that did not mean her suffering was any less acute.

Here was Bucklersbury with its pleasant apothecaries' smells. Here was the old home.

'I never enter it without a thousand memories assailing me,' he said.

And Mercy knew that he was glad to be here again, to recall those happy memories, to treasure them for that time when he would be unable to visit the house in Bucklersbury.

'Come, Father, you will be hungry. Let us eat at once.'

They were at table when the messenger arrived.

Mercy rose. She was not unduly disturbed. She did not expect them to come for him here. This must be a friend calling. No? Then a messenger from the Court. It must be someone for John, for he was now one of the King's physicians.

The man came forward. He carried a scroll in his hands.

'A message for me?' asked John.

'Nay, sir. I was instructed to deliver this to Sir Thomas More at Chelsea, but, hearing that he was at your house, I have saved myself the journey.'

Thomas rose to receive the scroll. 'Thank you. You were wise to save yourself the journey.'

He did not look at the scroll, but chatted awhile with the messenger in his friendly way; and when the man had left, he still held it unopened in his hands.

'Father . . .' began Mercy fearfully.

'Let us eat this excellent meal you have prepared for us, my daughter.'

'But . . .'

'After,' he said. 'There is time for that.'

Then he began to talk of the sermon he and Will had heard at St Paul's; but none of them was attending; their eyes kept going to the scroll which lay on the table.

'Father,' said Will angrily, 'keep us no longer in suspense. What is this?'

'Have you not guessed, my son? I'll warrant it is an instruction for me to appear before the Commissioners to take the Oath of Supremacy.'

'Then, Father, look at it. Make sure.'

'Why, Will, you fret too much. We knew this must come.'

'Father,' said Will in exasperation, 'your calm maddens me. Read it . . . for pity's sake.'

Thomas read. 'Yes, Will,' he said. 'I am to appear before the Commissioners at Lambeth to take the Oath.'

'It is more than I can bear,' said Will. 'It is more than Margaret can bear.'

'Take hope, my son. Let no trouble drive you to misery. If the trouble is lasting, it is easy to bear. If it is hard to bear, it does not last long.'

'Father, when do you go to Lambeth?' asked Mercy.

'Tomorrow. You see, today I need not fret. Today I may do what I will.'

'We must go back to Chelsea,' said Will.

'Why?'

'They will wish to have you with them as long as possible. Margaret . . .'

'Let her be. Let her have this day in peace. The sooner she knows this notice has been served upon me, the sooner will she fret even as you do, Will.'

'Is the knowledge that this has come any worse than the fear that it will, the knowledge that it must?'

'Yes, Will. For in uncertainty there is hope. Leave Margaret for a while. Come, let us eat, or Mercy will be offended. She and her servants have taken great pains to please us with these foods.'

Eat! Take pleasure in food? How could they?

They sat there at the table, and the pain in their hearts was almost unbearable.

And the only merry one at that table was Sir Thomas More.

*　　*　　*

They went along the river, back to Chelsea, in the early evening.

'Not a word yet, Will,' said Thomas. 'Leave them in peace. . . . Let them have this day.'

'But, Father,' said Will in distress, 'I doubt that I can keep my fears from them.'

'You have been displaying fears for many a day, Will. Smile, my son. They'll not know. They'll not think this could be served on me anywhere but in my own home. Let us have one more merry night at home. Let us sing and tell tales and laugh and be happy together, Will . . . just for one more night.'

Will did manage to curb his misery. He sang as loudly as the rest; and he was aware of his father-in-law's gratitude.

And that night, when he lay beside Margaret, he was sleepless, and so was she.

She whispered: 'Will, it cannot be long now, can it? There cannot be many more such days left to us.'

And Will said: 'It cannot be long.' He remembered his father's plea and he did not say: 'There can be no more such days. Today is the last, for tomorrow he goes to Lambeth.'

*　　*　　*

The next morning the family rose as usual. Thomas had an air of resignation which Margaret noticed: it was almost as though he found pleasure in this day. Alice noticed it too; she thought, I do believe he is going to do as the King wishes. I do believe he has come to his senses at last.

But after they had breakfasted he said: 'Come . . . let us go to church.'

They walked across the fields to Chelsea Church as they had done on many other mornings. And after the service, when the sun was high in the sky, he laid his hand on Will's arm and said: 'Will, 'tis time we were away.'

He called to two of the servants and said: 'Have the barge ready. This day I have to go to Lambeth.'

So they knew. The day had come.

Margaret took a step towards him, but his eyes held her off. Not here, Meg, they said. Not here . . . before the others.

'I have to go to Lambeth.' Those words might not sound ominous to the others as they did to Margaret and Will.

He is going to Lambeth on some business of the Parliament, they would think. He will be home ere evening.

But Margaret knew why he must go to Lambeth; and she knew what he would do when he was there. In her eyes was a mute appeal; Father, Father, do as they wish. What does it matter who is Head of the Church, if you are head of your family and continue to live with them to their delight and your own?

He was looking at Margaret now. He said: 'Do not come beyond the wicket gate. I must go in haste. Goodbye to you all.'

He kissed them all, and when her turn came, Margaret clung to him.

'Father . . .'

'Goodbye, my daughter, my beloved daughter. I shall be with you . . . ere long. . . .'

And he went over the lawns, opening the wicket gate, shutting it fast when Will had passed through, down the steps to the barge.

He took one look at the house which he had built, the house in which he was to have known perfect happiness with his family. He looked at the casements glittering in the sunshine, the peacocks on the wall, the blossoming fruit trees in the orchards. Who would gather the fruit this year? he wondered.

One last look at all that contained his happiness on Earth. Then he turned to Will, and as the barge slipped slowly away from the stairs he said: 'I thank the Lord, son Roper, that the field is won.'

* * *

He was sent to the Tower, and all the brightness had fled from the house in Chelsea.

There was no more pleasure in that house. There was nothing to do but wait in fear for what would happen next.

Margaret had begged to see her father, and because of the influence Dr Clement and Giles Allington were able to exert, she was at last allowed the privilege.

She had not slept at all the night before; indeed, for many nights she had had little sleep. She would lightly doze and wake with thoughts of her father in his comfortless cell. During the days she would walk along the river until she could more clearly see that grim fortress which had become his prison.

And now that she was to see him, now that she might take boat and go down the river to the Tower, she must be ready to offer him words of comfort. She must try not to beg him to do that which was against his conscience.

She reached the stairs; she alighted from the barge. Will helped her out, for he had insisted on coming as far as the Tower with her. Will would wait for her. Dear, good Will, the best of comforters, the dearest of husbands! She would bless the day her father had brought him to the house; for she must think of her blessings, not her miseries.

How she hated the place – the place that impressed her with its might and its horror! She looked up at the round towers, at the narrow slits which served as windows, at the dungeons with the bars across the slits. And here, in this place, was her father, her beloved father.

A jailer took her up a winding staircase and unlocked a heavy door. She was in a cell, a cell with stone walls and a stone floor; and then she saw no more of it, for there he was, smiling at her, hurrying to greet her.

She looked into his face and noticed how pale he was, how hollow were his eyes. He had changed. Yet . . . he could still smile, he could still feign a gaiety which he could not possibly feel.

'Meg . . . my own Meg!'

'My Father!' She was kissing him, clinging to him. 'Oh, Father, how are you? What have they done to you? You have grown thin and your beard is unkempt, and your clothes . . . Oh, Father . . . Father . . . what can I do? What can I say?'

'Come,' he said. 'Sit down, Meg. My jailer is a kind man. I have these stools. . . . Many people have been kind to me, Meg. My good friend, Bonvisi . . . he sends meat and wine . . . and I am allowed to have my good John a Wood here with me to look after me. You see, I am not treated badly. I am well looked after here.'

She tried to smile.

'Why, Meg, how are you? You are looking well. The sun has touched you. How are my dear sons and daughters? Bid them be of good cheer, Meg. You can do it.'

'To be of good cheer!' she cried. 'Father, let there be no pretence between us. Do not let us deceive ourselves and say, "This will pass," when we know there is only one way in which it could pass, and that you have determined against it.'

'Let us talk of other things, dear daughter.'

'How can I? What can I tell the children?'

'It may be, Meg, that you will have to speak to them of death. And if that be so, let them see it as a beautiful thing. Let them see it as release to beauty, to joy, to happiness such as this Earth cannot offer. Tell them that the man is dreaming who thinks in this life he is rich, for when death wakes him he will see how poor he is. Tell them that those who suffer at the hands of unjust men should take hope. Let kindly hopes console your suffering, Meg. He who is carried away by great wealth and empty pride, he who stands so bold among his courtiers, will not always be so bold. One day he will be equal with the beggars. Ah, what gift has life given that compares with death? You will find that he who can in life inspire fear, in death inspires nothing but laughter. Oh, Meg, Meg, lift up thy spirits. Do not grieve because I must come to that which awaits us all. My spirit is ready to break its shell. What matters it who cracks that shell? It may be the King. It may be the King's ministers. It may be the King's mistress.'

'Do not speak of her, Father. When you do, my hear. is filled with hatred. I think of her as when we first heard of her and she seemed naught but a frivolous girl. I did not know then that she was a wicked wanton . . . a would-be murderess of saintly men.'

'Hush, Meg! Do not speak ill of her. Pity her rather than condemn. For how do we know, poor soul, to what misery she may come?'

'I will not pity her, Father. I will not. But for her, you would be with us at home in Chelsea . . . all together . . . as we used to be. How can I pity her? How can I do aught but curse her?'

'Meg, you must have pity. She dances gaily at the Court, I hear; and these dances of hers will prove such dances that she will spurn our heads off like footballs; but, Meg, it may not be long before her own poor head will dance the like dance.'

'Father, what does it matter . . . what does anything matter if you but come home to us? Could you not . . .?'

'Nay, Meg, I know what I must do.'

'But what will happen?'

'We shall see.'

'My lord Bishop of Rochester is also in the Tower.'

'My jailer told me. I knew my dear friend Fisher must do this . . . even as I must.'

'The monks of the Charterhouse refuse to acknowledge the King's Supremacy, Father.'

'My good friends? It is what I would expect of them.'

'But, Father, is it right . . . is it lawful that they should imprison you for this? What have you done? You have merely refused to take an Oath. Is it then the law that a man may be imprisoned for this?'

'Ah, Meg, the King's pleasure is the law. It is a great pity that any Christian prince should, by a flexible Council ready to follow his affections, and by a weak clergy lacking grace constantly to stand to their learning, be so shamefully abused with flattery.'

'But, Father, is it worth it, think you? Could you not . . . take the Oath . . . and retire from Court life altogether? Live with us . . . your family . . . as you long to live. You have your library . . . your home . . . all that you love. Father, you are no longer young. You should be at home with your sons and daughters, with your wife. . . .'

'Why, have you come here to play the temptress, then? Nay, Mistress Eve, we have talked of this thing more than once or twice. I have told you that if it were possible to do this thing that would content the King, and God therewith would not be offended, then no man would have taken the Oath more gladly than I.'

'Oh, God in heaven,' she cried, 'they are coming to tell me I must go. Father . . . when shall I see your face again?'

'Be of good cheer, Meg. Ere long, I doubt not.'

She embraced him, and she saw the tears on his cheeks.

She thought : My coming has not cheered him; it has distressed him.

*　　*　　*

Alice had permission to visit him.

She was truculent, more full of scolding than usual; that was because she was so unhappy.

She stood in the doorway, her sharp eyes taking in the cell in all its comfortless gloom.

'What the good year, Master More!' she cried. 'It is a marvellous thing to me that you have always been taken for such a wise man. Here you are, playing the fool, as is your wont. You lie here in this close, filthy prison, and you are content to be shut up with mice and rats, when you might be abroad and at your liberty, enjoying the favour of the King and his Council. And all you must do is as the Bishops and learned men of this realm have done. And seeing you have at Chelsea a right fair house, your library, your gallery, your garden, your orchards and all other necessaries so handsome about you, where you might be in the company of your wife and children and with your household be merry, I muse what in God's name you mean, here so fondly to tarry.'

'Alice . . . Alice, it is good to see you. It is good to hear you scold me. Come, wife. Sit down. Sit on this stool which my good jailer has provided for me. We do well, here, John a Wood and I. My good friend Bonvisi sends more meat and drink than we need. Have no fear.'

'So you like this place better than your home. Is that it? Is that what you would tell me?'

'Is this house not as nigh Heaven as my own?' he asked.

'Tilly valley! Tilly valley! What nonsense you talk! All the prisons in the world could not alter that, I see.'

'But answer me, Alice. Is it not so?'

'By the good God, will this gear never be left?'

'Well, Mistress Alice, if it be so, and I believe you know it to be so and that is why you will answer with nothing but "Tilly valley!" that is well. I see no great cause why I should have much joy in my handsome house or in anything belonging to it, when if I should be but seven years buried under the ground and then arise and come thither, I should not fail to find someone therein who would bid me get out of doors and tell me it was none of mine. What cause have I then to like such a house as would so soon forget its master?'

'Tut and tut! Have done with this talk. What of your clothes? Have you anything for me to wash? And what a filthy place is this! And what does Master a Wood think he is doing not to look to your comforts more? It seems to me Master More, that you are a fool . . . surrounded by fools. . . .'

And he saw the bright tears brimming over on to her cheeks; he pretended not to see them. She scolded on, while in her way she was begging him to come home, even as Margaret had done.

*　　*　　*

From the windows of her husband's mansion, Ailie looked out over the park. She was tense and waiting. Soon, she believed, Lord Audley would come riding to the house in the company of her husband, and she had told Giles that when they returned he must leave her that she might have a word with the Chancellor.

'Oh, God help me,' prayed Ailie, more fervently than she had ever prayed before. 'Help me to do this.'

Lord Audley could help her, she believed. But had he the power? He was the Lord Chancellor, and when her father had been Chancellor many had brought their petitions to him.

Ailie could not bear to think of the house in Chelsea now. Margaret wrote to her often; so did Mercy. But the feigned cheerfulness of their letters only served to tell her how changed everything was. Would this dreary summer never pass?

She heard the huntsmen's horns and looked in the polished Venetian mirror which her husband had given her and of which she had once been so proud. Her eyes were hard and bright; her cheeks were flushed; she looked at her trembling, twitching mouth.

Then, composing herself, she ran down to greet the returning huntsmen.

Audley was talking excitedly about the deer he had killed in the park. What could it matter? There was only one thing that mattered now.

Giles was smiling at her tenderly, full of understanding. He led the way to the stables, where the grooms rushed forth to take the horses. Ailie was walking with Lord Audley, and Giles saw that they were left alone.

' 'Twas a good day's sport, I trust, Lord Audley?'

'It was, Lady Allington. Your husband is fortunate to have such happy hunting grounds at his disposal.'

'You must come often to hunt with us.'

'That I will.'

Ailie laid a hand on the arm of the Lord Chancellor and smiled up at him.

'My lord, you are a man of great influence at Court.'

Lord Audley smiled his pleasure.

'You could do something for me an you wished.'

'Lady Allington, I would willingly do anything in my power to please you.'

'You are gracious, my lord. It is of my father, I would speak.'

Lord Audley gave a quick, rather harsh laugh. 'Why, Lady Allington, he has all the means at his disposal to help himself.'

'That is not so.'

'I beg of you, forgive the contradiction, but it is so. He has but to sign the Oath of Supremacy, and he would be a free man tomorrow.'

'But that he cannot do.'

'Cannot! Cannot sign his name!' Lord Audley laughed. (He was proud of saying, 'I am no scholar!' which meant he had a certain contempt for those who were.) 'But we have always heard that he is such a learned man!' he went on.

'My lord, he feels this to be a matter of conscience.'

'Then he should reason with his conscience. My dear lady, I would do as much for your father as I would for my own . . . for your sake; but what can I do? The remedy lies with him. I marvel that he should be so obstinate in his conceit.'

'Could you not persuade the King that, in my father's case, this matter of the Oath could be waived?'

'My dear lady, you know the ways of Parliament.'

Then the Chancellor began to tell Ailie one of Æsop's fables. 'This,' he said, 'you, being the daughter of such a learned man, have doubtless heard before.' It was the fable of the few wise men who tried to rule the multitude of fools. The few were flogged by the many. 'Were they such wise men after all, Lady Allington? Were they, I wonder.'

Ailie looked into the cold, proud face beside her, and her heart felt leaden.

They had reached the house, and she stepped on ahead of him. Giles came forth and, seeing her state, engaged their guest in conversation so that she was free to run upstairs to her bedroom.

This she did, with the tears flowing down her cheeks, and her face set in a mask of utter hopelessness.

*　　*　　*

There were no more visits to the Tower, and the months were

dragging on. Christmas came; and it was last spring when he had been taken from home.

What a different Christmas was this from that which they usually spent! They were all together, but how could they be happy without him?

They lived for the letters they received from him. They were allowed to send a servant to the Tower to take letters to him and receive his. The faithful Dorothy Colly made the journey, for she was almost one of the family, and Thomas was fond of her. She would come back and tell them everything he had said.

'He wishes to know what you are doing, how you spend your days. No little detail is too small. It pleases him much to hear these things. He must have news of the latest sayings of the children.'

To Margaret, when they were alone, she said: 'He kissed me when I left. And I was to tell you, he said, that he loves me as one of the family. He said: "Have you married John Harris yet, Dorothy? You should. Tell Margaret. She will help you to arrange it, for marriage is a good thing; and if two people grow together in love and comradeship, there is no happier state in the world."'

Margaret kissed her maid. She knew that John Harris loved her; and she knew that her father meant: 'Be happy. Do not continue to grieve. Go about your ordinary business. If there is a wedding among you, rejoice and celebrate. Your father is with you in all you do.'

'I must see him soon, Dorothy,' she said. 'We cannot go on like this.'

* * *

He had changed very much since his imprisonment; he was thin and ill. He had his books with him, and they brought him much comfort. He was writing what he called *A Dialogue of Comfort*. This was a conversation between two Hungarians, an aged man Antonio and his nephew Vincent. These two discussed the coming invasion of the Turks. The allegory was easily understood by Margaret – for he sent his writings to her.

'I cannot read this to you,' he wrote, 'but I need your opinions as I ever did.'

Margaret guessed who the Great Turk was meant to be, for Thomas wrote: 'There is no born Turk so cruel to Christian folk as is the false Christian that falleth from his faith. Oh, Margaret, my beloved daughter, I am a prisoner in a foul place, yet I am happy when I take up my pen to write to you, and I would rather be Margaret's father than the ruler of an Empire.'

Rich, the Solicitor-General, paid him many visits. Thomas understood the purpose of these visits; they were to entrap him. Now they were trying to make him *deny* the King's supremacy; but Thomas was too learned in the ways of the law to do this. He was fully aware that he could not be condemned merely for refusing to sign the Oath. If he preserved silence on his views, he must be guiltless. There was no law under which it was possible to punish a man because he refused to sign an oath.

In vain did Rich seek to entrap him; Cromwell, Norfolk, Audley, the whole Council did their best to please the King by making a case against him; but Thomas was the greatest lawyer of them all. Not one of them – even Cranmer – could lure him to say that which would condemn him.

He knew that his friend Bishop Fisher was in the Tower. Fisher was a brave man, but he was no lawyer. Thomas wrote notes to him, and Fisher answered him; their servants found means of exchanging these notes, for the jailers were willing to make the incarceration of two such saintly men as Fisher and More as comfortable as was possible.

'Have great care, my friend,' Thomas begged the Bishop. 'Be on your guard against the questions which are put to you. Take great care that you do not fall into the dangers of the Statutes. You will not sign the Oath. That is not a crime in itself. But guard your tongue well. If any ask you, be sure that you say not a word of the King's affairs.'

The Bishop was a very sick man and his imprisonment had greatly affected his health.

One day Richard Rich came to the Bishop and, smiling in a friendly fashion, assured him that this was not an official visit;

he came, not as the King's Solicitor-General, but as a friend.

The Bishop, worn out with sickness, suffering acutely from the closeness of his confinement, from heat and from cold, bade the Solicitor-General welcome. The latter talked about the pity of this affair, the sorrow it was causing many people because such men, so admired and respected as were Bishop Fisher and Sir Thomas More, must lie in prison on account of a matter such as this.

'I talked to the King of you but yesterday,' said Rich, 'and he said that it grieved him to think of you in prison. He said that he respected you greatly, and that his conscience worried him concerning you. He fears that he may not have been right in what he has done. And indeed, where is the son that God would have given him had He approved the new marriage? He has but a daughter – a healthy child, it is true, but a daughter! The King's conscience disturbs him, and you could lighten it, my lord Bishop. The King has promised absolute secrecy, but he wishes to know your mind. He says that what you say – as a holy man of the Church – will be carefully considered by him. Now, my lord Fisher, if I swear to you that what you say is between you, myself and the King, will you open your mind to me?'

Fisher answered: 'By the law of God, the King is not, nor could be Supreme Head on Earth of the Church of England.'

Rich nodded and smiled: he was well pleased with himself.

Fisher had answered exactly as he had hoped he would.

* * *

There were others in the Tower for the same reason as were those two brave men.

The Carthusians had been asked to sign the Oath of Supremacy. This they had found they could not do in good conscience, and the Prior of the London Charterhouse, with those of Lincoln and Nottinghamshire, was very soon lodged in the Tower. Others quickly followed them there.

The King was growing more and more angry, and when he was angry he turned his wrath on Cromwell.

'By God's Body,' roared the King. 'It is this man More who

stiffens their resistance. We must make him understand what happens to those who disobey the King.'

'Sire, we have done all we can to bring a charge against him, but he is as wily as a fox in this matter of the law.'

'I know, I know,' said the King testily, 'that he is a clever man in some ways and that I am surrounded by fools. I know that you have tried in many ways to bring charges against him, but every time he has foiled you. He is a traitor. Remember that. But I have no wish to see him suffer. My wish is that he shall end his folly, give us his signature and stop working malice among those who so admire him. These monks would relent if he did. But, no . . . no. These fools about me can in no way foil him. It is Master More who turns their arguments against them and snaps his fingers at us all. Let him be reminded of the death a traitor suffers. Ask him whether or not that is the law of the land. Ask him what clever lawyer can save a man from a traitor's death if he is guilty of treason.'

Cromwell visited Thomas in his cell.

'Ah, Sir Thomas,' he said, 'the King grieves for you. He wishes you well in spite of all the trouble you are causing him. He would be merciful. He would take you to a more comfortable place; he would see you abroad in the world again.'

'I have no wish, Master Cromwell, to meddle in the affairs of the world.'

'The King would feel more inclined towards you if you did not help others to resist him. There are these monks, now lodged in this Tower. The King feels that if you would but be his good friend you could persuade these monks to cease their folly.'

'I am the King's true and faithful subject and I do nobody harm. I say none harm; I think none harm; and I wish everybody good. And if this be not enough to keep a man alive and in good faith I long not to live. Therefore is my poor body at the King's pleasure.'

'I repeat that the King wishes you well. He would do a favour unto you. Yet you would not accept this favour.'

'There is one I would accept. If I could see my daughter, Margaret Roper, there is little else I would ask of the King.'

Cromwell smiled. 'I will do what can be done. I doubt not that the request will soon be granted.'

And it was.

She came on that May day, a year after his imprisonment, when the four monks were to pay the terrible penalty which had been deemed their due.

This was as the King and Cromwell would have it; for, said Cromwell, the bravest of men would flinch when they considered the death accorded to these monks. It was the traitor's death; and there was no reason why a Bishop and an ex-Chancellor should not die the same horrible death as did these monks. Only the King in his clemency could change that dread sentence to death by the axe.

Let Master More reflect on that; and let him reflect upon it in the company of his daughter, for she might aid the King's ministers with her pleas.

So she was with him while preparations were being made immediately outside his prison. He and Margaret heard these and knew what they meant. The hurdles were brought into the courtyard below the window; and they knew that those four brave men were being tied to them and that they would be dragged to Tyburn on those hurdles, and there hanged, cut down and disembowelled while still alive.

To face such death required more than an ordinary man's courage, though that man be a brave one.

Margaret stood before him tight-lipped.

'I cannot bear it, Father. Do you not hear? Do you not know what they are doing to those brave monks?'

And he answered: 'Lo, Meg, dost thou not see that these blessed fathers be now as cheerfully going to their deaths as bridegrooms to their marriage?'

But she turned from him weeping, swooning to the floor; and it was he who must comfort her.

*   *   *

Mercy said to her husband: 'I must do something. Inactivity is killing me. I have a tight pain in my throat, so that I feel it

274

will close up altogether. Think, John. For a year we have suffered this agony. Oh, was there ever such exquisite torture as slow torture? Does the King know this? Is that why he raises our hopes and all but kills them before he seems to bid us hope again?'

'Mercy, it is not like you to give way, you . . . who are always so calm.'

'I cannot go on being calm. I dream of him as he was years ago when he first brought me to the house . . . when I would stand before him while he explained some small fault to me. I think of him when he told me that I was truly his daughter. I am his daughter. That is why I must do something. And you must help me, John.'

'I would do anything in the world for you, Mercy. You know that well.'

'Four of the monks have now suffered most barbarously at Tyburn, John. And there are others who are suffering, less violently, but in a horribly slow, lingering way. They are in Newgate and I am going to help them.'

'You, Mercy? But . . . how?'

'I am going to Newgate to take succour to them.'

'They would never let you in.'

'I think the King's physician could help me.'

'Mercy! If you were discovered . . . have you thought what it would mean?'

'He said I was truly his daughter. I would like to prove that to myself.'

'What would you do?'

'You know their sentence. Those learned monks are tied to posts in confined spaces. They cannot move; there are iron collars about their necks and fetters about their ankles. They are to be left thus to die. That is their punishment for disobedience to the King. They are given no food; they cannot move from that spot. They have been there a day and a night. I am going into Newgate with food and the means to cleanse them . . . so that they do not die of their plight.'

'It is not possible, Mercy.'

'It *is* possible, John. I have planned what I shall do. I shall dress as a milkmaid and carry a pail on my head. It shall be full of food and the means of cleaning them of their natural filth. And this milkmaid shall be allowed into the prison on the recommendation of the King's physician. You can do it, John. And you must . . you must . . . for I shall die if I stay here thinking . . . thinking . . . Don't you see it is the only way for me to live? I shall feel I am helping *him*. I must, John; and you must help me.'

He kissed her and gave his promise.

The next day Mercy, dressed as a milkmaid, with a pail on her head, walked into Newgate Jail and was taken to the monks by a jailer who had been paid to do this.

She fed the monks with the food that she had brought; and she cleaned them.

She was happier than she had been since her father had been taken to the Tower.

* * *

The King was growing angrier. He was also growing accustomed to the shedding of blood. He was being unfaithful to his Queen, and he was in urgent need of reassurance, for that old monster, his conscience, was worrying him again.

The Pope, hoping to save Fisher, had talked of giving him a Cardinal's hat.

The King laughed aloud when he heard this. 'Then he shall wear it on his shoulders,' he said, 'for he'll have no head to put it on.'

And on a day in June Bishop Fisher, after his examination in the Tower, during which the secret confession he had made to Rich was revealed by the treacherous Solicitor-General, was condemned to death.

But the King was generous. In view of the Bishop's age and position, though he was a traitor indeed, it was not the royal wish that he should suffer the traitor's death. He should die by the executioner's axe.

Now it was Thomas's turn, and on the 1st of July he was taken to Westminster Hall for his trial.

There Norfolk, his kindness forgotten – for he had become exasperated by what he called the obstinacy of the man for whom he had once had a liking – told him that if he would repent of his opinions he might still win the King's pardon.

'My lord,' was Thomas's answer, 'I thank you for your good-will. Howbeit, I make my petition unto God Almighty that it may please Him to maintain me in this my honest mind to the last hour that I shall live.'

Then he defended himself so ably that those who had been set to try him were afraid that yet again he would elude them. That could not be allowed to happen. There was not one of them who would dare face the King unless Thomas More came out of Westminster Hall convicted of treason. Then the resourceful Rich stepped forth and announced that he had had a secret conversation with More, even as he had had with Fisher.

'Ah,' cried Thomas, 'I am sorrier for your perjury, Master Rich, than for my own peril.'

But the jury was glad of a chance to find him guilty, as each member knew he must or earn the King's displeasure.

They brought him out of Westminster Hall, and Margaret, who was waiting with Jack and Mercy, felt numbed by her pain when she saw him between the halberdiers, and the blade of the executioner's axe turned towards him.

Jack ran forward and knelt at his father's feet. Margaret threw herself into his arms; only Mercy stood back, remembering even in that moment that she was only the foster-daughter.

Margaret would not release her father; and Sir William Kingston, the Constable of the Tower, stood by unable to speak because of his emotion.

'Have patience, Margaret. My Meg, have patience. Trouble thyself not . . .' whispered Thomas.

And when he released himself, she stepped back a pace or two and stood looking at him, before she ran forward to fling her arms once more about his neck.

Now Sir William Kingston laid gentle hands upon her, and

Jack had his arm about her as she fell fainting to the ground and lay there while the tragic procession moved on.

* * *

The King had been gracious. He would save the man who had been his friend from that terrible death which the monks had suffered.

'The King in his mercy,' said Cromwell, 'has commuted the sentence to death by the axe.'

'God forbid,' said Thomas with a touch of grim humour, 'that the King should use any more such mercy to my friends.'

There were certain conditions, Cromwell explained. There must be no long speeches at the execution. And if Thomas obeyed the King's wishes, the King would graciously allow his family to have his body to bury. The King was indeed a merciful king.

* * *

Death by the axe!

Now it was dark indeed in the house at Chelsea. They sat in a mournful circle, and none spoke of him, for they had no words to say.

That which they had feared had come to pass. He who had made this house what it was, who had made their lives so good and joyous, was lost to them.

They would never see him again.

Dauncey was weeping silently – not for frustrated ambition; that seemed to matter little now. He did not know what had happened to him when he had come to this house. He had dreamed of greatness; he had made an advantageous marriage that would lead to the King's favour; and whither had it led him? Being Dauncey, he knew more than the others. He knew that the King's hatred of Sir Thomas More would extend to his family; he knew that goods and lands would be taken from them; that it might be that their very lives were in danger. But he cared not. He, Dauncey, cared not. He would have given all the lands and goods he possessed, he would have thrown away his ambitions for the future, if the door could have opened and the laughing voice of Sir Thomas More be heard again.

His wife Elizabeth smiled at him. She understood and was grateful to him, for it seemed to her that in the midst of her black sorrow there was a touch of brightness.

Cecily and Giles Heron were holding hands, staring before them, thinking . . . thinking back over the past.

Alice was remembering all the scoldings she had given him, and wishing, more than she had ever wished for anything before, that she could have him with her to scold now.

Dorothy Colly slipped her hand into that of John Harris; and they were all very still until they heard the sound of horses' hoofs approaching.

It was a messenger who had brought a letter for Margaret.

She trembled as she took it, for he was to die tomorrow, and she knew that this was the last she would ever receive from him.

It was written with a piece of coal – all that was left to him to write with; for they had taken his writing materials when, some time before, they had taken his books.

She forced herself to read aloud.

'Our Lord bless you, good daughter, and your good husband, and your little boy, and all yours . . . and all my children and all my god-children and all our friends. . . .'

He then mentioned them all by name, and as Margaret spoke their names they hung their heads, for the tears streamed from their eyes.

But Margaret went on steadily reading.

He begged them not to mourn for him. He was to die tomorrow, and he would be sorry to live longer.

'For tomorrow is St Thomas's Eve, and therefore tomorrow I long to go to God. St Thomas's Eve! It is a day very meet and convenient for me. Dear Meg, I never liked your manner towards me better than when you kissed me last, for I love when daughterly love and dear charity hath no leisure to look to worldly courtesy. Farewell, my child, and pray for me, and I shall for you and all my friends; and may we all meet merrily in Heaven.'

Margaret had stopped reading and a silence fell upon them.

* * *

Early on the morning of St Thomas's Eve, Master Pope, a young official of the Court, came to tell him that he was to die that day.

The young man came with tears in his eyes, and could scarcely speak for weeping, so that it was Thomas More who must comfort Thomas Pope.

'Do not grieve, Master Pope,' he said, 'for I thank you heartily for these good tidings.'

'It is the King's pleasure that you should not use many words at the execution.'

'You do well to give me warning, for I had planned to speak at length. I beg of you, Master Pope, plead with the King that when I am buried, my daughter Margaret may be there to see it done.'

'The King will consent to that if you do not speak overmuch before your death. Your wife and all your children shall then have liberty to be present.'

'I am beholden to His Grace that my poor burial shall have so much consideration.'

Then Pope, taking his leave, could say nothing because his tears were choking him.

'Quiet yourself, good Master Pope,' said Thomas, 'and be not discomfited, for I trust that we shall, once in Heaven, see each other merrily where we shall be sure to live and love together in joyful bliss eternally.'

Shortly before nine o'clock, wearing a garment of frieze that hung loosely on his thin body, and carrying in his hands a red cross, Thomas More left his prison for Tower Hill.

There was only one member of the family there to see him die. Mercy was that one. She stood among the crowds about the scaffold, watching him, taking her last look at him. Later she would be joined by Margaret and Dorothy Colly for the burial of his body in the Church of St Peter ad Vincula.

Mercy did not stand near, for she did not want her father to witness her grief. She told herself that she should be glad, for he was not subjected to that ignoble death which those poor monks had suffered at Tyburn, while others of their brethren were rotting in their chains at Newgate. The jailer there, fearing discovery, would no longer allow her to visit those monks, and although she had made efforts to reach them she had not been able to do so, and they were slowly perishing where they were chained.

Oh, cruel world, she thought, that surrounds that island of peace and happiness in Chelsea like a turbulent sea. They had thought themselves safe on their island, but now the malignant waters had washed over it, destroying peace and beauty, leaving only memories for those who had lived there and loved it.

Thomas was mounting the steps which led to the scaffold. They had been hastily constructed and shook a little.

He smiled and said to one of the Sheriff's officers: 'I pray you, Master Lieutenant, that you will see me safe up. As to my coming down, you may leave me to shift for myself.'

The executioner was waiting for him. This hardened man looked into Thomas's face and, seeing there that sweetness of expression which had won the affection of so many, he turned quickly away murmuring: 'My lord, forgive me. . . .'

Thomas laid a hand on his arm. 'Pluck up your spirits, my friend. Be not afraid of your office . . . for such is all it is. Take heed that you strike not awry for the sake of thine own honesty.'

Then he knelt and prayed. 'Have mercy upon me, O God, in Thy great goodness. . . .'

He rose and the executioner came forward to bind his eyes.

'I will do it for myself,' said Thomas.

But first he spoke to the people who were waiting on his last words; very briefly he spoke, remembering the King's displeasure that could fall on those who were left behind him.

'My friends, pray for me in this world and I will pray for you elsewhere. Pray also for the King that it may please God to give him good counsel. I die the King's servant . . . but God's first.'

Then he bound his eyes and laid his head on the block, pushing his beard to one side, saying: 'That has no treason. Let it therefore be saved from the executioner's axe.'

There was a great silence on Tower Hill as the axe fell.

Thomas's lips moved slightly.

'The King's good servant . . . but God's first.'

* * *

News of the death of Sir Thomas More was brought to the King.

'So perish all traitors!' he cried.

But his little eyes were fearful. In the streets the people were murmuring. It was all they dared to do against the King. They had seen the terrible deaths of the Carthusians; and now the head of Sir Thomas More was on a pole on London Bridge beside that of the saintly Fisher, Bishop of Rochester.

'Come, Norfolk, what are you thinking . . . skulking there?'

Norfolk was a bold man. He said: 'That it was a pity, Your Grace. Such a man of talents to be so obstinate . . . so wrong-minded.'

'You seem sad that it should be so.'

'Your Grace, he was a lovable man . . . for all his faults. Sire, many loved him.'

Many loved him!

The King's eyes narrowed. The people would remember that the man had been put to death because he had obeyed his conscience rather than his King. The King's good servant, but God's first.

The King cursed all martyrs.

This man must not live in the memory of the people. He must be seen as a traitor, a man deserving death, a traitor whose head was in its rightful place, looking down from London's bridge on London's river.

But Henry knew that, as the people passed by the bridge, as they looked at the head of the man, they would mutter prayers and ask his blessing. Too many of them remembered his kindness, his piety and virtue.

Living, he had been Thomas More, the kind, good man; dead, he would be Thomas More, the saint.

That should not be; it must not be.

Had not More stated that he believed the sowing of seditious heresies should be prevented at all costs? During his reign as Chancellor one or two people had been burned as heretics. The King would have it bruited abroad that this great good man had not been averse to inflicting suffering on those who did not share his views. Could he then complain at the King's treatment of himself?

There would be some who would say: 'It is not the duty of a Chancellor to pass sentence on heretics. That lies in the hands of the clergy.' But who would examine that too closely? The Tudors and their friends, who had found it necessary to suppress many historical facts, would have no difficulty in supressing or garnishing wherever it was expedient to do so.

The King remembered the case of a heretic who had been ordered by Sir Thomas More to be flogged. The King had been amused at the time of the offence, for the man concerned had crept behind women kneeling in the church and, lifting their clothes, had cast them over their heads. The just sentence for such an act was flogging; but this man, as well as being a lewd person, was also a heretic. A little adjustment of the reports of such cases, and there was More, a flogger of heretics.

The King doubted not that his good friends would have no difficulty in providing the necessary evidence.

For, thought the King, we cannot have martyrs in our kingdom. Martyrs are uncomfortable men, and I like them not.

The King must always be right; and the King was uneasy, for he also found it hard to forget the man. Norfolk was right: More had been a lovable fellow.

I liked him, mused Henry. It gave me pleasure to honour him.

He remembered their pleasant talks together over the writing of the book; he thought of evenings on the balcony with his first Queen beside him, and Thomas More pointing out the stars in the heavens; he thought of the pleasant family at Chelsea and walking through those fragrant gardens with his arm about his Chancellor's neck.

'I loved the man,' murmured Henry. 'I . . . as well as the

others. It was not my wish that he should die. God bear me witness. I loved him.'

His Queen came in.

He was not pleased with her. She had not brought him all that he had desired. She had filled his heart with jealousy and his mind with misgiving.

He had noticed a quiet, pale girl among her maids of honour. Jane Seymour was her name; and although this young woman was modest, she had shown that she was not unconscious of the King's regard.

The King lost control of his temper suddenly as he looked at his Queen; and he was filled with fear because the murder of a great and good man lay heavily upon his conscience.

'You have done this!' he shouted at his Queen. 'You have done this. You have demanded of me the death of a good man and, God forgive you, I have granted your request.'

EIGHT

THERE WAS no sound on the river but that of the oars as they dipped in the water.

The stars in the July sky scintillated like jewels in the doublet of a king, and the outline of hedges was clear along the banks.

The bridge and its ghastly relics came into view.

The boat stopped and, when Margaret alighted, Will was beside her. He put his arm about her.

'Meg . . . Meg . . . you still insist?'

She nodded.

'''Tis a dangerous thing to do, my darling. I know not what the penalty would be if . . .'

'I know not either,' she said; 'and I care not.'

They walked away from the river's edge up and on to the bridge.

'Meg . . . go back to the boat. I will do it.'

'Nay. 'Tis my task and mine alone.'

The air of the hot summer's night caressed her face as she stood on the bridge and firmly grasped the pole in her hand.

'Meg, you torture yourself.'

'Nay,' she answered. 'Let be, Will. Let be.'

And together they pulled down the pole, and they took that which was set upon it.

Margaret wrapped it tenderly in the shawl which she had brought, and, putting his arm about her, Will led her back to the boat.

Tenderly Will Roper watched his wife and swore to cherish her until the end of their days. He and their children between them would give her such love that Thomas himself, looking down from Heaven, would smile upon them and bless them.

Now Margaret stared before her, her arms about the shawl which held that terrible and precious relic.

London Bridge was behind them, and they went swiftly up the river to Chelsea.

Jean Plaidy
The Wandering Prince £2.95

The Charles II Trilogy

Charles II, the most fascinating rake in England's history . . . the
years he spent in exile as a young man, seen through the eyes of
two women . . . an enthralling story of romance, escape and the
youth of a king for whom love always came first.

A Health unto His Majesty £2.50

Charles II's return to the throne meant restoration of all the gaiety
that had been suppressed during the previous years.

The King's fiery mistress Barbara Palmer could twist him round her
little finger. He could refuse her nothing, even if it meant hurting his
new wife, the naive and loving Catherine of Braganza. The
jealousies, intrigues and loves at the court of the 'Merry Monarch'
are seen from the viewpoint of both women – the wicked and the
wronged. Both, in their different way, loved him dearly.

Here Lies our Sovereign Lord £2.95

Charles II intrigues with Louis XIV for the money that will keep him
independent of Parliament and dispel the shadows cast over the
throne by his son Monmouth and his own brother, the Duke of
York. When politics tire the Merry Monarch there are always
women ready to please him – Nell Gwyn, Hortense Mancini,
Louise de Koroualle . . .

All these books are available at your local bookshop or newsagent, or can be ordered direct from the publisher. Indicate the number of copies required and fill in the form below.

Send to: **CS Department, Pan Books Ltd., P.O. Box 40, Basingstoke, Hants. RG21 2YT.**

or phone: 0256 469551 (Ansaphone), quoting title, author and Credit Card number.

Please enclose a remittance* to the value of the cover price plus: 60p for the first book plus 30p per copy for each additional book ordered to a maximum charge of £2.40 to cover postage and packing.

*Payment may be made in sterling by UK personal cheque, postal order, sterling draft or international money order, made payable to Pan Books Ltd.

Alternatively by Barclaycard/Access:

Card No.

Signature:

Applicable only in the UK and Republic of Ireland.

While every effort is made to keep prices low, it is sometimes necessary to increase prices at short notice. Pan Books reserve the right to show on covers and charge new retail prices which may differ from those advertised in the text or elsewhere.

NAME AND ADDRESS IN BLOCK LETTERS PLEASE:

....

Name ————————————————————————————

Address ——————————————————————————

————————————————————————————————

————————————————————————————————

————————————————————————————————

3/87